MW00442312

LIFE'S ILLUSIONS

MICHAEL KENNY

Life's Illusions

Copyright © 2022 Michael Kenny. All rights reserved. No part of this book may be reproduced or retransmitted in any form or by any means without the written permission of the publisher.

Published by Wheatmark®
2030 East Speedway Boulevard, Suite 106
Tucson, Arizona 85719 USA
www.wheatmark.com

ISBN: 978-1-62787-930-9 (paperback)
ISBN: 978-1-62787-931-6 (ebook)
LCCN: 2021923616

Bulk ordering discounts are available through Wheatmark, Inc. For more information, email orders@wheatmark.com or call 1-888-934-0888.

"Life can only be understood backwards, but it must be lived forwards."

—Sören Kierkegaard

"Is *all* that we see or seem but a dream within a dream?"

— Edgar Allan Poe, "A Dream Within a Dream"

For Beth, my love and guiding spirit.

VIRTUE VERSUS VICE

Even if your eyes are open and darting about and your lungs are pumping oxygen and your heart is pumping blood, you would not be reading these words if a virulent disease with no cure had already shriveled away two thirds of your brain. The morbid fear that your brain is queuing up in the enfeeblement line is one haunting reason why this jury trial had been so riveting and its climax was now so anticipated. Murmurs vibrated throughout the packed San Francisco courtroom as Jonathan A. Kent stood to deliver his closing argument to the jury of five women and four men who would decide his spellbinding case.

For three weeks nine attentive jurors were presented engrossing scientific evidence about the human brain and how a degenerative disease insidiously ravages it away. The disease is called Alzheimer's. It delivers a cruel death sentence for the afflicted millions of people, mostly sixty-five and older, and its prevalence is ominously rising. A terrifying game of who's next. The disease has no conscience and patiently waits for an anxious aging population to take their turn at death's roulette wheel. The jurors heard more than just the scientific evidence. They heard contemptible evidence of corporate corruption and chicanery that killed a quest for a cure and crushed the dreams of a devoted granddaughter. Now they were poised to listen and watch as this renowned lawyer from Washington, DC, prepared to put it all together in one complete, coherent, and compelling story.

Jonathan Kent represented the granddaughter and her small company, MSI—Memory Solutions, Inc. The granddaughter, Dr.

Anne Little, and her co-owner, Dr. Helen Elion, were both PhDs in molecular biology. Both were brilliant scientists. Both were inspired by family members robbed prematurely of life by the pernicious disease that relentlessly shrunk their loved ones' brains until their hearts and lungs and liver and kidneys surrendered and stopped cold. Heart and head caused Anne and Helen to dream big. Their high-wattage brains burned with a desire to discover a cure for this dehumanizing disease that steals identity, extinguishes life, and leaves trails of tears. The realization of their dream promised to benefit the human race.

The defendant was Jager Pharmaceuticals, an international corporate conglomerate headquartered in Hamburg, Germany. It was worth more than $50 billion. Its swaggering corporate executives had their pick from a fleet of Dassault Falcon corporate jets, and its overpaid chief executive officer made $45 million a year in cash and stock options. In a year when Jager fired 10,000 loyal employees, what the hard-hearted executives publicly boasted was "responsible rightsizing," its stock rose 27 percent, ensuring hefty year-end bonuses for corporate tycoons already raking in small fortunes. In this courtroom, Jager, which means "hunter" in German, stood accused of stealing MSI's revolutionary ideas for an Alzheimer's cure drug. Ideas protected by what the law calls intellectual property. Ideas protected by what ordinary people call honesty and decency. Ideas Anne and Helen generated from a fertile mixture of extraordinary intellect and love, hope, toil, and tears.

The defendant's motive was simple. Money. Lots of money. The market for Alzheimer's treatment drugs was already in the billions. With scientists predicting a doubling of the number of people who will live past 65, a miracle cure drug would be worth exponentially more. Drs. Little and Elion were on the cusp of developing that revolutionary drug. Then Jager went hunting and killed the young visionaries' dream through a perfidious trap of lies, deception, and outright fraud. The predator's primary defense was both arrogant and cynical: these brilliant young scientists were rubes who should have been better businesspersons. Jonathan would argue to the jury that heartless hunting might thrive in the law of the jungle, but lying and cheating and flouting moral codes should not survive in this courtroom. That nature, as the poet Tennyson wrote, might be red in tooth and claw, but in the civilized world of law and morals, such conduct must be denounced and punished.

Corporate lying and cheating motivated by unbridled and ruthless greed were the pieces of evidence Jonathan had presented to the five women and four men on the jury for the past three weeks. Now it was his final time to talk to them, to summarize the evidence and give it meaning by showing them how the seemingly scrambled pieces fit tightly together like a completed jigsaw puzzle. By reputation and performance, he possessed a certain concinnity, an eloquent gift for weaving together a morally compelling story. Now in his mid-fifties with a stunning string of courtroom successes to his credit, he was more than ready to speak one last time on behalf of Anne and Helen. Every eye in the hushed courtroom was on him.

With preternatural calm he stood, passed by the lectern in the middle of the courtroom, and walked over to the jury box. No notes, no fancy computer graphics, not yet. For now, it was just him and the five women and four men sitting in the jury box. He unobtrusively made eye contact with each one as he spoke in a conversational tone. No windy windup. No prattling on about civic duty. No unctuous pandering. Just his always-respectful acknowledgment of the judge, with "may it please the court," and a style described a century and a half earlier by Ralph Waldo Emerson as true eloquence, the power to translate truth in words perfectly understandable to the people you are talking to. So he began.

"May it please the court. Good morning, ladies and gentlemen. I ask you to imagine a vibrant and radiant woman who raised three good children. Got them through school and now watched with renewed hope and joy as her grown children were starting their own families. She had four young adoring grandchildren who were attracted by her magnetic charm. Nurtured by her warmth and caring. A woman who married the young man of her dreams and, with retirement approaching, was preparing to travel with him to places they had dreamed about for years. For her, what we hopefully call the golden years were promising indeed to be golden.

"Imagine a witty woman who penned poems. Some silly about her children, others serious about her loves. A charitable woman who contributed to her church and community and doted on her dogs. Fastidious about her appearance and proud of her position as the matriarch of a loving family extending multiple generations. A matriarch who instinctively understood that the love she showered on her children and grandchildren infused her life with meaning, beauty, and significance. A woman who embraced life and daily squeezed joy out of it. Never one to take herself too seriously, she made family and friends laugh in times of joy and was there to console them in times of sorrow.

"Now imagine that this lovely woman, like millions of our fellow Americans, even before her golden years, slowly lost her ability to live a normal life. Where at first awareness and trust gave way to delusion and paranoia.

"Then her downward spiral continued to accelerate. Her painful list of can't-do-anymores grew inexorably. Can't bathe herself. Can't brush her teeth. Can't brush her hair. Can't make coffee or tea. Can't clean her clothes.

"Can't pen her poems. Can't cook a meal. Can't feed her dogs. Can't plant her flowers. Can't shop at her stores. Can't answer a telephone. Can't tell time on the clock on her kitchen wall. Can't tell her adoring husband she loves him. Can't understand when he tenderly says to her, I love you. Can't remember. Can't breathe.

"Once an adoring wife and mother, she was mercilessly robbed of her ability to recognize her life's loves—husband, children, and affectionate grandchildren. Who saw only a stranger when she stared into a mirror. Who slowly became lifeless, inert, and finally dead. A noble life with an ignoble end. It started when she was fifty-nine and ended when she was sixty-six. The killer was identified as Alzheimer's.

"That wonderful woman was Dr. Anne Little's grandmother. The beauty of her life and the devastation of her death inspired Dr. Little to earn her PhD in molecular biology at the young age of twenty-three, impatient to find an Alzheimer's cure. She teamed up with her brilliant friend and colleague, Dr. Helen Elion, to start MSI. Together, they had but one mission. To find a cure for Alzheimer's. They worked tirelessly, seven days a week, to find a cure. That was their passionate dream.

"Their dream—until this predatory conglomerate hunted them down and stole their dream by stealing their ideas. Fifty *billion* dollars wasn't enough for these corporate cheats. They wanted more. They saw an opportunity to make billions more with a miracle Alzheimer's drug, but they didn't have the talent to do it themselves. So they concocted and executed a fraud scheme to steal it from a company that did have the talent. Members of the jury, only one company on the entire planet had that talent. That company is MSI. And the two women who were making it all happen—Anne Little and Helen Elion—are sitting right there at that table. Ladies and gentlemen, we are here today because Jager Pharmaceuticals ruthlessly defrauded them and stole their dream.

"The defendant had an unlimited budget to fight this lawsuit, which it almost exceeded. They hired four experts to be paid mouth-pieces for them, and an army of lawyers. Just look around the courtroom at all the suits and ties. Experts charging up to two thousand dollars an hour to smugly shill for Jager in one last effort to crush Drs. Little and Elion. Remember last week when I totaled it up for you? They've paid these hired guns more than seven million dollars to try to pull off their final con—in this courtroom with the nine of you as their marks."

He paused. He didn't need a bunch of grossly overpaid expert witnesses. He had something much better. He had his two genius-level clients, who had the added benefit of brutal and refreshing honesty. Dr. Little was a natural born teacher, Dr. Elion more of the pure research virtuoso. During the trial he had Dr. Little explain the brain. Astronomers tell us that the Big Bang created the universe almost 14 billion years ago. Earth formed 4.5 billion years ago. So far, the most remarkable known development in all that time is the human brain. Some say it is the crowning achievement of evolution. There are many extraordinary things brilliant scientists know about the brain, but there are still mysteries to be solved. Dr. Little taught the jury essential facts about the human brain and explained how Alzheimer's erodes it. Explained what cure MSI was on the cusp of developing. Dr. Little was spellbinding in a matter-of-fact sort of way. He always wanted his experts to speak like a good high school teacher when addressing jurors. Even the most complex

subjects can be explained by a gifted and enthusiastic teacher motivated to teach, not preach or be seduced by the sound of their own
voice. Dr. Little had gotten off the witness stand, stood in front of
the jurors, and taught. The students listened.

He spent thirty minutes walking the jury through Dr. Little's
testimony. This natural teacher had explained how the human
brain weighs about three pounds, has a texture similar to firm jelly, and needs proper hydration because 75 percent of our brains
consists of water. Dr. Little related to the jury. She had explained
that this three-pound jelly organ has a huge appetite. It consumes
about 20 percent of the oxygen and fuel our blood carries in our
bodies. How much blood actually flows through our brains, the
jurors might wonder? Every minute enough to fill a thirty-three-
ounce soda bottle. That is why aerobic exercise, which increases our
heart rates and blood flow to our brains and thereby allows more
oxygen to be delivered to our brains, is important for both physical
and mental health. And she amused the jury by letting them know
that our brains are the fattiest organs in our bodies, weighing in at
60 percent fat, but that weight doesn't slow down the brain's information highway, which clocks speeds of about 268 miles an hour.

Dr. Little's testimony was designed to do two things: to explain
how a normal functioning brain works so she could then explain
just how perniciously Alzheimer's destroys it. With that founda-
tion, Dr. Little then explained how so many brilliant scientists have
tried to unlock the mystery but have failed. So the jurors could understand just how pathbreaking MSI's research is. How dastardly
the defendant deceived, lied, and stole. How the promise of their
research provided hope, not dread, for an increasing number of human beings who live long lives. Hope that life can end with dignity,
not despair and desperate dependence.

He reminded the jury that the next part of Dr. Little's testimony
was a little harder to follow but was essential to understanding Alzheimer's. Dr. Little explained that our brains have an astonishingly
large number of nerve cells. They're called neurons. How many?
About 100 billion she told the jurors. Jonathan wrote the number on a big chalkboard—100,000,000,000. Dr. Little gave that
number astronomical perspective by explaining that the number of

neurons in our brains is about the same as the number of stars in our galaxy. Dr. Elion's animated color graphic perfectly punctuated the point. Like looking at the Milky Way in motion through the Hubble Telescope. He paused to let that extraordinary fact sink in.

Jonathan asked the jury to recall that Dr. Little explained that it all gets even more amazing. Even more staggering to comprehend. She explained that these 100 billion nerve cells are connected by branches at more than 100 trillion points. Our brains have tremendous difficulty comprehending large numbers, so Dr. Little told the jurors that scientists have estimated that if you laid 100 trillion dollar bills end to end, they would stretch from planet Earth to the Sun, ninety-three million miles away. Jonathan paused before returning to the chalkboard and adding three more zeros to the number—100,000,000,000,000. Remember, he told the jury, all of this activity in a piece of jelly that weighs three pounds. Brain scientists call this the neuron forest. All the time, Dr. Elion continued to display with dazzling computergraphics what Jonathan was explaining. Several of the jurors were on the edges of their seats as they watched in fascination how the visuals brought to life the complex inner workings of the human brain.

Jonathan paused again to let this all sink in. He recounted how Dr. Little had explained that the brain sends signals through the neuron forest. These signals give us our memories. Our thoughts. Our feelings. Astonishingly, all of this happens in individual, tiny, tiny cells. And really smart scientists have figured out that something called neurotransmitters carry our brain's signals from cell to cell. That is how a normal functioning brain works.

And that is the point of attack for Alzheimer's. Alzheimer's disrupts the way electrical charges travel within our cells. And it disrupts the activity of the neurotransmitters that carry the signals to our brain cells.

Using a harrowing visual that Jonathan showed the jurors again, Dr. Little explained how Alzheimer's kills nerve cells and causes tissue loss. Over time, Alzheimer's causes the brain to shrink dramatically. Jonathan remembered that when Dr. Little had explained the shrinking brain two weeks ago, jurors edged up on their chairs, so he lingered a bit and stood silent for a moment to let them stare at the dreadful picture of a shrunken brain. Jonathan could feel their fear. His gut told him that everybody in the courtroom was thinking the same thing: "That could very well be me one day." He could also feel their desperate hope: "Somebody *please* find a cure."

The courtroom was silent. As if paying proper respect to the visual of a shriveled brain. Jonathan made a mental note that several of the jurors glanced over at Drs. Little and Elion, in silent acknowledgment that there were two saviors in the courtroom.

In a soft but somewhat accusatory voice, Jonathan looked at the jurors and asked, "So what is the killer?" Dr. Little had explained that scientists don't know for sure, but she and Dr. Elion believe that there are two prime suspects. They are called plaques and tangles. Dr. Little unpacked this by explaining that plaques are deposits of a protein fragment called beta-amyloid, which build up in the spaces between our nerve cells. Tangles, she had explained, are twisted fibers of another protein called tau that build up inside our cells. Dr. Little had explained that all of us develop plaques and tangles as we age. But Alzheimer's patients develop far more of them, beginning in the memory area of our brains.

Dr. Little explained that these plaques and tangles are hungry beasts. They spread in our brain's cortex and don't stop until we die. In the process, Alzheimer's patients lose their capacity for daily existence. Talking, walking, bathing, eating, and, of course, remembering. They can't answer the basic question we all ask of ourselves from time to time—Who am I? Worse, they lose the ability to even ask the question.

Dr. Little had explained for the jurors the revolutionary nature of MSI's research. She explained how the federal Food and Drug Administration has approved some Alzheimer's drugs, but those drugs only treat Alzheimer's *symptoms*; they do not treat the underlying *causes*. Drs. Little and Elion and MSI have zeroed in on the underlying causes. They were working on medications related to beta-amyloid, the primary plaque component. And they were working on medications related to the tau proteins, the primary component of tangles. And they were close. Tantalizingly close. He asked the jurors to imagine what it must have felt like to be on the verge of solving the mystery of Alzheimer's and improving the quality of life for millions of people—only to have it stolen away so the stupendously rich could get even richer.

Jonathan then shifted gears from the aspiration of medical hope to the avaricious greed of the defendant's deceptive scheme, his voice slowly rising, his tone shifting from inspiration to accusation. A low-boil anger.

By the summer of 2018, MSI had ten employees in addition to Drs. Little and Elion. All were brilliant young scientists working on the same mission to annihilate Alzheimer's. Their small company worked out of rented space in Mountain View, California, and had eighteen patents but no revenues, just some seed money from an investor hoping that they would develop the drugs and then commercialize them at fair market value. They were getting really close.

That is when the hunter found its prey. Jager Pharmaceuticals had all the money and lots of scientists, but nobody with anything approaching MSI's Alzheimer's expertise. So the charlatans prepared the big lie. The apparent plan was to partner up. MSI would supply the medical and scientific expertise and the defendant would provide marketing support and the money to commercialize an FDA-approved drug. The parties executed a term sheet that also provided for a buy-out option allowing Jager to buy MSI for $2 billion. He wrote that figure on an easel next to the jury box.

Turning up the heat, Jonathan methodically marched the jurors through the evidence of the big lie to infiltrate MSI to figure out how to develop the Alzheimer's drugs and then leave MSI high and dry. He damned Jager with its own contemporaneous documents, emails, strategy presentations, and board of directors' minutes that proved that the corporate cheat's perfidious plan all long was to defraud MSI. Jonathan reviewed testimony from the defendant's own employees, where he secured incriminating admissions on cross-examination that Jager never intended to follow through with a partnership with MSI. It was all just one big lie. The courtroom was silent.

Jonathan paused. He resumed by revisiting the MSI testimony that explained how, after a year of working side-by-side with Jager, the hunter just walked away. Walked away but not before looting MSI's intellectual property secrets, smug in their arrogant but false assumption that they could now bring an Alzheimer's cure drug to market without the help of MSI. How, after a year's time, MSI was out of money and unable to go forward. He asked the jury to imagine Dr. Little's deteriorating grandmother and a dream destroyed.

Finally, Jonathan reviewed MSI's economic expert's opinion explaining how the defendant had harmed MSI. How Jager did a corporate spin-off of the division that had defrauded MSI and was able to raise billions of dollars after issuing a prospectus falsely trumpeting a forthcoming Alzheimer's cure. That never happened. Jager first lied to MSI, then to investors, and finally to the members of the jury. Jonathan paused and put the term sheet on the big screen, showing that Jager had valued MSI at $2 billion. Now it was worth nothing. The hunter reduced MSI to desiccated roadkill.

Jonathan, with purpose in his step, went back to counsel's table and stood behind Drs. Little and Elion. They were there every minute of the trial. A hand on each of their shoulders, Jonathan Kent proudly told the jurors that it was the honor of his lifetime to represent these two remarkable and inspiring scientists. He was almost finished.

Slowly walking back close to the jury rail, Jonathan spoke his final words to the five women and four men who would decide the case.

"Ladies and gentlemen, we are here today because this defendant refused to tell the truth. Fifty billion dollars wasn't enough money for their bonus-baby executives. So they lied. They lied at least thirty different times to Dr. Little and to Dr. Elion about their intent. And they lied to you in this courtroom. We exposed those lies with their own documents when we cross-examined them.

"In this courtroom you heard their lies. You heard their feeble explanations for their conduct. Did they ring true to you? We know from our everyday lives, from our common sense, that when an explanation is successful, we feel the key turn in the lock. Then we hear the click. When the defendant's lawyers offered up their explanations, did you feel the key turn in the lock? Did you hear a click? Or did the key stick, refusing to turn because the key was fake? Just like the explanations and excuses you heard in the courtroom to cover up the lies Drs. Little and Elion heard out of the mouths of corporate cons who attempted to steal a cure. To steal a dream. All because fifty billion dollars is not enough for them.

"So what is their defense? Ladies and gentlemen, it's a scoundrel's defense. The old standby when you have nothing else: it's called blame the victim. Jager claims that Drs. Little and Elion should have been more diligent and less trusting and should have been more lawyered up when they negotiated the term sheet. Think about the arrogance of it all. What Jager is really asking you to believe is that the good doctors were fools for believing a single word that came out of their lying mouths. That they should have equipped themselves with lie detectors when dealing with Jager's unscrupulous businesspeople. Ladies and gentlemen, that's not a defense to fraud, it's a damning indictment of their own deceptive conduct. And it's insulting.

"We all know that money cannot fully repay Drs. Little and Elion for the harm they have suffered at the hands of this corrupt corporation. But that's how the law tries. Money is how you can make Jager pay for its fraudulent conduct. Members of the jury, you will render a verdict in this case. I ask you to please keep in mind that there is no such thing as a big verdict or a small verdict. There is only a just verdict. And that is all we are asking from you, to deliver a just verdict.

"Allow me a word about justice. That is what you have the power to deliver. This defendant deliberately set out to defraud MSI and deserves to be punished. This isn't the law of the jungle. We're talking about trust, honesty, and integrity. They belong in corporate boardrooms. But they are not in Jager Pharmaceutical's corporate boardroom. Now you can send a message with your verdict that it is high time they should be. Because money is the only message these fraudsters understand, we are asking you to get their attention with one billion dollars in punitive damages.

"On your verdict form, we are asking for damages of two billion dollars to compensate MSI for the harm caused by the defendant. And for punitive damages to send a message loud and clear that lying and cheating and killing humanitarian dreams is not acceptable. The word *verdict* means 'speak the truth.' With your verdict, you will speak the truth about the kind of world you want to live in.

"Jager Pharmaceuticals thinks it's the kind of world where a mammoth corporation can hunt down and squish a small company with the potential to improve and save the lives of millions of ordinary people. Where lying to steal billions is perfectly acceptable. You have the power to tell them they are wrong.

"Ladies and gentlemen, I submit that for the past three weeks we proved to you that what Jager Pharmaceuticals did to MSI was wrong. Really wrong. On behalf of Drs. Anne Little and Helen Elion and MSI, I thank you for your time and attention. Our fate is in your hands."

It was eleven o'clock on Wednesday morning. The judge gave the jury instructions on the law, sent them off to lunch, and told them to begin their deliberations in the afternoon.

After thirty years of trying cases, this seasoned warrior thought this might have been his finest effort. Others told him the same thing. And he had tried difficult cases throughout the United States, some in this very courthouse. He felt good, but the case was now completely out of his hands and with the jury. No control. All he could do was wait. No control and waiting—he wasn't very good at either.

Wednesday ended with no verdict. Not surprising, Jonathan reasoned from experience. The jury had lots of evidence to review, and he was impressed with their commitment. They seemed smart, attentive, and diligent. He assumed they were just trying to get it right.

It was now early Friday morning. No verdict on Thursday. Jonathan had just finished his morning run along Embarcadero and the San Francisco Bay, about ten miles. Confident, yes, but the inevitable self-doubt that anxious waiting brings was creeping in. *What is taking the jury so long?* he wondered. *Do I still have it? Did I try the case the right way? Did I strike the right tone in closing argument, or did I offend some of the jurors?*

Running was usually a good distraction for him, but this morning the relaxing state of euphoria from his runner's high was giving way to anxious self-doubt.

Jonathan showered and, as was his long-standing custom, donned a tailor-made but understated navy blue suit with soft blue pinstripes redolent of understated elegance, white shirt with blue pinstripes, no cuffllinks, and an emerald-green tie. Black shoes, polished and shined, back to court he went.

At 11:30 a.m. the jury sent a note that they had reached a verdict. Anxiety and anticipation pulsated through his and everyone else's body. Slowly the jurors filed in, heads mostly hanging down, and took their seats. Placid faces giving no indication of the decision they had reached. The jury foreperson handed the verdict to the deputy clerk, who handed it up to the judge. The jury unanimously found that Jager Pharmaceuticals harmed MSI by committing fraud. The judge then read the damages verdict—$2 billion. Gasps in the courtroom. The judge next took a deep breath and announced that the jury awarded MSI $1 billion in punitive damages. The courtroom erupted. The heartfelt hugs from Anne and Helen, clients and friends, were electric and soul satisfying.

The press ran several praiseworthy stories about Jonathan and the case. It was the largest jury verdict of the year in the United States. And Jonathan, who in recent years had started to represent underdog plaintiffs rather than defend powerful corporations like Jager, with stiff resistance from his Big Law management, had taken the case on contingency, meaning that his firm would get paid only if they won and recovered. They did win, and the defendant had $50 billion. Jager could afford to share three billion of that dough with MSI and its accomplished avenger.

Already a trial lawyer legend, the MSI verdict further intensified the luminosity of Jonathan's star. He was on corporate America's shortlist for the very toughest lawsuits. With a free afternoon before heading back to DC in the morning, he did what he loved to do in San Francisco. Trek through the streets, content to follow where his feet led.

Out of his suit and into his Nikes, Jonathan wandered the streets and hills of San Francisco to decompress and reflect. As a young man, he had naively assumed that professional success was destiny. Now older and wiser, he acutely appreciated that his path to legendary trial lawyer at a major American law firm was far from preordained. In fact, with his humble origins, it was most improbable. But for most of his career, he was an arresting arriviste whose ascension to the top epitomized the amoral zeitgeist of Big Law in the twenty-first century. His professional biography represented an American paradigm for the generation referred to as the Baby Boomers. Now late in his career, he was changing. He had just won a fight on the side of the angels. It felt good.

Ascending Telegraph Hill and mulling around Coit Tower, with panoramic views of the Golden City and sparkling bay, Jonathan was feeling restless and introspective. Perched atop the Big Law pyramid, at the pinnacle of his storied career, but frustrated and disillusioned with the values and ethos of his firm and Big Law, he lay in the grass and drifted into a reminiscent trance, reflecting on the long arc of his life and career and wondering where it goes from here.

ESCAPE AND INDEPENDENCE

Born and raised in the Midwest, Jonathan attended a predominantly blue-collar high school, where he excelled in sports and studies. College was not destination central for most. But for as long as this restless romantic could remember, he was something of a dreamer. And Jonathan dreamed big. Dreams often naive in appreciating the obstacles and harsh realities that crush many a hope and aspiration of a young imagination from modest circumstances and no connections. Rags-to-riches stories excite the imagination, sometimes even inspire hope, but they are mythical precisely because they are so fanciful for the multitude. Black swan events might happen, but they are extremely rare. Jonathan's uninspiring high school guidance counselor, not one to think big or advise many college-bound students, envisioned no black swan when he recommended that Jonathan accept a baseball scholarship to a small college and pursue a job at a beer distributorship following graduation. At eighteen Jonathan wasn't sure what he wanted to do at twenty-two, but a job selling suds and recounting the glory days until time slips away was not the dream-come-true life he was envisioning. For him, there *had* to be something more promising for an escape out of a life dominated by the whims and caprices of ignoramuses and jerks.

Jonathan learned early that Henry David Thoreau was probably right that most men live lives of quiet desperation as he despondently watched his own father, uncles, and fathers of friends muddle frustratingly through life as workers and middle managers, always punching the clock and answering to the boss man. Boss men uncharitably but spot-on accurately referred to as a bunch of pricks and jackasses who, as his father complained, "don't have the brains God gave a goose." Whether the shop foreman or some corporate nincompoop possessing a meaningless title and imperious attitude, Jonathan was smart, really smart, and ambitious and did not intend to go through life kissing some halfwit's ass just to keep a job that had a countdown clock ticking away the days until he could get the hell out. Fear of ordinariness, ennui, banality, and especially subservience motivated Jonathan at eighteen and for the rest of his life. As did fear of a slumberous life. The dynamo exited his mother's womb in an agitated state of restlessness that gathered steam with each passing year. Reflexively, intellectual wanderlust caused him to crave action and new challenges. He determined to be alive before he died, not passing time circling the drain until nothing remains but death and pain.

There were no lawyers in Jonathan's family. That included the extended family of grandparents, aunts, uncles, cousins, and the entire family tree. He knew some guys in high school whose dads were lawyers, but as best as he could tell, they handled simple wills, divorces, and DUIs. In Jonathan's parochial world growing up, words such as *antitrust, torts, intellectual property*, and *securities* were as arcane and abstruse as Latin and Greek.

The lens of life would begin to broaden soon enough for the young man. By the time he enrolled in his midwestern college, he knew instinctively that the first biological lesson of history is that life is competitive, often nasty, and brutally competitive. It is also unsparingly impersonal and exceedingly short. The world did not give a damn about Jonathan Kent, and nobody anywhere was looking to help him out. He was and always would be on his own. Jonathan reasoned that he did not make the rules of the life he was born into and had no ability to change them. But he was a savvy survivor and fervently determined to be a rules master, not a slave. And he most certainly had no intent of being a slave to the world's pricks and goose brains. To be his own master, the ambitious young man determined that he would need money and independence, not just to say fuck you to the halfwits but to live life on his terms. He was hardwired to beat his own path and trusted nothing but his own instincts and ingenuity to survive and thrive.

A dreamer, but also a born probabilist, Jonathan thoughtfully considered and weighed the probabilities and consequences of potential courses of action before he made important decisions. His choice of college major and potential career was guided by the twin North Stars of money and its concomitant independence. Blue Bic ballpoint in hand, he listed out his options on a yellow legal pad. With his intellectual firepower and energy, not to mention self-assurance, he reasonably assumed that pretty much all options were on the table. Now was the time for the process of elimination.

Beginning a process that he repeated in his early professional years, the overachiever first looked outward rather than inward to begin his career calculation. *Not who am I and what do I want, but instead, who do Americans admire and financially reward the most?* he asked himself. That helped him narrow his focus and eliminate options. High on the American worship list were Hollywood celebrities and musicians, especially rock musicians. After all, Americans refer to megastars in various walks of life as "rock stars." Hollywood heartthrob Warren Beatty and skinny lead singers got the chicks back then, but Jonathan was looking for more out of life than random hookups, fornication prowess, and herpes. Jonathan quickly checked them off the list. Same with professional athletes, even the best of whom peak and fade before age forty, although he might have changed his mind if he were a left-handed pitcher with high heat, a fall-off-the-table curveball, nasty cutter, and a disappearing changeup. But he wasn't.

Military leaders in the twenty-first century, much more than when Jonathan started college, are admired and many have gone on to make money in business. But the still-fresh Vietnam War experience soured a lot of the American public on the military, and there was no denying that it was a long and potentially lethal slog to the top. More disqualifying for Jonathan, the military was about the last place to look at for a young man seeking independence. Then there was the hair: he preferred freak flag to peach fuzz.

Astronauts and civil engineers held appeal to the adventurous

Jonathan. He was a young boy in 1969 when Neil Armstrong and Buzz Aldrin landed the Apollo Lunar Module Eagle on the southeastern edge of the moon's Sea of Tranquility on that unforgettable July day, fulfilling President John Kennedy's famous challenge to Congress in 1961 to put a man on the moon in less than a decade. Why wouldn't a talented young boy reach for the stars when his country was landing men on the moon? To this day Jonathan gets chills thinking about the message Armstrong radioed back to mission control in Houston: "The Eagle has landed." Mars might be next, but not likely in Jonathan's lifetime. Ultimately, he concluded, there aren't too many opportunities to go boldly where no one man has gone before, so Jonathan scratched astronaut off his list.

He also thought civil engineering could be a cool job. Civil engineers can think big. Really big. He liked the idea of designing and building major infrastructure projects like the Hoover Dam or the Golden Gate Bridge. That takes imagination and execution, two of his trademarks. But, as with astronauts, there would likely be exceedingly few opportunities to do something grand unless he joined a major construction firm and risked getting stuck in middle management. Such a risk was paralytic for Jonathan.

Jonathan figured that accountants made money, how much he had nary a clue, but green shirts and brown hush puppy shoes didn't ding his beanie. Jonathan wanted to count his own beans, not some other guy's. Bankers also presumably made money, but the only thing he knew about bankers was what he learned from reading Mark Twain: they are fellows who lend you an umbrella when the sun is shining and want it back the minute it begins to rain.

As far as Jonathan was concerned, Wall Street investment bankers, hedge fund Huns, and private equity vultures made a lot of money, some obscene amounts of money, but for the life of him he could not understand the allure of money fetishism, money manipulation, and financial engineering. To be sure, Jonathan wanted to make a lot of money, but as a means to his end of individual independence and being the master of his own fate. Not as a way to prove his penis size by pillaging and plundering companies as he tooled around in a Porsche and named his yacht *Nauti Fortune*. And as far as he could tell, most of those gel heads were aliens by way of private prep schools and legacy admissions to Ivy League colleges. That seemed a real stretch for him. Besides, he didn't aspire to drain martinis at lunch and fret over the color and design of his suspenders.

Then there was the nebulous businessperson (at the time, businessman). Corporate America dominated American life and was the ineluctable destination of many college graduates, mostly by default. *But what the hell does it actually mean to be a businessperson,* Jonathan wondered, *and what does a businessperson actually do?* That could all get figured out, he presumed, but the idea of donning the proverbial gray flannel suit and melding into a faceless, obsequious conforming life of corporatism would be the very antithesis of the life he was longing for. A life where he would have to surrender originality and independence, a life with long odds of ever earning escape money. Jonathan scribbled that toady option right off the list.

So how about medicine? Jonathan was excellent in math and science, not afraid of blood or organic chemistry, and figured everybody likes doctors, except for ambulance-chasing lawyers. He did not know any doctors or doctors' kids socially, but to Jonathan they pretty much seemed to call their own shots in life. It also seemed like they made good money. After all, he thought, only the kids in the rich schools had doctors for parents. There was no doubt, in Jonathan's estimation, that doctors did admirable work.

And he did believe that the world would be a better place if all professionals, not just doctors, followed the basic principles of the Hippocratic oath. He gave medicine close consideration but decided that he had found something more enticing and to the liking of his competitive personality.

Lawyer. In the parochial world of his youth, Jonathan had never heard the cynical lawyer jokes. Indeed, saying he wanted to be a lawyer induced a collective exclamation of "Wow!" from family members who cheered him on. A son or relative who was a lawyer would create a halo effect and bring bragging rights in Jonathan's little familial orbit. All except his maternal grandmother, who harbored hope that one day he would become the first American pope. An aspiration with at least more inspiration than a beer distributorship. Neither Jonathan nor his family had any clue about what life was like for high-achieving lawyers in major American law firms, but they would learn in due course that professional success exacts a heavy personal price. Indeed, later in life he would shake his head in disbelief that rich, poor, and middle-class parents alike made sacrifices and incurred debt, often staggering debt, for their kids to get ahead in the hopes that one day their American Dream–chasing kids might land a job with a silk-stocking law firm, when those jobs unceremoniously chewed up and spit out most of the young men and women who began their working lives at those legal sweatshops. But that was later.

So Jonathan mapped out his plan. He would major in economics, which seemed easy enough, get all A's, graduate in three years, and then go to a top law school. He even visited local courthouses and watched some trials, convincing himself all the more that not only could he do this, but he could be very good. Unlike many college students who are good at school and go to law school because they are unsure about what else they can do and therefore default to the comfort zone of a classroom, Jonathan knew exactly why he wanted to go to law school. He wanted to become a trial lawyer.

The aspiring barrister confidently assumed that he would be a natural in law school. There, his classmates would be competitive foes he could vanquish in the pursuit of top grades, the holy grail in the soulless culture of American law schools and the yellow brick road to Big Law—the major law firms in the country. Grades, or class rank, would be an external validation, an objective measure, a reification of his intellectual prowess and, for Jonathan and so many others, his self-worth. So college had a tangible, teleological purpose for Jonathan: get A's and be accepted into a top law school. Learning for its own sake or as a means of self-exploration was not something he was initially seeking. But then life, Jonathan discovered soon enough, is a long, strange trip full of unanticipated twists and turns. And young love was about to twist and turn him around and around.

SHELLY

A man on a mission to zip through college with stellar grades, Jonathan was a fixture in his college library, where he studied when not in class. He staked out his place on the seventh floor, which housed the literature, classics, foreign languages, and art history books. Not much traffic on that floor. Better for solitary study. Jonathan laid claim to an isolated carrel by the windows and typically studied until the closing hour of midnight.

To graduate in three years, Jonathan took classes all year round. A scholarship relieved the burden of having to work in the summers, although he pocketed spending money by tutoring struggling calculus and statistics students, mostly in the social sciences and premed. The demand exceeded his ability to supply. It was the beginning of summer semester following sophomore year. Two advanced econ courses and a philosophy elective—God, Perfection, and Evil—filled his plate. He was parked in his carrel, on course to finish in three years and knocking out top grades, per his ambitious plan. It was that Friday night when he learned that some fates cannot be denied.

His watch read 9:30 p.m. His eyes followed perfection walk to the center table, where she dropped her books and took a seat. Couldn't take his eyes off her. Her lithe voluptuousness, flawless face, and mesmerizing eyes. Emerald green, more luminescent than jade, ensconced perfectly in her beautiful face. A face radiating intelligence and supremacy. His senses were on fire. He looked at his watch. It now read 10:15; he hadn't studied a lick in the last forty-five minutes. Barely looked at his books or notes. The brain's medulla controls involuntary functions, like reflexes. Jonathan's medulla directed him straight to this ravishing young woman's table. Without hesitation or abashment, he introduced himself.

"Excuse me, my name's Jonathan Kent. I basically own that carrel over there. Looks like you're the only other person on the floor, so I thought I'd stop by and introduce myself."

"How welcoming of you. My name is Michele. I haven't seen you around. Looks like I'm not the only lonely soul burning the Friday midnight oil. You a lit major?"

"Econ. I've commandeered a carrel up here because it's so quiet. The main floor seems to be more for socializing than studying." *Perhaps not the best line*, he thought, as he was obviously hitting on her.

"I know what you mean. I usually study in my apartment, but I'm working on a term paper about Jane Austen and her influence on the modern novel. Thought I would camp out here to be close to the stacks and source materials." *Something about this guy*, she thought.

"Sounds challenging, and pretty ambitious." Jonathan was smitten and searching for a way to keep the conversation going. "I read *Pride and Prejudice* in high school, but that's about it for me and Jane Austen. Good book." *That's the best line I can come up with?*

"Then, Mr. Darcy, you probably remember her iconic first sentence—'It is a truth universally acknowledged that a single man in possession of a good fortune must be in want of a wife.'" She thought, *Did I really just say that to a guy I never met before?*

Be still my beating heart, Jonathan said to himself. "That's a great opening to a book. Certainly makes you want to read on." As fate would have it, he had just read a book last semester in an elective literature course that was now going to come in handy for repartee with a lit major. "Just like the opening sentence in Dickens's *David Copperfield*, 'Whether I shall turn out to be the hero of my own life, or whether that station will be held by anybody else, these pages must show.'"

"Well played for one majoring in the dismal science. Are you going to be the hero of your own life, Mr. Kent?" she asked, with a slight degree of coyness slipping out of her remarkable eyes.

Oh, she's good. "That's my plan. But I suppose I'll need a little help along the way," he said, with a slight wink. "I do hope, down the road when the candle of my life is burning out, I'll at least have a good story to tell."

"Laudable ambition. I hope you make your way. Anyway, you ought to try out two of Jane Austen's other books, *Emma* and *Persuasion*. She is a master psychologist and so skilled in character portrayal and relationships, especially romance and the maturation of love. And the notion of persuasion, for good or bad, as fundamental to human communication. But listen to me. You didn't introduce yourself to hear me carry on about one of my very favorite novelists," Michele said, as she thought, *I don't want this guy to leave just yet.*

Are you kidding me? I could look into your emerald-green eyes and listen to you all night. "No, this is great, but I guess I should let you study. The library closes at midnight, and it's almost 10:30. Nice to meet you, Michele. Good luck with the term paper."

"Nice to meet you, Jonathan." *Why not?* she thought. *It feels right.* "Hey, I don't know if you're a night owl, but if you would like to unwind from studying and have a drink and listen to some good music after we get kicked out of here, KB's Keyboard Lounge is a happening place."

Seriously? This is moving fast. "Isn't that a jazz place? Don't know much about jazz, but I guess college is for learning. Sounds like a fun plan," he said. *I think I'll let Michele teach me anything she likes.*

The jazz and company were perfect. There was an electrical jolt from soul to soul that night, causing what the French-speaking Michele later in their relationship romantically described as a *coup de foudre*. Love at first sight that quickly developed into a dazzling relationship. Listening to jazz at KB's Keyboard Lounge, Jonathan received his first glimpse of Michele's passion for jazz. Later, there would be Miles Davis blowing trumpet on his iconic album *Kind of Blue*, and "Grazing in the Grass" is a gas of a song you can dig when Hugh Masekela is playing it. Michele turned Jonathan on to sax players like Charlie Parker, Sonny Rollins, Grover Washington Jr., Stanley Turrentine and *Pieces of Dreams*, and the incomparable John Coltrane and *A Love Supreme*, an album they played over and over. She loved the great jazz pianists McCoy Tyner, Les Mc-

Cann and "Compared to What," Thelonious Monk, Herbie Hancock and "Watermelon Man," as well as Dave Brubeck and "Take Five" and Keith Jarrett and his mesmerizing 1975 *Koln Concert*. The French-Italian jazz violinist Stephane Grappelli was a favorite, as well as the ethereal sounds emanating from the French jazz violin virtuoso Jean-Luc Ponty on *Imaginary Voyage*.

The jazz inflamed the passions pumping in their hearts. They met up a few days later at the student union for a study break that turned into an hours-long discussion of books, ideas, music, backgrounds, and life plans. Law school for Jonathan, graduate school, eventually, for Michele. More jazz at KB's Keyboard Lounge and late-night listening at Michele's apartment.

They discovered a mutual passion—long weekend bicycle rides on their ten-speed bicycles. A red Schwinn Continental for her, black Raleigh Competition for him, pedaling through pastoral lands and swimming in sparkling lakes. Movies and music, books and conversation, bicycle rides and long walks holding hands. Study sessions on the seventh floor until midnight closing, often interrupted by surreptitious and extended kissing and canoodling.

Early fall, they made love for the first time. Joni Mitchell's *Miles of Aisles* playing softly on Michele's stereo. Slow french kisses and gentle hand explorations causing mutual arousal. Foreplay with inevitability. "Jonathan, I'm ready," Michele whispered softly in his ear. "I want to make love. Go slow."

"I want you, Michele," Jonathan whispered back. "Let's help each other." Both were inexperienced. Both wanted the first time to be special. They guided each other along, providing the other particularly pleasing sensations. Jonathan intensified Michele's passion by entering her, staring into her luminescent eyes all the while, so each could see the special passion the other was feeling. One inhabiting the other through the silent communication of the eyes and the union of their bodies. As they stayed in each other's embrace, Michele whispered, "That was wonderful," then both drifted off into serene sleep.

Michele loved the romantic poets. Percy Bysshe Shelley and John Keats were her favorites. In the morning, she quoted Shelley and sweetly said to Jonathan that "soul meets soul on lover's lips. Jonathan, last night you touched my soul. You are my soulmate."

"And you are mine," he responded. "From now on I'm going to call you Shelly. That will be my pet name for you. Shelley, author of the poem "Love's Philosophy," where he wrote, 'Nothing in the world is single, all things by a law divine, in one spirit meet and mingle, why not I with thine?" You, Shelly, by a law divine are my romantic spirit."

"I love it," she said as she gave him a wonderful kiss. "And I have a pet name for you. I waited until we made love to share it."

"This should be good."

"I'm going to call you Jack."

"I like Shelly better."

"Not Jack, J-A-C-K. But Jak, J-A-K."

"Okay, but what's the difference. They sound the same?"

Jonathan was learning that Michele—Shelly—was whimsical. Yet something else about her he found so attractive. "Maybe to an econ major but not to a literature and art history double major. Your full name is Jonathan Andrew Kent, initials JAK."

"Darling, that doesn't sound too original."

"I'm not done. There is beautiful symmetry in your initials. The letter A is the number 1 in the alphabet. The letter J is number 10 and K is number 11. Together, they are 11011. Perfect symmetry and the binary code of the computer revolution! Ha! And you didn't think a humanities major was good with numbers."

"Well, I have to admit I never thought of that. Pretty cool."

"I've got more," Shelly teased with glee. "There are twenty-six letters in the alphabet. J, A, and K are the only three that so rhyme. Fourteen don't rhyme with any other letter. Nine rhyme with one another. B, C, D, E, G, P, T, V, and Z. Then there are J, A, and K. The magical three. In Latin omni trium perfectum means the perfect three. OTP. J, A, K are the perfect three, just like you," she beamed as she gave him another passionate kiss. "From now on, you're Jak. My Jak, my soulmate."

"And, soulmate, you're my Shelly."

By junior year, the soulmates were inseparable. "Jak, when soulmates meet, something wonderful happens," Shelly said to him. "A passionate desire and the need to be in each other's company. That's how I feel about us."

"I feel the same way," Jak said. "Even in class, I can't wait until it's over so I can be with you."

"You should read John Keats's poem 'Bright Star, Would I Were Steadfast as Thou Art.' It's how I feel about us. A desire to remain in my lover's company   forever. To have your head rest on my breast and feel it gently rise and fall while I breathe, awake forever in a sweet unrest. And let me die if this cannot persist forever."

"That's wonderful," Jak said, as he prepared to say three perfect words to his soulmate. "Shelly, my dear, I love you."

"Jak, I love you." Then three more perfect words: "I always will."

"As will I you."

"Jak, omni trium perfectum. OTP. That will be our special code. OTP, for I love you. And OTP, I always will."

"Shelly, I know we've been talking about this, but I've made a decision. I'm not going to graduate in three years. I want to spend senior year with you so we can graduate together. Take a bunch of lit and philosophy courses to round out more. Then I'll go to law school."

"Really, Jak? Really, that's wonderful. I know how eager you are to start law school. That you would do that for me, for us, so we can have a special senior year together. Oh, I do love you."

"What can I say, I'm hopelessly in love."

"Last one to the bedroom has to turn out the lights!"

PASSION

Shelly's ebullience and vivaciousness opened up Jak to an emotional world he never imagined could be so liberating. He was emotionally vulnerable and laying his soul bare to her. Passionate love was his reward.

One night as he sat down at his library carrel, he found a love note with some lines from Tennyson's poem "Locksley Hall": "For I dipped into the future, as far as my eyes could see/saw the vision of the world and the wonder that would be. Jak, I have a vision of the wonder of you and me, Love Shelly."

One night out of the blue, "Jak, let's take some classes in ballroom dancing," Shelly urged him.

"You must be joking. I don't dance. At my high school prom, I was practically forced at gunpoint to do one slow dance with my date. I was like a statue. It was awful. No wonder that was the one and only date with Susie Anderson." Jak was terrified at the thought. With Shelly's extraordinary legs and athletic grace, she would likely make him look like he had two left feet and suffered from spasticity.

"Don't be a stick in the mud. You'll be a natural. You're limber and a terrific athlete. Don't forget," she said suggestively, "I know how you can move those hips."

"Not the same thing, but I'll gladly show you some hip movement right now if you're game."

"Dance first, dessert later, if you're good."

"Okay, I'm game. But no pictures!"

And so Jak and Shelly learned to dance together. They learned the foxtrot, iconic waltz, and the Argentine tango. Jak loved it. So Shelly upped the ante and took Jak by the hand as they learned more sultry Latin styles.

The east coast swing, jazzy jive, pelvic-tilting samba, and Shelly's favorite, the intimate romantic rumba, the dance of love. On the dance floor, they learned to move their bodies alluringly, rhythmically together, from elegance and grace to fervent flair and burning orgasmic energy desiring to combust.

Combust is what their sexual energy was doing. Together they read the *Kama Sutra*, a sybaritic guide that took their lovemaking to erotic new dimensions. More than just a how-to manual on titillating sexual positions, the book taught them ethics and aesthetics and the art of living well.

Shelly especially appreciated the book's emphasis on how a man should unselfishly prioritize a woman's pleasure and admonitions for Jak to make sure Shelly climaxes first. An eager student of Shelly's sensual satisfaction, Jak learned the lessons well, allowing the exploratory soulmates to be even more attentive lovers.

Shelly and Jak were young and hormonal and passionate and concupiscent and horny and aroused and turned on and curious and imaginative and inquisitive and therefore more than willing to indulge steamy adventures in mutual sexual gratification. They experimented with many of the *Kama Sutra*'s illustrated positions, often, with Cowgirl's Helper becoming Shelly's favorite. The soulmates were reveling in the gratifying lesson of physical and emotional uninhibitedness.

Their love was joyfully expressive. "Jak, do you know what my favorite movie is?"

"Probably *Casablanca*—'We'll always have Paris'—or something based on a literary novel."

"Ha, good guess, close but that's not it. Ever since I first saw the *Sound of Music* when I was a little girl, it's been my favorite movie. I fell in love with Julie Andrews as Maria, and the music."

"When I'm feeling sad, I remember a few of my favorite things— you—and then I don't feel so bad." Shelly wasn't the only one who had seen the popular movie.

"Aren't you sweet, my raindrop on a rose? With you my heart wants to sing every song it hears. There's a scene in the movie where the stern Captain Georg Von Trapp, on course to marry another woman, suggests that his true love is Maria. In front of that shrew, Maria, and the children, the captain unexpectedly strums an acoustic guitar and sings the melodious song "Edelweiss." I cry every time I watch it. The movie is on TV this Sunday night. Let's watch it together."

They did. Shelly cried. When the movie ended, Shelly affectionately cooed, "Jak, you are my edelweiss, every morning you greet me, you look happy to meet me, please bloom and grow forever. And, Jak, my dream will need all the love you can give me." They retreated to the bedroom for gentle lovemaking.

The next night Jak came to Shelly's apartment for a late dinner after classes. He asked her to light candles and turn off the lights. He then did something she had never heard him do before. He sang to her. He softly sang "Edelweiss." It was beautiful. Shelly let loose a stream of tears of rapturous joy.

After Jak's rendition of "Edelweiss," Shelly played Claude Debussy's "Clair de Lune." Jak had never heard the song. Shelly loved it. Originally called "Promenade Sentimentale," the beautiful, hypnotic piano took Jak and Shelly on a journey of unique, personal emotions. Its ethereal beauty and sense of mystery, its frequent diminuendos, with elements of sadness and solitude, created for Shelly a sense of floating in the clouds and a dreamy suspension of quotidian life. Where for the duration of the playing, all that existed for the luminous moonbeam that was Shelly that night was the poetry in music and Jak's loving embrace.

A FUTURE UPON THEM

"Jak, I'm so excited. I can't believe we are going to Chicago. Joni Mitchell concert and the Art Institute to see the Renoir exhibition, on loan from the Musée d'Orsay in Paris. You know how much I love Joni and the Impressionists."

"I can't wait. Neither one of us has ever been to Chicago. This should be a great visit. The future is upon us."

It was senior year, Jak had been accepted into several elite law schools, and he'd narrowed his choices to the University of Chicago and Northwestern. The couple was inseparable. Shelly, accepted by Yale and Berkeley, intended to pursue her PhD in literature at the University of Chicago but wanted to take off a year or two to catch her breath and try something different than school. Maybe something in music or media, or even wait tables at a Rush Street jazz club. Having deferred graduation for a year, Jak couldn't wait and wanted to be in the same city with his soulmate. The timing was perfect: visit both schools over the weekend, see the Renoir exhibition on Saturday afternoon, and Joni Mitchell later that night.

"And I know how much you love Joni Mitchell. I think you're on your second and third copies of most of her albums. I love it when you sing "Both Sides Now" in the shower."

"You know that's my favorite song. Even more than "Clair de Lune." How mournfully she sings about the illusions of love and life. But right now both love and life feel so real to me. I know love and it is you, Jonathan A. Kent."

"Love you too, Shelly. It's going to be a great weekend. Maybe, in honor of Joni, we'll ride a big yellow taxi and sing about not knowing what we've got until it's all gone."

"This lady of the canyon knows what she's got and is not going to watch some taxi take away my old man, and we're going to see fabulous *art* in the museum, not a *tree museum* after paradise is paved to put up a parking lot," she gushed as she kissed her soulmate.

The law school visits went fine. Jak was leaning toward Northwestern and its beautiful Lake Shore campus. They both loved the Art Institute and the Joni Mitchell concert.

"I was blown away by the Art Institute. What a great location in Grant Park," Jak noted. "Man, does the wind whip off Lake Michigan! Now I understand why Chicago is called the Windy City."

"Hold onto your hat when you're in Chicago. The museum is huge and everything I expect of a world-class art museum. Glad we got to spend three hours in there. Can't wait to go back when we move to Chicago. Apartment hunting is going to be so much fun."

"Too many options! Agree the Art Institute rocked. So much to see. How cool it was to see Picasso's *The Old Guitarist*. The sad old man Picasso depicted looks like he could have been the inspiration for George Harrison's "While My Guitar Gently Weeps." And I loved seeing Edward Hopper's classic *Nighthawks*. So simple yet poignant. The loneliness it depicts is haunting. Hope I don't end up a sad old man sitting alone in a late-night diner."

"Never! We have each other to keep loneliness at bay. But, Jak, wasn't the Renoir exhibit fabulous? Just the opposite of loneliness. Love and togetherness. Didn't you just love his four dance-themed paintings? The *Dance at the Moulin de la Galette*, *Dance in the Country*, *Dance in the City*, and *Dance at Bougival*. We *have* to visit the Musée d'Orsay one day! Paris, the Côte d'Azur, the lavender fields of Luberon, the French Riviera, and then off to Rome. I'm loving our life together, Jak." Shelly, always vivacious in Jak's presence, was especially exuberant that day, confiding in him that she had "never felt more alive than our special day in Chicago."

"I love your travel dreams, my artistic one. Renoir's paintings are fantastic, and I think I appreciated them even more now that I'm a bona fide ballroom dancer … Not."

"You dance just fine. The way you have learned to move your hips has helped you in more ways than one, lover boy."

"Yeah, I suppose the dance lessons have conferred some collateral benefits."

"Joni at the spectacular Auditorium Theater. What a way to cap the day," Shelly reminisced as they snuggled.

"Another magnificent building with its Romanesque facade. I didn't realize that it is its own art museum with all of the mosaics and murals, stencils, and art glass. Even the carpets."

"A perfect venue to see Joni. You know, Jak, she is quite an artist herself. Her music is divine, but she is also an outstanding painter. As she sings in 'A Case of You,' a lonely painter living in a box of paints."

"When she sang that song in concert, it made you cry and squeeze my hand."

"Oh, Joni is so right that love is touching souls. Part of you, Jak, will always pour out of me. Never let me be a lonely painter. Never let our love get lost. I love you."

"Our love will never get lost, Shelly. OTP."

BE WARY THE LONG RUN

Two weeks before graduation. Jak and Shelly were both graduating with high honors, packing up their belongings, scoping out Chicago apartments, and readying for their next life adventure. Jak was in classes until very late afternoon and went to Shelly's apartment around six o'clock, expecting a light meal and a few quiet hours of study. Perhaps some late-night Miles Davis with a glass of wine. The table was set, which included fresh flowers in an oriental vase he had bought for Shelly as a spur-of-the-moment gift. A bottle of wine was opened with two glasses waiting to be filled. Celebration was in the air. Shelly's body language was suppressed eagerness. She was beaming. He thought, *Shelly is about to tell me something wonderful, and I have no clue what it is.* The suspense was palpable.

Shelly couldn't wait any longer to tell her soulmate the good news. She blurted it out: "Jak, we're pregnant."

Jak stood there stunned. Not the type of stunned she had hoped for, anticipated, and expected. "How long have you known?" he asked with a tinge of accusation.

"The test was confirmed this afternoon," Shelly responded with a perplexed look.

"When did you suspect?"

"A few weeks ago. But I wanted to confirm it before I told you. What difference does it make? Jak, Jak, can you believe we're going to have *our* baby!"

Then the dagger to the heart. "Shelly, you should've told me once you suspected. We can't have a baby now. I've got law school, and in a year or two, you have graduate school. We have no time for a baby!"

"Jak, what do you mean we don't have time for our baby? What are you saying?" She was stunned by his matter-of-factness and immediate dismissal of having their baby.

"I'm saying we can't have a baby now. You need to get an abortion. Obviously, I'll help pay for it."

"Jesus Christ, Jak, listen to yourself. I tell you I'm pregnant with our baby and the first thing you think about is law school and getting rid of our baby? What's wrong with you?"

Like many young people of that Baby Boom generation, Jak and Shelly had discussed among friends and in the classroom the morality and legality of abortion, a woman's right to choose and reproductive freedom, and society's interest in protecting the unborn. Until now, the discussions had always been abstract and removed from actual decision-making. Now there was an actual decision to be made. The Supreme Court had legalized abortion a little more than a decade earlier. Jak believed a woman should have the right to choose. To him abortion wasn't so much a religious or moral issue as it was a practical issue. He didn't see abortion as ending an inchoate life but as a way to stay on a chosen career path that would enable him to escape the life of his upbringing. In the moment, he buried all emotion and was in deep denial about two things: he was young and scared. His imagination of what life could be like with the baby in Shelly's belly completely failed him. He compartmentalized his emotions and reduced the decision to a narrow, rational calculation of career choice. As if the variable of time had no stretch to it. As if the little heart beating inside of Shelly's belly, with his DNA, was some type of abstraction.

For Shelly, the issue was also one of choice. Not some abstract rational choice. But her personal choice based on her heart and head and life. She was a young existentialist who believed that actions have consequences and individuals are responsible for their choices. After two years with Jak, and after suspecting that she was pregnant, Shelly realized even more profoundly that she was passionately in love with Jak, and any baby conceived by these two soulmates must be brought to life, loved, nurtured, and joined with them. To Shelly, right then and there, at that very moment, they were now three, emotionally joined together, not two, rationally calculating whether to include the third.

For Shelly, her choice was about a face she could already imagine seeing, an extension of her and Jak. Having their child would not be constraining, it would be unifying and fulfilling. An expression of the maturation of beautiful love. The perfect antidote to the evanescence of young love consumed by the exploration of physical pleasure.

"Shelly, nothing's wrong with me. Calm down and think about this rationally."

"Damn you, don't patronize me. Don't tell me to calm down. We're talking about our baby, not whether we should get a one- or two-bedroom apartment when we move to Chicago, Jak."

"I know, I know, but we can't have a baby now. There's no way we can do both school and have a baby."

"Why not? We're smart, we're resourceful, we can figure out how to make it all work," Shelly said, resolutely pleading what to her was an easy case.

"We're just a little more than four months away from law school; there's no way we can work it all out. Look, Shelly, let's get an abortion, finish school, I'll get a law firm job, and then we can talk about having a kid if we decide we want one. Let's face it, neither of us planned to have this one."

"Jak, how can you be so cold, so cavalier? And don't call our baby a kid, like it's some strange inanimate object, like it's a goat. This baby is ours, yours and mine, flesh and blood. Body and soul."

"I'm not. But look, we never sat down and said let's have this baby. Obviously it was an accident."

"Seriously? Yes, you're right. We didn't plan this baby. But we did make love and our lovemaking produced this very baby. This isn't a fuck baby, it's a love child. This is you and me inside my belly, Jak. Don't you understand that?"

"Of course I understand. But in a few years we can have a baby, a baby we planned to have."

"Jak, listen to me, we can never have *this* baby ever again," Shelly shouted. "This baby, Jak, this love child, this union of you and me. This baby, *our baby*, with a beating heart inside my belly right now. This precious baby, Jak. We'll never be able to have this baby again. And I don't want to lose *this* special baby. This is our choice to make, and I choose you and the baby. The three of *us*."

"That's the wrong choice, Shelly."

"I don't believe what I'm hearing."

They just sat in silence and stared at one another. He stared, she glared. As if their eyes might be more persuasive than their words, they each tried to take their understanding of the other to another level. It wasn't working. After twenty minutes or so, Jak said, "Look, let's call a timeout for the night. I want to take a walk. Let's finish our discussion tomorrow." Shelly said nothing. She just shrugged her shoulders and let him walk out, thinking, *Who the hell are you really, Jak?*

After a restless night, Jak spent the day weighing options. That was doing him no good. He loved Shelly, he recognized that she completed him in ways he never could have imagined. He deluded himself into thinking that he wasn't rejecting the baby. Instead he convinced himself that an abortion was the only way to avoid "the trap." The trap that would dash their dreams and consign them to a life he was resolved to escape. He was scared and could imagine only one way out. He would stand firm and convince Shelly to have the abortion so they could get on with their career plans.

That evening Jak headed back to Shelly's apartment. She gave him a welcoming kiss and walked over to the table. The flowers and wine were still there. John Coltrane's *A Love Supreme* playing softly on the stereo.

"Jak, I've thought about this all night and day. I *know* we can make it all work out. Let's postpone law school for a year, just a year, get jobs, have the baby, get a small apartment, save a little money, scrape by, and then you can start law school next year. I was already going to put off graduate school for at least a year. It will be romantic, and we will look back years from now and remember these days as some of the best in our lives.

"Come on, Jak, we can do this. Just close your eyes and imagine how wonderful our life will be with this baby. Boy or girl, it won't matter. The precious baby will be ours."

"Shelly, you know I love you. And someday we can have a kid—sorry, I mean a baby. But what you're proposing isn't realistic. If we veer off our career paths at this point, there's no telling if we'll ever get back on them."

"But why? Realism is only what we make it. And what's so magical about sticking to plans? Two years ago you and I were on certain paths until we unexpectedly met. That wasn't planned. And look where that took us. It's been wonderful. Jak, use your imagination. Why can't you believe in us and what, together, we're capable of? The two of us, soon to be the three of us? Why can't you see that together we can live our dreams and make it all work out? Make it all work beautifully. Our three lives. Jak, OTP. *Omne trium perfectum.* Just the three of us. It will be perfect. A life of love is the best plan of all, Jak. Don't you see that? That's the plan we should hug and embrace."

"Shelly, that's different. We were always going to go to law school and graduate school. That's why I'm in college. If I veer off that course, no telling where I'll end up. I knew a couple in high school, Peter Zanotti and Mary Kowalski. We were in honors math and science classes. Peter and Mary were a great couple, both headed to the University of Michigan to study premed. End of senior year, Mary gets pregnant and the Catholic couple have the baby and put off college. They never made it to college. Poor Peter is punching the clock, stuck working in a tool-and-die shop and Mary is pregnant with baby number two. So much for becoming doctors. They'll never escape the home town.

"Same with a cousin of mine, Dawn Chamberlain. Scholarship student at Case Western studying biochemistry with plans to get her PhD. Got pregnant sophomore year, dropped out to have the baby, and never finished. Working as a hospital admin now at the Cleveland Clinic. They all said they would go to college and graduate, but none of them did. All smart as hell working dead-end jobs. They're trapped. Dreams dashed. Now it'll just be bowling on Friday nights and maybe some Caribbean cruise at retirement. I can't do that, Shelly."

"Come on, Jak, that's different. We're not trapped. We're graduating from college in two weeks and it's not in your DNA to land in some dead-end job. Having our baby isn't going to change that. Have more faith. Just like our love has helped to complete you, so will *your* baby. You should be excited about our future with the baby, not scared."

"Shelly, I appreciate what you are saying, but if we put off law school and your graduate school, the odds are too great that we'll never go there, and I'll get stuck in some run-of-mill job having to kowtow to some jerk boss, just like my dad. An abortion is the best decision we can make at this time. We can keep our options open about the future."

"Jak, are you really not even going to listen to me? To believe in us? To give it a try with me? With me, your loving Shelly?"

"Shelly, believe me, this will be the best for both of us in the long run."

"Are you joking, the long run? You once told me that your economics hero John Maynard Keynes says that in the long run, we're all dead. I don't want to give up my life in the short run, Jak, for some vague long run. We're in the here and now and right now *we* have *our* baby inside of me. Our baby and our opportunity to expand our love. Why can't you see the beauty in that?"

"Shelly, you won't be giving up life in the short run; you'll be saving the life you've been working for these four years in college."

"That's pathetic. Damn it, Jak, life isn't some linear, straight and narrow, preordained path. Don't you see that? Like jazz, we improvise as we go. Improvise life with love. A love supreme. Love with your soulmate. There's no better way to live. The life I want is the life I'm living. And that life is with you and now our baby. "

"Shelly, I do see that, but I also see the clear choice we have. Why don't you? We have the abortion, get our graduate degrees, and then move on with our careers. If we then decide that we want to have a baby, so be it."

"So be it? Seriously? Just another rational decision for you, huh, Jak?"

"Shelly, it's the best way to make decisions. Try to take the emotion out of it."

"I can't believe what I'm hearing, and I don't believe you believe what you are saying. Jak, you're scaring me. I feel like I don't know who you are right now. Are you really not going to change your mind? You really are insisting that I have an abortion? There's nothing else I can do or say?"

"No, Shelly, this is for the best. I *won't* change my mind. No chance. This is what we *have* to do."

"I can't believe it. This is too surreal. Okay, Jak, you win. You're leaving me no choice but to have the abortion ..."

"Shelly that's the best ..." His sense of relief only aggravated the anger and hurt consuming her.

"Stop! I'll have the abortion. But we're done. I can never love you again. I can't love a man who refuses to sacrifice a year or two chasing a career over having a beautiful baby with the woman he professes to love. A man who has no faith in me and us. Jak, it's over. I want you to leave, and I don't want to see you ever again."

"Shelly, please, no need to be so dramatic and drastic."

"Jak, I want you to leave. Now. Please go."

Jak, Jonathan, feeling like he had no choice, walked out her door.

He was devastated. He wasn't going to change his mind, but he wanted to comfort Shelly as she had the abortion and then convince her to reunite. So smart, yet so clueless. He let a few days pass, hoping for a cooling off period, and then tried to reconnect over the ensuing weeks and months. Phone calls not returned. Letters unanswered. It was as if Shelly had vanished. No reconciliation or romantic rapprochement. What had been inseparable torn asunder. Dissolution leading to disillusion.

Alone after two years of togetherness, Jonathan had no choice but to move on with life and head to law school. But, like the poet Dylan Thomas, he felt as if he was raging against the dying of the light. Raging, and all he felt was darkness. His soul was shattered. Emotionally crippled, he needed an outlet. He resolved to exert all his energy to becoming a superstar trial lawyer. An obsession that would become his monomania. Motivated by fear to escape the life of his father, his singular ambition now was magnified by a sense of rage at a world that brought him Shelly only to see her disappear completely from his life.

That summer Jonathan read Gustave Flaubert's book *Madame*

Bovary. He was haunted by Emma's literary imagination and suicide, her craving and restlessness, and by one passage in particular:
"Emma tried hard to discover what, precisely, it was in life that
was denoted by the words joy, passion, intoxication, which always
looked so fine in books." With emotions raw, he too wondered about
joy and passion, sensations, and impermanence. *What is joy in life
when ecstatic love so quickly turns to heartache?* he wondered. The jilted
lover understood that law school is not a place where sane people
find joy, but now, alone, he was back on track to pursue a singular
professional passion for becoming a star trial lawyer. And he was
searching for a substitute for a passionate future extinguished by a
failure to imagine love's possibilities with a special soulmate.

LAW SCHOOL

Law school is tediously long at three years, but Jonathan knew at the outset that the first year was probably the most important year of all. First-year grades largely determine which law firms will make offers for summer intern positions after the second year and determine the career direction of the majority of students. Jonathan understood this competitive landscape and was determined to navigate his way to the top. Not one to lack confidence or self-assurance, before he had met a single other student, before he had stepped foot into his first class, there was no doubt in Jonathan's mind that he would rise to the top. As in a Greek tragedy, it was his destiny.

Just as Jonathan set out to master the competitive rules of biological life and survival, he was determined to master the rules of litigation and jury trials. He therefore zeroed in on civil and criminal procedure and evidence. Every lawsuit and trial involved procedure and evidence. They were the rules of the road; they determined how the litigation game was played.

Jonathan would become their master. First up, first semester civil procedure class. Others thought it was masochism. When Jonathan went to law school in the 1980s, the top schools had at least one professor who struck mortal fear into the strong and faint of heart alike. Like the army, there was a callous social ritualization process where intellectual humiliation seemed to be the endgame. Not all made it through. It was as if there was a professorial ogre factory whose assembly lines produced pedagogical mutants with a seemingly singular purpose in life: to terrorize first-year law students. There were even books and movies glamorizing these sadistic beasts.

At Jonathan's law school, the bugbear had an ominous name that must have been invented—Professor Gladstone Bulldozen (accent on the second syllable). Stage name or not, Gladstone Bulldozen was all too real. Students dropped out after being thrashed in class by him. Others didn't wait that long. Gladstone Bulldozen could have played the ruthless, larger-than-life, scalp-hunting Judge Holden in Cormac McCarthy's chilling book *Blood Meridian*—when lost lambs in the mountains cry, "Sometime come the mother, sometime the wolf." There were no rescuing mothers to protect the shivering lambs in Bulldozen's class. At six foot seven and a solid 265 pounds, with a shaved head and thick chocolate-brown goatee, Gladstone Bulldozen was scarily, physically imposing. His basso profondo voice shook windows. He roamed the classroom. Up and down the aisles like an unfrozen woolly mammoth seeking revenge on the human species. This time, law students, not beasts, would face extinction. But he was more than beast and brawn. Eyes the shade of lapis lazuli, he exuded a hyperintelligence that enabled him to earn the highest three-year grade point average in the history of the law school. Those glistening deep-blue eyes were corrosive, allowing Bulldozen to penetrate deep into the core of any problem or person. Like a jeweler's loupe, separating fake from authentic, zircon from a sparkling gem. After clerking for two federal appellate judges, including a U.S. Supreme Court justice, Professor Bulldozen returned to the law school, students feared, to eat the school's young. While others cowered, Jonathan prepared to confront.

Somewhere along the way, the young upstart had read a quip by the aesthete Oscar Wilde, one of his favorite writers, that "the first duty in life is to assume a pose. What the second duty is, no one has yet to find out." Jonathan was angry and fearless and determined to assume a pose in Professor Bulldozen's civil procedure class. He parked in a center seat in the middle of the classroom so Bulldozen could not miss him and every other student could hear him. A classmate who commandeered a seat in the last row, prized real estate in Bulldozen's class, told him, "You got balls." That would not be the last time Jonathan heard himself so described.

This was not going to be a fair fight, nor would Professor Bulldozen ever relinquish the upper hand. Like most law school professors, Bulldozen used a totally one-sided version of the Socratic method to interrogate his students, meaning he got to ask all the questions and never had to supply any answers. No law student, certainly no rookie, could win at a rigged game with an opponent as formidable as Gladstone Bulldozen. It was like stepping into the ring to box a young Mike Tyson with one hand tied behind your back. Good luck with that. After the first week of class, five students dropped out of school. Two were college valedictorians who, like the confused butterfly wondering whether it was a butterfly dreaming it was a man, or a man dreaming he was a butterfly, left school wondering whether they were morons dreaming they could actually have ever succeeded in law school. Whether their stellar college grades were just a fraudulent dream now that Gladstone Bulldozen had exposed their idiocy.

Jonathan took his punches. In the beginning he needed to, as Bulldozen exposed flawed reasoning and excavated layers of unsupported assumptions in Jonathan's arguments. Jonathan's classmates were amazed at how nonplussed he seemed to be with his verbal floggings, but they marveled at the formidable fencer he had become by the end of the first semester. By the end of the second semester, it was as if Jonathan and Bulldozen were going one-on-one while the rest of the students were there to spectate a verbal chess match. The mutual self-respect of the two grandmasters was plain to see. Jonathan would encounter some churlish trial judges throughout his career, but nobody would put him through his paces and test his mettle as relentlessly as Professor Bulldozen did.

At the end of the first year, class grades were posted. Jonathan finished number two in his class. Number four was Lisa Sheldon, a charismatic woman from Tiburon, California, in Marin County north of San Francisco. Jonathan would get to know her in his third year. Jonathan had a remarkable first year and was well positioned to pursue his dream of becoming a young trial lawyer in a top law firm.

In the summer between first and second years, Jonathan assisted Professor William Church, a professor of criminal law, on a study he was doing on plea bargaining in the criminal justice system. Professor Church had received a research grant from the U.S. Department of Justice to study the dynamics and prevalence of plea bargaining. An empirical study with some statistical analysis. Jonathan was well suited to assist.

In the 1980s the plea-bargaining debate boiled down to this: supporters of plea bargaining argued that, in fact, most people arrested for crimes are guilty as charged and plea bargaining fosters a more efficient administration of the overcrowded criminal justice system by avoiding a bunch of time-consuming trials where those arrested will likely be convicted in any event. Life is about trade-offs, and plea deals trade off maximum punishment with huge strains on the system for certain punishment and less resource allocation. Critics of plea bargaining argued that plea bargaining makes a mockery of the presumption of innocence by effectively coercing the accused to accept much less severe punishments by pleading guilty, or risk much more severe punishments if they are tried and convicted. Professor Church, with Jonathan's assistance, designed a study to tease out this debate. Part of the study involved interviewing judges in various criminal courts in the country. Two in particular left an indelible impression on Jonathan that he shared with younger lawyers in later years.

In the early 1980s, Jonathan watched a movie starring Paul Newman called *Fort Apache, the Bronx*. The name came from the depressing fact that the 41st police precinct resembled an army outpost in a foreign country. Throughout the 1970s and 1980s, the South Bronx was a crime-ridden war zone. Name the crime, it occurred in the South Bronx. Often in broad daylight. Often with plenty of eyewitnesses. A depressing miasma of fear and despair enveloped the festering crime problems of this forsaken part of New York. Professor Church's and Jonathan's first stop on the interview trail was the Bronx County Courthouse and the irascible and inestimable Judge Paul McCracken.

Young Jonathan had led a sheltered life, and this would be his first time on an airplane. His first time donning anything other than jeans and flannel shirts. His first mistake was dressing like a prep boy out of a Brooks Brothers catalogue. Khaki pants, blue blazer, white button-down shirt, red and blue rep tie, and mahogany loafers. The second mistake was lugging his luggage with him as he taxied straight from LaGuardia to the courthouse. The only thing missing from his walking I'm-a-mark-ass-bitch advertisement were dollars dangling from his pants pockets. From the bottom of the courthouse steps to Judge McCracken's chambers, all the wide-eyed midwestern young man saw were pimps, streetwalkers, dope dealers, delinquents, and dozens of bad asses accompanied by harried public defenders. Jonathan was called more profane names, and more different combinations of profane names, than he thought semantically possible. By his unofficial count, he was called at least twenty-five different combinations that included the word *motherfucker*. Many were creative, none were flattering, all were threatening. All in the twenty minutes it took him to reach the judge's chambers.

Professor Church was already there. Judge McCracken looked like the Lou Grant character on the old *Mary Tyler Moore Show*, with his bald head, permanent scowl, white short sleeves, loosened tie around his beefy neck, and a thick, cheap cigar billowing plumes of odious, greenish smoke. The crusty judge took one look at Jonathan, rolled his eyes, blew smoke straight in his direction, and said, "Son, you got balls. You got shit for brains, but you got some set of balls walking around the Bronx looking like that." Jonathan sheepishly shook the skeptical judge's strong, thick-fingered hand. He already had little doubt where the judge with the bone-crushing handshake stood on the issue of plea bargaining.

The Bronx had one of the highest bargains-to-convictions rates in the country. When Professor Church asked the judge why he thought that was so, he puffed on his cigar, tilted his head upward, blew a ring of smoke, turned to Jonathan like he was about to make a revelation, and bellowed, *"Because they're all fucking guilty!"* The surly, street-smart jurist knew he was getting a rise out of the fresh-faced student and seemed to be enjoying it. But he relaxed and said, "Look, I've been doing this judge job for twenty years, and I'm telling you the Bronx is on fire. It's lawless. The cops could arrest fifty people at random and forty-nine of them would be guilty of something. When I say the guys who copped a plea are guilty, I'm not some hairy knuckle-dragger making a moral judgment. Facts are, they are guilty because crime is out of control and the cops only catch the bastards who are too damn dumb not to get caught. It's like shooting fish in a barrel. It ain't pretty, but that's the way it is, fellas."

That was sobering. Seeing is believing. The Irish-Scots descendant took Jonathan and Professor Church on a tour of the Bronx in a police car with tinted windows. He wanted them to see firsthand where the plea bargaining they were studying was taking place. He railed against academics who write about crime and the criminal justice system with "their heads in the clouds." In his lilting brogue he said, "Fellas, if you want to understand criminal justice, get off your asses and put down the goddamned books and get out on the messy streets." He would be their Bronx tour guide. There were no scenic routes.

"Look out your windows. You guys gotta understand that the crimes that are coming to my court are happening right out here." Judge McCracken sighed, pointing to a war zone.

"Not even the south side of Chicago looks this bad," Jonathan observed in dismay. Everywhere he looked, he saw burned-out buildings, busted windows, boarded-up windows, cars in the streets stripped to shells, profane graffiti sprayed on virtually every building, street corner dealers, street corner hookers, strung-out men and women drinking cheap booze out of bottles in brown paper bags, lethargic people smoking and passing joints, others using needles and syringes, wasted people urinating on the sidewalks and in the alleys, garbage in the streets and on the sidewalks, rats scattering everywhere, sweat-soaked half-naked people popping open fire hydrants to cool off from the scorching summer heat, and skinny kids, lots of skinny kids.

"No place is this bad," snapped the judge. "You want to talk about crime and urban decay, just look out the window. No saints and saviors are strolling these streets. Hell, for years landlords have torched their own fucking buildings for the insurance proceeds. It got so bad people started saying the Bronx is burning. And it is. Then the city went into massive debt and started cutting the funds to the cops, fire department, and sanitation."

"What happened after that?"

"The fuck you think happened? Crime soared. Robberies up, murders up, assaults, everything went up. Nobody doing shit to stop it. Hey, Atticus Finch, ever hear of muggin' money?"

"No, Judge, what's that?" Jonathan was definitely curious with that scary tease.

"Say you got thirty bucks. You put ten bucks in your wallet and twenty bucks in your shoes. That way, when you get mugged and the bastards take your wallet, they'll think that's all the money you got. Muggin' money, like a tariff just to walk the sidewalk."

"Incredible."

"Ever see that movie *Death Wish* with Charles Bronson? That's what it's like here. Vigilante gangs roam the streets. And by the way, stay away from the subways, especially at night."

As they continued to drive around, all Jonathan saw was urban blight, squalor, and a breeding ground for crime. Nothing could be plainer to his naked eye — poverty and crime go hand in hand. Some correlations are what statisticians call spurious, but not this one.

Judge McCracken interrupted the silence. "You guys gotta get out of the tower. Sure it would be nice if every accused criminal could get a trial with a good lawyer. Maybe every kid can also get a pony for Christmas. But that's not real life. Not here in the Bronx anyways. Society out there is producing criminals a dime a dozen. Perfect justice in the Bronx is a pipe dream. Plea bargaining at least lets us get something like imperfect justice. We process them through the system here, knowing most will be back on the streets in a year or two and hoping that at least some of them avoid coming back to us. When there are no jobs and no hope, when society don't give a fuck, the Bronx is what you get. The niceties of plea bargaining are the least of our worries. It's like Billy the Bard Shakespeare said, 'Striving to better, oft we mar what's well.' Guys, let's not mar what's working well. Plea bargains ain't the problem, society and its indifference, they're the fuckin' problem. Us lawyers, we're just pawns in the system. What are ya gonna do, you know?"

Finished in the Bronx, Jonathan headed to Detroit for his next interview. On the airplane to Detroit, Jonathan thought that he had learned more about criminal justice in America from a few hours with Judge McCracken than he had in a year of law school. He was particularly struck by the judge's emphasis on jobs and hope and society needing to give a fuck if there was going to be any meaningful strides in crime reduction and a better society. Hard to argue with that. Judge McCracken was working the tail-end of the system. If the system was rotten, he said, "throwing the book" at the arrested or tinkering with plea bargains wouldn't do a "god-damn bit of good in solving crime or improving the criminal justice system." Jonathan would soon hear a similar sentiment expressed in Detroit.

He interviewed Judge Harvey Gellman, a judge in Detroit Re-corders Court. Judge Gellman was a political liberal, lived through the Detroit race riots in 1967, and had defeatist ideas, but what he resolutely believed were realistic views when it came to plea bargaining. Like Judge McCracken, the son of Holocaust survivors believed that most of the criminal defendants who appeared before him were unfortunately factually guilty. He pinned most of the blame for crime squarely on society, poverty, and systemic racism and economic inequality. Sure, he said, life produces bad apples, but in the nature versus nurture debate, the conscientious Motor City jurist strongly believed that American society and poverty cul-tivated a nurturing ground of crime and fertilized it with racism and indifference. He thought systemic socioeconomic issues re-duced way too many poor and minorities to a vicious cycle of crime and the criminal justice system. In the affluent suburbs, wealth and opportunity are inherited. In the inner city, poverty and crime. He said, "Here in Motown it's like Marvin Gaye's soulful song, 'Trou-ble Man'—taxes, death, and trouble are the only three things, for sure. You don't make it by playing by the rules." To Judge Gellman, the plea-bargain debate was more of interest to academics than it was to prosecutors, defense attorneys, and the judges who toil away daily in the overcrowded criminal justice system and have to figure out some Band-Aid solution for administering it.

Judge Gellman acknowledged that a sample size of one doesn't move the debate's needle, but he thought his anecdotal example made his point. To Judge Gellman, the guilty are caught not because cops have the detective abilities of Sherlock Holmes. He had a very low opinion of cops and their detective abilities. According to Judge Gellman, "Suspects are caught because they are desperate or dumb and there are eyewitnesses." To Judge Gellman, the cops don't catch the smart criminals. His example—8 Mile Road in Michigan is the northern border of Detroit. It is lined with seedy bars and strip joints, more recently made famous by the rapper Eminem.

Judge Gellman told this true story. "A guy walks into a bar one afternoon on 8 Mile. He whips out a pistol and demands that everyone put their wallets in a bag he passed around. After gathering up the wallets, the guy leaves. The cops arrive and find a pile of wallets right outside the bar. Everything but the cash. The cops go back into the bar and return the wallets to their owners. There was one left. The dumb ass robber threw his own wallet into the pile, with his driver's license. So the cops go to his run-down apartment and find him and some floozy chugging Colt 45 and doing Acapulco Gold water bong hits. Mr. Addled Brain was higher than a kite. Easy bust on multiple charges. What public defender wouldn't cop a plea for him? Sure, not all cases are this clear cut, but the crooks are more like the 8 Mile moron than Professor Moriarty in a Sherlock Holmes story. Guys, the real question isn't how much due process they should get. It's how much time they should serve. That's just how it works here in Detroit."

Jonathan also got an up-close look at crooked and shady police practices. Cops on the take and racist cops. When Judge McCracken said put down the books and get out on the streets if you want to understand the criminal justice system, that experienced boots-on-the-ground jurist knew what the hell he was talking about.

By the end of the summer, Jonathan had developed a much better appreciation of the complicated real-world operation of the American criminal justice system. The importance of facts and data to inform theories and opinions, not the other way around. Like he learned in physics classes, the only reliable way to learn about the world is by observing it. By observing, Jonathan got a firsthand glimpse of an imperfect system in an imperfect world. His first lesson about being wary of grand ideas and plans and to look for progress one pragmatic step at a time. And an eye-opening account of what can happen when a society lacks a common humanity.

Jonathan graduated number three in his law school class, right behind two aspiring tax lawyers on their way to Big Law wealth-planning departments to help the super wealthy dodge Uncle Sam by protecting their fortunes with trusts and off-shore tax shelters, and just ahead of Lisa Sheldon, an aspiring litigator with a definite plan. She was going to work for a prestigious Wall Street law firm for a couple of years to experience life in New York City and then return to California and work in San Francisco. She even talked about maybe doing something in music. She encouraged Jonathan to give San Francisco a try.

Lisa had caught Jonathan's eye in his first year, but his all-in pursuit of grades and lingering love for Shelly doused any potential romantic flame. By the end of his third year, and clueless about what Shelly was doing with her life, Jonathan was tepidly willing to re-enter the mating game. Lisa was whip smart, physically attractive—alluring actually—exuded cool confidence, and had something of a slinky gait and seducing, supplicatory eyes.

No doubt there was a spark between them. Competitive banter about case subjects would sometimes take teasing turns with evocative eyes. Lots of double entendres. Lisa could be sassy and acerbic, with a wicked wit.

Clever and coquettish, she was adept at the tantalizing game of amorous cat and mouse. Jonathan could sense a smoldering desire longing for combustion. This went on until graduation.

The graduation ceremony occurred on an unusually balmy Chicago morning. The night would be even steamier. Jonathan hosted a quiet celebratory dinner for Lisa. Celebrate they did, but they didn't quite make it to the dinner part. Jonathan was not a champagne connoisseur and was congenitally incapable of overspending on a label bottle like Dom Perignon. The guy at the wine shop seemed knowledgeable and steered him to a bottle of Veuve Clicquot. Jonathan figured that if the champagne is French and sexy to pronounce, it would do the trick of suggesting an appropriate level of sophistication and creating a mood for what the evening had in store. It did.

Lisa arrived at Jonathan's apartment and looked stunning. She glowed wearing a sleeveless, sultry summer dress and, apparently, nothing else except her sandals. They shared a toast from generously poured glasses. Then another as they bided their time, both erotically sensing what was soon to unfold. His body was being overcome with her come-hither manner and wooing smile. Later, he would have barely a clue what these law graduates talked about, but their seductive body language was unambiguously communicating mutual offer and mutual acceptance. Lust, not law, was the libidinous signal vibrating in their dopamine neurotransmitters.

As Jonathan's loins aroused, he moved forward to give Lisa a congratulatory kiss. They started slowly but soon picked up the carnal pace. Jonathan was correctly sensing that they were about to engage not so much in lovemaking, but in an exhausting, athletic contest of sport fucking. Barely missing a stride, they playfully explored erogenous zones as they disrobed one another and clumsily entered Jonathan's bedroom completely naked. Fully ready, Jonathan whispered that he had protection. Lisa winked, cracked a pun saying she had it covered, and led him into bed.

They explored each other's naked bodies with lustful aggression. Lips everywhere, sometimes lingering to taste hungrily. Heat on heat, they were both on fire. In their game of copulatory conquest, Lisa released first, accompanied by a feline moan of satisfaction. Lisa lay firmly on top of Jonathan, regathered her strength, and rode like a sailboat on a windy sea as he thrusted until they both released with relish and power.

Catching their breath while they eagerly switched positions, Lisa looked up at Jonathan, part submissive, part hungry for more. Fully rejuvenated, Jonathan thrusted at the pace of an eight-hundred-meter runner while Lisa was giving as good as she was getting. Finished with their last round of release, they lay still in sweat-soaked sheets and bodies, like two spent cheetahs on the savanna.

As he lay in bed, Jonathan was both exhilarated and exhausted. Yet he felt haunted. He and Lisa had not been a union of two into one. There was no soul touching soul. Sex for its own sake with no emotional commitment.

As beautiful as Lisa's curvy body was, as physically and technically accomplished as she was in his bed, the memory of Shelly and the passionate way they melded into one when they made love overwhelmed him. Achingly reminded him that there was only one Shelly. His temporary feelings of exhilaration and exhaustion quickly gave way to a longer lasting feeling of emotional emptiness.

After a couple of hours of quietly lying in bed, Lisa slipped her dress back on, kissed Jonathan on the forehead, winked, said she would see him later, said goodnight, and saw herself out. With no expectations and no energy, Jonathan escaped into a deep sleep, believing that he would probably never see Lisa again.

JUDGE LUKE ROY

"**M**ake love, not war" was an antiwar slogan chanted by hippies and peaceniks during the Vietnam War. Fought far off in jungles in a country most Americans couldn't then find on a map, for vague, ideological, and speculative geopolitical reasons conceived by the so-called whiz kids and the best and the brightest, against a foe that had committed no act of aggression on American soil, the war left both physical and emotional scars on the men and women who fought in and survived that war.

Inscribed on the somber black granite walls of the Vietnam Veterans Memorial in Washington, DC, are the names of more than fifty-eight thousand American soldiers who were killed or are missing in action. Wars invariably kill the young and progenitors of future generations. Approximately 60 percent of the dead were under the age of twenty-one and 30 percent were married. For many of the soldiers who survived, their scars bear witness to a war of misguided purpose and lies and deceit by the authoritative voices who were in charge.

One of those scarred, surviving soldiers was a former marine and now prominent federal judge in Chicago. Like Jonathan's first legal mentor, Professor Bulldozen, Judge Luke Roy had a profound influence on Jonathan's early development as an aspiring trial lawyer. Over the two years the trial lawyer in embryo worked as a law clerk for Judge Roy, he would come to idolize this eccentric and remarkable man. Judge Roy's experience in Vietnam helped to forge his character and seared into his moral fiber a profound respect for the rule of law, truth, professionalism, humanity, facts, hypothesis testing, and evidence. Real, concrete, verifiable evidence.

The judge was six foot two and ramrod straight with a chiseled jawline. He moved quickly, with agility, authority, and purpose. An ascetic diet and demanding exercise regimen kept his taut frame at a rock-hard 180 pounds. A body toned by doing one hundred fingertip push-ups and one thousand stomach crunches every (very early) morning, jumping rope for thirty minutes four times a week, and yoga and boxing on a regular basis.

The "boxing judge" had a galvanizing path to the bench. A double major in physics and philosophy at Princeton, upon graduation he joined the marines and did a life-changing, death-defying tour of duty in Vietnam. A reflective man with an empirical bent, Judge Roy preferred facts to theories, experience to speculation, and skepticism to both idealism and cynicism. After an honorable discharge, the decorated veteran went to law school at Northwestern, where he graduated with high honors. From there he earned a coveted job as a federal prosecutor in Chicago, ultimately making it to the top spot as US Attorney for the Northern District of Illinois. As a trial lawyer, he won fraud convictions of a former Illinois governor and two state senators. He won racketeering convictions of drug lords as well as several executives of three construction companies. He also won antitrust bid-rigging convictions of four electrical contractors who tried to cheat a bidding system designed to eliminate graft for government contracts at Midway Airport. Judge Roy had a sterling reputation for integrity and was considered a brilliant trial strategist and charismatic jury trial lawyer.

The conscientious judge had a profound respect for the rule of law and a contemptuous disdain for those in law enforcement who abused and corrupted the system. Neither Pollyannaish nor sanctimonious, but a pragmatist who believed in duty and public trust. As an assistant US attorney, he worked on a major undercover operation that investigated and then prosecuted corrupt judges, cops, and court personnel in the Cook County judicial system. This three-year investigation was a coordinated effort of the FBI, the IRS Criminal Tax Division, and branches of the Chicago and Illinois state police departments. This sting operation included planting listening devices in targeted judges' chambers and presenting fabricated cases to unsuspecting judges who proceeded to fix them in exchange for duffel bags of cash. Judge Roy was able to secure a number of mail fraud and racketeering convictions in high-profile jury trials as well as guilty pleas from crooked judges, cops, and lawyers.

In another bust of law enforcement personnel in positions of power and trust, the dutiful public servant secured convictions of several southside Chicago cops who took hefty cash bribes from local cocaine dealers for the Guadalajaran cartel and its leader, known mysteriously as "the Boss." The cartel smuggled cocaine out of Mexico and into Arizona through an elaborate series of tunnels where couriers, euphemistically known as mules, retrieved the cocaine and transported it to various major cities, including Chicago. They then supplied the cocaine to local dealers. These lowlifes were brazen, and in time their white-powder racket became a notorious open secret on the streets of Chicago. The feds suspected that local cops must know. They did. Judge Roy was able to flip several local dealers who wore wires to record conversations and turn state's evidence against the cops. These convictions solidified Judge Roy's reputation for integrity, fearlessness, and legal brilliance and helped to pave his path to the top prosecutor's spot and then on to the federal bench.

Jonathan likely would have gotten his clerkship under any circumstances, but, like all successful people, he was helped by fortuitous circumstances. Several antitrust class action lawsuits had been filed around the country against the major home building materials suppliers for alleged price fixing and were consolidated into one case and sent to Judge Roy for trial. The discerning jurist thought Jonathan's economics major, including statistics classes, would be particularly useful in helping him manage and resolve this massive antitrust case where both sides would put forward expert economic witnesses using complicated statistical equations to evaluate—or obfuscate or even fabricate—reams of pricing data.

In antitrust cases, both sides rely heavily on expert witnesses. Red alert for Judge Roy. The wary jurist recognized that experts can sometimes help juries make sense of complicated and technical issues, but he maintained an abiding skepticism of testifiers who get paid staggering amounts of money to offer opinions for the purpose of winning in court. The inherent conflicts of interest and financial incentives are too great for them not to fudge the truth and data to help their benefactors win lawsuits. The street-smart judge taught Jonathan an invaluable lesson about expert witnesses he would pass on over the years to younger lawyers: "Remember, always remember, courtroom expert testimony is *paid opinion* testimony. It is not factual testimony. It is not testimony about what actually happened in the case, and invariably it is slanted and flawed. So hold onto your wallet and be wary."

Physics classes taught a young Judge Roy the importance of empirical testing of ideas and hypotheses, philosophy classes the importance of questioning assumptions and conclusions from faulty premises. Outside the classroom, real-life experiences honed the young man's skepticism of pronouncements from authoritative voices, starting with his experience as a marine in Vietnam. Judge Roy was there in 1968 at the battle of Khe Sanh and told Jonathan about his experience in harrowing detail.

The young marines were ordered "to hold the base at all costs." Battle raged for seventy-seven days. It was one of the longest and bloodiest battles of the Vietnam War. The Americans were badly outnumbered, close to six thousand marines surrounded by twenty thousand North Vietnamese and Viet Cong who kept the marines under constant fire. The attack came during the monsoon season, making it even more difficult for the airmen of the 834th and 315th air divisions to resupply the beleaguered soldiers on the ground. At one point, the marines engaged in hand-to-hand combat with bayonets in the trenches. Judge Roy was there. He remembered the *thunk, thunk, thunk* of enemy mortar rounds and shell fragments. The black smoke, dirt, and debris meant death was everywhere. The putrid smell of death was a permanent presence in his nostrils. Judge Roy fought and killed enemy combatants and watched the enemy kill his buddies and fellow soldiers, his brothers in arms. Ultimately, a combination of US Army, Marines, and South Vietnamese, in what was called Operation Pegasus, relieved the base and ended the siege by mid-April 1968.

Then, after the bloody battle to hold the base at all costs, the United States closed the marine base at Khe Sahn. Judge Roy told Jonathan that he listens to Bruce Springsteen's song "Born in the U.S.A." over and over—the Viet Cong still there in Khe Sanh and lots of Judge Roy's brothers dead and gone. What was the purpose of this battle, the valiant warrior wondered. "Why did I have to kill men I didn't know and watch my brothers die?" he asked himself, in disgust, then and for years to come.

The best and brightest behind their desks in DC looked pretty damn dumb and dangerous to this courageous soldier and recent college graduate. It got worse.

Ten months later, May 1969, Judge Roy was wounded and scarred in another senseless battle. He earned a Purple Heart and saved lives, but he told Jonathan he is still haunted by the thought that he had not done enough for his brothers in arms, what psychologists once specifically called survivor syndrome and now refer to more generally as post-traumatic stress disorder. What Judge Roy said should be called NETSD, as in never-ending traumatic stress disorder, because the horrors of war permanently torment the psyche.

Dong Ap Bia was located in the dense jungles of the A Shaw Valley in South Vietnam, a little more than one mile from the Laotian border. The Vietnamese called it "the mountain of the crouching beast." To American soldiers who fought there, it would come to be known horridly as Hamburger Hill. The hill had no technical significance. The battle ostensibly was waged to thwart the North Vietnamese from infiltrating from Laos.

Beginning on May 10, 1969, the battle raged for ten grueling, bloodletting days. The Americans' foes were fearless and formidable, battle-tested veterans of the infamous 1968 Tet Offensive, where as many as fifty thousand North Vietnamese and Viet Cong soldiers were killed. It was total warfare. Heavy air strikes, artillery barrage, and infantry assault. Tropical rainstorms at times reduced visibility to near zero. The young Princeton Tiger was fighting in the middle of the hill. A dead man's land. At one point, after fighting on the hill for six straight days, an exhausted and famished Luke Roy carried a wounded marine down the hill to safety. He could have stayed safe at the bottom of the hill. His brothers on the hill were still fighting and dying. He would not let them fight alone.

Running on fumes but propelled by the singular cause of loyalty to his brothers, the determined marine slowly cleaved and clawed and fought his way back up the hill to fight side by side with his trapped and doomed brothers. In dense fog he was shot in his side. Bleeding, he fought on.

Only after another soldier was badly wounded did he, another wounded soldier slumped over his shoulder, weave his way back down the hill. With a patchwork of gauze and bloody bandages, the young marine once again climbed back up the hill, retrieved another wounded soldier, and carried him to safety. He then collapsed in total exhaustion. A few days later, on May 20, American soldiers captured the hill.

The judge told Jonathan that soldiers and reporters on the front lines of battle, unlike double-talking politicians, describe things as they really are in language that does not obfuscate plain truth. Because of the high casualty rate, the battle to capture "the mountain of the crouching beast" was dubbed "Hamburger Hill" by some wartime correspondents. One nineteen-year-old enervated sergeant had said to a reporter: "Have you ever been inside a hamburger machine? We just got cut to pieces by extremely accurate gunfire." Judge Roy told Jonathan that the image of being trapped inside a hamburger machine perfectly captured the horror of war and what he experienced on that awful hill.

Just sixteen days after capturing Hamburger Hill, the Americans abandoned it. It was abandoned because it had no strategic value. Seventy-two American soldiers killed and 372 wounded, including Judge Roy. And yet General Melvin Zais had the gall to say, "People are acting like this was a catastrophe for the US troops. This was a tremendous gallant victory." Hearing that, Judge Roy called to mind Lady Soul—Aretha Franklin's song "Chain of Fools."

Marine Luke Roy was awarded the Purple Heart and Silver Star Medal and then honorably discharged. His scarred abdomen is a permanent, everyday reminder of the brutality and senselessness of war. To him, it is also a constant reminder of the tragic consequences of imbecilic leadership, lying and deceiving by those in power, and reliance on experts who fudge data, ignore inconvenient facts, and pretend to be experts in subjects when they are not. Jonathan would never forget these stories and lessons. Nor would he ever forget Judge Roy's exemplary display of sacrifice for something greater than self.

For two years, Jonathan clerked for a special man in a special place. Most federal courthouses are imposing, and some are even awe-inspiring buildings. This was true of the Everett M. Dirksen Courthouse in the Chicago Loop. Named after Senator Dirksen of Illinois, who once famously said, when criticizing out-of-control federal spending, "A billion here, a billion there, pretty soon you're talking about real money." Jonathan thought that the courthouse was magnificent, and Judge Roy's chambers on the twenty-fifth floor was something like a temple. He could not imagine a physically better place to work.

Throughout his legal career, Jonathan stood in awe of courthouses and what, at their inspiring best, they represent. He loved the majesty of the marble and wood and pillars and elevated benches. The solemnity. The seals and flags. The witness stands and jury boxes. The counsel tables. The rituals. The ceremony of a trial. The crucible of the competition. The substitution of law, reason, and persuasive argument over guns, bombs, force, and combat as a civilized way to resolve disputes. Every time he stepped foot into a courthouse, he mentally genuflected. Some courthouses with Renaissance revival architecture, some with Romanesque architecture, some with vaulted ceilings, some with clock towers, some with grandeur, others with simplicity.

But it is what the courthouses symbolize that inspired Jonathan the most. The rule of law and the liberalizing democratic aspiration of judging citizens not by status, political views, party affiliation, gender, race, or arbitrariness, but by general laws evenly applied and by evidence. Real, not doctored evidence. Where ordinary citizens, not the high and mighty, get to sit in judgment and decide cases. Where the state is not all powerful and where whim and caprice can be rejected by the people. Where widows and orphans with the help of a good lawyer can hold powerful corporations to account when they break the law and wreck lives. Where the right of cross-exam-

ination can expose false testimony. Jonathan profoundly appreciated Judge Roy's sagacious insight that "the great experiment in
democracy is still in its precarious youth, and properly functioning courts are vital for its continuing success." Imperfect justice for
sure, if nothing else his plea-bargaining work showed him that, but
courts are still a sanctuary of hope for democratic government and
fairness. And now, at the age of twenty-five, Jonathan was working
in a fabulous courthouse under the tutelage of a bona fide war hero
and brilliant federal judge.

Then there was spectacular Lake Michigan, the only Great
Lake entirely in US territory. Beautiful and sublime. Jonathan liked
nothing more than very early morning runs up and down Michigan
Avenue and over to Lake Shore Drive and the banks of the great
lake to watch a sunrise of bright orange, yellow, and red hues reflecting on the crashing waves while his heart was already pumping
faster from the run. He especially enjoyed watching the sunrise at
Fullerton Beach north of downtown with its panoramic view of the
lake and sun reflecting off the towering downtown skyline. The
stuff of dreams and poetry.

All his life, early mornings were special for Jonathan. In his lyrical book of poems, *Odes*, the Roman poet Horace more than two
thousand years ago introduced the concept of *carpe diem*, meaning
"seize the day and let tomorrow take care of itself." For Jonathan,
mornings were magical. Often he had trouble sleeping through the
night because he was impatient to start the new morning and new
adventure. Caffeine was not necessary to kickstart this congenital
energy machine. While many slowly eased, Jonathan bounded out
of bed. Mornings represented renewal and new beginnings. Evinc-
ing a profound appreciation of the impermanence and contingency
of life, for him each new morning represented some new opportunity, some new adventure, some new fact or idea or lesson to learn
about life. Some new opportunity to continue to *create* himself.
He fervently agreed with the attitude that life is not about finding
yourself, it's about a never-ending process of creating yourself. Every waking hour is an opportunity to create, to be the author, the
artist, of me. The reality of mortality, its conditionality and ephem-

erality, its finality, imbued in Jonathan an urgent vitality that there was not a day to waste, but to create.

That is why Jonathan was intrigued by the mournful Japanese expression *mono no aware*, the awareness of the impermanence of things with a gentle sadness for their passing and a deeper sadness that this is the reality of life. Symbolized by cherry blossoms, where Japanese people picnic under them not because they are lovelier than other blossoms but because of their transience—they fall from their branches only a week or so after first budding. This quick evanescence is at the heart of the world weariness of *mono no aware* in the eyes of the viewer. Jonathan, jilted in young love, painfully experienced the quick evanescence in matters of the heart and appreciated full well that his blossom would fade and fall lifeless all too soon. Until then he intended to seize each day and the opportunities that came his way.

THE MENTOR

They were in chambers eating lunch—the judge his standard steamed vegetables and walnuts over wild rice and Jonathan a bowl of broccoli cheddar soup. After a morning listening to a series of lousy arguments from ineffective lawyers, the agitated judge said, "Too many trial lawyers are unpolished professionals who think flashy style and bombastic rhetoric can substitute for hard work, attention to detail, and a carefully crafted presentation. That's bullshit. I call them lubricious lawyers, dildos without batteries. Look, Jonathan, that's probably a bit harsh, but if you want to be a great trial lawyer, you better have an iron butt—by that I mean you have to park your ass in the study seat and learn your case inside and out before you ever walk into a courtroom to try a case to a jury. There are no shortcuts in trial work." As Jonathan was nodding his understanding, the judge put his robe back on and said, "Let's go into the courtroom. Let's see if an old warrior can teach you something about how to be a jury trial lawyer."

The judge-turned-teacher grabbed a large easel and markers and stood next to the jury box. He instructed Jonathan to sit at counsel table. "A morality play." That was Judge Roy's didactic answer to his own question as he wrote it down. "What is a trial in an American courtroom?" Jonathan knew immediately that this was going to be a special moment, one of those mentor/protégé bonding moments he would never forget.

"Think about it, Jonathan, a group of ordinary citizens gets summoned to a courtroom, a place many have only seen on television or in the movies. They've been told nothing about the type of case they might get picked to judge. Then, in front of total strangers, they get asked a bunch of personal questions by some lawyers they don't know to see if they will be picked to be on a jury. At the start, they are only given some sketchy details about the case. And the case will then be presented to them by total strangers."

"Sounds scary when you put it that way," Jonathan ruefully noted.

"It is scary. That's why jurors tend to sympathize with many witnesses, especially if the attorneys appear to be unnecessarily aggressive and rude to them."

"I imagine many people try to get out of jury duty."

"Some do, but most folks, once they're here, take their civic duty seriously. That's why great trial lawyers don't waste jurors' time. You come to court totally prepared, have all of your exhibits at your fingertips for each witness, and get to the point in your examinations. Keep a good pace and move everything along. If you do it right, the jury will follow along with you. And they'll appreciate you for not wasting their time. And the last thing you want to do is anger the jurors by wasting their time."

"I suppose that takes a lot of discipline."

"It sure does. And a lot of practice. But that's the only way to command the courtroom. And no bullshit. Jurors see right through it. Your credibility is your best asset. You blow that, and the jurors will tune you out. For that matter, so will the judge."

"Got it. But why a morality play?" Jonathan thought, *Alexander the Great hit the jackpot when he got Aristotle for a tutor, and now I'm getting Judge Luke Roy. Pretty damn lucky.*

"For two reasons. Morals and a play. Jurors are like the rest of us: they want the good guys to win and the bad guys to lose. It's instinctive, unless you're a psychopath. That doesn't mean you always have to demonize the other side, but you do want to wear the white hat. Not like some unctuous, sanctimonious moralist, just somebody who's on the right side of the issue the jury has to decide. Give them an emotional reason to go your way.

Another reason why, as the lawyer, never, ever blow your credibility with the jury. Never." He wrote CREDIBILITY on the easel.

"But why a play?"

"This is why you become a trial lawyer. This is the fun, creative part. Think performing artist. Pop quiz, what's a fact?"

"Is this a metaphysics quiz?"

"Close. A fact is not some 'thing' seen by everybody the same way. The facts of the case at trial are what you, the trial lawyer, present to the jury and how you present them. The philosopher Jeremy Bentham once said, the power of the lawyer is in the uncertainty of the law. He should've added, and in the facts. In any case of any complexity, there are innumerable ways to present facts and frame issues. Innumerable ways to expose an opponent's obfuscations, euphemisms, and double talk. And never, ever, assume that different people, with different life experiences, will look at the so-called facts and see them the same way. Not happening. People have different centers of gravity. Never forget that."

"But don't you have to still keep it simple?" Jonathan asked.

"Yes, you do. And that's the creative part. That's what makes the trial lawyer the playwright. You choose the story you want to tell, how to tell it, and how to arrange the parts. Most importantly, how the jurors will see and hear what you present to them. That takes imagination, and the more powerful your imagination, the better storyteller you will be. Constrained only by actual facts, rules of evidence, and common sense. And remember, like a Broadway play, there are no rewind buttons once the trial starts. You get one shot with each part."

"Not so simple after all."

"Very hard work. That's why you need an iron butt. Early on in any case, your instincts will give you an idea of what type of story you'll want to tell. But it's not until you master your facts and the controlling law that you can develop and prepare the precise story you'll want to tell the jury. But nothing ever goes precisely according to plan. What's that saying about everybody has a plan until they get punched in the mouth? You'll get punched, so you have to be prepared to improvise and think quickly on your feet. Impossible to do unless you are thoroughly prepared and think through contingencies. Muscle memory is the trial lawyer's best friend."

"I can see where that will start to separate great trial lawyers from good lawyers."

"You bet. Preparation, preparation, preparation. Write and revise, write and revise, and then write and revise the lines of the play some more. Get rid of jargon and legalese. Write like ordinary people talk. Then put away the script and rehearse. You want conversational tones. Rehearse with your witnesses and rehearse your opening and closing arguments. It takes a lot of preparation and practice to ad lib and be spontaneous," the sly master said, with a wry grin and a wink.

"A lot of work but a lot of fun," Jonathan enthused.

"It gets even better. The great trial lawyer is not only the playwright, producer, and director. He, or she, is also the lead actor. Never upstage your own witnesses, but otherwise, the jurors' eyes are always on you. Always."

"Another character in the play, so to speak," Jonathan observed.

"Yes, and a main character at that. Don't preach, scream, or condescend. Talk to the jurors in a conversational tone. And for heaven's sake, don't read to them. Make eye contact." The judge walked to the center of the jury box, about twelve feet away from the railing, and scanned the box to show Jonathan how to do it. "Put yourself in the jurors' shoes. How would you like to be talked to if you were sitting in their place?"

"Like an adult who has to make an important decision about who wins and needs honest guidance to understand the case."

"That's exactly right. Like an adult. And never forget what the brilliant orator Winston Churchill said about public speaking: have and show conviction. If you want somebody to believe what you are saying, you damn well better sound like you believe it yourself." He wrote CONVICTION on the easel.

Jonathan thought, *Most new top law grads are slogging through tedious document reviews at their law firms right now and here I am being schooled on the ways of the Force by Obi-Wan Kenobi.*

Jonathan wound up spending most of his clerkship on the building materials supplier price-fixing case. The case was in full steam when Jonathan got involved. Judge Roy had already given the green light to let the case proceed as a class action. That was an important decision because most defendants in class action cases settle to avoid a potential crippling jury verdict due to the aggregated damages claims. It's one thing to fight a single plaintiff with a $2,000 claim. It's quite another to fight 150,000 aggregated claims that total $300 million. So it was not surprising that some of the building suppliers settled after Judge Roy's class decision. More surprising was the decision by others to dig in and take their chances at trial. Jonathan was thrilled—an actual antitrust class action trial and he was going to be in the front row.

In some respects the building supplier case was easy enough to understand. At the time, most houses in the United States used plywood in their construction. Plywood is a standard commodity, and its sales do not generate much of a profit. There were eight major manufacturers. They were the defendants. They were accused of raising plywood prices by coordinating strategic plant shutdowns to reduce supply and by signaling future price intentions through an industry trade publication. The case was interesting because there were no whistleblowers or insiders ratting them out. Nor were there any truly incriminating documents, although plenty generated some smoke. More smoke: the plaintiffs' expert economist had conjured up some statistical models purporting to show that plywood manufacturers tended to charge very similar prices. Judge Roy predicted that this would be a close case and economic expert testimony from both sides would be important. It might even determine the outcome.

The plaintiffs were a class of direct homebuilder buyers. They bought plywood directly from the manufacturer defendants. They then in turn sold the plywood to home buyers as part of the overall construction cost of the homes. Judge Roy told Jonathan that many people might wonder why the homebuilders and not the home buyers got to sue, especially if, as is likely, the homebuilders just passed along any higher plywood prices to the home buyers. The simple answer, he said, is that the Supreme Court, out of whole cloth, made up that rule long ago and has stuck with it. But, the judge told Jonathan, clever defense lawyers will still try to plant that very seed in the minds of the jurors—that the homebuilders didn't suffer any harm because they passed on any extra cost to the home buyers—in the hopes that the jurors would have zero sympathy for the homebuilders if the case came down to damages. The defense will want the jurors to ask themselves this question: "Why should we award any money to the homebuilders when they just stick it to the home buyers? It's always the little guys like us who get screwed in the end. If anybody should be getting money, it should be us."

Judge Roy would be impartial during the trial, but he did tell Jonathan that the plaintiffs' lead lawyer was a "preening peacock." A former marine, the judge didn't appreciate courtroom lawyers who were "out of uniform." He expected male lawyers to wear suits, preferably dark suits. Not loud sports jackets, tan slacks, stupid-looking ties with baseballs, or slick loafers with tassels, like Mr. Peacock. Lawyers "in clown garb" think they are signaling to the jury, "I'm not some corporate tool." To Judge Roy, it signals, "You're a dickhead." An injudicious view he wisely kept to himself.

Some lawyers think that the opening statement is the single most important part of a trial. Judge Roy was not dogmatic about it, and cases can vary, but he generally agreed with that sentiment because that is the first time lawyers get to lay out, in extended fashion, their theory of the case. A lot of lawyers flub this opportunity. The mentor told his protégé that the best opening statements, especially for a defendant, give the jury the theory of the case in the first two minutes, tell a compelling story that the jury can believe, address bad facts, and give the jury a reason to believe. Judge Roy encouraged Jonathan to pay particular attention to the opening statement of Cyrus Wright, the lead defendant's lawyer, a wily Chicago trial lawyer veteran knocking on retirement's door. This trial was likely his swan song.

In his opening statement for the plaintiff homebuilders, Stan Butler—Mr. Peacock—told the jury that instead of competing on prices, the defendants conspired to jack them up. He told them that they, in concert, shut down production lines and plants when prices dropped as a way to decrease supply and raise prices back up. Butler told the jury that the defendants used an industry trade magazine to signal pricing intentions and coordinate price increases. He flashed on the big screen documents from the defendants' own files that he contended showed price-fixing intentions. Butler talked about trade shows that the executives attended together and how they provided an opportunity to conspire. Motive, means, and opportunity, Butler stressed. Finally, Butler talked at length about how his expert economist, Dr. Karl von Hutton, would explain how conditions in the plywood business made price-fixing attractive for the manufacturers and how he calculated damages in the amount of $1.3 billion, based on the assumption that there was a conspiracy.

As Jonathan listened to Butler's opening statement, he thought that the jurors had already decided the case. Plaintiffs win. He had seen most of the evidence in the pretrial proceedings and thought the defendants would win. But after listening to Stan Butler, he changed his mind and thought they would lose. It underscored for him the importance of a powerful opening statement to create a persuasive first impression for how a case should be decided, in order to lead the jurors down the path of confirmation bias, where they filter the witness and documentary evidence to support their initial assessment of who wins and who loses. Defense attorneys who do not counter the plaintiff's opening statement with a strong counter-narrative will find themselves in a deep and likely inescapable hole.

Then the crafty Chicago veteran Cyrus Wright rose to speak. Wright delivered his opening for his client, Northwest Manufacturing, Inc., and also addressed allegations about industry conditions and damages. Wright started strong.

"May it please the court. Members of the jury, good morning. Beginning in the mid-1970s and continuing to this very day, Northwest Manufacturing made the strategic decision to be the strongest plywood competitor by being the lowest-cost producer. To be the strongest competitor, Northwest got rid of some small older plants, bought big new plants, and then sold a bunch of its other businesses to raise money to make even more investments in plywood. With an energized focus, Northwest has increased its plywood production, spent more than half a billion dollars on plywood plants, and increased its plywood production output. Out here in the rough-and-tumble real world, that's called competition. Competing, not conspiring, is the story of this case."

Wright then zeroed in quickly on three points he wanted the jury to remember. He put his three bullet points on the big screen.

"So, ladies and gentlemen, what will the evidence show? It will show three things.

"*Point one*. The evidence will show just the opposite of what you just heard from Mr. Butler. Northwest charted its own course and has gone its own way. Northwest never stopped competing with anybody. Northwest increased supply and increased production by spending a half a billion dollars to compete. Northwest did all of this to put the competitive hurt to the other players, not to lend them a cooperating hand.

"*Point two*. There were never any uniform plywood prices. They say a picture is worth a thousand words. Let's look at this picture. It's called a scatterplot. A scatterplot of plywood prices to these homebuilders over time. The actual prices charged, not the laboratory model prices that their paid expert conjured up for this lawsuit. The real prices vary dramatically, sometimes by hundreds of dollars per sale. The picture here tells a story of competition, not agreement. And that brings me to my third point.

"*Point three*. These plaintiffs must prove an agreement to fix prices. Please ask yourselves this question: What agreement? What's the evidence? There is not a single witness in this case who has said there was any price agreement, any production agreements, or any other agreements among the eight plywood manufacturers. Their own expert admitted under oath that he assumed—that's right, *assumed*—that there was a conspiracy and then, based on that assumption, ginned up a damages number."

Wright then elaborated in detail on his three points. Every step of the way, the crafty Chicagoan spoke in plain language and didn't try to con the jury with blustery and hyperbolic rhetoric. For this Chicago jury, it was like turning on radio station WFMT and listening to Studs Terkel deliver an oral history of plywood. The only thing Wright was missing was Terkel's trademark cigar. Wright took an unglamorous subject—certainly not anything that was made for Hollywood or television—and made it sufficiently interesting to keep the jury's attention. Like Terkel giving voice to ordinary Americans, Wright made plywood, a ubiquitous product in the houses of ordinary Americans, an important matter, and then he stressed that his client was the industry leader in making it better and more affordable. He was giving the jury a reason to believe.

A master in the courtroom, Wright quickly addressed what he thought plaintiffs thought was their best evidence and stripped it of any fizz and carbolic acid. Finally, he showed that the emperor had no clothes by explaining the critical faulty assumptions and mathematical mistakes in Dr. Karl von Hutton's damages model, effectively delivering a TKO before the shameless shill even took the witness stand.

Wright then wrapped up by thanking the jury for their patience and attentiveness and quickly recapped his three overarching points. His very last words in his opening were these:

"Ladies and gentlemen, as you review all of the evidence, we are confident that you will conclude that the absence of evidence is evidence of the absence of any imaginary conspiracy. This is a case about competition. The antitrust laws these plaintiffs are relying on are on the books to promote competition in the marketplace, not class action lawsuits in our nation's courtrooms. Northwest has been investing, expanding, and intensifying competition against fierce competitors. Northwest has been competing with, not conspiring with, its competitors. At the end of this trial, this hard-nose competitor will ask you to return a verdict in favor of competition and Northwest. Thank you."

As Cyrus Wright returned to his chair, Jonathan looked around the courtroom and over at the jury. He thought everyone was thinking the same thing. This case is over. Three weeks later it was. A complete win for the defense. As Judge Roy read aloud the jury verdict, Jonathan shook his head in wonderment at his great fortune to start his law career by clerking for a fabulous judge and teacher and to watch and learn from a master trial lawyer who commanded a courtroom.

Jonathan's clerkship ended two weeks after the plywood trial. On the night of his last day, Judge Roy took Jonathan to a small jazz club off Rush Street. One of his favorite local acts was playing, Judy Roberts, a jazz vocalist and pianist. The scarred marine loved when she played jazzman Mose Allison's song "Your Mind Is on Vacation" and the line about your mouth working overtime. The judge laughed and said Judy Roberts could be singing about half of the lawyers he sees in his courtroom.

They stayed for a couple of sets, reminisced some, shared some laughs, and talked about Jonathan's future. Jonathan had accepted an offer to join Cabot, Lodge & Biddle, a large, old-line, nationally prominent law firm based in DC with a strong reputation in complex litigation and antitrust, almost exclusively in defense of corporate America and corporate interests. Jonathan thought about following his war hero mentor's recommendation to go to the US Attorneys Office for trial experience, but he was eager to move on to his preferred path. As they were about to leave, the wounded warrior grew plaintive and advised Jonathan to remember Shakespeare: "To thine own self be true," and said, "Don't let Big Law do to you what Vietnam did to me—eat your soul."

Walking out of the club, the remarkable mentor gave Jonathan an envelope with a laminated 3 x 5 card inside. Jonathan opened the envelope when he got back to his apartment. The card was engraved with a quote from Michel de Montaigne, a sixteenth-century humanist philosopher who wrote wonderful meditative essays: "There is nothing so beautiful and legitimate as to play the man well and properly, no knowledge so hard to acquire as the knowledge of how to live life well and naturally; and the most barbarous of our maladies is to despise our being."

How to live life well, what a profound aspirational goal, Jonathan thought, *and self-loathing, what a malady to avoid*. He would never forget Judge Luke Roy, the judge and the man.

AGAINST THE ODDS

Jonathan was twenty-seven years old when he packed up his Chicago apartment, rented a small U-Haul truck, and drove seven hundred miles to DC. Plenty of time to wonder about the future and reflect on the past. Confident though he was, he was nonetheless amazed how improbable his road less traveled had been. Starting in a family of no lawyers, modest means, no social standing, and a rather sheltered upbringing, he was an honors graduate from a top law school, with an impossible-to-get judicial clerkship with a remarkable judge and true war hero, and now he was preparing to start his career at one of the elite law firms in the United States nestled in the nation's capital. In some sense, it seemed to the wunderkind that he had already lived a lifetime, yet he realized that he was starting all over, at the very bottom of a rigid hierarchical pecking order, in a world that was completely foreign to him.

Almost completely. In the summer before Jonathan's third year of law school, he did what most law school creme de la creme did. He worked as a summer intern at an elite law firm. Big Law, as the country's most prestigious law firms are called. In Jonathan's case he interned at two elite Big Law firms, one in Chicago and one in New York City. Six weeks at each firm. Firms that were pompously known as "white shoe," although any lawyer caught wearing white shoes would likely have been fired, and if he was also wearing a pinky ring, summarily executed or perhaps worse, made to work in a plaintiff's personal injury firm that advertised on the backs of buses and billboards on the highways, appropriately juxtaposed between signs lewdly advertising adult toy stores and those moralizing that Sin Has Consequences—REPENT.

Jonathan's mid-1980s experiences as a summer intern were eye opening, even mind blowing. First there was the pay. Even for entitled yuppie Baby Boomers, $1,500 a week, annualized to $78,000 a year, was serious walking-around cash. *Are law firms crazy?* he wondered. A summer internship is nothing more than an extended job interview and audition. What other businesses pay this kind of money to job interviewees? When Jonathan's father retired after forty years from his auto company employer, he made $32,500. And Jonathan's dad had to actually work hard for every penny. Jonathan knew going into his summer job that interns were pampered and wined and dined, but he assumed he was still going to have to do *some* work for the dough. That proved to be an unwarranted assumption. Jonathan's first glimpse of the life of Big Law was so far removed from the experiences of most Americans. Not a place to go to sanctify one's soul.

These elite law firms inverted the Greek motto "nothing in excess" by having seemingly nightly outings where alcohol did not have an off switch. Some weren't shy about sharing nose candy arranged in white lines on a mirror. Many a midmorning, interns rolled in with cotton mouth, massive hangovers, breath mints, and Visine. Work assignments were few and far between. Lots of lazy afternoon Cubs games at Wrigley and leisurely boat outings on the Hudson River. No wonder interns pined for a stoppage of time so they could indulge in Saturnalian revelries forever. But of course there was a catch.

Jonathan understood that Cabot, Lodge & Biddle (CLB)—cynically referred to as Crush, Lobotomize & Burn 'em Out—was no different and was also suffering from no delusions about what life would be like once the interns bit on the big-bucks bait and were reeled into firms as young associates. Big Law dollars may glitter, but life was anything but golden. In many respects, Jonathan appreciated that working in Big Law threatened to be a dreary descent into a black hole, causing the light of ordinary life to vanish. Money and prestige on the gilded surface, but scratch just a tad to

discover below a Sisyphean grind. Partner demands and life-drain-
ing billable hour requirements meant long, mind-warping tedious
workdays and nights, with plenty of drudge work on the weekends.
Young lawyers in suits toiling away in a hoity-toity version of the
"dark Satanic Mills" decried in William Blake's poem "Jerusalem."

For young lawyers in Big Law, the first (survival) skill required is
stress management. Hordes of young lawyers grinding away tracking their every breathing moment in six-minute intervals. They all
thought the same thing: What sick psychopath invented a billing
tracking system that made a person account for her work life every
six minutes? Such an impersonal time-management system works
for robots and automatons, but could it be any more dehumanizing? Yet very smart kids throughout the country—the "most likely
to succeed" crowd— seeking status and external validation and encouraged by parents, bust their butts for seven years of college and
law school and rack up huge student debts to start their working
lives this way. Most grow disillusioned and weary. For most, it's all
about the money, paying off debts, doing some time, and then getting the hell out for a better quality of life elsewhere lest they perish
in a slow fire. And yet every year law schools are flooded with ap-
plications from young, ambitious, talented college students—rich,
poor, and middle class—seduced by the siren song of status and
salary and hoping one day to land a job in the satanic mills known
as Big Law. Some even dream of being trial lawyers.

Judge Roy had warned his protégé that trial opportunities would
likely be few and far between in Big Law and that he would need
to be patient. The stark news Judge Roy spared him was that Big
Law is where aspiring trial lawyers go to die. Jonathan was shocked
to learn that fewer than 1 percent of Big Law cases actually go to
trial, and most of those cases don't even get close to a trial. Many
partners in Big Law, including those at CLB, have never tried a case,
certainly not as the lead trial lawyer. When third-party presidential
candidate Ross Perot in the 1992 campaign talked about a "giant
sucking sound," Jonathan thought it was the sound heard in Big
Law litigation departments sucking out the hopes and dreams and
aspirations and vitality and optimism and very life of young trial
lawyer wannabes. In a bit of gallows humor, he once joked to anoth-

er young litigator that "there should be a sign on the litigation door at every Big Law firm—Trial Aspirations, RIP."

Jonathan recognized this depressing state of affairs. But he was a probabilist. Sure, he thought, most cases don't go to trial, but some do, and my firm does try *some* cases. At least some partners do, including antitrust and complex corporate cases. Jonathan thought that most of his fellow associates would sensibly drop out of the rat race, so he determined that nobody would impress more than he, and nobody did, and by God, nobody would work harder, and nobody did. The ethos and value system of Big Law was the perfect environment for a brokenhearted lover to forget about life for more than awhile and commit to a twenty-four seven work pace and compete in a Darwinian system where only a very few would ever make it anywhere close to the top. He was going to move all of his career chips to the center of the table and place a big bet on himself. No matter the cost.

More poetically, his career was going to be metaphoric, like a long bus ride from one coast to the other coast. He had only one life and probably not more than forty years to try cases and make his name. If the stars aligned, he might get lucky and get twenty to forty trials, fifty if he was really lucky and his clients were not. If he missed the next bus, he would be left standing at the station, getting no closer to his coastal goal. The ambitious young man was determined not to miss any bus along the road of trial life. He would make it to the other coast. Nothing would stop him, at least nothing that he could even remotely control. Scarred by love and desirous of independence and achievement, Jonathan's passion was his profession.

TRANE

Before starting with Cabot, Lodge & Biddle, the intrepid warrior was inspired by the oldest story in the world—*Gilgamesh*, the story of an ancient Sumerian king who one day departed his kingdom to journey to the Cedar Forest with his companion Enkidu to slay the monster Humbaba, who did not deserve to die. But why, and why take the risk? In a speech to Enkidu, Gilgamesh explained his quest for fame:

> *"We are not gods, we cannot ascend to heaven,*
> *No, we are mortal men.*
> *Only the gods live forever. Our days*
> *are few in number, and whatever we achieve is a puff of wind.*
> *Why be afraid then,*
> *since sooner or later death must come?*
> *I will cut down the tree. I will kill Humbaba. I will make a last-*
> *ing name for myself.*
> *I will stamp my fame on men's minds forever."*

Mortality renders life short, Jonathan recognized, and he would not be the first successful person to indulge the self-delusional fantasy that his achievements would be more memorable than a "puff of wind." Like his literary and cinematic hero, the fictional baseball player Roy Hobbs from *The Natural*, he wanted to make a lasting name for himself "as the best there ever was." Like Roy Hobbs, he wasn't going to just hit home runs, he was going to knock the cover off the ball and bring down lightning from the heavens. Little did it occur to the man of twenty-seven that it could all just be building castles in the air, that it could be life's illusion. An illusion that had already blinded him to the poignant possibilities of shared love and a fuller life.

So where to start? In Jonathan's first year at CLB, he diligently did his work and impressed, sometimes overwhelmed, more senior lawyers with his analytical and writing skills. In particular, he caught the eye of a young partner who was trying to keep a high-profile defamation case against a newspaper publication from going into the ditch until the senior trial lawyer returned from a leave of absence. This was the second time the senior lawyer had to call a timeout for substance-abuse treatment. Specifically, alcohol. His name was Jack Kenneth Coltrane. He was recovering and he was returning. This brilliant, melancholic man would have a profound effect on Jonathan's career, but even more important, on his life.

Jonathan maneuvered himself onto Jack Coltrane's defamation case. It was set to go to trial in ten months. Excited, sure, but Jonathan had some trepidation about working with this unruly character. He had survived, even thrived, in Professor Bulldozen's classes, and a decorated war hero and formidable boxer had taken Jonathan under his judicial wing. But Jack Coltrane looked to be an entirely different kettle of fish. Coltrane, like Judge Roy, was six foot two. But unlike the judge's 180 pounds of taut muscularity, Coltrane tipped the obesity scales at around 310 pounds. If that were not imposing enough, his full head of sandy brown hair started a few inches north of his eyebrows and completely covered an 8¼-inch head, giving him an ursine appearance. His Irish surname was the Anglicized form of Gaelic O Caltarin, but to most everybody who knew him, he was just Trane. Trane because he was a locomotive of a man. He had what they called presence. Literally and figuratively, a very big presence.

Schooled in the halls of privilege at Exeter, Princeton a year early, and Yale Law, Trane was a lucid and laconic writer who believed that adjectives and adverbs in legal writing were rat poison, part Ernest Hemingway and part Raymond Chandler, with a near photographic memory. Colleagues joked that the extra storage capacity explained the skull size. He quoted poems and literary texts from memory and had an unexpected and peculiar penchant for doing the same with rock 'n' roll songs.

Trane was an unreconstructed liberal. After graduating number two in his class from Yale Law, he joined with the Freedom Riders, civil rights activists riding buses throughout the South, protesting segregated busing by racist companies acting in defiance of the US Supreme Court.

President John F. Kennedy, with his eloquent words and enlightened vision, was an inspiration to the young Trane. To Trane and many of his coming-of-age generation, Kennedy represented hope and change. A white president who went on national television to persuade Americans that the black civil rights movement was a moral battle "as old as the Scriptures and as clear as the American Constitution." And Trane was among the crowd of 250,000 at the National Mall and the Lincoln Memorial on August 28, 1963, to hear the Reverend Martin Luther King Jr. deliver his soul-stirring *I Have a Dream* speech. From Dr. King, Trane learned that the mastery of language should always be the servant of the cause. Trane was roused when Dr. King said, "We have also come to this hallowed spot to remind America of the fierce urgency of now." And immediately preceding Dr. King, Joachim Prinz, the president of the American Jewish Congress, spoke passionately about his days in Berlin during Hitler and the Nazis, exhorting the gathered throng: "America must not become a nation of onlookers, America must not remain silent." Those rallying calls to urgent, enlightened action were the words that had inspired Trane, then a young, northern white Princeton and Yale grad, to join with the Freedom Riders. An abiding hope for a better world and a more perfect union.

Disillusionment would soon follow. In 1939, the poet W. H. Auden had written that "the music must always play." Trane felt it stop playing on November 22 with Oswald's bullet, just three months after Dr. King's spellbinding speech. Trane's spirits were buoyed a little later when President Johnson, carrying on JFK's legacy, and completing what the persistent moral agitation by black civil rights leaders made possible, signed the Civil Rights Act of

1964 and the Voting Rights Act of 1965. In President Kennedy's inaugural address, he had spoken eloquently about renewal and change and of a new generation of Americans going forth "knowing that here on earth God's work must truly be our own." To Trane, that work was finally being done. Then more disillusionment.

The year 1968 was like no other. The North Koreans captured the USS *Pueblo*, race riots continued, the Tet Offensive and My Lai massacre and escalating Vietnam War, student protests, street violence, the 1968 Democratic National Convention and the Chicago Seven, and assassins' bullets that took the lives of Dr. King and a transforming and hope- inspiring Bobby Kennedy. Trane had been working in the firm for a few years, but those tragic, culminating assassinations crushed his hopeful soul. He would later say, "I felt lower than whale shit." He likely was in a state of undiagnosed depression. With Nixon's election in November 1968, followed by his racist appeal to the "silent majority," Trane sunk into a weltschmerz from which he never fully recovered. It was then that his turn to liquid relief began. In heavy doses.

The early signs of a drinking problem were all there. As a young partner in the early 1970s, Trane was already racking up trial victories. He excelled in all facets of trial work and had a knack with juries. How does one explain charisma? Trane had the uncanny ability both to impress juries as the smartest person in the room and as a world-weary soul who likely was muddling through life with many of the same troubles and griefs they had. He had the most important jury trial talent of all: he could relate. But he was a troubled soul with little self-control. At a partner retreat, while CLB's managing partner was droning on superciliously at dinner about firm values, Trane, four sheets to the wind, rocked back and forth, eyes unable to focus, and collapsed his giant noggin, face-first, into his sauce-soaked steak and garlic mashed potatoes. At the time, partners thought it was funny. Not Baxter Hodges, the priggish managing partner, but issues like this weren't generally taken too seriously. Heavy drinking was part of the warp and woof of Big Law social activities.

Over the next several years, Trane was still trying cases but increasingly showing ominous signs of fear of failure. Always a bit lazy, that would not change, but no case was too difficult for him, at least not conceptually. With his outstanding pedigree and, what he believed, attendant extraordinary expectations, Trane began to be overwhelmed by the paralyzing belief that anything less than stellar achievement would be an abject failure. A jury trial loss would be the lowest of the lows. Johnny Walker Black became his coping mechanism. Trane's wife said enough, intervened, and checked him into a rehab facility. This was before Jonathan had even started law school.

Trane returned to practice and stayed sober for five years. Then he began to drink prodigiously. Eight to ten beers at lunch, always ordered two at a time. Bobby Zussman, the young partner Jonathan would work with on Trane's defamation case, told the story of his first time traveling with Trane when he was a first-year lawyer. Trane downed three double Johnnies at the airport bar, swilled an entire bottle of wine on the airplane, and ordered two more at dinner at the hotel restaurant. Bobby, sensing a rite of passage, tried to keep up. Until, in the middle of dinner, he rushed to his room and spent the night worshiping at the great white commode. In the morning, Trane admonished the painfully hungover rookie by saying, "You should have stayed for dessert and Courvoisier XO Cognac."

Two days later, Bobby showed up at Trane's hotel room at 6:30 a.m. to help him prepare for an important deposition he was going to take that morning. Trane's breakfast room service arrived at the same time—six scrambled eggs with ham and cheese, two orders of bacon, extra hash browns, six slices of toast and butter, and six Budweisers. Trane drained all six by 7:00 a.m. Bobby took the deposition.

Trane did his second rehab stint during Jonathan's first year at the firm. Six months earlier, Trane had been hired by a milk producer to defend a slew of antitrust price-fixing cases, alleging that the country's major milk producers conspired to overcharge grade-school children for their lunch milk. The cases were filed throughout the southern United States. Now, if only the firm could hold onto them while Trane tried to get sober, there would be plenty of opportunities. But first, Jonathan was about to catch his first bus on his coastal journey.

He was picked to work with Trane and Bobby on the defamation case. His job was to help them get the case ready to present to the jury. Jonathan was ecstatic. Bobby was a good young mentor and gave him valuable tips on working with Trane, a volatile partner with a bad temper who did not suffer fools gladly. He was especially harsh on poor writing. Bobby told Jonathan that he was assigned to work with Trane on his first day at the firm. After six months, Bobby thought his name had been changed to "Goddammit" because all he ever heard from Trane was "Goddammit, Zussman" this and "Goddammit, Zussman" that and "Goddammit, Zussman, my ten-year-old son writes better than the shit you give me." Trane, who was a funny man but had an unfortunate prick gene, one day even came to Bobby's office wearing a gas mask and rubber gloves holding one of Bobby's legal memos, bellowing, "This shit is toxic." Things were different then.

But Bobby also told Jonathan that, with Trane, game knows game and never, ever back down. Bobby advised Jonathan, "You're really good and Trane will respect you, so hang tough." Bobby also told Jonathan that for all of Trane's gruffness, he actually had a soft side, that two stints in rehab or, what Bobby indelicately called the drunk tank, had mellowed Trane, and that Trane was brilliant in the courtroom. There was a hell of a lot Trane could teach him about how to try a case before a jury.

Understandably wary about his new assignment, Jonathan nonetheless was eager to start. So he girded up his loins, enveloped himself in an invisible shit shield, and went to Trane's office to meet his new mentor and prepare for trial. The first thing he noticed when he entered Trane's office was an engraving from the gateway to hell in Dante Alighieri's *Inferno*: "Abandon hope all ye who enter here." Jonathan thought, *Why am I not surprised?* and reminded himself that only fools rush in where angels fear to tread, and he took a seat.

Jack Coltrane's first words to Jonathan: "Anybody ever call you Jack?"

"Yeah, once, but that was a long time ago. I go by Jonathan."

"Well, Jonathan, I have two things to tell you. First, Zussman is being pulled off this case because he is needed for another trial that starts in a couple months. So right now it's you and me. You up for it?"

"Absolutely, Mr. Coltrane."

As Trane slowly crushed his thin cigar/cigarette into his ashtray, he glared at Jonathan and said, "I hate when people say 'absolutely.' Don't like 'totally' or 'awesome' either. Or, for that matter, 'amazing,' 'incredible,' 'literally,' 'unique,' 'interesting,' 'clearly,' 'really,' 'very,' 'egregious,' 'disingenuous,' 'you know,' and, especially, 'like, you know.' Same goes for gerunds and dangling participles and pleonasms. Stay away from verbal crutches and make your words count. Don't be trite, hackneyed, or clichéd. Get to the point. We're in the business of persuading ordinary jurors and busy judges, not gag-me-with-a-spoon Valley girls or other airheads. The second thing is, I hate to lose. Understand?"

"Abso ... yes, I understand," Jonathan stuttered.

"That's all," Trane said, in a dismissive tone. "One other thing, call me Jack." Jonathan walked out after just a few minutes feeling like he was lucky to still be alive and wondering what in the hell he was getting himself into.

For the next several months, Jonathan worked pretty much without incident helping Trane prepare for trial. Trane occasionally flashed some anger but seemed to enjoy working with Jonathan. From time to time while Jonathan was working at his desk, Trane would wander in with his beloved *New York Times*, sit in Jonathan's guest chair, open the paper, and inevitably start inveighing about yet another one of life's outrages. But mostly Trane read and Jonathan worked in quiet, comfortable silence, like well-worn friends. A bond was developing between Trane, the Knight of the Sad Countenance, and his highly driven, immensely gifted protégé. Jonathan would realize only much later in his career that he was the only person Trane never called by his last name. And Jonathan always called him Jack, not Trane.

Jonathan couldn't believe his good fortune to be working on a defamation case as his first trial. The case was in Nashville, Tennessee. He and Trane were representing Billy Joe Wynn, a popular country-and-western singer, especially with the Christian crowd, which is basically the entire South. The married singer's wholesome image, sad-sack lyrics, and mellifluous voice endeared him to a large audience of admiring fans. Billy Joe was a big star. The kind trash tabloids and gossipmongers love to bring down a peg or two. Where truth never gives pause to a salacious story that sells. In this case, a New York tabloid called *The Sun Sensational* published a callous calumny—"Billy, Booze and Boys"—falsely claiming that Billy Joe was a booze hound who bedded a young male bartender in Biloxi, Mississippi. After the publication, Billy Joe lost gigs and record sales. The trial was going to be a thriller.

The Sun Sensational's New York lawyers defended their client on the grounds that the tabloid had a First Amendment right to publish the piece, and then they tried to argue that anybody who read it would think that it was parody. Just a few years earlier, *Hustler Magazine*, another purveyor of pornographic provocation, published an advertisement claiming that Jerry Falwell, then leader of the short-lived Christian right-leaning moral majority, whom critics claimed was more like the hypocritical pretender to piety in Molière's play *Tartuffe*, had engaged in incest with his mother. The ad, entitled *Jerry Falwell Talks about the First Time*, was a fake interview with Falwell, suggesting he did the rumpy pumpy with mommy in an outhouse and displayed a bottle of liquor. At the bottom of the ad there was a disclaimer: "Ad parody not to be taken seriously." The case made its way to the Supreme Court. The high court, famous for its inability to define pornography but confident in its ability to know it when it sees it, ruled for *Hustler* on the grounds that the ad was "obviously ridiculous" and "clearly not true." Conclusions the sanctimonious evangelist presumably would be hard-pressed to dispute.

Before the trial started, Trane argued to the judge that Billy Joe's case was nothing like *Hustler*'s farcical hit job on Jerry Falwell, didn't have any disclaimers, and didn't pretend to be anything other than a supposed factual account of Billy Joe's ribald escapade with boy and bottle. So, Trane argued, the case should go to trial for the jury to decide three issues: (1) whether the article was false; (2) whether *The Sun Sensational* knew it was false or published it with reckless disregard of whether it was false or not; and (3) how much money the tabloid trash traducement had cost Billy Joe. The judge agreed with Trane but admonished him not to refer to the

defendant as tabloid trash in front of the jury. With a grin, Trane
nodded an intent to comply.

Jonathan had worked tirelessly, seven days a week. Work, sleep,
run. Work, sleep, run was his schedule. Trane did something he
rarely did: he genuinely praised Jonathan. Better yet, he assigned
him a couple of witnesses to examine at trial. Before trial, Trane reminded Jonathan that emotion trumps reason in decision-making,
so the goal was not so much to convince the jury with logic and
rational arguments but to tap into their emotional impulses and
persuade them with evidence that comports with their common
sense and sense of fair play. "Put the facts out there and lead them
to the three conclusions we want them to land on without beating
them over the head," he instructed. Trane said he felt very good on
the falseness issue. *The Sun Sensational* had no fact witnesses to back
up its salacious story, and Billy Joe had plenty of witnesses to attest
to his moderate drinking of Bud Light beer and his heterosexual
fidelity to his voluptuous wife, Honeysuckle, a name given to her
at birth because her mother loved honeysuckle's beautiful aroma
and sweet nectar. Honeysuckle would be an irresistible and colorful
witness.

Like the popular blue-eyed sensual soul singer Dusty Spring-
field, Honeysuckle was a peroxide blonde with bouffant/beehive
hair who turned heads with her onyx collar and spray-on fuchsia
leather miniskirt that was so short the prurient prying eyes of Bible
Belters could see clear to the promised land. Preferring décolletage
to decorum and pink, six-inch, knock-me-down-and-fuck-me heels
to closed-toe black flats, Honeysuckle would leave the jury with
little doubt as to which way Billy Joe's peter teeters, Trane dead-
panned. Trane also thought that they would prove that the article
was false based on handwritten notes from the tabloid reporter's
files that said, "I need to find some dirt somewhere fast on BJW
or we're toast." At a minimum, Trane believed that the jury would
conclude that the tabloid was reckless.

Shortly before trial, *The Sun Sensational* made a take-it-or-leave-
it confidential offer of $1 million and no retraction. That amount
confirmed for Trane that the defense had sized up the case pretty
much the same way: it would come down to actual damages and

possibly punitive damages. Billy Joe was claiming $3 million in lost gigs and record sales. In this heavyweight bout, Trane thought he also had a puncher's chance at punitive damages, but only if he could get the right jury.

Billie Joe Wynn was straight out of Tennessee country-and-western typecasting. Mellifluous voice with a soft twang, boots, buckle, Bullhide hat, and his six string, Billy Joe wrote most of his own songs, usually on napkins. He sang love ballads and songs about failed relationships, drinkin' and hell-raisin', songs about betrayal and hard luck times, and forgiveness and redemption. Trane just needed to find eight jurors he could lather up enough to get them stoked to award punitive damages.

Trane taught Jonathan that in every jury trial the most important people in the room are the jurors. Echoing something Judge Roy had told him, Trane bemoaned that many lawyers are lousy at jury selection, what the law calls voir dire. The tabloid sent its New York lawyers to try the case, and Trane was laying odds that they would stink at jury selection here in Music City, where they don't sell the thousand-dollar Italian suits and Bruno Magli loafers favored by these Big Apple lawyers. Trane would have bet his last silver dollar that they could not name one song by country-and-western legends Merle Haggard, Hank Williams, George Jones, Waylon Jennings, Charlie Pride, Roger Miller, or Patsy Cline. Nor could Trane three weeks earlier. That is why he dragged Jonathan down to Nashville two weeks before trial and had Billy Joe give him a crash course on country and western. Lesson done, Trane said he could listen to Patsy Cline sing "Crazy" one hundred times and it would still give him chills.

Trial day finally arrived. Given the celebrity of Billy Joe and the pretrial publicity, the judge brought in seventy-two Nashville-area residents to be interviewed as potential jurors in jury selection. Eight would ultimately sit on the jury. Even though each side would be able to strike three for basically any reason they liked, the judge figured that many more would not be able to serve for the scheduled two-week trial, either because of some hardship, like a single mom with no childcare help, or because they already had made up their minds who should win. There were plenty of those. During jury selection a number of folks said, "If it's in the paper, then there must be some truth to the story," while others said, "I wouldn't believe a single cotton-pickin' word from any fast-talkin' New Yorker."

Billy Joe was the plaintiff, so he went first. Trane taught Jonathan that "the key to jury selection is to ask open-ended questions and let the jurors do the talking." As Trane admonished him, "You're learning nothing when you're talking. We want to find out what jurors are thinking; we want them to open up so we can figure out which jurors would be bad for our side and get them the hell off the panel." That was priority number one, two, and three. And Trane wanted to figure out which potential jurors would be unlikely to award punitive damages. Some devout Christians believe that it is only God's place to punish, a view he sure enough respected, just not on this jury. Trane spent his first thirty minutes asking several jurors about their backgrounds, what they did at work, what they liked to do in their spare time, and got a dialogue going among some of the jurors about how the press covers celebrities and politicians.

Unless struck, juror number ten, Ricky Jones, was likely going to be on the jury because Trane was going to strike juror number two and the judge was going to strike number six for cause. Ricky owned a honky-tonk bar called Moonshine Blackouts, as his black T-shirt with white letters emblazoned on it said, was skinny, and wore a ponytail, earring, and shaggy beard. But he had bright, intelligent eyes, not the lethargic and lugubrious eyes made dull and weary by too much weed and whiskey. Trane's first impression was that Ricky could go for either side but could also be a ringer for him, so he explored with a particular line of questions. After some clipped, cautious answers to Trane's first few questions, Ricky responded to Trane's question about some of his favorite songs by providing several song titles:

"How Can I Miss You If You Won't Go Away?"

"How Come Your Dog Don't Bite Nobody but Me?" Trane barely suppressed a laugh. He knew the feeling.

"Her Only Bad Habit Is Me." To which Trane told the jury,

"Hey, that could be my wife's song." The panel got a good laugh out of Trane's self-deprecation. He relates.

"I'm So Miserable Without You, It's Just Like Having You Around."

Ricky paused, but Trane encouraged him to continue.

"My Best Friend Run Off with My Wife and Boy Do I Miss Him." Juror number 27, donning a Jack Daniels T-shirt and a red bandana around his neck, hooted out, "Love that tune, man." Jurors 17 and 18, also young men, gave each other a high five. The judge gaveled them to be silent.

"Thank God and Greyhound You're Gone."

"You Done Tore Out My Heart and Stomped That Sucker Flat."

Trane had no more questions for Ricky. Jonathan thought Mr. Moonshine Blackouts was one toke over the line, sweet Jesus. So too, apparently, did the Gucci lawyers because they didn't strike him. Trane knew Ricky Jones belonged on his jury.

That left juror number nine. Trane wanted to ask her a few questions just to confirm a hunch and plant a seed. Her name was Dr. Sarah Claybaugh, distinguished university professor of English at Vanderbilt University, just down the road from the Nashville courthouse. She had a captivating, velvety voice with a trace of honeydew and elongated the pronunciation of her vowels. *No wonder*, Trane thought, *her classes were so popular.*

Professor Claybaugh was fifty-three years old, had majored in English at the University of Mississippi, said her beloved Square Books in Oxford was her home away from home, especially during Ole Miss Rebels football season, had a particular fondness for Faulkner and Shakespeare, and received her PhD from Emory University in Atlanta. Her doctoral dissertation— "Eudora Welty: The Humanizing Pedagogy of the Short Story in Southern Literature"—was published in a respected academic journal.

She was going on her twenty-second year at Vanderbilt. Trane learned these details in his casual questioning of the professor and also learned that she enjoyed Broadway plays in New York, was an amateur poet, and was an avid fan of the Atlanta Braves and one of its star pitchers, Tom Glavine, whom she adoringly called Tommy. She reminded Trane of Susan Sarandon's character Annie in *Bull Durham*, a wonderful movie about life and baseball. Trane didn't distinguish between the two.

Wrapping up his questions, Trane asked Professor Claybaugh if she ever taught Shakespeare to her undergraduates. She replied that she taught introductory courses and also taught an upper-level course on Shakespeare's tragedies. Almost indifferently, Trane asked if the course included the study of Shakespeare's play *Othello*. The vivacious professor grew animated and said, "Why, yes, *Othello* is one of my favorite plays because Shakespeare created a wonderfully sinister, Machiavellian villain in the character of Iago." With a slight smirk, Trane told the judge he had no further questions. When the judge finally seated the jury, Professor Claybaugh was on it. Trane was feeling better.

The trial was surprisingly fast and smooth. Trane handled Billy Joe's testimony, most of the cross-examinations of the tabloid's witnesses, and both sides' damages experts. Jonathan did the direct examination of Honeysuckle. It was entertaining and powerful. Certainly revealing. Some puerile press writers called it titillating. It got better on cross-examination. Even law students know that it is playing with fire to ask a witness on cross-examination an open-ended question if you don't know what the answer is going to be, especially if the answer could be consequential. Yet *The Sun Sensational*'s lawyer must have been a pyromaniac because his first (sarcastic) cross question, in a phony southern accent, to Honeysuckle was, "Now, Honeysuckle, how can you be so sure that Billy Joe only has eyes for you?" Honeysuckle's bountiful upper-body assets almost tumbled out of her reveal-more-than-conceal diaphanous silk top as she bent over to pick up her thirty-two-ounce Mountain Dew and moistened her ruby-red lips before taking a long, slow suck on the straw, swallowed, and responded in a kittenish, honey-tongued voice that could sweeten a horseradish pickle, "Because when I smile at Billy Joe and tell him it's BJ time, he rises to the occasion, knowin' he's gonna be a cum ... in ... when I *sluuuuurrrrrrp* his straw." The courtroom exploded in laughter and that put an end to

the cross-examination of Honeysuckle Wynn. When Honeysuckle left the witness stand, the jury was left with little doubt about
where Billy Joe's love train did its choo choo chooing. She certainly
gave sensual meaning to the expression morning, noon, and night.
Honeysuckle left everyone in the courtroom wondering where Billy
Joe ever found the time to compose and sing. More than once the
judge had to ask for silence in the courtroom.

Trane went first in closing argument. He cogently laid out all of
the evidence for the jury. The tabloid's lawyer's closing was off-put-
ting. Speaking very fast, he was caustic and abrasive and attempted
to belittle Billy Joe's case. He even made an edgy comment about
Honeysuckle's testimony, which raised many an eyebrow in the
courtroom. Ricky Jones scoffed in disbelief. The lawyer didn't even
mention damages.

It was now Trane's time for the final remarks before the judge
instructed the jury on the law and sent them off for their deliberations. The large man with a large head rose slowly. The courtroom
was silent. Jonathan was mesmerized. Trane began by pointing out
that one sleazy, scandalous, salacious piece of trash masquerading
as investigative journalism from malicious keyboards in New York
City cost Billy Joe $3 million in lost gigs and record sales and incal-
culable damages to his well-deserved reputation. Trane then went
for the jugular. He pounded on the theme that the tabloid knew the
article was false and published it anyway. It was a calculated smear
job, and it was *reprehensible*, a standard Trane knew the judge would
tell the jury that it must find to award punitive damages.

Trane paused and stood before the jury in the middle of the
room. No notes. Standing directly across from Professor Claybaugh,
his predicted jury foreperson, he said in a soft but commanding
voice, "Ladies and gentlemen, on behalf of Billy Joe, I want to
thank you for your service and attention. This is a very important
case for Billy Joe. Millions of people read the article that brings us
to the courtroom today. It was false, and that defendant knew it
was false. No verdict, no back-page retraction, no belated apology
can undo all of the harm done to Billy Joe and his reputation. Y'all
know from your daily lives that once something is printed in black
and white in a paper, many people will believe it. They will believe

it forever. That is Billy Joe's cross to bear. And for that *The Sun Sensational* deserves to be punished. They deliberately chose money and mendacity over honor and honesty. From here in this Nashville courtroom, you now have the power to tell them and all the world that what they did was wrong. Tell them it was terribly wrong.

"So allow me to end by quoting something written long ago that applies to how this defendant stole Billy Joe's good name, the jewel of his soul, and made him poor indeed." Sounding eerily like the wonderful Shakespearean actor Sir Ian McKellen, Trane flawlessly delivered these lines:

> *"Good name in man and woman, dear my Lord, Is the immediate jewel of their souls; Who steals my purse steals trash; tis Something, nothing, 'twas mine, tis his, and has been slave to thousands; but he that filches from me my good name robs me of that which not enriches him, and makes me poor indeed. Ladies and gentlemen, Billy Joe's good name and fate are now in your hands. Thank you."*

Professor Claybaugh could not suppress a smile. She, and only she, knew that Trane had just quoted Iago from *Othello,* and indeed, sounded like Ian McKellen as she imagined him with the Royal Shakespeare Company performing in Stratford-upon-Avon.

This was Jonathan's first trial. He learned one of the most poignant lessons about trial work: the wait for the jury to return with their verdict is excruciating. There are no real distractions, just a mindless passing of time and increased anxiety in thirty-minute intervals. Jonathan would learn what stomach churning means with a long wait. But not today. After just two hours of deliberations, the jury sent a note that it had reached a verdict.

As the jury filed in, Trane noticed that Professor Claybaugh was holding the verdict form in her right hand. She was the foreperson. After the jurors were all seated, the judge called for the verdict form and then read it aloud. On the charge of defamation, the jury found for Billy Joe Wynn. The jury further found that Billy Joe was entitled to damages in the amount of $3 million. Jonathan was about to hyperventilate. The judge paused for a moment and reflected. He even checked something in a law book. Jonathan was anxiously muttering to himself, "Come on, come on." The judge raised his head, looked at the defense table, and announced that the jury awarded punitive damages in the amount of $10 million. The courtroom erupted while Billy Joe hugged Trane and Jonathan and everyone else in sight.

The Sun Sensational would go on to file an appeal and lose. Billy Joe walked away with $13 million, plus millions more in interest. No one could figure out how the jury had arrived at the punitive damages amount. Ten million was never mentioned in the courtroom, and ten is not a multiple of three. Trane had more than a clue but kept it to himself. While questioning Professor Claybaugh in voir dire, he asked her how many tragedies Shakespeare had written, including *Othello*. She answered ten.

When Trane asked her if she thought each one was worth a million dollars, she said, "Oh, I don't know about that, but I do know they are all priceless to me." Then, as now, Trane moved on.

In a bit of poetic justice, Nashville style, after Billy Joe collected his money from *The Sun Sensational,* he and Honeysuckle divorced. The terms of the divorce were never disclosed, but local gossip rags noted that Honeysuckle quickly married the heir to a scrap metal empire, bought a 10,000-square-foot yellow and pink mansion on the Gulf Coast, and was a frequent visitor to Babies R Us. As for Billy Joe, he added a Chuck Mead song to his repertoire, "She Got the Ring and I Got the Finger." Patrons of Moonshine Blackouts sang along in out-of-key commiseration each time Billy Joe played it.

SOUTHBOUND

The Billy Joe Wynn trial was career altering for Jonathan. Sure, he dreamed since college of being a trial lawyer on a big stage. But the bright light of reality often vanishes away dewy dreams the way the morning sun evaporates the fog. To be in the courtroom participating, anxiously awaiting to see if your story resonated with the jury, knowing that it's either win or lose, was an indelible experience, an adrenaline rush a litigator could find nowhere else in the law. Now he was living his professional dream. He was hooked. He was craving another opportunity. His next coastal bus ride. He did not have a long wait.

Jack Coltrane was keenly perceptive. He appreciated that there was something special about Jonathan. All could see that he possessed off-the-charts legal smarts. In the courtroom, Trane saw something else that he rarely saw in Big Law litigation departments—genuine jury trial ability. A knack, an instinct, an ability to relate and take the pulse of the room, and a burning desire to be in the arena and fight, to get on the stage and perform without a net. Duly impressed, Trane asked Jonathan to work on the new school milk price-fixing cases. Cases where a trial was very likely. Maybe even more than one. Jonathan took a zeptosecond to say yes.

These cases were going to be a formidable challenge. In Billy Joe Wynn's case, it was not hard to assume the role of the good guy, the avenging angel, sword in hand, sent to right a grievous wrong. But Cabot, Lodge & Biddle, like Big Law generally, rarely sided with plaintiffs. Their bread and butter, their raison d'être, was defending powerful corporations, the bigger the corporation and the nastier their legal problems, the better. Defenders of the Dark Side. For Jonathan, defending the price-fixing cases was going to be an entirely different experience.

Throughout the southern United States, from the Carolinas, across Florida, Georgia, Alabama, and Mississippi, and including Tennessee, Arkansas, Louisiana, and Texas, grade school children in public schools drank a carton or two of milk every day at lunch, five days a week. Nutrition for healthy, growing bodies. All well and good until the Department of Justice announced that it was launching a sweeping criminal investigation and convening federal grand juries to investigate whether greedy milk producers in the southern states were conspiring to overcharge the school kids for their milk. Shortly thereafter, like hungry hyenas and lappet-faced vultures on the savannah searching for carcasses to feast on, plaintiffs' lawyers throughout the south filed tag-along civil class action lawsuits in each of the states seeking billions of dollars. The named defendants were the top seven milk producers controlling 95 percent of all milk sales. There was not going to be any sympathy shown to big corporations ripping off little kids for something as essential as lunch milk. The avenging angels were all on the other side, even if many of those plaintiffs' lawyers comported themselves more like black-backed jackals than halo-wearing paragons of virtue.

Big Law worships money on bended knee and thus salivates to join the defense side of the fee-feeding frenzy these types of sprawling antitrust cases generate for billable hours and enormous fees. They employ armies of lawyers, charging by the hour, working around the clock, and they typically last for several years. *Cha-ching* is the silk-stocking sound echoing through the gilded halls of these powerhouse law firms. Partners who bring in these cases usually get top compensation. Time to test-drive the Porsches and S-Class Mercedes.

Younger lawyers often can ride the golden surf all the way to partnership if they perform well. But scratch the surface and there is a dismal dreary underside for younger Big Law lawyers. For most assigned to work on these cases, they disappear into a black hole of endless document review and midnight memo writing that dulls then deadens senses and zaps creative energy. They become like zombies in the land of the walking dead. Spouses and significant others see these meter machines on Saturday nights, but that's about it. Trane assured Jonathan he would be riding the wave, not submerged somewhere in the abyss of zombie land.

True to his word, Trane assigned Jonathan to be his point person for the defense of the case filed in Birmingham, Alabama. The judge, John Pointer, comported himself with stoic gentility and was well known for quickly moving along his cases. In short order he set a rigorous pretrial schedule with a trial date in eighteen months. Warp speed, in antitrust litigation. Besides Trane, there were lawyers senior to Jonathan and a horde of contemporaries and junior lawyers working on the case. The zombies. Jonathan sensed that this would be the next case for him to leave his mark and catapult his career. In ways he never could have anticipated, this experience was about to transform him both professionally and personally.

The Alabama case, as well as the related cases, took Jonathan on an eye-opening journey all over the southern United States. The Billy Joe Wynn case in Nashville had given the midwestern boy an authentic feel for the colorful language and vivid similes, metaphors, and analogies used by southern lawyers and judges to make their arguments and convey their messages. In the school milk cases, Jonathan spent the eighteen months before the Alabama trial in the offices of southern law firms and courthouses taking and defending depositions and attending hearings. He was introduced to a new smorgasbord of language as well as the actual food.

Jonathan learned quickly that southerners praise the Lord and the Lard. He wondered if southerners even fried their water. Fried chicken, fried pork chops, fried catfish, fried shrimp, fried potatoes, chicken-fried steak, fried BLT, fried okra, beer-battered fried pickles, even fried green tomatoes, the one fried vegetable he enjoyed. As Jonathan heard more than one Deep South gourmand say, "Lorda mercy, this eatin' will fill you up fuller than a tic." Keep chowing down the buttermilk cornbread and counting the calories—buttermilk biscuits and (sausage) gravy, collard greens, turnip greens, shrimp and grits, mac and cheese, pimento cheese, hush puppies (more deep-fried treats), Brunswick stew (wild game of choice), po'boy sandwiches (with the arresting motto "put a piece of south in your mouth"), tomato and mayo white-bread sandwiches followed by tomato, cheddar and bacon pie, or pecan pie or key lime pie or peach cobbler or banana pudding. Deviled eggs and country ham, iced sweet tea, and a barbecue joint on every street corner. Jonathan thought, *no wonder the southern states virtually run the table in the obesity sweepstakes.*

Southern food was largely indigestible for him, but he ate up the way colorful southern lawyers talked. Drawl and language and locution. Jonathan, who had started in college to develop an appreciation for the protean richness of the English language, was fascinated by the evocative expressions he heard in the South. Especially considering the blandness of the plain speaking he had been accustomed to growing up and going to school in the Midwest. This recreational philologist was developing an acute sensitivity for the southern patois.

Southern lawyers (loyers) sure enough have a hankering for animal references. Dogs and pigs are especially popular. If an adversary's argument falls flat, the southern lawyer says, "That dog don't hunt." Or if an issue doesn't concern his client, the lawyer will say, "I got no dog in that fight." Or if the witness is a liar, "He's lyin' like a no-legged dog." Then there are the pigs. To ridicule overkill, the southern lawyer might say, "Y'all don't need to burn down the house to roast the pig." If something is futile, "Son, don't try to perfume that pig." Greed is a universal vice; in the South it is encapsulated in this prudential admonition, "Pigs get fat, hogs get slaughtered." Speaking of hogs, good trial lawyers will make certain that their defenses are "hog tight, horse high, and bull strong."

Don't forget the other animals. A linguistic Noah's ark for litigators. The first time Jonathan heard a lawyer say, "Bring down the grass so the goats can eat," he scratched his head trying to figure out what that meant. He's still scratching. Easier to understand is the improvement on the difficulty of herding cats: "Getting that group fast on the same page is like herding turtles barefoot over coals." One of Jonathan's favorite expressions to mock a lawyer who is all talk is to say, "That boy's all hat, no cattle." Or all he has is "rodeo evidence, a point here and a point there, but all bull in between." About a lawyer who talks nonsense, Shakespeare's King

Lear might say, "I want that glib and oily art to speak and purpose not," while a low-brow southern lawyer says, "His words made no more sense than the bubbles issuing from the mouth of a fish." When a northern lawyer makes his final and best settlement offer, he will unimaginatively say, "That's as good as it gets," whereas a southern lawyer will tell you, "That possum's on the stump." When a witness is slick and hard to pin down, a northern lawyer calls him evasive, but a southern lawyer says, "Dag gum, ain't he slicker than owl shit." A northern lawyer might call an adversary underhanded, while a southern lawyer will say, "That rascal's lower than a snake's belly in a wagon rut."

Jonathan himself was the target of a southern barb. A favorite trick of the older lawyer is to slyly use a younger lawyer's age against him. In the Alabama case, Jonathan argued a tough motion that had several components. He prepared intensely, practiced in front of a mirror the way Winston Churchill used to do, and delivered his argument eloquently and flawlessly. A young Daniel Webster in the making. Then the sixty-year-old plaintiff's lawyer stood up, thumbs inside his clip-on suspenders, belly bouncing over buckle, jiggling jowls a saggin', and wisecracked, "Listenin' to that young fella's argument is like drinkin' a margarita. It sure is intoxicating, but it's best appreciated with a grain of salt." Jonathan lost his motion.

Jonathan wasn't drinking margaritas, but he was intoxicated with his work and time in the South. For the entire eighteen months before trial, he didn't take off a single day, including the holidays. Even Trane admonished him to relax from time to time, but Jonathan kept a singular focus on the case and advancing his career at CLB. And he certainly wasn't going to miss his next bus stop. At the same time, Jonathan was growing more distant from his fellow younger lawyers, all working similarly insane hours, but most wallowing in the abyss, stuck in the daily grind of life behind a lonely desk, and most updating and shopping their résumés to get the hell out before dying in the slow fire. Unlike Jonathan, with his monomaniacal focus on partnership and career, most of his contemporaries had little hope of ever making partner, were desperate for some semblance of work/life balance as they married, had babies, and unsuccessfully tried not to be absentee parents. Premature gray and periorbital dark circles brought on by stress, sleep deprivation, failed relationships, and exhaustion were causing them to cry out in despair, "Lord, there's gotta be a better way." But for the golden handcuffs of their low-six-figure salaries, most of them would have flown from the gilded cage yesterday.

Not Jonathan. He was obsessed with winning his Alabama trial, now three months away. It promised to be a blockbuster. There were seven defendants, and his client was the fifth biggest milk producer in the South. As Trane explained to him, "This is a conspiracy case, so each defendant needs to have its own lawyers and defense to avoid giving the jury the appearance that it's one for all and all for one. Savvy plaintiffs' lawyers will tap dance on our heads with that optic." But there would be some common defense themes, and some where the two largest producers, both of which were under federal grand jury investigation, would take the lead at trial. Given the huge number of lawyers in the case, Jonathan was not expecting to get what lawyers called a stand-up role at trial. Trane would handle all speaking roles before the jury for their client.

Jonathan was encouraged with the positive feedback he was getting from the client. The client, Southern Dairy, was a multi-billion-dollar company and had its own internal legal department. They handled most of Southern Dairy's legal issues, but not litigation. The head of the legal department, the general counsel, a former Army Ranger, was hard charging, demanding, irascible, stern, terse, and, many thought, an asshole. At times his vocabulary seemed to be limited to variants of balls and bust, as in grow some, bust some, and shave some. His name was Richard Weiner, and no one dared call the former Army Ranger Dick, at least not to his face.

The hard-charging soldier thought Jonathan was fantastic and marveled at his twenty-four-seven dedication to winning and the superlative quality of his work. He was not alone. Senior partners at the other defense firms thought Jonathan was as fine a young lawyer as they had ever seen. A couple of them even tried to hire him away. Weiner told Jonathan he had high hopes for him and was glad he was on the team.

Nashville might be home to country-and-western music, but two hundred some miles to the west is Memphis, Home of the

Blues and the Birthplace of Rock 'n' Roll. Trane had to meet with a witness who happened to be in Memphis and asked Jonathan to join him for the interview. Several years earlier, Trane, on behalf of entrepreneurs wanting to build a hospital in the city, won an anti-trust conspiracy trial against the state of Tennessee and incumbent hospitals run by Baptists and Methodists that conspired to block Trane's new-entrant client from getting state regulatory approval to build the hospital. Defeating Caesar and God was no mean feat, but victory was not the only reason Trane grew fond of this sleepy city on the muddy banks of the Mississippi River.

Trane dragged Jonathan to the "best meal on Beale" for food and blues at the legendary Blue City Cafe on Beale Street. Sitting in the cafe, Trane talked excitedly about the music legends but for some reason also seemed anxious and distracted. He talked about the great B. B. King and his rise from the cotton fields of Mississippi to become the King of the Blues. He ruefully said, "Like B. B., I lived on after the thrill was gone." Jonathan thought to himself, *Don't I know that sentiment*. Trane talked about Johnny Cash ("life ain't easy for a boy named Sue") and the famous Sun Studio where King, Cash, and many other blues and soul greats recorded albums. There was Al Green and his velvety tenor voice on "Let's Stay To-gether" and "I'm Still in Love With You," Isaac Hayes and his grav-elly voice on the soulful, funky "Shaft," and piano man Jerry Lee Lewis and "Whole Lotta Shakin' Goin' On" and goodness gracious "Great Balls of Fire." Jonathan was amazed that Trane knew all of this and more. And of course, there was the omnipresent King of Rock 'n' Roll: Elvis. Elvis the Pelvis. Trane still harbored some ill will toward Elvis for meeting with Richard Nixon in the White House in December 1970 as a prop for the ill-conceived war on drugs, including his own narc badge, but Trane begrudgingly admit-ted that anybody who shows up at the White House for a photo op with Nixon dressed to the nines in a purple velvet suit, gold belt, and a Colt .45 pistol had some real cojones. Or more likely, popped too many prescription drugs that morning.

Elvis was addicted to an assortment of prescription drugs. For Trane, it was the bottle. It first manifested itself in 1968 after the King and Kennedy assassinations. A white man, James Earl Ray, shot King dead shortly after 6:00 p.m. on April 4, 1968. Five years earlier King had written his eloquent *Letter from Birmingham Jail*, where he wrote powerfully that injustice anywhere is a threat to justice everywhere. Trane loved that letter and told Jonathan that King was in Memphis in 1968 to march on behalf of striking Memphis sanitation workers. He was standing on a second-floor balcony of the Lorraine Motel when Ray gunned him down. Trane ostensibly wanted Jonathan to accompany him to Memphis for the witness interview, but the real reason was to show his protégé the now-closed motel and visit the National Civil Rights Museum, built around the motel.

Trane let down his guard with his protégé. He confided in Jonathan that he was filled with hope when JFK was elected president and was crushed when Oswald's bullet took the oxygen out of JFK's body and hope out of a renewed nation. He talked about King and his *I Have a Dream* speech and his *Letter from Birmingham Jail*. How as a jury trial lawyer he had a profound appreciation for King's marriage of words with cause to inspire change and progress. He talked about King's courage and unwavering conviction that the "arc of the moral universe is long, but it bends toward justice." Trane wanted to believe in these inspiring words, but the experience of real life made him more than skeptical. Then Ray aimed a Remington Model 760 rifle and fired a single bullet into King's right cheek, which traveled through his body, severing his jugular vein and major arteries. An hour later he was pronounced dead at St. Joseph's Hospital. Trane lowered his head and sadly, in a quiet voice, sighed, "How tragically poetic that this peaceful man who believed that the time is always right to do what's right, and that life's most persistent and urgent question is what are you doing for others, was murdered in the city known for gospel and the blues." Mentor to protégé, "Jonathan, as you go through life, periodically stop and ask yourself, what am I doing for others?"

Trane continued with his lugubrious memories of that tragic night. On the evening of April 4, another hero, who would also be felled by an assassin's bullet just two months later, delivered an impromptu speech that brought him to tears. He remembered it vividly. Bobby Kennedy, candidate for president, was in Indianapolis on the night of April 4 when he got the news of King's assassination. Standing on the back of a flatbed truck, in a ghetto section of the city, Kennedy delivered consoling words and told the predominantly black crowd that he knew all too well what it's like to have a loved one killed by a white man. He spoke of compassion and love and healing. From memory, Trane told Jonathan that Kennedy, quoting his favorite poet Aeschylus, told the shocked crowd, "In our sleep, pain which cannot forget falls drop by drop upon the heart until, in our own despair, against our will, comes wisdom through the awful grace of God." Trane remembered that Kennedy concluded his poignant plea for racial harmony by asking that we "dedicate ourselves to what the Greeks wrote so many years ago: to tame the savageness of man and make gentle the life of this world."

But savageness is a hard beast to tame. On June 5 there was no moral arc in the universe, no gentleness in the night: Kennedy was shot in the head and died. Trane, choking up, told Jonathan that he felt the music die and started drinking the next day. Not as an excuse, not as a justification, just a sorrowful fact. In Memphis, the perceptive protégé was learning that his brilliant mentor was a multifaceted, compassionate, well-intentioned, tender, tormented, tortured soul and a hugely complicated man.

The start of the trial was now three weeks away. In two weeks, Trane, Jonathan, and the litigation team would depart DC and decamp at the historic Tutwiler Hotel in downtown Birmingham, half a mile straight shot down Sixth Avenue from the 16th Street Baptist Church. The place of worship where, in September 1963, four cowardly members of the Ku Klux Klan planted nineteen sticks of dynamite beneath the church's steps and killed four innocent black girls. The murderers injured at least fourteen more in what Dr. King called a "vicious and tragic crime against humanity." And so it was. In the long shadow of the church, the Southern Dairy trial team set up their litigation headquarters.

Trane had scheduled a Saturday morning team meeting to map out their final strategy, review all of the logistics of moving operations to Birmingham, make final case assignments, and plan for the final three weeks of trial preparation. Everything was in order, and Jonathan was keenly eager for the meeting to start. It was 9:00 a.m., starting time.

Everybody was there except Trane. Not a big surprise, Trane was habitually a few minutes late for his own meetings, and very late for meetings of his partners. 9:30 a.m. and still no word from Trane. Somebody suggested they check his office, maybe he was on the phone. Closest to the door, Jonathan volunteered. Trane was there, slumped in his chair, looking half past dead, an empty fifth of Johnny Walker Black on the floor and another half a fifth on his desk. More than a dozen snuffed out cigar/cigarettes in his ash tray. One still burning.

Jonathan darted back to the conference room to break the news. A partner returned with Jonathan to Trane's office. They checked for a pulse. Trane was still alive, but barely. They woke him up. He was incoherent. By 6:00 p.m., eight and a half hours later, he wasn't much better, just muttering, "This case is a fucking loser, this case is a fucking loser."

To say the firm had a problem would be an understatement of epic proportion. Hours earlier they had called Baxter Hodges, the managing partner and a man with an exaggerated sense of his own dignity, to report the depressing news. Hodges was all too familiar with this drill and was furious with himself for giving Trane a third chance. Trane had already done two stints in alcohol rehab, and this latest massive bender was going to send him right back. Right back immediately. Immediately, three weeks before a blockbuster trial for a major client that had already paid the firm millions, and would pay millions more through trial, and millions more for all of the other milk cases in the south. With every swig of Johnny Walker Black, Trane had put it all in jeopardy and had exposed the firm to an embarrassing lawsuit by the client. Jonathan was wondering if Baxter Hodges was going to pick up the half-empty bottle of Johnny Walker and polish it off himself.

There was no finessing or delaying the issue. Baxter Hodges had to place an immediate call to Richard Weiner and tell him the news. It was 4:00 p.m., just hours after Jonathan had found Trane passed out drunk. The client call was short. Hodges got straight to the point. With no emotion in his voice, Weiner curtly said, "I'll get back to you."

By 9:00 a.m. Sunday, Trane was back in rehab. His wife told Hodges that she would "deal with this later, but this is the last straw." As it turns out, Trane would be released from rehab in three months and divorced in nine. But right now it was Sunday morning, and nothing but uncertainty was in the air. The firm didn't know if it was going to be fired. Or whether another firm would be hired to work with them on the case. Or, if they were not fired, which partner would step into Trane's role as lead trial lawyer—there weren't many viable choices. At 6:00 p.m. that Sunday night, Richard Weiner called Baxter Hodges but first said he needed to speak with Jonathan. Hodges summoned Jonathan to his office and together they called Weiner. Weiner took them both by surprise. The former Army Ranger had a short wish followed by a short question. "Jonathan, I want you to be my lead trial lawyer. Can you do it?" Hodges tried to stall for time, but Weiner was in no mood for delay.

Taking a deep breath, Jonathan cleared his nervous throat, disguised his are-you-shitting-me reaction, and responded, "Yes, sir, I'll be ready."

As Hodges glared at Jonathan, Weiner said, "Good, now get back to work and win my case." Hodges, taciturn by nature, sternly said to Jonathan, "You heard the man, get back to work," and dismissed Jonathan with a wave of the hand.

DARE TO BE BOLD

In terms of knowing the case, Jonathan was indeed ready. He had read all the trial documents, the most important ones several times. He had read all the pretrial sworn testimony, worked with client witnesses, and even prepared cross-examination questions for the defense expert witnesses. In a mock trial conducted by all the defendants three months earlier, Jonathan played the role of the plaintiff's attorney and received rave reviews from the mock jurors as well as the client. That performance likely gave Richard Weiner the confidence to put Jonathan in the role of lead trial lawyer. Weiner probably also took some comfort knowing that the other defendants were represented by senior trial lawyers who would do a lot of heavy lifting at trial. Unless, that is, they settled before trial. But they didn't.

In law school, where angels fear to tread, only fools rushed in to spar with Professor Gladstone Bulldozen. Jonathan was no angel nor, as it turns out, a fool. He had planned to master trial procedure and evidence and he did. That classroom knowledge was fortified by courtroom experiences working for Judge Roy, especially the building supplier plywood trial. It was Jonathan's mastery of the rules that spurred an idea of how to defend Southern Dairy at trial. A bold idea. An especially bold idea for a young lawyer who had never been the lead lawyer in a jury trial. So bold that he knew he had to get it approved by Richard Weiner, the former Army Ranger who knew a thing or two about bold strikes and calculated risks.

But first Jonathan double-checked his memory to confirm his operating assumption for his bold plan. Jonathan watched as Trane had grown increasingly pessimistic about their odds of winning at trial, culminating in his drunken mumbling that "this case is a fucking loser." For starters, they were talking about milk. Milk that school kids bought and drank every day for strong minds and strong bodies. Yummy for the tummy, was one defendant's insipid motto. Trane cracked a pun that the crafty plaintiffs' lawyers would milk that optic for all it was worth. So too would they milk the fact that many of the school kids were poor, as would be the case for at least some of the Birmingham jurors. Rich, powerful corporations ripping off poor innocent kids to be judged by poor parents—enough to drive any defense lawyer to drink. Then there was the inconvenient fact that the two biggest defendants were being investigated by a federal grand jury. Trane wasn't sure whether that fact would come into evidence, but as one who lived by the motto hope for the best but prepare for the worst, he assumed that, by hook or crook, the jury would find out.

Trane also believed that a chain is only as strong as its weakest link. In any multidefendant trial, the defense attorney loses an element of control. In the milk trial, there were seven defendants with more than seven lawyers presenting to the jury, with scores of witnesses being prepared or examined by other lawyers. Trane used to preach that there is no such thing as a surprise at trial, just insufficient planning and figuring out contingencies. He threw that little homily out the window in the face of a trial with six other defendants and a gaggle of egomaniacal lawyers. "A cluster fuck waiting to happen" was Trane's gloomy prediction.

Jonathan understood Trane's concerns, understood that this trial was going to be an uphill climb, and understood that the real fight, once again, might come down to the proper amount in damages. But the defendants had calculated that this was the case to make a stand. With the cases in the other states queuing up for trial, Birmingham is where the defendants decided to fight in the hopes of tempering the plaintiffs' astronomical settlement demands. Jonathan's adrenaline was in overdrive.

In his southern travels, Jonathan learned the carpenter's credo, measure twice, cut once. To double-check his memory, he squirreled himself away in a conference room and re-reviewed every document on everybody's trial exhibit list. The rules were demanding and un-forgiving: if a document was not on the list, it could not come into evidence. And Jonathan knew that Judge Pointer would rigidly fol-low those rules. At trial, sworn testimony taken before trial in depo-sitions may be used at trial if it satisfies the rules of evidence. That testimony must be meticulously designated before trial, or it doesn't come into evidence. And trial expert witnesses must disclose their opinions in written reports before trial. Jonathan intensely re-re-viewed every last sentence of all this material. He was indefatigable, including consecutive all-nighters reviewing this material. When he finished his exhaustive review, he was bleary-eyed and worn out. Yet anxious and inspired. Perhaps the delusion of a young, naïve, and inexperienced trial lawyer, but he had faith that his trial plan could work. He was ready to share it with Richard Weiner. Just in case it was rejected, he had a plan B. He never used plan B.

With Weiner on board with plan A, Jonathan finished his prepa-ration and was intellectually ready for trial. Emotionally, not as far along. His stomach was in knots. Faith in plan did little to assuage the fear of being torched in his first trial by fire. He kept telling himself that the nervousness would abate once the action started, but he wasn't so sure. Besides the palpable pressure and tension of winning and losing, Jonathan knew that a win in a case of this magnitude would add rocket fuel to the trajectory of his career. But if his bold plan flamed out and crashed to earth, he would be lucky to land an assistant manager's job at a Piggly Wiggly supermarket. He needed some more water.

After a full day of jury selection conducted entirely by Judge Pointer, he announced that opening statements would begin first thing in the morning. Each side was allotted two hours. That meant that each of the seven defendants would get seventeen minutes if they divided their time equally. That caused a knockdown, drag-out fight among the defense counsel, including a couple of windbags who could not even recite a limerick in fewer than twenty minutes. The group finally agreed that the lawyers for the two biggest de-fendants would each get thirty-five minutes and the remaining five lawyers would each get ten minutes. Knowing that Judge Pointer would take a break after the first seventy minutes of the defendants' opening statements, Jonathan saved his bargaining chips to go first after that break. The others shrugged and said sure.

The next morning, the plaintiffs' two lead trial lawyers evenly split their time. They both tended to be grandiloquent and light on the minutiae of case details. Just as Trane had predicted, they spent a lot of time on the optics and playing the sympathy card. One played the race card. Jonathan listened carefully, took a few notes, and generally thought their presentations persuasively told a conspiracy tale. More importantly, their presentations renewed his faith in his plan.

At the break after the first two defense opening statements, Jonathan informed the remaining four defense lawyers that he was going to waive his opening statement. Looks of surprise poured over their faces. Was the young guy experiencing an acute case of performance anxiety, they wondered. A crippling case of stage fright? Not their problem, so the remaining four lawyers delivered their openings after the break. There was no mention of Jonathan or Southern Dairy.

Judge Pointer scheduled the trial for six weeks. He split the time evenly between the two sides. Jonathan let the other defense lawyers sit at the main counsel tables while he receded into the shade. Sitting behind the others, he was barely visible to the jurors. He neither craved nor needed the spotlight. Not based on the facts of this particular case. The singular goal was to win, not strut. Anonymity would be his ally in this fight. At least that was the plan.

Toward the end of the third week, the plaintiffs' case was winding down. Jonathan had not stood up a single time to address the judge or jury. It was as if he were invisible. One smart-ass, sixty-two-year-old defense lawyer asked, "Hey, kid, are your legal malpractice insurance premiums paid up?" Plaintiffs then called their final witness, their damages expert. He calculated damages by running a statistical analysis on the seven defendants' milk sales data. Stripped of its incomprehensible jargon, where the egghead actually lectured the by-now somnolent jury about something statisticians call heteroscedasticity, Dr. Propeller Head's damages model was surprisingly simplistic. Albert Einstein had famously advised that "everything should be made as simple as possible, but no simpler."

Jonathan thought: Dr. Propeller Head ignored the sage's advice. He simply assumed that all seven defendants participated in the alleged conspiracy in Alabama by overcharging for every single carton of milk for ten years by a fixed percentage markup. In the course of his testimony, he pointed out the total sales, by name, of each of the seven defendants. He proceeded in alphabetical order. Southern Dairy was last on the list.

When Dr. Propeller Head finally mentioned Southern Dairy, Jonathan bolted out of his chair, moved to the corner of the main defense counsel table, and in full sight of the jury, bellowed out, "Your Honor, may the court note for the record that the clock on the wall says that the time today, September 25, is 10:43 a.m.?" Judge Pointer, as perplexed as he was annoyed, over snickers and sniggers, said, "Noted. Anything else, Mr. Timex?" Jonathan had nothing else. When the commotion died down, Dr. Propeller Head finished his testimony, offering his opinion that the damages amounted to $724 million. The plaintiffs then rested.

The defense took eight days to present their case. Jonathan did not stand up a single time. It was late afternoon, so Judge Pointer announced that closing arguments would begin in the morning and dismissed the jury for the day. He allowed each side three hours, with plaintiffs going in the morning and the defendants in the afternoon. Judge Pointer paused, peered over his half-moon reading glasses, and pointedly asked Jonathan if he was planning to honor the court with a closing argument. Still mad at Trane, Jonathan firmly said, "Absolutely."

The defense divided their time by giving the two largest defendants forty minutes each, and the remaining five defendants twenty minutes each. This time the other defense counsel, leery of their young, unorthodox co-defense counsel, insisted that Jonathan go last. No objection from Jonathan.

Jonathan had been fastidiously preparing his closing argument from before the start of trial. Nothing really unexpected happened at trial to alter his intended argument, so he spent an hour or so going over his outline, went for a long run, and turned in for an early night's sleep. Not that he would get much sleep, but at least he would be lying in bed resting, in the dark, and thinking through his argument and any opening plaintiffs might provide in their arguments. The next day was going to be long and emotional and he was going last. He just hoped it wasn't going to be the last time he ever delivered a closing jury argument.

By habit, Jonathan awoke at 4:00 a.m. sharp, as if the sleep-cycle of his circadian rhythms was synchronized to buzz precisely at that early morning hour. He lay still in bed, lights off, eyes closed, and spoke his closing argument. When he finished, the digital clock beside his bed read 4:19 a.m. He was ready. Restless, he went for another run, through the dark streets of Birmingham. On his return, half a mile from the hotel, he stopped outside the 16th Street Baptist Church. He thought of Dr. King's hopeful words in August 1963 at the Lincoln Memorial, and his despairing words just one month later after four little girls were blown up simply because they didn't share the same skin color as their killers. Craven killers who deprived those innocent little girls of the opportunity to grow up and be judged by the content of their characters as they went through life. Head bowed, and remembering a conversation with Trane, Jonathan thought of Dr. King's hope, his "hope that the dark clouds of racial prejudice will soon pass away and the deep fog of misunderstanding will be lifted from our fear-drenched communities." He stood for a moment of respectful silence before running back to the hotel. It was going to be a very long day.

Jonathan got to court early. He milled outside the courtroom doors and finally went in ten minutes before game time. Listening to the plaintiffs' lawyers' arguments was painful. One would have thought that the defendants had committed the most devilish conspiracy of all time. The spitfires wound up and delivered southern stem-winders. Lots of fire and brimstone with biblical quotes and references liberally sprinkled here and there. He heard his opening. From Proverbs, "Open your mouth, judge righteously, defend the rights of the poor and needy." From Psalms, "The Lord gives righteousness and justice to all who are treated unfairly." And Isaiah, "He will bring full justice to all who have been wronged. He will not stop until truth and righteousness prevail." When those courtroom evangelists finished, Jonathan was certain the jury was going to conclude that there was a satanic conspiracy. And then deny the defendants any absolution when it came to damages.

The main defense closing arguments, in Jonathan's real-time estimation, offered no reason for redemption. The arguments were technical and dry and focused on the fine points of antitrust law and the legal instructions the judge was going to give the jury. No emotional connective tissue. No morally compelling alternative narrative for the jury to consider. Jonathan also thought that these defense lawyers were avoiding, not explaining away, some of the weaker facts for the defense and worried that the plaintiffs' lawyers would pounce on those failures when they got the last opportunity to speak to the jury. Pounce they did.

After a break, the five other defense lawyers spoke. Three of them pretty much repeated what had already been said, a blundering waste of precious time. All three read from typed-up outlines, a guaranteed way to lose the jurors in the first thirty seconds. Madder than an old wet hen, the fourth defense lawyer, who spoke right before Jonathan, had only two gears: loud and angry. Frothing at the mouth, he screamed at the jurors that it was a travesty that his client was made to stand trial for six weeks against outrageously false charges. As he was finishing his embarrassing display of feigned righteous indignation, he ended with a flourish by slamming a notebook on the table in phony-baloney disgust. *What did Trane say about cluster fucks and weak links in the chain?* Jonathan thought, as he was about to deliver his first-ever closing argument by following Captain Batshit's burlesque act?

Judge Pointer peered over at Jonathan and in stentorian voice asked, "Mr. Kent, do you *now* wish to say something to the jury as your closing argument?"

"Yes, Your Honor" was his respectful response. At this point, Jonathan was an enigma to the jury. What this curious young lawyer would finally say to the jury was the question on the mind of everyone in the courtroom. Many were fearing the worst and hoped that Jonathan would not embarrass himself too badly. One elderly woman in the back even made the sign of the cross as he arose to address the jury. The rubberneckers in the room were craning their necks and rearranging in their seats, all the better to gawk as the disaster unfolded.

No notes. No notebooks. No lectern to hide behind. With purpose, Jonathan walked over to the jury box, respecting their space, just as he had watched Trane do. Standing still, he paused for effect as he made eye contact with each juror, as Judge Roy had taught him to do. Confident and relaxed, he began in a soft voice, causing some jurors to lean in.

"May it please the court. Good afternoon, ladies and gentlemen. My name is Jonathan Kent, and I represent Southern Dairy. You have seen and heard from a lot of lawyers these past six weeks. But this is only the second time you've heard from me. The first time was very brief. I want to tell you why that is. Some of you might think it's because I don't try hard enough. Maybe you look at me and see a young lawyer and think maybe he is scared. Well, truth be told, I am a little nervous, but I'm not scared one bit. Want to know why? I'm not scared because Southern Dairy did not participate in any conspiracy. That is why those lawyers over there didn't even try to prove a case against Southern Dairy. Ladies and gentlemen, they didn't even try. Those plaintiffs' lawyers sure do like to quote a lot of Bible verses, but they forgot the one that applies to Southern Dairy. It's from the Gospel of John—"The truth shall set you free.""

"So I want to talk about the truth. Now you might have been wondering what the heck I was doing on the morning of September 25 when I asked Judge Pointer to take note that the clock on the wall said it was 10:43 a.m. Do you know why I did that? Because that was the very first time in this trial that anybody even said my client's name. When those lawyers in their opening statement said they would prove a conspiracy, they didn't mention Southern Dairy. That's the truth. When they put on fact witnesses, nobody mentioned Southern Dairy. That's the truth. When they showed you trial exhibits, they didn't have Southern Dairy's name on them. That's the truth. The first and only time you heard the name Southern Dairy is when their damages expert said he looked at their sales data. He simply assumed—he *assumed*—Southern Dairy was part of a conspiracy, so he threw their sales data into the damages pot. But ladies and gentlemen, an assumption is not proof of anything. It's nothing. And that's the truth.

"If you take out Southern Dairy sales data, there's not a single document in evidence that even mentions Southern Dairy. Nor did any witness who took the stand, raised their right hand, and swore an oath to tell the truth, give any testimony that Southern Dairy was part of a conspiracy. No witnesses. No documents. No proof. They have nothing on my client.

"So I wasn't going to shadow box in this long trial. Six weeks is a long time for you to be away from your work, your family, and your friends. They have the burden of proof. If they weren't even going to bother to try to prove a case against Southern Dairy, I certainly wasn't going to waste your precious time by talking when there was nothing to say.

"When you go back to your jury room, you'll have to decide two things right off the bat. First, was there a conspiracy? If you conclude there was not, full stop. You're done. If you conclude that there was a conspiracy, you then will need to decide who was in it, just like this verdict form I'm showing you lays it out. In the box next to Southern Dairy, I submit you should leave it blank.

"Ladies and gentlemen, the other side has an army of lawyers. Believe you me, they looked under every rock. If there was something incriminating against Southern Dairy, they would've shown it to you. But they didn't find anything. Because there is nothing there to find. So they didn't waste their time trying to prove a case against Southern Dairy that they could not prove. On behalf of the good folks at Southern Dairy, I ask that you and the truth set Southern Dairy free and return a verdict in its favor. Thank you."

As he sat down nineteen minutes after he started, Jonathan's mind wandered back to his interview of Judge McCracken from the Bronx. "Son, you got balls, shit for brains, but you've got some balls." With a sigh, he was now fervently hoping that the old curmudgeon was only half right.

The jury began their deliberations on a Thursday afternoon. No surprise they didn't return a verdict that day. They reconvened Friday morning. With the weekend just ahead, Captain Batshit, the defense lawyer who screamed his closing argument and slammed his notebook on the table, confidently placed his betting money on a verdict that day so the jurors could finish before the weekend. Good thing he didn't put real money where his loud mouth was because the jury finished the day without reaching a verdict. It was going to be a long weekend.

Jonathan had not been back to DC for seven and a half weeks and was tempted to fly home and return to Birmingham on Sunday. He opted instead to rent a car and make the two-hour drive to visit Atlanta, a city he had never seen before. A city that advertised itself as the "city too busy to hate." The same city that was nine months away from hosting the 1996 Summer Olympics. Jonathan had a special reason to head east to Atlanta.

Joni Mitchell was playing at the majestic Fox Theater Saturday night and Jonathan secured a ticket. Joni was magnificent. But when she played "A Case of You," Jonathan winced remembering how Shelly had once exhorted him not to let her become a lonely painter. And when she sang "Both Sides Now," all Jonathan could think was how lovely Shelly sounded when she sang the song in the shower. Now, years later, it was love's illusions he was remembering. As time moves on, it leaves behind many memories but takes some indelible ones with it.

It was a fabulous Sunday morning. From Jonathan's Midtown hotel, he was able to map out a refreshing eight-mile run from the hotel to and around Atlanta's Piedmont Park and back. A park bigger than New York's Central Park. Jonathan had a premonition that he would return to the capital of the South one day. Before heading back to Birmingham, Jonathan drove over to see Ebenezer Baptist Church, where Dr. King served as copastor until an assassin's bullet took his life in April 1968. He remembered Trane telling him in Memphis that one of his favorite quotes from Dr. King was "Forgiveness is not an occasional act, it is a constant attitude." Forgiveness provides a release from resentment and revenge and the grip of the offender. A constant attitude of forgiveness, Jonathan thought, good for both personal and societal health. He wished Trane was with him now.

Refreshed and rejuvenated, Jonathan returned to Birmingham. That Monday morning he could already feel his stomach tightening as he anxiously anticipated the jury's verdict. Jonathan had stumbled across a seldom-used Old English word that perfectly described his predawn morning after a restless night—uhtceare, referring to the anxiety experienced before dawn that causes one to wake up too early and not fall back to sleep, no matter how tired, because you are worried about the day to come. He thought, as long as there are jury trials, that spot-on descriptive word should re-enter the trial lawyers' vernacular.

With a stomach full of butterflies, he headed to court, but there was no need to hurry because Monday came and went with no verdict. Waiting for a jury's verdict, many anxious lawyers pass the time doing crossword puzzles, swapping embellished war stories, or just prattling about nothing in particular. Jonathan's CLB colleagues spent their time sucking up to Richard Weiner. Put a Big Law lawyer in front of a corporate client who controls which lawyer gets the business and witness the profligate disregard of dignity: fawning, flattering, groveling, wheedling, brown nosing, sniveling, bootlicking, toadying, oleaginous, obsequious, unctuous, ingratiating, prostrating, and begging. Weiner enjoyed being the center of attention but was never fooled by lawyers' transparent motives. They were like the family dog hovering around the dinner table hoping food would fall their way.

It wasn't until Tuesday afternoon that the jury reached a verdict. The nervous tension in the courtroom was palpable. There were a number of items on the verdict form, but three in particular riveted everyone's attention. In his closing argument, Jonathan covered the first two. The first question asked if the jury found that there was a conspiracy to overcharge school kids for lunch milk for ten years. The jury said yes. Jubilant reactions in the gallery. Judge Pointer demanded silence. The defendants were now fearing the worst. The second item asked the jury to put a check in the box next to each defendant that it found participated in the conspiracy.

Lots of hearts in throats at this point. Judge Pointer read the list one by painful one. There were checks next to the names of the first six defendants. After Jonathan heard the judge say that there was no check next to Southern Dairy, he zoned out and didn't process the rest. Only later did he realize that the jury awarded the plaintiffs $615.4 million in damages. Only later did Jonathan and the rest of the defendants learn that the jury subtracted 15 percent of the requested damages, or $108.6 million from the plaintiffs' expert's estimate of $724 million. The 15 percent was the amount of Southern Dairy's sales.

The litigants learned all of this after Judge Pointer allowed one lawyer for each party to go to the jury room and ask the jurors about their verdict. The jury agreed to do this for thirty minutes. The lawyers learned that the jurors agreed quickly that there was an overcharge conspiracy and who was in it, but they bogged down on the question of the proper amount of damages. Then one of the jurors turned to Jonathan and, in amazement, said, "Man, when you stood up to tell the time on that clock, I thought you must be some kinda dumbass; what's the point of that? But then I thought, the dude's young but he must have some trick up his sleeve. So I kept waiting for it. Then when you put it all together in your closing speech, I shook my head and thought that's one smart motherfucker. You got my vote right there. Loved your 'truth shall set you free' zinger." The other jurors nodded in admiring agreement.

Walking back to the hotel to pack up, Jonathan thought maybe, just maybe, I have both balls and brains. Either way, he was ready to hop his next bus. And it was not destined for cleanup on aisle six at a Piggly Wiggly.

ANTITRUST STRATEGY

Jonathan returned to DC and Cabot, Lodge & Biddle a conquering hero. He pulled off a stunning victory. Seven defendants: six with senior lawyers got walloped, and one young one trying his first case as lead lawyer walked away with a storybook victory. With a single, strategic comment in the first six weeks of trial and an intuitive and inspired nineteen-minute closing argument, Jonathan followed King Lear's admonition to "have more than thou showest, speak less than thou knowest." Jonathan, an associate, managed to secure a jury verdict when six other defendants, represented by senior Big Law partners, miserably failed. He connected emotionally with the jurors. His audacious trial strategy took guts and confidence, but it also displayed imagination and a creative, intuitive mind rooted firmly in the rules of the litigation game.

Creative imagination and disciplined execution. These would be Jonathan's defining jury trial trademarks throughout his career. But immediately, Richard Weiner rewarded him in two ways. In Big Law, the way to the top of the compensation ladder is big client billings. Some deny it, others resist it, but Big Law insiders know that rainmakers, those who bring in the business and control the clients, go to the top of the money pyramid. And that Big Law trend would accelerate as if on pecuniary steroids in the twenty-first century. Big Law is a Big Money game. Jonathan was not yet a partner when he got the call from Richard Weiner.

"Jonathan, my man, you pulled a rabbit out of the hat for me and Southern Dairy. You know my old Army Rangers motto is Rangers lead the way, and you led the way for us to a most improbable victory. And to think you had to do your first closing argument after that nut job Captain Batshit. Well done. You have one happy client."

"Thank you, Richard. And thanks for having confidence in me and trusting that our risky trial strategy would actually work. I'm deeply grateful."

"Look," Weiner continued, "I want you to know that I know how young lawyers, hell, all lawyers, get ahead in Big Law—client billings. For that reason, I'm transferring Southern Dairy's billings to you. You've earned it, and you deserve it."

"Wow, I don't know what to say." Jonathan knew that it was virtually unprecedented for a Big Law associate to be the billing attorney for a major client. He understood immediately what that would mean for his path to partnership. "So I'll just say what my mom taught me to say when someone does something nice for you: thank you."

"I'm not done. As you know, we have another trial in February, four months out, in Atlanta. I want you to be my lead trial lawyer in that case also. Ready for round two in the milk cases?"

Jonathan's first thought—*I must be dreaming, this is not really happening in real time, in real life, to me.* He snapped to quickly, once again suppressed his palpable nerves, and said, "You bet I'll be ready. Once again, Richard, thank you very much. We'll do everything we can to bring home a W."

"I expect no less. Go bust their balls."

Here he stood: new status, new responsibility, new opportunity. And new pressure. Lots of pressure. In the fast lane you can surely lose your mind. Jonathan had every intent of keeping his head and his newly achieved inside pole position to partnership. In the fast lane, he was ready for action and gung ho for the game.

After a long and important trial, especially an out-of-town trial, most lawyers take some time off to rest and recharge. Take a lazy victory lap. Jonathan was not like most lawyers. Not then and certainly not in the future. He knew the second trial was going to be different. Sure, the plaintiffs would still go hard after the other defendants, especially the two biggest players, but this time there would be no hornswoggling the plaintiffs' lawyers with a clock-on-the-wall gambit. Certainly the plaintiffs would put in *some* evidence against Southern Dairy. And some problems were not going away.

Jonathan still had the problem of being part of a weak chain with weak links. To his surprise, the other defendants were sticking with the lawyers who had already whiffed once in a crushing defeat. Even Captain Batshit, whose hyperbole and histrionics would be a haunting presence in trial number two. But Jonathan thought he had two things going in his favor. Although the trial judge, Marvin Shuman, was known to have a plaintiff's bent, defense lawyers complained about a thumb on the scale; he put the trial on a fast track—four weeks, six days a week. The 1996 Summer Olympics were being held in Atlanta starting July 19, the city too busy to hate was feverishly in construction mode, and Judge Shuman wanted the trial finished by Saturday, March 2. The other thing working in Jonathan's favor was that the plaintiffs' Georgia case against Southern Dairy was not much stronger than its Alabama case. That was not going to change before the start of trial. If he could distance himself once again from the other defendants, Jonathan believed he might pull off another upset win. This time, though, he would have to figure out a way to do it early in the trial.

No rabbit out of the hat at the very end of trial.

Jonathan remembered what his war hero mentor taught him in the building materials supply case. It was an instructive lesson, and he would now apply it in his next antitrust conspiracy trial.

In a pensive mood over lunch—steamed vegetables and walnuts over wild rice for Judge Roy, broccoli cheddar soup for Jonathan—the judge said, "Look, Jonathan, there are two basic ways to prove an antitrust conspiracy case. The best way, if you have the goods, is by direct evidence. Suppose there are four companies that make and sell automobile tires and their presidents meet privately and all agree to raise their prices and do, in fact, raise their prices. If one of the presidents later goes to the prosecutor and rats out the others, that would be direct evidence of a conspiracy. He was there, participated in the formation of the agreement, and therefore had firsthand knowledge of the conspiracy. No need to make any inferences to connect the evidentiary dots.

"Another way is with tape-recorded evidence, manna from heaven for prosecutors. Let me show you a copy of a 1983 *New York Times* infamous report of a phone call that two airline executives had about airfare prices. American Airlines, and its leader Robert Crandall, and Braniff Airlines, and its leader Howard Putnam, were competing hard with one another to win customers in Dallas by dropping prices. Neither was gaining any competitive advantage. Both were losing money. What do you do?

"Well, the hyper-aggressive Crandall had had enough and called Putnam. But Crandall, who had what my virtuous mother used to call a potty mouth, didn't realize the call was being tape recorded, a naive, crackbrained oversight when talking on the phone with a competitor about fixing prices. Here's how it went:

'Mr. Crandall: I think it's dumb as hell for Christ's sake, all right, to sit here and pound the shit out of each other and neither one of us making a fucking dime.

Mr. Putnam: Well…

Mr. Crandall. I mean, you know, goddamn it, what the hell is the point of that?

Mr. Putnam: But if you're going to overlay every route of American's on top of every route that Braniff has, I just can't sit here and allow you to bury us without giving our best effort.

Mr. Crandall: Oh sure, but Eastern and Delta do the same thing in Atlanta and have for years.

Mr. Putnam: Do you have a suggestion for me?

Mr. Crandall: Yes, I have a suggestion for you. Raise your goddamn fares twenty percent. I'll raise mine the next morning.

Mr. Putnam: Robert, we…

Mr. Crandall: You'll make more money, and I will too.

Mr. Putnam: We can't talk about pricing.

Mr. Crandall: Oh, bullshit, Howard. We can talk about any goddamn thing we want to talk about.'

"Crandall was wrong and lucky that Putnam declined his invitation to raise Braniff's fares. Had he done so, the recording would have been direct evidence of a conspiracy and the whippet-thin Crandall might have been swapping out his gray pinstripes and Salvatore Ferragamo saddle leathers for prison gray and leg irons."

Jonathan knew there were no recordings or other direct evidence to incriminate Southern Dairy. If there were, people would be in federal prison.

Instead, just like in Birmingham, the plaintiffs were going to have to prove their case with circumstantial evidence. Evidence that requires the jury to make an inference from certain evidence to draw a conclusion. Judge Roy was also his legal instructor on circumstantial evidence.

"It's like footprints in the sand. So, for example, if Mom and Dad didn't see Day-Glo Donnie pilfer the fudge cookies from the cookie jar they had just filled to capacity an hour ago but saw pudgy Donnie with a shit-eating grin on his face with fudge smeared around his lips and on his thick little fingers and noticed that the jar was half depleted, it would be a reasonable and legally acceptable inference for them to conclude that their chubby delinquent was the cookie culprit."

Jonathan knew that the plaintiffs' proof was not so sweet. Jonathan thought their proof was more similar to the ambiguous situation of four gas stations that Judge Roy used as an example of how to defend against antitrust conspiracy claims when there is no direct evidence of an actual agreement.

Judge Roy said, "Suppose there are four gas stations, each on one of the four corners at the intersection of State and Madison Streets in the heart of the Chicago Loop. Each one has a tall sign showing its price for gas. Each one charges the same price. Is that circumstantial evidence of a gasoline price-fixing conspiracy? Or is it just smart business because as soon as one station lowers its price, the other three will follow suit or risk losing customers to the price cutter because customers have four immediate and convenient options of where to buy their gas?

"Virtually any economist would say that lowering prices in that situation just means all four stations will do the same volume of business, but at lower prices and therefore lower profits. No smart businessperson needs to agree with her competitors to avoid that result. Each owner, even without consulting a PhD economist, would have enough walking-around sense to independently figure that out on her own. They wouldn't need a weatherman to figure out which way the wind blows."

Hmm, you don't need a weatherman, an expert, to figure out the obvious. That would be Jonathan's overarching trial theme—Southern Dairy made smart independent pricing decisions, not, as plaintiffs were alleging, decisions based on secret agreements with its competitors. Now he had to figure out a way to sell that story to the jury. And sell that story right off the bat in his opening statement.

The milk defendants tended to charge the same prices to the Georgia public schools, so Jonathan knew that his challenge at trial was to provide an explanation to counter what jurors would be inclined to believe, that it must be a conspiracy, just as the Birmingham jury had unanimously concluded for six of the defendants. Jonathan knew he had to persuade the jury that Southern Dairy's milk prices were smart business prices. That Southern Dairy, as the number-five player in the game, played follow-the-leader, just like so many other smaller players do in so many other industries. That, and emphasizing the theme that the plaintiffs had scant evidence against Southern Dairy. Those would be his twin trial themes.

In early January, Judge Shuman held a morning pretrial conference to make sure everything would be ready for the February 5 start date. The conference went just fine. That afternoon, Jonathan journeyed to Warm Springs, about an hour and a half south of Atlanta. After Franklin Roosevelt was diagnosed in 1921 with poliomyelitis, he eventually made his way to Warm Springs, hoping to find healing power in its natural spring. Raised as an aristocrat in Hyde Park, New York, FDR, a "traitor to his class" in the estimation of blue bloods, was enamored with Warm Springs, so much so that he built a cottage there that became known as the "Little White House." It was there he died from a cerebral hemorrhage in the early afternoon of April 12, 1945, hours before he was planning to watch a children's musical show. Eighteen days later, Adolf Hitler, who was responsible for the deaths of millions of innocent children, committed suicide by swallowing a cyanide capsule and putting a bullet in his head. FDR and Hitler both rose to power in 1933 and both died in office in April 1945. One in honor and admiration, the other in disgrace and contempt. One helped to save a nation and its most vulnerable, the other tried to destroy Western civilization and a race and religion. One was a hero to humanity, the other an antichrist. Jonathan agreed with Judge Roy, who idolized FDR and, in his assessment, was the greatest US president after Lincoln. In a nod to his mentor, he wanted to pay his respects to the pragmatic leader who sailed the ship of state out of the Great Depression, catalyzed freedom from fear, and rallied the country to join the Allies to defeat Nazism, fascism, and imperial Japan.

IT'S ELEMENTARY

Jonathan and team were back in Atlanta one week before the February 5 start date. The federal courthouse is located in the Richard Russell Federal Building, close to CNN's world headquarters and what would soon become Centennial Olympic Park, ground zero for NBC as the television host of the 1996 Summer Olympics. Although Richard Weiner, a notorious penny pincher who one southern lawyer described as tighter than a bull's ass at fly time, initially balked at the idea, Jonathan and team decamped at the downtown Ritz-Carlton, about a mile walk to the courthouse. Perfect brisk walking weather in Atlanta in February. Jonathan would have enjoyed an even longer walk, but that might have caused a team mutiny.

The trial started promptly at 9:00 a.m. on February 5. This time Jonathan took a seat at the main defense counsel table. Richard Weiner, Southern Dairy's corporate representative, sat behind him. As Judge Pointer had done in the Birmingham trial, Judge Shuman had the prospective jurors complete a lengthy questionnaire before coming to court. He also asked some questions and allowed one lawyer for each side to ask limited follow-up questions. The lawyer for the largest defendant, from a major Houston law firm, was the defendants' designee. His questions were ineffective but harmless. When jury selection concluded, Jonathan felt good about the draw, which included a Coca-Cola marketing assistant, UPS package driver, Home Depot store clerk, CNN audio technician, Morehouse University professor, Delta flight attendant, Fulton County grade school teacher, unemployed auto mechanic, and a retired private detective who would likely understand and appreciate his opening statement.

Jonathan was the last defense lawyer to present. This time he did not follow Captain Batshit's burlesque act. The defense group made that crackpot go fourth, exactly in the middle, hoping—praying—that the primacy/recency effect would cause the jurors to forget every inane, fevered word he uttered. Jonathan had fifteen minutes. Since he did not want to repeat what six other lawyers had just told the jury for two hours and fifteen minutes, he thought fifteen minutes was sufficient time to make his point. An elementary point he intended to make with an indelible character and one prop.

"May it please the court. Good afternoon, ladies and gentlemen of the jury. As I sat listening to the plaintiffs' lawyers make their opening statements, I couldn't help thinking about a case cracked by the brilliant detective Sherlock Holmes. Holmes and his sidekick, Dr. Watson, were on the trail of trying to solve a whodunit murder. Scotland Yard thought that the evidence was pointing in one and only one direction. They consulted Holmes, whose experience and sagacious judgment were suggesting to him that the evidence was pointing in precisely the opposite direction. But the mystery had yet to be resolved.

"One day Holmes and Watson were walking on a path through the woods. They had started from the north and were headed due south. Holmes quickened the pace as they came upon a long stick laying straightaway in their path. Holmes stopped abruptly. The clue was plain to see. He turned to Watson. 'I say, Watson, which way do you say that stick is pointing?' Watson, perplexed, responded, 'Holmes, whatever do you mean? The stick is obviously pointing south.' Holmes then took Watson by the arm, walked to the other end of the stick, turned Watson around, and asked again, 'Now, Watson, which direction is the stick pointing?' Watson humbly responded, 'Well, Holmes, the stick obviously is pointing north.' Holmes had just cracked the case.

"Ladies and gentlemen, the plaintiffs told you a story to get you to believe that the stick is pointing south to conspiracy. But in which direction will the evidence, not a lawyer's imagination, point? It will point north to competition. You heard these lawyers talk for hours. What you should have heard is what they did not say about Southern Dairy. No eyewitnesses, no tape recordings, no admissions, no documents showing that Southern Dairy joined some pricing conspiracy. They want you to believe that Southern Dairy, the number-five player in the game, willingly broke the law just because its prices were the same or close to the price leaders. But, members of the jury, as a small player, Southern Dairy is what you call a price follower. That just means that they tend to charge what the big guys charge. Not because of some agreement but because Southern Dairy's pricing strategy is smart, independent business conduct. And that's what the evidence will prove. The plaintiffs are going to call to that witness stand a couple of PhD economists, charging them more than a thousand dollars an hour to try to sell you pipe smoke about an imaginary conspiracy theory, but in this case you won't need a weatherman to figure out the competitive winds. Just use your common sense because the wind blows in the direction of competition and independent pricing decisions.

"This is an extremely important case for Southern Dairy. The plaintiffs are asking for a lot of money, about one billion dollars. So every time they put a witness on the stand, please listen carefully to what they say about Southern Dairy. Listen for the sounds of silence. Every time they show you an exhibit, please do what Sherlock Holmes would do if he were in this case and take out a magnifying glass like the one I'm holding in my hand right now and try to find the name Southern Dairy anywhere on it. You might want to make sure you have some eyedrops to relieve the strain, as you try in vain, to find the name … Southern Dairy. Because whatever the plaintiffs say this case is about, it's not about Southern Dairy.

"At the close of the case, when all the evidence has been presented to you, I'm going to stand right here and ask that you find, like the brilliant Sherlock Holmes, that Southern Dairy's stick is pointing north toward competition and return a verdict for Southern Dairy. Thank you."

That night Richard Weiner canceled the quick dinner he had planned to have with Jonathan and the team, citing a pressing engagement. Then, the next morning, Weiner was a no-show for the start of the morning session and the plaintiffs' first witnesses. Judge

Shuman liked to break for lunch between 11:45 a.m. and noon for forty-five minutes. At 11:45 a.m., Weiner entered the courtroom with one of the lead plaintiffs' lawyers, but not one of the trial lawyers. He was known as "the Fixer." He was the negotiator, the guy who leads settlement discussions for the plaintiffs. He looked like the twin brother of Tony Sirico's character Paulie Walnuts on the HBO show *The Sopranos*. Sounded like him, too.

After the jurors cleared the room, the Fixer approached the bench and asked Judge Shuman if he and Weiner and Jonathan could see him in the judge's chambers. Jonathan had a clue but not much else as to what was happening. In chambers, the Fixer announced that he and Weiner had been negotiating for two weeks to settle the Atlanta case as well as all the other milk cases in the south. What lawyers call a global settlement. They reached an agreement on the major points, but the final terms would have to be ironed out in a written settlement agreement and approved by Judge Shuman, who indicated he would approve it in due course. He also agreed that Southern Dairy was released from the trial. Walking out of the judge's chambers, the Fixer winked at Jonathan and said, "Hey, Sherlock, you are a pain in our ass, and we want you and your weatherman and your friggin' magnifying glass the hell out of this case." The plaintiffs wisely decided to keep their focus on the big players.

The settlement was a win/win, a spectacular success for Southern Dairy. The company admitted no liability or wrongdoing and paid no money. Instead, the company agreed to donate milk, free of charge, to inner-city school systems in each of the southern states. The deal was made all the sweeter when the Atlanta jury returned a verdict against the remaining six defendants in the amount of $820 million. Under the antitrust laws, damage awards are automatically tripled. The Birmingham verdict of $615.4 million plus the Atlanta verdict added up to $1,435,400,000. Times three, the remaining defendants were on the hook for $4,306,200,000. As former Illinois senator Everett Dirksen used to say, a billion here and a billion there, and pretty soon you're talking about real money. But none of that very real money was Southern Dairy's money.

Jonathan's intellectual and strategic imagination and trial skills

once again saved Southern Dairy a lot of money. While Southern Dairy's competitors were paying their lawyers tens of millions
of dollars to lose billions and billions of dollars, Southern Dairy
reaped the benefit of favorable publicity for donating milk to inner-city school systems and increased its sales by 20 percent, good
enough to move from number five to number three in the market.
Jonathan was flying high on cloud nine but would soon return to
earth to catch his next coastal bus.

PARTNERS, PIGS, AND PERCEPTIONS

That fall, to no one's surprise, Jonathan was elected into his firm's partnership. He was a can't-miss superstar. Baxter Hodges called him a "franchise player." Both as a practicing attorney and, even more important to a Big Law firm, a developing rainmaker. Jonathan was already light-years ahead of his contemporaries in terms of trial experience. The others were push-the-paper lawyers. Discovery lawyers. Never-in-a-jury-trial lawyers (they mockingly, self-pityingly, called themselves the "No JTs" and even had black T-shirts emblazoned in white with NO JTs). In reality, they were going nowhere. They drafted legal filings but spent most of their tedious, long hours reviewing documents, engaging in endless letter-writing battles about documents, writing motions and briefs, and maybe taking and defending some inconsequential depositions from time to time. What they did not do was step into the arena of a jury trial, and most never would. They were dead-end lawyers in Big Law. That distinguishing factor alone would enable Jonathan to survive and thrive in Big Law's Darwinian milieu. He was a rarity.

That advantage also gave Jonathan a huge edge in attracting clients. When it comes to jury trials, corporate America is not looking for courtroom virgins and novices. Driven by a just-win-baby motto, they demand lawyers with experience in the big trials. Paper pushers might work well in the back room, but they don't get hired to be lead lawyers. And lead lawyers are the ones who attract and control the business and ascend to the top of the compensation ladder. To the outside world, partners in a Big Law firm might appear to be prestigious equals, but Jonathan had read George Orwell's *Animal Farm* and knew the swinish truth: when the pigs are in control, all partners are equal but some are more equal than others. Jonathan knew this asymmetrical Big Law truth from day one and set his sights on getting the business and ascending the ladder. Being more equal meant being more independent, or so he thought.

Jonathan was realizing that there was something ironic about being voted into the partnership of Cabot, Lodge & Biddle. A cause of celebration for most young Big Law partners considering the long anxious slog to get there, but for Jonathan it merely meant once again starting over at the bottom of a long ladder. It made him even hungrier and more impatient for success. Compensation success, because that is the way to keep score in Big Law, and everybody knew it. On the animal farm of Big Law, better to be a pig than not.

Jonathan was realizing another irony about joining his firm's partnership. At his first partners' dinner, in a cavernous dining room with fine china and silver, water goblets, and a liquor spigot with no off switch, Jonathan surveyed a room that reeked of entitlement, and thought, *No wonder Richard Weiner took a scalpel to his Big Law legal bills.* Jonathan quickly formed the view that many firm partners were pompous prima donnas who thought "their shit don't stink." He, a product of humble circumstances and public schools, disdained both the to-the-manor-born crowd as well as the parvenus. He abhorred the elitism, the swank country clubs—historically reserved for white males only—with $100,000 initiation fees paid just to walk through the front door so the clubs could fleece them even more for annual dues, golf, tennis, meals, and drinks. With their second-home enclaves that bordered on the incestuous, all the while oblivious to their privileged lives and extraordinary luck in life's lottery. He thought they suffered from a collective case of spiritual halitosis.

Over the years, he came to the disquieting conclusion that many of his partners, like so many partners in Big Law, were psychologically tormented with an acute case of imposter syndrome where they lived in mortal fear, an insecurity bordering on neurosis, that their status and income relative to their actual skill and talent were giant frauds and could disappear faster than stratocumulus clouds with rising CO_2 levels. He thought again of Thoreau and the many partners who live lives of quiet desperation and wounded pretensions and frustrated expectations. Jonathan felt alienation; he was a stranger in a strange land and would beat them at their own game. Not by blending in, but with brains, sheer talent, and force of will. But he deluded himself by believing that he could be the best among them without being one of them. He couldn't have it both ways.

Yet he shunned the clubby herd instinct of Big Law life. Big Law partners, he thought, exhibited a lot of mediocrity and conformity—Big Law Babbitts. Very few with the will, much less the talent, to be great and fewer still with the will to be an original, content to mimic the thoughts and ideas and behaviors of other people, believing that if they drift with the current they'll get somewhere in the end. For most, it was keep your head down and don't rock the money boat. Highly paid, no doubt about it, but timid and insecure and nothing more than cogs in a well-paying wheel being turned by someone else.

The bell curve proves the point. In both talent and pay, most Big Law partners cluster in the middle, and many don't even achieve average accomplishment in their firms. Jonathan never understood why, just for the money, so many would accept the psychological torment of being in a firm that regarded them as no better than average, or find solace in the self-delusion that, sitting in the middle, they nonetheless considered themselves better than average. Jonathan had no desire to howl with the pack; he needed herd separation. Only the exceptional ones ever make it to the right tail of the bell curve, where this stranger in a strange land intended to find a home.

VENALITY AND VALUES

A week after Jonathan made partner, lady luck as well as controversy struck. Richard Weiner left his position as general counsel at Southern Dairy and took a similar position at a publicly held company in Virginia that had a monster of a legal mess on its hands. The no-nonsense, hard-charging, ball-busting former Army Ranger was hired to clean it up.

Hazard Waste, Inc. specialized in the treatment and removal of hazardous and dangerous chemical waste materials generated by manufacturing companies. It was a multibillion-dollar company traded on the New York Stock Exchange. In a story as old as Eve tempting Adam with an apple, forbidden fruit was the downfall of mortal human beings. Hazard's senior officers, including its chief executive officer, chief financial officer, and chief investment officer, were placed on administrative leave based on charges that they had manipulated the company's financial books and records in order to inflate Hazard Waste's stock price. Not surprisingly, they all owned a slew of stock options, including the CEO, who owned two million shares and had a plan to pump then dump a number of those shares.

Unchecked, these executives would have made tens of million dollars treating the company's financials as their own private piggy bank. But they were caught.

Hazard's board of directors, tipped off by a whistleblower in the company's accounting department, hired an outside law firm of seven former federal prosecutors to conduct an internal investigation. What the sleuths working with an honest forensic accounting firm unearthed wasn't pretty. It was ugly, really ugly. Massive manipulation of Hazard's financial books and records over several years. A staggering scheme to defraud shareholders and investors. The federal securities laws required that Hazard come clean and make a public disclosure. So the board of directors issued a press release announcing the discovery of "material financial errors and irregularities," accounting jargon for "this is really bad shit." So bad that Hazard had to issue a restatement of the financial documents to correct all of the false information and lies on the books. A restatement of the financial documents is milquetoast corporate speak for a harsher investor truth. In plain English, what a restatement is really telling shareholders and investors is this: "The documents y'all relied on to buy our fraudulently overpriced stock are so fucked up we had to shitcan them and start all over. Our stock is worth a boatload less than what y'all paid for it. Y'all got royally fucked. Sorry, our bad." The Edenic apple-munching executives were placed on administrative leave and expelled from the corporate garden soon thereafter. Once the truth of Hazard's real financial condition was disclosed, its stock price tanked.

What immediately followed was a predictable legal nightmare for Hazard. The US Securities Exchange Commission launched an investigation and the US Attorney's Office in eastern Virginia opened a criminal grand jury investigation. Hazard's shareholders filed class action lawsuits. Hazard had to make the strategic decision to file for Chapter 11 bankruptcy protection, legal code for the only way the company can save its sorry ass is by making its creditors take it on the chin. Hazard's creditors would be lucky to get ten cents on the dollar. All of this happened a year before Richard Weiner arrived. Also, Hazard filed a lawsuit against the huge accounting firm that was paid millions to audit Hazard's financial documents to prevent the very thing that happened—crooked, greedy senior executives defrauding shareholders and investors by cooking the books so they could illegally pocket tens of millions in addition to the millions they were already being paid. That case was pending in Charleston, South Carolina.

Weiner realized immediately after his arrival that Hazard was hemorrhaging money on the gaggle of lawyers billing outrageous fees by the hour, on the hour, every hour. Their failure to produce results enraged him even further. Hazard spent $30 million on lawyers in year one alone after the press release and stock plummet, and there was no end in sight. Lots of churn-the-file lawyers were getting rich while Hazard was firing hapless employees and getting squeezed in every direction. Weiner determined to get this shit show better organized, streamlined, and most important, fire the no-results lawyers and hire ones who could get him some results.

Judge Peter Beauregard, a descendant of Pierre Gustave Toutant-Beauregard, the Confederate general who started the Civil War by leading the attack on Fort Sumter, was no nonsense, had a light docket, and probably thought he was doing Hazard a favor by scheduling the Charleston trial eighteen months after Hazard filed its lawsuit against the accountants. Maybe so, but not with Hazard's current lawyers. They were defense lawyers from Big Law with offices all over the country. The lawyers in charge were from Los Angeles and New York and had no clue how to prepare and try a case like a plaintiff. It only took Richard Weiner two weeks on the job to realize he needed to change horses. He called Jonathan Kent. Jonathan, metaphorically speaking, hopped on his bus to Charleston.

Hazard's negligence lawsuit against its accounting firm, FHM Advisers, was languishing and without direction. And therein lay the controversy.

An excited Jonathan walked into Baxter Hodges' office with the great news that Richard Weiner had called him to take over the defense of the securities lawsuits and government investigations as well as the prosecution of the accountant malpractice lawsuit. CLB stood to earn tens of millions in fees. Pop the champagne. Hodges immediately recorked the bubbles.

"Jonathan, that's great news about the defense work, but I'm not sure about suing a major accounting firm," the ever-cautious managing partner noted.

"I did the conflicts check; we don't represent FHM and have no legal conflicts, so we're good to go," Jonathan duly noted.

"That's not the end of the inquiry," Hodges responded. "Our corporate and securities partners are dead set against us suing the big accounting firms because they are potential referral sources. We like to be on the same side with them. Want to avoid a business conflict."

The newly minted partner was incredulous but suppressed that emotion. "Understood, Baxter, but we're not talking about *potential* business, we have an *actual* bird in the hand and that bird will pay us millions to sue the accountants who screwed up big time and harmed Hazard big time. Those buffoons should have their licenses revoked."

"Look, Jonathan, we are a Big Law firm, and suing major accounting firms, even if they make mistakes, is not our bread and butter. Wouldn't be good for our reputation in the corporate world."

"Mistakes? Baxter, we're not talking just about mistakes. FHM sat by and watched Hazard's greedy senior executives ruin the company and now it's fighting for its very corporate existence. They need us. Maybe it's above my pay grade as a first-year partner, but in my judgment we shouldn't shun a client in desperate need just to avoid pissing off some accounting firm that has *never* hired us in the *hope* that one day it *might* refer us a few bread crumbs."

"There is something unseemly about suing major accounting firms." Hodges couldn't conceal his blue blood background. "Why can't we represent Hazard in the defense work and let another firm handle the FHM case?"

"That won't work. The cases are all related. Weiner is apoplectic with his current lawyers who are bleeding him dry and wants one firm—me, us—to get it all coordinated and streamlined and resolved. And he strongly believes the FHM case will go to trial and wants me to be his lead trial lawyer."

"This makes me nervous, Jonathan. We don't like working on the plaintiff's side and don't sue major accounting firms. Lots of partners will be strongly opposed to this."

"Are you telling me I can't take the representation?" Jonathan was feeling crushed. The Billy Joe Wynn trial had given him a taste of what it's like to be on the plaintiff's side, and he liked it, and now another avenging-angel case was falling into his lap. Then there were the huge legal fees. This is how to get ahead in Big Law, and these opportunities don't fall like apples off the trees on a sunny autumn day. This was the career break Jonathan or any other young Big Law partner needed to catapult up the ladder.

"No, I'm not saying that, exactly." Hodges always played his cards close to the vest and rarely staked out a position until he knew in which direction the political winds were blowing. "I don't think it's a good idea to take the accounting case, but if you're telling me it's all or nothing, I'll take it to the management committee for a vote."

"It is all or nothing. Weiner is a former Army Ranger and needs to know that his law firm is all in for every battle in a brutal war he is fighting on multiple fronts."

CLB's fifteen-person management committee met for six hours. It was contentious. One member threatened to move to another firm if CLB took the case. Another said, "If a fucking rookie partner wants to be a sleazy plaintiff's lawyer, why doesn't he just pack his bags and take that sorry-ass accounting case with him? We're a white-shoe law firm and we don't sue major accounting firms, for crying out loud." The vote was eight to seven in favor of taking the representation, with all eight in favor noting that they would have voted to decline if it were only the malpractice case against the accounting firm. In the mission-critical name of partner profitability, they voted in favor of collecting the huge Hazard fees the firm stood to gain in all the lawsuits. There were a number of royally upset partners.

Magnanimous in victory, Jonathan simply said thank you. He would never learn that Baxter Hodges voted against accepting the representation.

After a few weeks of learning the accounting case, Jonathan thought he had figured out a way to give it direction and to simplify it for the jury. A tall task because the technical accounting was both complicated and boring. FHM Advisers is a name only an overpaid, coked-up marketing consultant could conjure up. F for Benjamin Franklin, H for Alexander Hamilton, and M for Henry Morganthau Jr. The first two luminaries everybody presumably knew. Morganthau was FDR's treasury secretary and likely unknown to many living Americans. What was clear was that all three men were dead and not doing accounting audits for publicly traded companies currently under investigation and defending shareholder lawsuits. It was also doubtful that they were providing any halo effects to help FHM's clients. Jonathan thought that it was suitably ironic that these venal accountants apparently were oblivious to Ben Franklin's perspicacious warning that he who lies down with dogs shall rise up with fleas.

FHM is a firm of certified public accountants, or CPAs. At the time, it was the fourth largest accounting firm in the world. Billions in global revenues, with a vomit-inducing motto the witless marketing gurus actually thought was appealing: Where Quality Meets Trust. For substantial fees, FHM performed audit work of a client's financial books and records to ensure that they accurately reflected the client's true financial condition. In fact, the federal securities laws require that public companies like Hazard hire CPAs to do annual audits and announce the results to the shareholders and the investing public. This helps prevent fraud and a rigged game. The Supreme Court even has a cute name for this type of work—"public watchdogs." The auditors are supposed to be public watchdogs protecting the integrity of the system so investors and shareholders don't get bamboozled by fraudulent managers of public companies. In theory, at least, that's how things are supposed to work. When the public watchdogs fall asleep, or wag their greedy tails in response to two masters, corrupt corporate clients can run amok.

FHM wasn't satisfied making billions doing audit work for huge corporations. Like other major accounting firms at the time, FHM had a sizable consulting practice. Often it had lucrative consulting contracts with the very same corporations whose books it audited. In many cases, these consulting contract fees dwarfed the audit fees. That was precisely the case with FHM and Hazard. Recalling an expression he had heard in Atlanta, Jonathan could smell a conflict of interest that stunk stronger than zoo dirt.

Jonathan thought, *Suppose FHM's audit team discovered problems with Hazard's financials, but exposing them would risk pissing off Hazard's senior executives and losing the consulting fees. That tension, that potential loss of millions of dollars, created a clear incentive for FHM to look the other way, fudge the audit, or go ostrich and bury their heads in the sand.* This gave Jonathan an idea for a human interest story for the jury. A sto-

ry of greed, an inversion of FHM's fatuous motto—no quality and
no trust. A story that would not put the jury to sleep with a lot of
technical accounting mumbo jumbo. That is where Hazard's prior
lawyers had floundered badly. They had been developing a technical case of accounting, skillful even, but not one any jury on the
planet would ever understand, and one with all of the persuasive
moral force of a bowl of soggy cream of wheat.

Jonathan realized he still had one whale of a problem he had
to overcome for his Low Country jurors. Hazard was suing FHM
for more than $1 billion for not detecting and reporting a mas-
sive fraud. Fraud that Hazard's own top executives had committed.
Sure, Hazard's board of directors fired the crooks, but any competent defense attorney was going to harp on the theme that Hazard
has no one to blame but themselves. Yes, FHM's lawyers should put
up some defense of the quality of the audit work, but that was going to be a challenge because it was piss-poor, or even worse. When
the books and records were corrected and restated, it was revealed
that there were five hundred errors that had to be corrected. Those
five hundred errors overstated Hazard's true financial condition by
$500 million.

Jonathan thought, *Hazard's fired executives didn't just manipu-
late the financial statements, they mauled them. How in the hell could the
watchdogs miss all of those errors?*

Jonathan had learned from Trane that great trial lawyers figure
out how they would try their cases if they were on the other side
to better appreciate their clients' weaknesses and make sure they
address them. So, the real jury play, Jonathan thought, if he were
representing FHM and not Hazard, would be to pound away at the
greed of Hazard's own executives. If he were FHM's lawyer, Jonathan would tell the jury, "This case is simple: if those greedy executives at Hazard had not phonied up their own company's financial
statements, we wouldn't be here today. This case is kind of like
the kid who murders his parents and then complains that he's an
orphan." Jonathan feared that is exactly how the jury might size it
up—steal a line from Mercutio in Shakespeare's tragedy *Romeo and*

Juliet, and exclaim "a plague o' both your houses." Now *that* would be a tragedy, he joked to himself. That would mean no money for Hazard. Which would mean a loss for him. Jonathan did not intend to lose. He could hear Arthur Schopenhauer whispering that talent hits a target no one else can hit.

MABEL

The trial lasted four weeks. Closing arguments were the next day. Jonathan had anticipated that FHM's lawyers would try to defend the quality of their client's audit work, but he was surprised that they had spent so much time on that dry and dull subject matter. They even enlisted a $1,200-an-hour expert in accounting, from another large accounting firm, who had never testified against an accounting firm, and they put him on the witness stand for a day and a half. On cross-examination, Jonathan quickly made that partisan point—he was an apologist for accountants who could not be trusted to call balls and strikes. He then used the bulk of his time methodically dissecting those bogus accounting entries.

There were five hundred in total. He highlighted that the FHM auditors missed every single one. FHM's lawyers and their $1,200-an-hour shill were trying to con the jury into believing that the fraud was so sophisticated that even the high-priced auditors from a world-renowned accounting firm missed it. In his cross-examination of the expert, Jonathan was calling bullshit with the popular proverb fool me once, shame on you; fool me twice, shame on me. Jonathan carried it one step further: fool me five hundred times, and I'm either a dumber-than-dirt saphead or a flea-infested enabler who snuggled in bed with the fraud dogs for a few million bucks. There wasn't much left of this expert by the time Jonathan finished his cross.

Jonathan liked the jury. They were engaged, took a lot of notes, and seemed genuinely interested in the case. But they were not professional accountants, so throughout the trial he wanted to keep the case themes simple. Remembering Einstein, not so simple as to insult the jurors' intelligence. His jury was a diverse group. An energetic regional planner who took copious case notes, an empathetic healthcare social worker, a restaurant waiter at an oyster bar who obviously blows blunts and likely would still be there in ten years, a retired high school history teacher who now led walking tours of Charleston, an unemployed dockworker who was working on a southern novel about a down-on-his-luck bluegrass singer, an old electrician with tattoos covering his thick arms and running up his neck, a diagnostic medical stenographer, a young dental hygienist who worked nights at a popular restaurant to earn extra money for college she hoped to attend in a year or two, and a veterinarian's office manager named Holly who was wearing a T-shirt with the mug of a smiling golden retriever. Jonathan predicted that Holly, the office manager, would be picked to be the jury foreperson. At a minimum, this organized, strong-willed woman would likely be a leading voice in the jury's deliberations. In his closing argument, Jonathan wanted to strike a chord with her and now had a vivid idea how to do it.

It was 9:00 a.m. and time for Jonathan's closing argument. He needed to stress that this particular case ultimately was about accounting negligence, not executive fraud, but he would have to address the fraud issue. And he needed to give the jury a reason to look past the fraud of Hazard's executives and focus on tagging FHM.

"May it please the court. Good morning, ladies and gentlemen. Four weeks ago I stood before you and told you that we would prove that things can go terribly wrong in corporate America when highly paid professional accountants fail to do their job. You will decide if I kept my promise. This morning I want to review the evidence that you have seen and heard that shows, I submit to you, that I did keep my promise.

"From the beginning of the trial until right now, we have told you that this case is about accounting. *One*, it's about accounting errors, accounting mistakes, and accounting problems. *Two*, it's about an accounting firm, FHM, that failed to live up to its professional standards and obligations to detect and report those mistakes. And

three, it's about FHM's refusal—and you have heard that refusal
for four weeks now—to take any responsibility for its professional
failures.

"FHM was supposed to be a public watchdog. Not a sleeping
dog. Hazard paid them more than one million dollars to do their
job. What job was that? To competently inspect the financial statements to ensure that they were accurate. To be a safeguard and
guard rail against the executives doing monkey business with Hazard's financial books and records. FHM is licensed by the state to
do just that. It was paid by Hazard to do just that. Paid more than
one million dollars to do their job of ensuring the accuracy of Hazard's financial statements.

"Well, what did more than one million dollars buy Hazard?
You saw the evidence in all of its fraudulent detail. Five hundred
errors and mistakes in Hazard's financial statements. And what did
this watchdog find? Nothing. FHM did not identify a single problem. Five hundred chances to hit the ball and they whiffed every
single time.

"And the result? Hazard's financial statements were overstated
by $500 million. Five hundred mistakes and $500 million. That's
on FHM. And we are here in this courtroom because FHM refuses
to take responsibility for anything.

"Ladies and gentlemen, in baseball and on the job, batting
averages matter. When you whiff going oh for five hundred and
cause $500 million worth of mistakes, you don't even get to play
for Charleston's Class A River Dogs, much less play in baseball's
big leagues. These guys claimed and represented to Hazard's board
of directors before they were hired that they are big-league players.
And remember when I showed their website and all the bragging
they do, calling themselves 'world class accountants' who do the audit work of many of the world's leading corporations? Where they
brag that their motto is Where Quality Meets Trust? But what they
showed you by their performance in this case is that they couldn't
even make it in the bush league. Hazard's millions bought them
neither quality nor trust."

At this point, Jonathan paused. He wanted to give the jury a
few moments to absorb his basic theme of five hundred mistakes

and $500 million in overstatements. If the jury wasn't buying this theme, he might as well sit down right now. And, in jury selection, several of the jurors had told him that they were big fans of baseball and Charleston's River Dogs minor league baseball team. He sensed that they were with him, including the office manager, who seemed to be inching up in her seat. So for now he switched gears to deal with the elephant in the room—Hazard's own executives being the ones, after all, who cooked the books. He couldn't ignore the most compelling reason for the jury to overlook FHM's botched audit and award Hazard nothing in damages.

"Let's ask ourselves this question: What is FHM's real defense to five hundred mistakes? It's the defense of last resort. You've heard it from them for the past couple of weeks—blame the victim. You heard their evidence, and I suspect that opposing counsel will get up after me and talk about Hazard's fired executives and how they are the ones who cooked the books. But, ladies and gentlemen, please do not be conned. Let's get one thing straight, as I told you in my opening statement. We're not proud of what those fellows did and we're not here to defend or excuse their conduct. Some of the things they did were just wrong. Plain and simple. You didn't hear us once try to defend them in this trial. And that's why we fired them.

"But those fired executives are not Hazard Waste. Hazard Waste is owned by the people who buy its stock. From individuals to 401(k) retirement plans to teacher's pension funds. These owners of the company, just like Hazard's board of directors, depended on FMH to blow the whistle if executives abused the trust placed in them to run the company honestly by stepping over the line to commit fraud to line their pockets. FHM was supposed to blow the whistle on executives who cooked the books, not swallow it and look the other way. But FMH swallowed the whistle for three years in a row."

Jonathan paused again. He set up an easel about twenty feet from the middle of the jury box. On it he put his favorite visual for the jury, a graphic showing five hundred errors overstating the financial records by $500 million. Throughout the trial, Jonathan worked and worked on simple yet gripping themes to cut through

the complexity of all of the arcane accounting. Now he was about
to deliver the embracing message that was the essence of his case.
He was banking on Holly the dog lover who managed the veterinarian's office to be listening intently. Pointing to his chart, Jonathan
delivered his final words.

"Ladies and gentlemen, five hundred accounting errors and irregularities overstating Hazard's financial condition by $500 mil-
lion. There is no question that some of Hazard's former executives
were behind the fraud. But that is precisely why FHM's auditors
were paid millions of dollars. Why Hazard's board of directors
and shareholders paid them millions and relied on them. Relied
on them to exercise their professional training, skill, and judgment
first to detect the fraud, and then to speak up. If those CPAs, those
public watchdogs, had done their job, we would not be here in
this courtroom right now. So please ask yourself this question—Did
FMH behave like watchdogs or lapdogs?"

Jonathan took a long pause. Eyebrows slightly raised, he made
eye contact with each jury. Then he resumed, in a soft, slow voice.
The jurors were leaning forward.

"I'd like to share with you a story about a real watchdog. When
I was a little boy, Mom and Dad got me a dog. A pound puppy from
the Humane Society. We named her Mabel. Mabel was part beagle,
part springer spaniel. I loved Mabel. Mabel received and gave a lot
of love. And Mabel was loyal. As time marched on, Mabel grew
old. By the time Mabel was fifteen, she was deaf and nearly blind.
Didn't move real well either. But dutiful Mabel would still lie down
by the front door like she was guarding the house. And you know
what else? Mabel could still smell. And when Mabel smelled something funny, something that stunk, you know what Mabel did? Mabel barked. My watchdog Mabel barked.

"Did the watchdogs at FHM bark at a single one of these five
hundred putrid smells? No they did not. Not once. So when you
go back to the jury room, I want you to ask yourself this question:
What would Mabel have done?"

Jonathan then spent two minutes reviewing Hazard's damages
request for $1.5 billion. On behalf of Hazard, he thanked the jury
and sat down.

The jury began their deliberations on Thursday afternoon. Jonathan and his team ate a light and early dinner and then enjoyed a long walk around and through Charleston's scenic Battery, a promenade not far from the main drag. They gawked at some of the beautiful waterfront homes and watched the boats sailing lazily in the harbor. Mostly they just enjoyed the breezy saltwater air and weather. A pleasant distraction from the nervous wait for the jury's verdict. That night there was a beautiful full moon.

Jonathan thought about Hippocrates, the father of modern medicine, who said that "one who is seized with terror, fright and madness during the night is being visited by the goddess of the moon." Jonathan thought the goddess of the moon sure likes to mess with trial lawyers, making them toss and turn and gripping them with night terrors during trial.

Any terror Jonathan felt that night was relieved in the morning. At 10:00 a.m. the jury sent a note with a question. The note read: "Are punitive damages permitted if we find the defendant liable for negligence?" Judge Beauregard sent back a one-word answer: "No." Jonathan had been taught by Judge Roy that it was a mistake to read anything into jurors' deliberation questions. They could mean just about anything. Jonathan was trying to heed Judge Roy's admonition, but he couldn't help feeling pretty good about that question.

At 11:00 a.m. the jury had a verdict. They filed in and were seated. The jury foreperson, the office manager of the vet's office, handed up the verdict. The jury found FHM liable for negligence and awarded Hazard Waste $1.5 billion in damages. Judge Beauregard asked the lawyers to remain seated as he dismissed the jurors, who had to walk past the counsel tables on their way out. As she approached Jonathan, Holly winked and whispered, "Mabel would have barked."

LOUSY CASES AND LOSING

Jonathan was a bona fide superstar. The national press ran stories about him, and he was receiving an increasing number of calls from corporate America. As the twentieth century was drawing to a close, he defended a major airline in consolidated antitrust class action lawsuits in Philadelphia brought by customers alleging that the airlines were conspiring to overcharge them by signaling price increases through a computerized reservation system. The airlines also coordinated retaliatory price decreases against any non–hub carrier that dared to try to win customers away in a carrier's hub by lowering prices. Some tactics were too cute by half. The airlines use alphanumeric codes to identify particulars flights. Two letters—the carriers' identity—and flight numbers. Then there was the letter code for the retaliatory prices—FU. Hard to mistake that message. They were also sometimes referred to as RAT fares. The low-price offender would quickly get the threatening message and raise its prices to match the hub-carrier's prices and the hub carrier would then raise back its FU/retaliatory prices. During the four-year period of the alleged conspiracy, the airlines reported billions of dollars in record profits. The case settled without any money payments. Instead, airline passengers could mail in a request for a coupon for a teensy-weensy discount off their next airline ticket purchase. A clever deal for the airlines, maybe not such a bargain for the over-charged customers, only 2 percent of whom even bothered to mail in a request.

Big Law salivates to defend Big Banks and trip all over them-selves to get their work. Curious because banks are notorious slow

pays and whack the hell out of firms' bills. To get their foot in the
door and prove their worth, hoping for bigger cases down the road,
on behalf of a major bank with its own multibillion-dollar credit
card operation, Jonathan led a team of mostly young CLB associates in suing delinquent card holders in mid-Atlantic states. The
client, Trust & Treasure Bank, decided to "play hardball" by "un-
leashing the junkyard dogs" on customers uncharitably described
in an internal memo as "dregs and deadbeats." One such described
customer was a sixty-one-year-old woman with a heretofore high
credit score who had maxed out her credit card in a futile attempt
to pay for her husband's cancer treatments. He died. Six months
later she lost her job and home. No time for tears at Trust & Treasure, they sued this judgment-proof widow for unpaid principal,
interest (which exceeded the principal), and attorney's fees. Penni-
less, the widow defaulted, and the bank gave the order to garnish
her wages if she got another job. The soft-headed and hard-hearted
skinflints at Trust & Treasure praised CLB's young lawyers for being "pit bulls" and "sending the right message to deadbeats." CLB's
management apparently had no moral or business qualms about being plaintiffs if the defendants were penurious widows rather than
venal accounting firms.

In Miami, Jonathan defended Cayman Island Banking & Investment, another major bank, in a federal racketeering Ponzi scheme
where the bank conspired with a fly-by-night seller of oil and gas
leases by telephones—what fraudsters and the feds refer to as a
boiler-room operation—from the lower floor of an old warehouse
building. A classic get-rich-quick scheme. With slick brochures
fraudulently touting the "mother lode of all geological findings" by
so-called expert geologists and high-pressure sales pitches, the seller promised a "limited opportunity" for extraordinary investment
returns if the buyers acted quickly before other "savvy" investors
beat them to the punch. Blinded by greed and forgetting the ad-
age "that if it's too good to be true, then it's not true," more than
ten thousand investors (or suckers, Jonathan thought), including
two federal judges and a midwestern governor, were swindled in
this scam. The bunco artists were not busted until several of the
fraudsters, including a senior vice president of Jonathan's client,

were arrested by the Coast Guard when they raided a cocaine and Cristal champaign celebration; entertainment of another sort was provided by filles de joie from Saint Barthelemy, on a yacht in the Atlantic Ocean. Jonathan managed to get the bank out of the case, but it was a substantial settlement. True enough, one of the federal judges who got bilked in the scam was himself later arrested and pled guilty to a felony charge of speedballing by supplying and sharing cocaine and meth with a stripper, known by her risible nom de guerre Candy Canesucker, who performed more than just lap dances for her sexagenarian supplier.

By the fin de siècle, Jonathan was humbled by his first jury trial loss. The case was tried in federal court in Detroit, the Motor City. Jonathan defended a major automobile company that plaintiffs alleged conspired with its largest dealers to maintain high resale prices to car buyers by imposing several competitive restrictions on the dealers. From the start, Jonathan thought his client had stronger legal defenses than it had factual defenses. This assessment was confirmed when the client did two mock jury exercises to test the strength of their case. They lost both times. The third time, the real trial, was no charm. Jonathan lost. The only silver lining was the jury awarded the plaintiffs only half of their claimed damages. And a year later, the appeals court, stacked with pro-business judges, agreed with Jonathan's legal argument, favored more by abstract theoreticians than cash-outlaying consumers, ruling that the resale prices agreed upon by Jonathan's manufacturing client and the dealers did not violate the antitrust laws. Left undisturbed was the jury's finding that those prices did, in fact, cause car buyers to pay higher prices.

In the meantime, Jonathan was devastated by the jury's verdict. His emotional ego eclipsed his rational faculties telling him that the car buyers only got half of what they asked for and would probably lose even that on appeal. No matter. The air of invincibility was destroyed forever. The feeling of personal rejection and failure depressing. The sense that he was nothing special unnerving. Jonathan now had to confront the hard lesson that all trial lawyers must

confront: Try enough cases and you are going to lose. Jonathan
sulked in his office. He needed to talk with someone who understood the painful, humbling lesson of losing a jury trial. Someone
outstanding who had lost a jury trial. He knew who he had to see.
So he walked out of his office, took the stairs up to the next floor,
and walked into Jack Kenneth Coltrane's office.

BUDDHA OF THE BELTWAY

After Trane's third stint in rehab, before the Birmingham school milk trial, he took some time off. His personal life was in shambles. His wife and the mother of his two kids hit her breaking point and divorced him. Trane didn't blame her and had the good grace to do what she wanted. He had become estranged from his kids, both now out of college and living on the West Coast. Even Trane's beloved English bulldog, Winston, had died while he was in rehab.

Then there was the question of whether Trane's "other family," his law firm, would also abandon him. Representing clients again was out of the question. The firm could not risk the legal liability, and corporate America would not trust a three-time rehab patient with its most important cases.

Trane's days as a practicing jury trial lawyer were over. Many of his senior partners wanted him back in some capacity, albeit at a vast reduction in compensation, but the question was, what could he do? Ironically, a law firm consultant had the idea. Ironic because Trane had for years complained about the money Baxter Hodges spent on consultants spouting the latest fad in organizational behavior.

Trane one year sent a memo to Hodges and the management committee grousing that legal consultants did seagull missions: they fly in, make a lot of noise, crap all over everything, then fly the hell away. In the memo he called them ultracrepidarians, a bunch of opinionated know-it-all nonlawyers who don't know the first thing about lawyers or how to run a law firm. Then the firm's litigation department head, with the befitting name Oliver Truckle, hired a consultant to help him figure out what to do about the fact that his paper-pushing younger generation of discovery lawyers was not developing any courtroom skills and was increasingly agitated about the paucity of trial opportunities.

Truckle was a curious choice to head the litigation department. He had never been the lead lawyer in a jury trial. He defended companies in class action cases and did a smattering of regulatory work. His own client base, what lawyers call "book," was meager, and he mostly depended on others in the firm to supply him work. But he excelled at office politics and had unctuously ingratiated himself with Baxter Hodges. Trane thought Truckle was a sniveling sycophant, telling one partner that "Truckle's only mark of distinction is a brown nose and that Hodges's decision to make that kiss-ass department head was the worst patronage decision since the ancient Roman emperor Caligula made his horse a Roman senator." Only half in jest did Trane quote his beloved King Lear: "When we are born, we cry that we are come to this great stage of fools."

Just two years earlier, Truckle had had a brainstorm—Trane called it a brain fart—for how to get junior lawyers into court. He arranged with a bank client—Invicta (Latin for "unconquered")—to have first- and second-year lawyers handle residential eviction proceedings for the unforgiving bank. Often the reasons why the down-on-their luck mortgage holders were behind or in default included loss of job or illness. No matter, Invicta was the dubious leader in the annual three and half million residential eviction filings in the United States. Plenty of hearing opportunities for princely paid young lawyers to learn how to put struggling families out on the streets, where disproportionately Invicta's evictees were people of color. After a year of doing Invicta's dirty work, the conscientious young lawyers threatened mutiny if the firm continued to make them do this merciless work. Management, in a split decision, capitulated. Invicta fired CLB and hired another Big Law firm.

Truckle was none too pleased. Back at the drawing board, the idea Truckle and the consultant landed on was both a recognition of reality and cynical. The reality was, young lawyers in Big Law don't try cases. Period, full stop. Many will muddle through their associate years, eight to ten years, and never see the inside of a courtroom, much less a jury trial. They don't examine witnesses at trial or make arguments to a jury. Most of the N0 JTs don't even take their first deposition until their second or third year of practicing law. A whole generation of Big Law lawyers were litigators in name only. Feeling desperate for some pugilistic palliative, they began clamoring for training programs and something to give them at least an inkling of what it's like to stand on their feet and try a case.

It was decided that Trane would be a good choice to run a training program. They dubbed it Trial College. Cynics snarked that the youngins' might get the diploma, but they would never get a trial lawyer job. The younger lawyers would get some practice drills, but that's all they would ever be, practice players. Trane had been back and running the college for about a year. Jonathan rarely saw him. There were a couple reasons. Jonathan was rarely in the office, as his cases took him all over the country. His last trial in Detroit had kept him away for the better part of two months. The protégé was also still harboring some angry feelings toward his mentor. Jonathan was a young associate when Trane fell off the wagon for the third time, a few weeks before the Birmingham trial. At the time, Jonathan was furious and couldn't understand how Trane could be so weak. To the young Jonathan, it was a matter of will, not disease.

Now thirty-seven, Jonathan had matured, at least with his understanding of addiction. At first he could not fathom how a person as brilliant and talented as Trane could let himself be conquered by brown liquid. But it was Trane's extraordinary intellectual gifts that made the ambitious protégé appreciate that not everything in life is a simple matter of will. The human brain—life itself—is far too complex for such easy explanations. Jonathan appreciated that since at least his time with Trane in Memphis the man with the sad countenance was far too complicated a human being for facile labels and pigeonholes. Then there was something else gripping Jonathan's emotions. The chemistry of "it." There was something ineffable, something emotionally irreducible about the bond between him and his old mentor. An emotional bond of another sort he had acutely felt in what now seemed like a lifetime ago.

Jonathan sat in Trane's office looking morose, almost boyish. Trane, about forty pounds lighter and now supporting a gray-flecked

beard, looked peaceful and relaxed. Slowly he puffed on his favorite cigar/cigarette, a habit Jonathan thought was vile but somehow
gave Trane the look of a deep thinker. *The Buddha of the Beltway*, Jonathan thought, as if Trane was now enlightened and mellowing by
seeking compassion and wisdom and following the Noble Eightfold
Path. Trane's intuition and his affection for the dejected young trial
lawyer enabled him to sense immediately why Jonathan had shown
up unannounced.

"Well, well, the intrepid warrior has returned from battle in
faraway lands. Welcome back, Jonathan."

"Thanks, Jack, how are you doing?" Jonathan never called
Trane by his last name, or Trane. Always Jack.

"I'm doing fine, running the college and trying to develop the
next Jonathan Kent. So far with no success. This month we're working on direct examinations."

"That's not surprising, you always told me that direct examination is underappreciated and often the hardest examination,"
replied the protégé, in a nod to his mentor.

"You learned well. And you've learned many trial lessons well.
Now, the look on your face is telling me that you are trying to learn
the hardest trial lesson of all," Trane reflected, as he took another
slow drag.

"No kidding. I never dreamed losing could hurt this bad. I al-
ways thought that by outthinking and outworking the other side,
I would never lose." Like nervous or agitated people tend to do,
Jonathan was fidgeting and rubbing his thighs as he spoke.

"Jonathan, you can control many things, you can outprepare
your opponent, but the facts are the facts, and sometimes the Great
Dealer deals you a losing hand. As the song goes, sometimes you're
out of aces."

"You're not going to go Kenny Rogers and 'The Gambler' on
me, are you? Every hand is a winner and a loser, so the best you can
hope for is to die in your sleep, or something like that. Jack, I think
you liked Nashville too much." When Trane and Jonathan were in
Nashville for the Billy Joe Wynn trial, Trane loved his tutorial in
country-and-western music. He even splurged on a pair of peanut
brittle ostrich cowboy boots by Tony Lama, which he conspicuously

wore from time to time. Folks were kind not to tell him they made him look ridiculous.

"That's good. I did like Nashville, and some of those country-and-western tunes are terrific. I still get chills when I hear Patsy Cline sing 'Crazy.' But these days I'm favoring Frank Zappa's song 'Montana,' think I'll be goin' to Montana soon and try livin' me a life as a dental floss tycoon. Life seems more absurd the older I get, I suppose. Gotta love Zappa's songs 'Jesus Thinks You're a Jerk' and 'Broken Hearts Are for Assholes.'"

"I come here for consolation and advice and you're talking about a dead rocker who wrote 'Don't Eat the Yellow Snow' and named his daughter Moon Unit and another kid Dweezil?" Frank Zappa wasn't going to make Jonathan forget his crushing loss, but Trane did understand how to lighten his mood, at least a bit.

"Even Jimmy Buffett knows that we would all go insane if we couldn't laugh. But look, Jonathan, sometimes losing hands lose, and in Detroit you had a losing hand. A lousy, losing hand. Let's face it, our car manufacturing client and its dealers did agree to maintain and charge higher prices to the car buyers. Jurors have common sense, and no jury on the planet was going to let them get away with screwing the buyers. Hell, the jurors are all car buyers themselves. Only right-wing ideological judges, kooky antitrust professors, and some of those blinkered wackos at the Federalist Society, an insidious ideological incubator, who are nothing but sycophantic shills for big business, think that bullshit is actually good for consumers."

"Careful, that's my lead argument on appeal. I need some of those right-wing judges on the appellate court to pull out their Federalist Society Bible, swig the Kool-Aid, and overturn this knock-me-on-my-ass jury verdict. But that's not why I'm here. Aren't great trial lawyers supposed to win with losing hands?"

"Yeah, and sometimes they do. And sometimes juries decide cases based on which side should win, not which side has the better lawyer," Trane sagely schooled him. "Don't lose all perspective. Sure, you will always give it your best shot, but when you are a mercenary for corporate America, let's face it, sometimes you are going to be on the side that probably should lose. I can think of plenty of trials where the world would have been less fair, less just, if the corporate defendants had won."

"Jack, you didn't lose many. Did it hurt this much when you lost?"

Laughing and shaking his head, Trane advised, "Always. Losing hurts like hell and it will always hurt like hell. It better damn well hurt like hell, or you are in the wrong business. I can remember every loss, remember the losses much better than any of the wins. I second-guess myself to this day. But you have to move on. Trial work is like baseball, my man. You have to play another game the next day, so you can't wallow in the gutter. You give it your all, learn from your mistakes, and move on. Great trial lawyers don't go undefeated. That's a bullshit myth. Every trial lawyer worth a damn who has tried more than a couple of cases has lost some. Nobody, I mean nobody, bats a thousand. And take it from me, never, ever, think the bottle will ease the pain. It damn well will not."

"Understood. But how do you keep from doubting yourself? By the time I'm ready to try my case, I'm convinced one hundred percent that I should win."

"Well, you better go in with that kind of conviction or you are sure to lose. But just because you think you should win doesn't mean the rest of the world sees it that way too," Trane admonished as he shrugged his shoulders and put his palms out. "You work your ass off for months, often years, to get a case ready for trial, and you convince yourself there is only *one* right outcome—you should win. But your mind is playing a trick on you. That's why jury trials are crapshoots. Always will be. We human beings have different belief systems and values, different biases and prejudices, and we process information differently for all types of different reasons. As the wise philosophers have taught us, there is no single answer, no single solution to our problems, so we muddle through and do the best we can."

"I hear you." Getting up to leave, Jonathan said, "Jack, I really appreciate you sparing some time to let me vent."

"Just a minute. Do you remember what I told you before the Billy Joe Wynn trial in Nashville about human facial expressions?"

"Yeah, something about how there are six universal facial expressions."

"That's right. Happiness, sadness, fear, surprise, anger, and disgust."

"You said four of them are negative and surprise could be either positive or negative. Pretty depressing."

"It says something important about the human condition. Only happiness is an unqualified positive expression and feeling. And it's fleeting; it inevitably gives way to one of the other five."

"Don't I know that, but that's a whole different matter. But, yeah, I suppose my face is not projecting much happiness right now."

A student of Shakespeare, Trane understood like Henry IV that there is a history in all of our lives, and he suspected that something from Jonathan's past was both unforgettable and contributing to his obsession with work and achievement. "No, it is not. You need to go find some. Away from work, Jonathan. You're not going to find it here. Not now. Just think about it, okay? For years now you have put all of your time and energy into this job and advancement. As best as I can tell, to the exclusion of all else. In some ways your ambition and the values and reward structure of Big Law are a perfect marriage. But they all too easily can result in a relationship of co-dependency, of emotional enfeeblement, mental fragility, and shallowness. And abuse. Try out William Butler Yeats's penetrating poem "The Choice": 'The intellect of man is forced to choose perfection of the life, or of the work … when all the story's finished, what's the news?' Yeats got it right—the singular pursuit of work will not fulfill; ultimately it will leave you 'raging in the dark,' where the 'night's remorse' might be your life's fate. I'm just saying there's a lot more to this short life than this all-consuming job, and however much you might pretend otherwise, it's just a job. Don't let the trappings of achievement, money, and status turn it into a treadmill. There's a lot more to life for a mind as keen as yours. Keep that in mind. The candle will burn out before you know it."

"I hear you. We'll see. Thanks again, Jack," Jonathan said, as he thought, *Buddha of the Beltway*.

"Jonathan, you know my door is always open. Don't be a stranger. And one other thing. Don't ever blame the jury if you lose— that's the surest way to start a losing streak. Consider taking some time off. Get away from the law for a spell. It will do you good."

"Thanks, Jack," he said as he walked out. He knew he would be back many more times, and that lifted his spirits already.

LA VILLE-LUMIÈRE

After a few more sleepless nights, Jonathan decided to do something he had yet to do his entire time with Cabot, Lodge & Biddle. Take a vacation. Moved by memories of lost love he continued to keep stowed away in the locked vault of his mind, he knew where to go and what to do. What Shelly long ago wanted to do with him. He was going to France. First stop, Paris. He even hummed Joni Mitchell's incandescent line about losing and gaining something by living every day from her meditative song "Both Sides Now." A mournful song with special meaning. Jonathan tried to gain something every day. Paris would not disappoint.

Jonathan left for the City of Light on a Wednesday night and planned to return to DC eleven days later, arriving back in the early afternoon. He would land in Paris Thursday morning, clear customs, and likely get to his hotel, the Park Hyatt at Vendôme on the Right Bank of the River Seine, by the noon hour. He was advised to take a nap to ward off jet lag, advice he could safely ignore. He required only five hours of sleep and would get that on the plane. Plus, he naturally burned with energy. He never even tried coffee. Caffeine would only cause this human energy machine to bounce off walls. Jonathan always assumed there would be plenty of time to sleep after he died. While alive, sleep was no more than a quick recharging necessity. Since his youth, Jonathan wanted to be alive before he died.

The free man in Paris was off the plane, out of customs, and into a taxi with a note card written in French with directions to the Park Hyatt. Jonathan didn't speak French, so he memorized a few

French phrases and greetings and otherwise intended to rely on a French/English dictionary and bilingual French people to get by. After checking in and unpacking his light bags, the young explorer did what he did in every city he visited. He headed out the door for a walk to explore. Map in hand, he made his way to the magnificent Champs-Élysées, a breathtaking tree-lined avenue bustling with Parisians and throngs of tourists from the world over. Hearing the speaking tongues of different languages, the curiosity seeker thought he was ambling amid a horizontal Tower of Babel. Quickly he was overwhelmed with a feeling that it was impossible not to feel free, vibrant, and alive on the Champs-Élysées. Even the air smelled different—fortifying and invigorating.

Jonathan made his way to the Place de la Concorde, the large public square on the eastern end of the Champs-Élysées, cars whizzing by in controlled chaos. Getting his bearings, he headed west on the Champs-Élysées for the mile-long stroll to the Arc de Triomphe, taking his time to sponge in all the smells and sounds emanating from the shops and cafes lining the most famous street in the world. Nobody in a hurry, folks reveling in the moment. Arriving at the Arc de Triomphe, Jonathan was amazed at the sea of humanity on the pullulating boulevard he saw when he looked back in the direction of the Place de la Concorde. Beneath the Arc's vault lies the Tomb of the Unknown Soldier from WWI, a war described by some as the Great War, the War to End War, but it was neither: it was a ghastly war and a prelude to an even more horrific war. But the feeling was strangely serene, and Jonathan felt a vague, transcendental connection to world history. There was so much more to come in the city aptly described as a moveable feast.

A natural peripatetic, Jonathan strolled a couple of kilometers over to the sixteenth arrondissement and the Passy Cemetery to visit the gravesite of the first Impressionist composer, the legendary Claude Debussy. Composer of "Clair de Lune," meaning moonlight, one of Shelly's favorite songs. Shelly, a moonbeam pulsating with the sound of music, once told him that Debussy believed that "the beauty of a work of art will always remain a mystery." So too, he mused, the beauty of love.

Returning to the Arc, Jonathan crossed over to the south side of the Champs-Élysées and headed back east. Along the way he veered off path to see the spectacular Pont Alexandre III, the ornate bridge that spans the River Seine. Described by his travel book as the most beautiful bridge in the world, Jonathan had certainly never seen another bridge so exquisite and extravagant. He walked across and back, enjoying the floating boats below and admiring the golden nymphs at the center of the bridge's arches. He even snapped a requested photo for a horde of Japanese tourists nudging their way into the scene who wanted a picture with the arches in the background.

Back on the Champs-Élysées, Jonathan continued past the Place de la Concorde and the Musée de l'Orangerie and spying, across the Seine on the Left Bank, the must-see Musée d'Orsay. Jonathan wandered through the Tuileries Garden and marveled at the massiveness of the Louvre, an incredible museum, but one he decided not to visit on this short trip because of the long lines that snaked around forever. For now, the *Mona Lisa*, *Venus de Milo*, *The Winged Victory of Samothrace*, *The Cheat with the Ace of Diamonds*, and I. M. Pei's Pyramid would have to wait.

Jonathan exited the Tuileries Garden, meandered over to the Rue de Rivoli, and sauntered for a while on that famous commercial street. Heading back toward the Park Hyatt, he stopped at the Place Vendôme, the small square with fancy shops and offices, as well as the Vendôme Column. The wandering soul also had to pass by the Ritz-Carlton Hotel, perhaps the world's most iconic hotel, whose loyal guests over the years have included Marcel Proust, Charlie Chaplin, Maria Callas, and the Prince of Wales. And then there was the bacchanalian louche, Ernest Hemingway. The Ritz houses Hemingway's eponymous bar where the gin-guzzler "code hero" reputedly downed fifty-one straight dry martinis after Paris was liberated from the Germans in 1944.

Good thing the prodigious imbiber had already written *The Sun Also Rises* because the odds were exceedingly low that he saw the sun rise the next day, more like a farewell to brain cells. Jonathan figured that if Hemingway could swill gin martinis until his liver surrendered, he could safely liberate a beer and toast French independence. When in France ... He ordered a Kronenbourg 1664, a

French favorite. After exhausting his French with "l'addition s'il vous plait," he about choked on his warm beer when he saw the tab. Jonathan thought, *Did Hemingway stiff the bar back in 1944 and now this young American must pay the Papa piper?* That was the last time Jonathan patronized Papa's watering hole.

So much to see in Paris, but so little time on this trip. Remembering Shelly's romantic dreams, a few museums were must-sees on his list, as were some gardens. In search of a visual, romantic, and reflective experience, he surprised himself when his spirit moved him to wander over to the Pantheon the next morning. Only a day in Paris and Jonathan was beginning to feel inadequate and incomplete. In the states, language was his stock-in-trade, what set him apart from the crowd, but in Paris he couldn't even speak the language of taxi drivers, street cleaners, and hotel clerks. On the streets, he was amid grandeur and splendor on a scale he had never seen before, testament to human genius and ingenuity that made him feel small and diminished. For all the sophistication of his law practice, he was feeling insignificant, une personne insignifiante, as the French might say. A minnow in the sea of humanity. Then he met Marie Curie.

Actually Marie Curie is dead. She is interred in the Pantheon, in the Latin Quarter, where the French have buried many of her famous heroes and luminaries. The writer Victor Hugo, author of *Les Miserables*, is there, as well as Voltaire, a genius product of the Enlightenment and author of *Candide*, a lively satire on the polymath Gottfried Wilhelm Liebniz's philosophy of optimistic determinism—as in, if "*this* is the best of all possible worlds," then we're all screwed. Jonathan especially liked two of Voltaire's enduring quotes: "I disapprove of what you say, but I will defend to the death your right to say it," and, "Those who can make you believe absurdities can make you commit atrocities." But it was Marie Curie, previously unknown to Jonathan, who stopped him in his tracks.

Jonathan learned that Marie Curie was extraordinary. She was the first woman to win a Nobel Prize. Why stop at one? She won two. In two different scientific fields. Jonathan was experiencing an "I'm not worthy" moment. Somehow, representing a country singer against a trashy tabloid, a milk maker that bilked school kids, a corrupt company suing venal accountants, and stony-hearted banks didn't seem so impressive. In 1903, Madame Curie, along with her husband, Pierre, and another Frenchman, won the Nobel Prize in physics for developing the theory of radioactivity. Marie Curie actually coined the word "radioactivity." Apparently not one to rest on her laurels, Curie won her second Nobel Prize in 1911, this time in chemistry. She discovered the periodic table elements polonium, number 82, and radium, number 88. She made those discoveries using techniques she had invented for isolating radioactive isotopes. Jonathan was truly inspired.

Inspired and humbled. Of course, he knew that there were geniuses throughout time and countries. In his own field of economics, he thought that John Maynard Keynes was a genius, and he knew that physicists Isaac Newton, Albert Einstein, Wolfgang Pauli, Neils Bohr, and Richard Feynman were geniuses. Of course Shakespeare and da Vinci, Goethe and Michelangelo, Erasmus and Galileo, and Mozart and Beethoven also qualify for the lofty designation. But there was something about being in Paris, unable to speak the language, learning about a two-time Nobel Prize winner, who also made contributions to finding cancer treatments, that made Jonathan feel diminished and insignificant and selfish. Like he was no more accomplished, no more significant, than an ant searching about for its next calorie. *When I die*, he asked himself, *who the hell will care or remember me or anything I ever did? The earth managed for billions of years before me, and after my insignificant and infinitesimally short time on the planet, it will manage for billions more. Just a cosmic piece of dust lasting for a blink of an eye.*

Jonathan forced himself to sit down and take a breath. He was undergoing existential angst, the alienating experience of realizing that he was a faceless nobody in an indifferent universe. With no prospect for change. And no smelling the roses. Whizzing through life, working twenty-four seven, defending faceless corporations in the civil litigation game of money changing hands, or not, where, truth be told, it usually really doesn't matter who wins or loses, with the pointless goal of climbing a compensation ladder so he could make more money than he would ever spend. He wondered,

Is this really what I'm doing with my life? He was feeling like an emotional oyster. No wonder Hemingway downed fifty-one martinis.

Back on his feet, disillusionment directed him to some more dead folks. Off to Père Lachaise Cemetery, the world's most visited necropolis.

Celebrated luminaries from authors, musicians, painters, and politicians are buried there. So too, mere mortals under unadorned headstones. *Perhaps*, he thought, *the propinquity of the gravesites reflects a certain congruity, even acuity, of our common humanity, or the French being French, maybe just a recognition of the otiosity, fatuity, and vacuity of it all, for rich and poor, famous and anonymous alike.*

Either way, Jonathan could not figure out why in the world people flocked to a graveyard to stare at tombstones of folks they don't know. When in France ... So he joined the rubberneckers and wandered the grounds. Frédéric Chopin, Molière, Èdith Piaf, and Marcel Proust are all buried there. So are the medieval intellectuals and lovers Abelard and the much younger Héloïse. Poor Abelard, castration was a high price to pay for platonic and carnal lust. *Ah, the French*, thought Jonathan.

Two writers Jonathan especially admired, Oscar Wilde and Honoré de Balzac, were also laid to rest at Père Lachaise. Wilde's *The Picture of Dorian Gray*, the tragic story of a young man who sells his soul for eternal youth and beauty and a life of decadence, only to die in the end, was a favorite. With his artistic sensibilities, Jonathan especially admired Wilde for aggressively defending his immersing book from critics who thought the book offended moral sensibilities on the grounds that art should be judged aesthetically, for art's sake, and not on some prig's view of morality. And *Dorian Gray* is a hell of a good read.

So too are many of the books in Balzac's collection of books referred to as *The Human Comedy*. Jonathan especially liked *The Wild Ass's Skin*, *Lost Illusions*, *A Harlot High and Low*, and *Le Père Goriot* and the character Eugène de Rastignac, a young law student from the South of France who decides to abandon law and climb the Parisian social ladder by any ruthless means necessary. Jonathan thought *Le Père Goriot* should be required reading in Big Law. He admired Balzac as a master realist who had an uncanny ability to expose the harsh realities that lurk just beneath gilded surfaces. He could only imagine the vivisection Balzac would do to Big Law's neurotic, money-grubbing underbelly.

So then why, Jonathan wondered incredulously, *is Jim Morrison of the rock band the Doors not only buried here but such a gawking favorite that extra security patrols the site?* The druggie died of a heroin overdose in a Paris bathroom, ignoble, but apparently the stuff of a certain type of legend, Jonathan supposed. But when he learned that adoring fans still pour beer on his grave and leave the cans in some sort of tribular worship, it began to make sense to him. *Besides,* Jonathan thought in fairness, *Morrison's performance of "L.A. Woman" was virtuoso and his belting baritone and foreboding "Roadhouse Blues"—if the future is uncertain and the end is always near, why the hell not pop the top and swill a morning beer—probably appeals to fatalistic French existentialists. Or,* Jonathan japed to himself, *maybe poor Abelard sang "Light My Fire" to Héloïse and she, no more hesitating, obliged and set their night on fire, causing Abelard's (lusting then thrusting) hard drive to be cooked on a funeral pyre. How did that work out for the gelded scholar?* Jonathan made a mental note to throw back a Budweiser and crank up the Doors's "People Are Strange" when he returned to DC.

Food lovers love Paris because the food loves them right back. But Jonathan was a foodie outlier. Five-course Michelin meals he would forgo for salmon at the hotel or an omelet at a brasserie, preferably on the Left Bank. But this fan of Bacchus did indulge one inestimable French contribution to civilization. Before time was lost and in search of things vinous, Jonathan discovered an old wine shop favored by Marcel Proust on the Boulevard Haussman— Les Caves Auge—where he purchased a couple of bottles from Bordeaux. Bordeaux, the shop's oenologist explained to him, is on the west coast of France and is split by the Gironde Estuary, which divides into the Dordogne and Garonne Rivers. The major wine regions are on the Right Bank and the Left Bank. So Jonathan went with the expert's recommendations and bought a bottle of a Chateau Léoville Poyferré from Saint-Julien on the Left Bank and a bottle of Château Figeac from Saint-Emilion on the Right Bank. Over the course of his Paris stay, Jonathan would enjoy these fine wines, with fabulous French cheeses he bought at a fromagerie around the corner of the hotel, as he people-watched in the evenings in the Tuileries Garden.

After a day of thinking about dread and dead people, Jonathan decided to come alive by starting his early morning with a long run. He charted his course: to the Champs-Élysées, past the Arc de Triomphe, to Montmartre and the spectacular white-domed Sacré-Coeur Basilica in the eighteenth arrondissement and a glorious sunrise, and then back. He spent the rest of the day walking through the narrow tributary streets on the Right Bank, getting lost a few times, and otherwise wandering with no particular plan. Jonathan wistfully thought that it had been a long time since he did something so unorganized, so unplanned, so spontaneous and carefree. Precisely what Shelly had once dreamed they would do together. He was Joni Mitchell's free man in Paris, unfettered and alive. *But for the work I have taken on*, he ruefully realized, *I might be strolling Paris hand in hand with Shelly*.

The simple pleasures of Paris. Jonathan spent a couple of hours in the afternoon strolling through the Marche aux Fleurs, a flower market on the edge of the Île de la Cité. The vibrant colors and pungent smells were delightful, and he even bought a small bag of lavender from Provence, which he put in his left shirt pocket. He topped off his afternoon by moseying over to Square du Vert-Galant. There, Jonathan stretched out on the grass of this beautiful park with its gorgeous views of the Seine and enjoyed Parisian songs, including Èdith Piaf's mesmerizing "La Vie en Rose," being played by an old accordion musician. Listening to the melodious masterpiece—it took your kisses to reveal that love indeed is real—on a glorious day brought back to him words from Shelly that haunted him still: "A life of love is the best life of all." *Of course*, he thought, *life cannot sanely be lived with a fixed stare in the rearview mirror, but a treasured part of it is not easily forgotten*.

Thinking about his visit with Shelly years ago to the Art Institute of Chicago, Jonathan remembered something the American realist painter Edward Hopper once said: "If I could say it in words, there would be no reason to paint." The linguistically inexpressible given meaning on a canvass is what Jonathan experienced the next day at the Paris museums. The museums Shelly had talked about so much. At the Musée de l'Orangerie, Jonathan stared in awe at eight enormous *Water Lilies* murals by the impressionist painter Claude Monet. Monet called them an extension of his life, observing that without water, lilies cannot live, "as I am without art." Jonathan let that sentiment sink in. How diminished life would be without great art.

With the calm intensity of a birdwatcher, he spent hours enraptured by Monet's sublime genius. To take the simple foundational elements of water, lilies, and the sun and transform them through paint, brush, and imagination into aesthetic treasures was astounding to Jonathan. How many times did Shelly ask, What is life without art and music? He enjoyed works by the other greats, including Renoir, Matisse, Cézanne, and Picasso, but Jonathan was mesmerized by the *Water Lilies*. He thought that if he lived in Paris, he would be a weekly visitor. He thought, *No wonder Voltaire called Paris "terrestrial paradise."*

Jonathan anticipated that his next visit would be emotional but was not prepared for how enthralled he would be until he stepped inside the Musée d'Orsay. The building itself, the former Gare d'Orsay railway station, a magnificent building, harmonizing architecture with art. In particular, impressionist art. Where once the building transmitted trains, it now transmits culture and the legacy of immortals. Shared for all the world to treasure are works by Van Gogh, Monet, Manet, Renoir, Degas, and so many others whose artistic creativity enriches life, art that stirs passions, excites imagination, arouses emotions, and evokes memories. *Objects,* Jonathan thought, *only in a literal sense because they transcend into ideas and fill our brains with a sense of wonderment and an escape from the raw reality of the pedestrian impermanence of life.* He mused that, *in a former railway station on the banks of the Seine, in one marvelous city on a blue/green microscopic dot of a planet, fueled by an average star, in an infinite universe, 14 billion years after Big Bang, resides objective evidence that perhaps it's not all just particles and forces obeying differential equations. Okay, maybe there is no transcendental purpose to the world, but great art teaches us that there is meaning in our individual lives.*

Feeling as if he could relate, Jonathan took a deep breath when he saw the terribly tormented depiction in Van Gogh's *Self-Portrait*. The artist's *Church at Auvers*, and *Starry Night Over the Rhône* were more comforting. He admired Paul Sèrusier's iconic *The Talisman*, which inspired young painters calling themselves Les Nabis who were dedicated to renewing the art of painting. His solitary soul was intrigued by the lonely, vacant-looking faces of a man and woman drinking a glass of absinthe, a potent spirit known as "the green fairy," in Edgar Degas's *L'Absinthe*. This poignant painting, Jonathan was amused to learn, was initially derided by English critics as degrading and uncouth and a debasement of morals. Jonathan agreed with the French—art is art; it is not politics, sociology, or moral instruction. He was captivated by the quiet, calm, reflective expressions on the faces of two gentlemen card players as they sat across a small table from one another in Paul Cézanne's *The Card Players*. And he sheepishly spied Gustave Courbet's still somewhat shocking-when-you-see-it *L'Origine du Monde*. Courbet's simple yet vivid depiction of a vagina made Jonathan think, *No wonder some refer to a vagina as a penis fly trap*, and, *No wonder somebody eventually invented the Brazilian wax*.

And then more Claude Monet. Shelly had told him that Monet famously said that London without fog would not be beautiful, so he painted *London, Houses of Parliament. The Sun Shining through the Fog* as if to prove his point. Jonathan marveled at Monet's artistic genius with paintings such as *Women in the Garden, Regattas at Argenteuil,* and *Luncheon on the Grass*. Monet bequeathed to the human race his spectacular garden creation at Giverny, a must-see on Shelly's bucket list, and in those sensual surroundings painted countless gems. He called the garden he created and tirelessly cultivated his greatest masterpiece, saying he abhorred bare earth. It was there, Jonathan learned, that Monet constructed his lily pond and painted *Blue Water Lilies* and the arrestingly beautiful *The Artist's Garden at Giverny*, with its rows of irises in various shades of pink and purple under trees. Purple—lavender—was one of Jonathan's two favorite colors. The other emerald green. To Jonathan, those two colors represented joy and passion and love's possibilities—Shelly, sight and scent. And Jonathan was mesmerized by *Coquelicots*, a sublime painting of a young woman and child strolling through an undulating poppy field with vibrant red flowers on a cloudy yet sunny day. He remorsefully thought, *What if?*

A melancholic question punctuated by four Renoir paintings that caused Jonathan's pulse to quicken and his heart to palpitate. Feeling like he could not move, he sat down and just stared and stared. For twenty minutes Jonathan stared at Renoir's *Dance at Le Moulin de la Galette*, a snapshot of life on a Sunday afternoon at Moulin in Montmartre district. Then there was Renoir's *Dance in the Country*, with its theme of dancing at a ball. He wiped a tear. Two other dancing theme paintings also sent him back in time: *Dance in the City* and *Dance at Bougival*. Jonathan felt a yearning, a wistfulness overcoming him. He was awash in emotion. Ingrained in his memory was that wonderful day in Chicago at the Art Institute where Shelly embraced him and gushed that she had never felt so alive. He whispered her name to himself. He needed to leave.

Jonathan exited and headed to the banks of the Seine. Walking along the river, he reflected on a past that missed its future. Oh how he admired the impressionist painters for their recognition of the fleeting nature of what we see and experience, the ephemerality of our realities. He knew it to be all too true. As if it were all quickly vanishing glimpses. He sauntered back to his adopted bench at the Tuileries Garden. There he sat in quiet solitude. Just him and his thoughts. What ifs and choices dominated his thinking. What his life is, what it might have been, and what the future might have in store for him. Without the sanctuary of his twenty-four seven law practice to escape self-reflection and bury the rest of his life, Jonathan realized in the moment that it had been quite some time since he allowed himself to be so acutely aware of the profound consequences of choices he had made earlier in life. But then life seems to have more in store for us than we can ever anticipate. He sat and wondered.

SUBLIMITY, SERENITY, AND SACRIFICE

Jonathan's plan was to spend time in Paris, visit Normandy, return to Paris for a day or two, then fly home. The shadow of lost love made him consider visiting Provence and the Côte d'Azur, but on this visit time would not permit. So off he went to the Gare St. Lazare station to take the three-hour train ride from Paris northwest to the town of Bayeux and the Hotel Tardif, which would serve as Jonathan's base to explore the five beaches of Normandy and the American Cemetery, an emotional experience impossible to feel from reading books or watching films and newsreels.

First Bayeux, an enchanting, idyllic town. Just four miles south of the English Channel, this commune in the Calvados department in Normandy turned out to be a fortuitous find. Jonathan even enjoyed the apple brandy from the region, known simply as calvados. What Jonathan liked most about historic Bayeux, founded in the first century BC, was the pace and events of quotidian life. Where time seems to have slowed down and living life, being there, living life in the moment, family and friends, seemed to be the essence of existence. Not career, not ambition, and certainly not the unattainable quest for validation from external sources. He was being transported to a world far from the life he was otherwise living.

On Jonathan's first night, the Tardif's proprietor, with his faithful dog, Atlas, by his side, recommended that Jonathan walk over to the town center and check out the magnificent Cathédrale Notre-Dame, consecrated in 1077, and then enjoy music night, a summer midweek eclectic celebration of music and life. At various places throughout the main part of town, families enjoyed jazz, choirs, a cappella groups, rock, and symphony music as they sipped their wine, mingled with friends, and played with their children. Jonathan loved the festivities and camaraderie of the night, but he was also overwhelmed with a feeling of depressing lonely incompleteness. It was the enchantment of the evening that spurred him to do something unplanned and spontaneous. In the morning he would rent a motorbike and scoot over to Honfleur, an old port city where the Seine kisses the English Channel, roughly one hundred kilometers east of Bayeux.

Jonathan fell in love with Honfleur. As did many painters, including Monet, Courbet, and Boudin, who were entranced by the timber frames and slate-covered frontages of the houses and featured them in numerous paintings. Honfleur has a long history, but its present is what seduced Jonathan. He meandered through the quiet streets and popped in and out of what seemed like countless art galleries. Many of the paintings in the galleries were painted along Honfleur's splendid harbor, the Vieux Bassin, dating back to the seventeenth century. On this sunny day, Jonathan must have spotted fifty artists with paints and brushes and easels and canvasses sitting in wooden chairs around the harbor painting away, seemingly without a care in the world. Attentive only to the details of what they were observing and inspiringly re-creating and reimagining on a flat surface with colors and brushes and vivid imaginations. One hundred years before, Monet had encouraged artists to abandon the studio and paint on the spot. The Honfleur artists were heeding his call. Jonathan wandered back through the town and its narrow streets and cobbled alleys before ordering an egg baguette and a Perrier from a vendor. Midmorning meal in hand, he found a bench along the harbor and whiled away an hour or so watching the boats and the artists at work. Breathing in the refreshing air, feeling the sun, listening to the sounds, and forgetting about time. Just living life in the moment.

Feeling rejuvenated, Jonathan hopped on his motorbike and scooted back to Bayeux early afternoon and headed to the Bayeux tapestry. Described by the tapestry's conservator, a woman who

displayed an infectious passion for her work, as "one of the supreme achievements of the Norman Romanesque," Jonathan was
in awe of this eleventh-century masterpiece. The meticulously em-
broidered cloth, 230 feet long and 20 inches tall, depicts the events
leading up to the Norman conquest of England in 1066 and, to
Jonathan and those who visit it, is visually stunning and tells a vivid story without saying a single word. The trial lawyer in Jonathan
had often fantasized about trying a case completely with visuals,
and there he stood staring at evidence that it could be done with
the proper amount of imagination and execution. Jonathan agreed
wholeheartedly with the tapestry's conservator who offered the
opinion that "the tapestry's exquisite workmanship and the genius
of its guiding spirit combine to make it endlessly fascinating." Ever
the lawyer, Jonathan thought that the conservator would be a terrific jury trial graphics consultant.

With Honfleur and the tapestry fresh in mind, Jonathan completed his day with a meal at La Rapière. This quaint restaurant,
located in a small alleyway in the town, offered a few vegetarian
options and seated Jonathan in a stone room from the sixteenth
century. Perfect ambiance for an old Bordeaux, a half bottle of 1986
Haut-Brion. Haut-Brion was such an imbibing favorite of Thomas
Jefferson, Jonathan's waiter said, that he bought six cases when he
was in France and had them shipped to his Virginia estate, making
Haut-Brion the first of Bordeaux's famous five first- growth wines
to be imported into the United States. A bit of history to finish an
unforgettable day. More was in store.

Jonathan only had a couple of days left, so he hired a tour guide
for his D-Day experience and lessons. Serendipity struck. A Parisian transplant who had been doing Normandy tours for ten years,
Nicole Laurent was stylish in silk scarves she flaunted with pa-
nache and possessed a certain French insouciance and savoir faire.
She was knowledgeable, urbane, a tad haughty, and unfortunately,
a chain smoker. A habit Jonathan detested but many French apparently believed was de rigueur. He immediately bonded with his
witty guide, who somehow blended the virtue of French fatalism
with the vice of American optimism for just the right mixture for
an engaging personality. Nicole also seemed to know every square

inch of the beaches, five in all, stretching for fifty miles along the Normandy coast.

Listening to Nicole effortlessly talk about American history caused this emerging Francophile to remember something Professor Bulldozen used to despair about law students and lawyers. He called them intellectual eunuchs. The professor with the corrosive eyes complained that they don't know "stuff." He called them process thinkers who don't have much substantive knowledge of anything. Bulldozen used to say that even the best and brightest typically had "river mountain brains." Like the water rushing down a mountainside as the snow was melting in the spring, their minds are quick and energetic but not deep. Their brains can't stay in one place for more than a nanosecond. They see clearly but almost always through a very small keyhole. Jonathan couldn't help but think that Gladstone Bulldozen would enjoy Nicole's company.

From west to east, the five Normandy beaches had code names: Utah, Omaha, Gold, Juno, and Sword. The invasion, part of Operation Overlord, was an allied effort of 150,000 American, British, and Canadian soldiers, most of them young—very, very young. The Great Invasion, beginning on June 6, 1944, was Hitler's greatest defeat, Nicole defiantly told Jonathan. Affecting the snide manner of a supercilious Parisian sophisticate, Nicole jeered that "we French drink wine and make love while Germans drink beer and fornicate."

General Dwight D. Eisenhower, supreme commander of the Allied Expeditionary Force, had forebodingly feared before the invasion that unpredictably rough weather could foil meticulous plans. As Nicole led Jonathan on long walks along the various beaches, he was transported in time and experienced firsthand the blustery vagaries of the coastal tides and weather that so complicated planning and logistics. Jonathan had a surreal feeling as he climbed into the German bunkers that he would look out to the channel and see the Americans disembarking the ships and storming the beaches. His heart swelled with patriotic pride as he appreciated for the first time the courage of the young men who changed the direction and allied fortunes of World War II. How historic, audacious, and brilliant battle plans conceived by the elders depend for their success on the brave and courageous execution by very young soldiers, many not too far removed from puberty.

The allies came in overwhelming forces by air and by sea. Nicole told Jonathan countless stories of the bravery of British and Canadian soldiers at Sword and the Canadians at Juno, and she showed him the fishing village of Arromanches captured by the British after they had stormed and secured beach exits at Gold. With excitement and her hands moving rapidly, Nicole recounted how, "between the hours of 3:00 a.m. and 5:00 a.m., approximately one thousand British RAF bombers strafed the German defenses east of Bayeux with five thousand pounds of deadly bombs. At the moment of landing—the H Hour—the Americans sent an additional twelve hundred bombers to support the RAF to bomb the areas around Omaha Beach. It was a massive display of arial power.

"The naval display was equally impressive," Nicole marveled. "A vast fleet of ships filled the channel, the largest convoy ever assembled. The soldiers, sailors, and airmen who were part of D-Day understood that they were embarking on a heroic mission of destiny." Nicole shared with Jonathan a copy of the message Eisenhower sent to them on the eve of the mission. It read in part:

> You are about to embark upon the Great Crusade, toward which we have striven these many months. The eyes of the world are upon you. The hopes and prayers of liberty-loving people everywhere march with you. In company with our brave Allies and brothers-in-arms on other Fronts, you will bring about the destruction of the German war machine, the elimination of Nazi tyranny over the oppressed peoples of Europe, and security for ourselves in a free world. ... I have full confidence in your courage, devotion to duty and skill in battle. We will accept nothing less than full victory!

American duty and skill were on full display on the beaches of Utah and Omaha. As Jonathan and Nicole traversed the beaches, it was only then that the young lawyer used to parsing words realized how misleading it was to think of these vast swaths of coastline as a "beach." They seemed to go on forever, haunted by death yet symbolic of liberation. At Utah Beach, which turns northward to form the eastern side of Cotentin, the Americans suffered their fewest casualties.

The bloodiest battle was on Omaha Beach, west of Bayeux, where Jonathan and Nicole spent the most time. She knew the details by heart. "Two thousand four hundred troops were killed there. Vertical stone cliffs, especially at Pointe du Hoc, made it impossible for vehicles to scale, and almost but not quite impossible for the courageous Americans on foot. Omaha has a twenty-five-mile stretch of coastline, and the Germans were well fortified with bunkers and an antitank ditch." Nicole recounted how one American soldier described the horror as he was about to leave ship for sand: "As our boat touched the sand and the ramp went down, I became a visitor to hell." Jonathan was emotionally overwhelmed, especially as Nicole described how Army Rangers had valiantly sealed a massive promontory at Pointe du Hoc and eventually took out heavy German artillery. Nicole said, "That was probably the toughest of the toughest assignments on all of D-Day." Jonathan was overcome with eerie stillness as he imagined the carnage on the beach, with scattered piles of young dead men who so bravely fought against Nazi and fascist tyranny.

Nicole's last stop was the American Cemetery, located in Colleville-sur-Mer, about eleven miles northwest of Bayeux. The first American cemetery on European soil. From D-Day through August 21, 1944, more than two million allied troops landed in northern France. Almost seventy-three thousand were killed and 153,000 were wounded or missing. Nicole and Jonathan arrived at the American Cemetery shortly before the noon hour. Jonathan was not prepared for the raw emotion he was about to experience.

It was a surprisingly sunny day with a soft cool breeze blowing off the English Channel. The cemetery has a semicircular colonnade with a loggia at each end with WWII maps and narratives of military operations. In the center stands a bronze statue with an apt description, *Spirit of American Youth Rising from the Waves*. To the west ten thousand perfectly aligned graves with ivory crosses cover the undulating grounds. As the clock struck noon, dozens of British WW II veterans assembled on the platform. These heroes were bedecked in blue double-breasted blazers, some wearing berets, all wearing medals. Some stood on their own, others with the help of canes or crutches. Still others were in wheelchairs. The lines, creases, spots, and wrinkles on their faces reflected both age and war. It was impossible to look into those noble faces and not see valiant soldiers. Defenders of democratic values and Western civilization. They were gathered to hear a small group of high school girls from Minnesota sing the national anthem. Their soft, beautiful, mezzo-soprano voices brought the old warriors to tears. Jonathan joined them.

Nicole let Jonathan slowly stroll alone through the gravesites. Again, he was astonished while reading the crosses, many with the Star of David, at the ages of the young men, boys really, who courageously fought and ultimately defeated Hitler and the Nazis. When Jonathan was eighteen, nineteen, twenty, he was in a safe classroom majoring in A's so he could go to law school and make a lot of money in pursuit of a life of independence, or he was in a warm bar drinking cold beer and listening to the syncopated rhythms and bent notes of improvising jazz musicians. These buried young men only heard the baleful sounds of bombs and bullets and shrieking pain as they breathed their last breaths making a better life possible by saving Western civilization.

Jonathan thought about these selfless young men, and he thought about Judge Roy and Hamburger Hill. He thought about their extraordinary sacrifices, with blood, scars, lost limbs, and lost lives to show for them. Disgusted with himself, he angrily thought, *What the fuck have I ever sacrificed for another human being? Not a damn thing.* He felt ashamed. His life felt selfish and trivial. He shared his feelings with Nicole, who had heard similar sentiments before echoed at the American Cemetery. Philosophical in response, Nicole wisely advised, "Yes, yes, but why feel this way? Feel lucky that you have never had to face the brutality of war. It is hell. Live life, embrace its possibilities, it ends soon enough. If faced with a difficult choice, just hope you do the honorable thing. What else can be expected? C'est la vie." Jonathan would not soon forget Nicole.

The next morning Jonathan returned to Paris and spent a gloriously sunny afternoon at the Jardin du Luxembourg, a beautiful, large public park a few kilometers south of the hotel in the sixth arrondissement. Tree-lined promenades, gorgeous flowerbeds, the Medici Fountain, a sensual and visual treat. In the moment, he remembered the Beltway Buddha's admonition to seek out more in life than an all-consuming job and heeded his counsel by reading Yeats's poem "The Choice"—about the need to choose between the perfection of life or work. Far away from work, he sat and watched people perfecting life. People living their daily lives. People ambling, kids playing, blowing bubbles, people laughing, people forgiving, roller-skating, skateboarding, jogging, walking pooches, pushing strollers, having picnics, reading *Le Monde, Liberation,* and *Le Parisien*, decompressing, sitting on blankets, listening to music, strumming guitars, playing frisbee, tossing balls, chatting with friends, painting pictures, reading poems, writing poems, clicking cameras, sharing secrets, soaking sun, napping, reading books, holding hands, pressing lips, sharing love. *What is lovelier than a sweet kiss in a beautiful park on a gorgeous day?* he wondered. Young and old lovers alike. Jonathan smiled and thought, *Maybe they all know Nicole.*

This was Jonathan's last night in Paris. Determined to go out in memorable style, he splurged on a fabulous dinner/music cruise on the magnificent Seine. *What a spectacular way to see the City of Light*, he thought.

Jonathan sat at a table with two welcoming couples from London who looked to be about his age and encouraged him to join them. After some champagne, Jonathan decided to treat with the wine. His companions were more than willing recipients, drinking their fair share of three incredible bottles of 1992 Claude Dugat. From the oenologist at Les Caves Auge on the Boulevard Haussman, Jonathan learned that the eponymous Claude Dugat winery is located in Gevrey-Chambertin in Burgundy, has some of the oldest vines in the region, and Claude Dugat himself tends the vines that produce his wines. Jonathan, suppressing a hint of jealousy that his companions were couples, thought there was probably no better way to end his stay in France than by slowly floating down the Seine, sipping a fine Claude Dugat, and listening to a jazz violinist play "Over the Rainbow"—and the dreams that you dream of once in a lullaby. An evening of joie de vivre. Bonsoir, Shelly. Viva la France.

PERFORMANCE ART PERSONA

Travel vacations in search of new experiences can be cathartic, offering outlets for reflection, expanding horizons, self-realization, and even personal renewal. But then, like New Year's resolutions, they can also quickly fade from mind as the demands of everyday life, making a living, and old routines reassert themselves. Perhaps not always to be forgotten, but buried somewhere in the recesses of the brain. So it was for Jonathan. Back in the states, his focus once again narrowed. He acutely realized that when you are in a rat race, you either run, get run over, or get out. He was in the rat race of Big Law competition and was not about to get run over and had no plan to get out. So he continued to run, at a pace that far eclipsed the pace of the other competitors. In Big Law there is no standing still or calibrating the pace. It's a full-throttle race.

He returned to DC re-energized but not reevaluated. Feelings of insignificance, inadequacy, alienation, despair, perfecting life, and sacrifice faded away. Desires for the challenge of the biggest cases, money that can buy independence, flowing from having the biggest clients and cases, marching to his own tune, fear of ordinariness and mediocrity, all raced back to front of mind in an intense rush. But he returned from Paris with one intangible in particular: the fervent belief that life, and certainly trial work, is, in major part, performance art. He thought of Shakespeare's Jaques in *As You Like It:* "All the world's a stage, All men and women merely players; They have their exits and their entrances; And one man in his time plays many parts." Jaques explained the seven evolving parts of short life one by one, ending depressingly with a man's "second childishness and mere oblivion, sans teeth, sans eyes, sans taste, and sans everything." Jonathan wasn't looking that dreadfully far ahead, and instead had something more dapper in mind as he double downed on playing one part, trial lawyer, with a carefully crafted persona for the stage of the courtroom that would now fully emerge from its embryonic development. Even more separation from the dreaded herd in Big Law and on the stage of life where, like cherry blossoms, he would exit soon enough.

The architect of his own persona started with diet and dress. He was already trending in this dietary direction as the year 2000 approached, the feared apocalyptic Y2K. Now he exerted his inviolable will with even more discipline. Morning breakfast consisted of blueberry yogurt with additional blueberries, a banana, vitamins, and twelve ounces of orange juice. He would substitute an omelet with green and red peppers from time to time, especially when he was on the road. For dinner, it was grilled salmon and a steamed green vegetable and carrots, with a small arugula salad with broccoli and avocado, with some accommodations when he was on the road. During the day, water and almonds, often a Granny Smith green apple.

Jonathan varied his dinner regimen on the weekends. On Saturday nights he dined out, alternating Indian and Italian. Sunday night, he mostly experimented with vegetarian soups, always with a red burgundy from Chambolle-Musigny or Gevrey-Chambertin and jazz. For this increasingly solipsistic soul, there was no better way to chop garlic, onions, and peppers and escape for a few hours than to sip a pinot noir treasure while listening to the smooth, smoky sophisticated intelligence of Diana Krall playing piano and singing jazz tunes or Grover Washington Jr. blowing his suave soprano saxophone on "Winelight" or "Mr. Magic."

Jonathan's diet, combined with his exercise routine, kept him slim and full of stamina. Running and swimming were his predominant forms of exercise. On the road and in bad weather, he would use rowing and elliptical machines at hotel health clubs, which were invariably unoccupied at his 4:45 a.m. start time. Jonathan loved early morning runs, for him an ideal way to explore cities when he traveled. And throughout his career, he would travel to virtually every American city. For upper body tone, besides swimming, the performance artist did lightweight arm exercises and stretch ropes. Any adversary would be hard-pressed to match his mental and physical stamina and discipline.

After Paris, Jonathan wore his last Brooks Brothers suit and button-down shirt. A certain understated elegant solemnity had always been to his liking, and as one who made a living trying to persuade everyday Americans on juries, he was careful to avoid flash and conspicuous displays of money. From Judge Roy he learned that trial lawyers should be in uniform. No gaudy Gucci, Armani, Savile Row chalk stripes, silk pocket squares, bow ties, or cufflinks. His apparel needed to authoritatively refine, not ridiculously caricature him. Jonathan eventually found an old-world tailor who made his suits. Precisely, for each new year, two navy blue with thin, light blue pinstripes, and two solid royal blue suits. Colors that represent trust, integrity, knowledge, reliability, and professionalism. His tailor also made his shirts. A dozen white, straight collars with thin blue pinstripes. Classy, not flashy. And two pair of black Allen Edmonds dress shoes. Perpetually polished. All complemented by six ties, three emerald green and three of slightly different shades of lavender.

It was always four suits. Typically there are twenty-one working days in a month. Two hundred and forty in a year, minus a few for holidays. Jonathan wore each suit in order, fifty-five to sixty times a year. At year-end he donated suits, shirts, shoes, and ties to charity and started over. To Jonathan, the world and his profession dodged the apocalypse of Y2K when the clocks worked at midnight on January 1, 2000. But years later the apocalypse came in full force with the advent of the casual clothes catastrophe in business and law firms. Jonathan feared, *What's next, the ten plagues?* Not surprisingly, he bucked the frumpy revolution and wore suits while the male herd unimaginatively switched to khakis, Oxford cloth or polo shirts, and scruffy shoes. Recalling Oscar Wilde's admonition that the first duty in life is to assume a pose, Jonathan was poised for the twenty-first century. Or so he thought.

MONEY, GRAVITATIONAL
FORCES, AND BLACK HOLES

The year 2000 arrived without incident. London's Big Ben struck twelve midnight and heralded the new millennium. The months of January and February blew westward winds of good fortune for Jonathan and Cabot, Lodge & Biddle. In rapid succession he was hired by powerful corporate defendants in cell phones, cigarettes, and car repair parts and insurance. Each one of his new clients had been sued by classes of consumers for violating the antitrust laws by conspiring with competitors to charge them higher-than-competitive prices. Jonathan didn't smoke or own a car and barely used a cell phone. Perhaps a curious counsel choice, except for what mattered most: he had a track record of success. The winds of fortune were blowing westward because all the cases were filed in San Francisco. Soon to become Jonathan's adopted city.

About each of the three cases, Jonathan felt conflicting emotions, and it had nothing to do with being on the side of the alleged wrongdoer. These were prized clients and cases for a Big Law firm. They were going to pay Jonathan and his law firm tens of millions of dollars to crush their customers who dared to complain and challenge the extra-high prices his clients were conspiratorially charging them. It was the money that created the tension, though not because of the pang of a conscience. Morality had nothing to do with it. Class-action lawsuits were becoming pervasive in civil litigation and representing corporate defendants facing the onslaught pumped firm profits. Jonathan very much wanted the big bucks and the rainmaker moniker that came with the money. Instead, it was about the nature of the performer's stage. Class-action cases rarely make it to the jury. Yes, his two milk cases did, but they were the extreme exception and most of those cases ultimately settled. Indeed, Jonathan's Atlanta case, as well as the cases in the other southern states, settled shortly after his opening statement.

In the main, class-action cases are for paper pushers and brief writers, not courtroom warriors. They almost always follow one of three paths, none of which pulsated the blood in Jonathan's jury trial lawyer veins. Path one, the defendant wins the case on some legal motion before any trial. Path two, the judge rejects the individual plaintiff's argument that the case should be treated as a class and the case goes away or settles for a nominal amount of money. Path three, the judge decides to treat the case as a class action and the defendant settles because the monetary risk to the defendant of trying and losing the case is too daunting. Jonathan wanted to try cases before juries, not push legal papers and negotiate settlements. As a monied tool for corporate America, he wanted to be fighting on the battlefield, not futzing around the peace table.

Ay, the money, therein lies the rub. Jonathan was an up-and-coming young partner in Big Law, and bringing in three big corporate clients shelling out huge legal fees would catapult him way up the compensation ladder, when most other partners, at best, slowly climb rung by rung and usually hit a plateau ten time zones away from the top. Cabot, Lodge & Biddle, like Big Law everywhere by the year 2000, was laser-focused on money. Lots and lots of money. The pretense that law was a clubby profession rather than a cutthroat business was quickly eroding away. Big Law was unquestionably big business, and the trend would only intensify in the ensuing years. Firms were partnerships in name only, and the expansive gulf between the majority of partners on the low end of the compensation ladder and the very few at the top was continuing to widen. Jonathan aimed to be far away from the howling herd by securing his rightful place on the right tail of the bell curve, where Big Law's animal farm pigs rolled in their dough.

Some partners managed to climb the ladder through office politics and firm management, but by and large, the golden rule was the ticket to the top: those who had the gold ruled. When deciding whether to accept new business, the amoral questions overwhelmingly reduced to: "One, will the matter generate huge fees, two, can the client pay, and three, do we have a conflict, and if so can we get a waiver or maneuver around it?" If the answers are yes, yes, and no/yes, then full speed ahead. No speed bumps, no pumping the brakes, to figure out whether the cases are actually interesting or ethically challenging.

Trane, still an unreconstructed liberal with a moral compass and a curmudgeon about the money-centric obsession of Big Law, wandered into Jonathan's office. As was his wont, he embraced the role of provocateur of principles. "So, I hear we're now representing one of the merchants of death and doubt. I suppose blood money is still green."

"Bad morning, Jack? I'm guessing you mean our new cigarette company client?" By this time in their relationship, Jonathan was used to Trane's jousts and jabs. Like most Big Law firms, Jonathan's firm had two tiers of partners. The first class were the equity partners, the ones with ownership and voting rights. Even among them, there was great stratification and a wide gulf between those few at the top and everybody else. Then there was the second class of partners, nonequity partners, mostly young partners without their own clients or older partners running out of gas and on their way out. The second tier were partners in name only—a rose by any other name ... indeed, it matters what one really is, not what one is called, and what nonequity partners really are, is something qualitatively different than the equity partners. Increasingly their ranks were as large as that of the equity partners. In reality, the second tier of partners were highly paid associates, making even less than the lowest paid equity partners. Trane returned to the firm after his third stint in rehab as a member of the second tier. Not surprisingly, this group tended to be even more cynical about Big Law and its obsession with money and pandering to the rainmakers, frequently asking, How much is enough?

"That's the one. I suppose since we're defending banks and mortgage lenders for perpetuating racial discrimination by systemic redlining, defending a major pesticide manufacturer that poisons crops and farmers, a pharmaceutical giant promoting anti-psychotic drugs for dangerous off-label uses and paying kickbacks to complicit doctors, and a breast implant manufacturer whose products mess up silicone sisters' autoimmune systems, we might as well carry a spear for big tobacco."

"You getting particular in your older years? Come on, Jack, everybody is entitled to a defense, and it pays the bills. That's how it works in Big Law."

"Yeah, and for these cancer peddlers, the best their dirty money can buy."

"What's the problem, you smoke?"

"Please, one lousy addiction at a time. I'm now sober and these damn little cigar/cigarettes are next on my break-the-bad-habit list. Your client is a real gem, a twofer with both addiction and cancer. Not to mention a peddler of misinformation about the causal link between tobacco and cancer and paying off some smarmy scientists to prostitute themselves by lying about the health risks of smoking. Aren't we proud?"

"What would be the point of turning down the work? They would just go to another Big Law competitor and we would be out millions in fees. You know profitability is the name of the game now."

Exasperated, Trane complained, "Jesus Christ, since when did everything hang on the issue of partner profitability? Look, I know we have to make a lot of money and pay our partners big bucks, but why do we have to act as if maximizing profits is the be-all and end-all of what we do? It's like Big Law managers are worshipping at the altar of that conservative economist Milton Friedman who preaches that the sole—the *sole*—social responsibility of business is to maximize profits. And that's supposed to be enlightening? Give me a break. Can't we at least sue some of these noxious corporate scofflaws, for crying out loud?"

"That's not happening. Hodges and Truckle would have a conniption if we took a plaintiff's case against a major corporation. But get with the times, Jack. You might think it's a Faustian pact with the devil and money, but partner profitability is Big Law's raison d'être. No doubt about it."

"Bullshit." In the world of *is* versus *ought*, Trane knew Jonathan was right, but the old warrior was not one to easily give up the good fight.

"You might not like it. You might not think we *should* worship at the altar of profitability, but that *is* the market reality. Everything else is just window dressing."

"Don't you think you are overstating the case?" Trane, now himself a teacher of the youth, admired Socrates, who enjoyed teasing out moral issues with penetrating questions exposing contradictions and going to the heart of the matter.

"Not at all. Lawyers in Big Law are free agents now and have little loyalty. Money mercenaries. And money, make no mistake about it, is the only glue that holds firms together. Profits drop even slightly, and watch the best ones head for the exits. And then the herd will stampede out.

Rainmakers are Big Law's best assets, and they go up and down the elevators every day. The only thing that keeps them put is the money, and lots of it. And the only way to get the most money is to shill for corporate America and their big-ass problems."

Dissatisfied, Trane said, "Yeah, I gag every time I hear some smug Big Law managing partner brag and blather on about firm culture when money is the only thing they really care about. And by the best you mean the lawyers with the biggest clients. They aren't necessarily the same, present company excluded, of course."

"No need to get metaphysical, Jack, but the fact is Big Law, us, needs to pay top dollar to the top rainmakers or risk losing them. Look what's happening in New York where shallow, avaricious lawyers are leaving elite firms where they are already making millions just because some other firm dangles a few more pieces of gold and silver in front of them. They'll offer up some bullshit reason for leaving like, 'I couldn't pass on this unique opportunity to grow my practice,' or 'My new firm has a better platform for my practice,' when everybody with half a brain knows it's always for more money. Or, supposedly, they don't feel they get enough respect—translation: they feel underpaid. But lose your rainmakers and watch your firm collapse or sink into mediocrity. And we both know that firms don't have a lot of rainmakers."

"Did Baxter Hodges pay some fucking consultant $100,000 to

provide that bullshit cover so he could coddle some sorry-ass, narcissistic prima donnas?"

"Funny," Jonathan laughed. "The consultants do say that, but this time they're right. And you and I both know that the only time the consultants get it right is when they tell us something we already know. Not bad work, if you can get it."

"Maybe it's a good thing I'm teaching the young folks something useful, like how to try a case they'll *never* get to try, and not practicing anymore," Trane said with dripping sarcasm. "I think this way of running a law firm sucks. Dollars, dollars, fucking dollars. That's all Big Law partners ever think about anymore. Some moral compass. Is that any way to live a good life?"

"Like it or not, that's the nature of the beast, and it's only intensifying. It's like crack cocaine: the more money Big Law partners make, the more they want. It becomes like a sense of entitlement. And the more rewarded a habit is, the harder it is to break."

"Yeah, Big Law partners think they have a moral right to increase the millions they make year after year. What a crock of you-know-what. And don't I know about bad habits. ... You know I'm not a particularly religious man, but maybe Big Law partners should read some Matthew 19 in the Bible, when Jesus says it is easier for a camel to go through the eye of a needle than for a rich man to go to heaven."

"Jack, maybe you should help out on the pro bono committee."

"Don't yank my chain, Jonathan, you know Big Law only pays lip service to pro bono, and their smug, self-satisfied public bragging about it is a marketing fraud. But that's a conversation for another day."

"Yeah, talk about fig leaves. But look, Jack, there's no standing still in Big Law, and if we want to run with the big dogs, we have to be a big dog. And that takes money and big corporate clients with big-ass problems. Big Law in the twenty-first century, or something like that."

"You know, Jonathan, when Tennyson wrote "The Charge of the Light Brigade," he was extolling the suicidal cavalry as heroes when he wrote about them, 'Ours is not to reason why, ours is but to do and die.' Perhaps blindly following blundering orders in the name of duty is appropriate for soldiers in war, but it seems to me we need to be more discerning in asking why we are representing some of the clients we represent."

"Look, Jack, the bigger the troubles our clients are facing, the more they need our help. And every one of our competitors is falling all over themselves to defend the biggest corporations with the biggest problems in the biggest lawsuits."

As he stood up to leave, Trane groaned, "Whatever gets you through the night, do it wrong or do it right, it's all right. I miss John Lennon. It all sounds like self-serving bullshit to me. I can hear Springsteen singing in my ear, 'Oh, baby, Big Law rips the bones from your back, it's a death trap, it's a suicide rap, the associates better get out while they're young.' Okay, Jonathan, this tramp is born to run, too much depressing talk for one day."

"Wait a minute. Think about this. When you started here at the firm, how many lawyers were there?" Jonathan agreed with F. Scott Fitzgerald that highly intelligent people can simultaneously hold two opposing ideas in mind and still function, and even though Big Law had spiraled down the degenerate path of money fetishism, he admired Trane's insistence on trying to improve the state of affairs. Although he didn't mind at all when Trane challenged him for being an apologist for the money-centrism of Big Law, he constantly felt a need to explain and justify, which gave Trane a reason to hope. He continued to believe that his protégé would one day grow weary of the one-dimensional life of Big Law.

"I was number forty-five."

"And I bet you knew everyone in the firm."

"Well, I did. And when I started, we were more selective in the cases we took on, by the way." Score one for Trane.

"And when you started, the firm had its main office in DC and a small office in New York. Now we have eight hundred lawyers and counting in ten offices across the country and one in London. We'll likely have more international offices in the near future and continue to increase our headcount. How many partners do you think know one another?"

"I get the point. It's a lot more impersonal now," Trane sighed.

"Impersonal? The fact is most partners hardly know one another and half of them I wouldn't recognize if I saw them in the elevator. We're all mostly strangers to one another and having an annual partner retreat only underscores the fact that we're better off that way. I always come away from the few retreats I have attended thinking, How in the hell did Goober, Gomer, and Forrest Gump ever make partner where I practice? Partner get-togethers make me think divorce, not vow renewal."

"So your point is money is the glue that holds it all together?"

"It's the only glue that keeps firms together. Why would I or any other successful partner stick around with a bunch of folks I don't really know, many, honestly, I don't professionally respect all that much, unless I was getting paid damn well for it? I wouldn't and neither would you and neither would anybody who had options."

"So all of the happy talk about firm culture is just bullshit?" Trane rhetorically asked as he puffed away on his smoke and stroked his bearded chin a few times. Trane was delighting in forcing Jonathan to say the words. He thought of James Baldwin ("Not everything that is faced can be changed, but nothing can be changed until it is faced").

"Honestly, yes, it is. But you know that. Every Big Law firm brags about its culture, but what is it really? Partners are only satisfied if they are making a lot of money, both at their firms and in comparison to the firms they consider to be like them. Even then, ninety percent of them still bitch about being underpaid. If the money starts to go south, the culture will quickly be one of abandon ship. It will be a cold day in hell before you hear some partner say something like, 'You know, the money sucks, but the culture is great, so I think I'll stay.' That will never happen. Never in a million years."

"So, Jonathan, what you are really saying is that there is some type of inexorable gravitational force in Big Law that pulls everything to the altar of money and profitability. That firms actually have no choice in the matter. Either keep making more and more money or die."

"That's a good way to put it, Jack. Maybe even a black hole. Big Law has gotten too close to the event horizon of money and profitability; there is no escape and no returning. And as long as Big Law partners continue to have insatiable wants for more money, the rules of engagement are clear as a goat's ass, an expression I heard in Atlanta in the milk cases. Get the biggest cases that pay the most money. Pay your rainmakers top dollar and deal with the rest of the partners as best as you can. Sure, they'll grumble from time to time, but they know as well as anybody that they can't go anywhere else and make more money. And if a few do, who really cares? Besides, they wake up every day pinching themselves over the money they're making and praying that it won't all go away."

"Nothing like worshipping the golden calf, and that didn't end well for the Israelites. Money fetishism like the fucking private equity vultures. That's what Big Law is becoming, or already is," Trane bemoaned, as he slowly shook his large head. "And I like your black hole analogy—the light goes out in a black hole, you know. Has the light gone out in Big Law?"

"I suppose it depends on your perspective. But it's nothing but a big money game. A few pro bono efforts here and there and insipid happy talk about culture, but it's all about the money. Like I said, Jack, Big Law in the twenty-first century."

"Okay, on that note, I really am out of here. But do me at least one favor: work on upgrading the quality of the clients you bring into the firm."

"I'll see what I can do." But for now, Jonathan was playing by the values and rules of Big Law success.

GOLDEN CITY

Bringing in just one of the three new San Francisco cases would have been a boon for the firm and Jonathan's career. Bringing in all three was a bonanza. More than twenty lawyers worked full time on them. The legal fees generated in 2000 made Jonathan one of the top five producers in his firm, an extraordinary achievement for a young partner. At the end of the year, the firm's management put him in the top half of all partners on the compensation ladder. He was well on the way to being the master of his own fate, his overriding life ambition.

The young warrior's new cases introduced him to San Francisco and Northern California. It was love at first sight. With its rich history, cultural diversity, temperate climate, and spectacular bay views, Jonathan could not get enough of the Golden City and surrounding area. Most of all, he simply liked being there. He liked how it felt and how it made him feel. Many a trip he would fly out a day early or stay an extra day to explore some aspect of the city or surrounding area. Peripatetic by nature, he loved to walk, walk everywhere around San Francisco, climb its famous hills, and take his morning runs along Embarcadero.

He delighted in catching a boat at the Ferry Building, cruise through the bay past Alcatraz, and arrive at the seaside village of Sausalito at the northern end of the Golden Gate Bridge. There, he would enjoy Sausalito's Mediterranean climate, stroll around, take in the sights, peruse the various art galleries, and enjoy a splendid

California cabernet, preferably an older Dominus or Shafer Hillside Select, as he watched the evening fall on San Francisco to the south. Sometimes he would stay the night at the wonderful Casa Madrona with its splendid views of the bay, other times return amid the cool evening breezes wafting off the sparkling water. He fondly remembered one stay at the Casa Madrona where he hitchhiked one early morning to the magnificent Muir Woods eight miles away and hiked its six miles of towering redwood trails before thumbing a ride back to Sausalito. He felt something of a transcendental connection to this spectacular place when he learned that the land was donated by some congressman with the surname of Kent and that an antitrust crusader, President Teddy Roosevelt, the "Trust Buster," was the one to declare the land a national monument.

Like so many who journey north from San Francisco to the Napa Valley and Sonoma wine country, Jonathan was seduced by the scenic views and sensuous, sybaritic life. He toured Napa Valley by bicycle and loved peddling on the Silverado Trail and journeying over to beautiful Pope Valley and back. Spa and mud baths in Calistoga were treats he experienced for the first time, as well as a hot air balloon ride down the valley. But what Jonathan enjoyed most was tasting and learning about the wines, especially the cabernet sauvignons of Napa and the pinot noirs of Sonoma and the Russian River Valley.

A trip Jonathan would never forget, and years later would sentimentally revisit in an effort to save his soul and restore his faith in love, was the time he rented a Harley-Davidson and rode from San Francisco to Napa and Sonoma, continuing on to a quaint coastal artist community called Jenner. Journeying to Jenner, Jonathan traveled Highway 116 west from the rustic town of Guerneville to the Pacific Coast. The road follows the magnificent Russian River, offering breathtaking views along the way. Jonathan pulled off the side of the road as he approached the mouth of the Russian River and watched it peacefully empty out into the ocean. How beautiful and sublime, he thought. Arriving in Jenner, he parked his Harley and walked down from a cliff to watch the sea lions, elephant seals, and harbor seals frolic in the water and sleep on the shore. It all seemed so timeless, so detached from the rat race of his life. He stayed the night at a cabin inn, sipping a 1997 Robert Mondavi Reserve as he watched a glorious sunset over a panoramic view of the Pacific Ocean. As he sipped his wine, he drifted off into lazy, hazy daydreams about existence, lost love, his past, chance, and choices. Only the disappearance of the sun over the water disturbed his remembrances.

IT'S JUST BUSINESS

Of Jonathan's three California cases, the first one to have a major hearing was the automobile replacement parts insurance case. The question of the day was whether to treat the case as a class action. The judge scheduled the hearing for a full day. Jonathan was selected by the group of defendants to deliver one of the two main defense arguments. Prepped and ready, he headed out for an early-morning run along the San Francisco Bay. He returned to the hotel at 6:30 a.m., 9:30 a.m. in the east. Life seemed so normal. He was on automatic pilot, in a groove and feeling good, anticipating that the day was going to go well. Then the new reality of life in the United States in the twenty-first century shook Jonathan to his core, as it did to Americans everywhere. It was Tuesday, September 11, 2001. When the unsuspecting lawyer clicked on CNN to catch some news, he watched the Twin Towers inferno in horror. There would be no class-action hearing that day. Jonathan didn't know it at the time, but he would soon learn about the 9/11 events in painful detail, for reasons that would infuriate Trane and make others, especially younger lawyers at CLB, seethe with anger.

At 8:45 a.m. on 9/11, American Airlines Boeing 767, loaded with twenty thousand gallons of fuel, barreled into the north tower of the World Trade Center in lower Manhattan. An inferno exploded on the eightieth floor of the 110-story skyscraper. Innocent human beings were immediately incinerated. Hundreds of innocent lives horrifically extinguished by gas and fire. Hundreds more were trapped on the upper floors. Eighteen minutes later, a United Airlines Boeing 767 crashed into the south tower near the sixtieth floor. These wanton acts of international terrorism on American soil unfolded before the eyes of shocked and disbelieving Americans who sat glued to their television screens. Like the 1963 JFK assassination, years after the event, people would tell you exactly where they were on the murderous morning of September 11.

Nineteen deranged terrorists, primarily from Saudi Arabia, and some living in the United States for years, had easily smuggled box cutters and knives through security at three East Coast airports and boarded four early-morning flights bound for California. Warped by ideology and possessed by a murderous monomania intent on maximum destruction, these maniacal killers had deliberately, dastardly, chosen their particular planes—planes loaded with fuel for long, cross-country flights. These soulless saboteurs commandeered four passenger jets, carrying business and leisure travelers, and converted the jets into fiery murder missiles.

As Americans watched death, destruction, and disintegration in lower Manhattan, they would soon shockingly learn that the carnage was not over. Two hundred and thirty miles south of New York, American Airlines flight 77 circled over DC like a suicidal vulture before heading straight for the west side of the Pentagon and a direct assault on the country's military headquarters. This happened at 9:45 a.m., before workers on the East Coast had their morning coffee break and people on the West Coast had finished breakfast and getting their children ready for school. More murdered Americans. One hundred twenty-five Pentagon personnel and civilians were murdered, as were all sixty-four passengers on the Boeing 757. Those killed included fathers and mothers, sons and daughters, spouses and lovers, neighbors and friends. As in New York, the wanton killing of innocent Americans was intentional, impersonal, and indiscriminate. The only criterion for death was living in the USA. These barbarous attacks on American soil were shocking and unprecedented. In real time, Americans were recoiling in fear and panic.

There was more. United Airlines flight 93 from Newark, New Jersey, was delayed in taking off. By the time it was hijacked forty minutes after takeoff, passengers were learning about the tragic news from New York and DC. They were learning the news on their individual cell phones and the phones on the plane. Brave patriots recognized that they were aboard a suicide mission and decided to fight. One fatalistic husband called his wife and said these last words to her: "I know we're all going to die. There's three of us who are going to do something about it. I love you, honey." From liberty-loving atoms embedded in their democracy bones, the passengers engaged in the quintessential act of free people: they voted whether to fight. Democracy won. So they fought. Passengers stormed the cockpit with a fire extinguisher and fought the four hijackers. These American heroes saved the intended target from the bloodthirsty terrorists, but sadly could not save themselves, the plane, or the passengers on the plane. At 10:10 a.m., UA 93, at a terrifying speed of five hundred miles an hour, plowed into a rural field in Pennsylvania. All forty-four people on board were killed. The intended target of the hijackers is uncertain. Authorities conjectured that potential targets included the White House, the Capitol, Camp David, or one of several nuclear power plants along the Eastern Seaboard.

The mastermind of those horrific attacks was Osama bin Laden, founder of al-Qaida. It took nearly ten years, but on May 2, 2011, US Navy SEALs found and killed bin Laden inside a private compound in Abbottabad, Pakistan. The French Enlightenment philosopher Voltaire had prophetically said, "Anyone who can make you believe absurdities can make you commit atrocities." Osama bin Laden brought home the point at the beginning of the twenty-first century. He preached to his terrorist acolytes that, in the name of jihad, it was legitimate to kill civilians from enemy countries, including innocent women and children. He preached absurdities, they committed atrocities, and innocent Americans died. As Americans across the country opened their doors and windows, they heard the same thing: the wailing of a grieving nation. Some wanted answers, many wanted revenge, all wanted justice.

Monetary relief through civil lawsuits can never adequately compensate victims and their families of a terrorist tragedy, but it is at least one way to help and one way to exact some justice. After 9/11, numerous victim lawsuits were filed in New York and consolidated into one case. They sought billions in relief from Saudi

Arabia and many others who had aided and abetted the nineteen terrorists. The ones who had made it all possible to slaughter thousands of innocent Americans. Those defendants included a web of Saudi Arabian entities officially and disgustingly designating themselves as charities. But the plaintiffs alleged that they were charities in name only because they laundered and funneled blood money to al-Qaida in support of terrorist acts. They were controlled by Saudi Arabia.

Right up there with bin Laden and the nineteen hijackers, these so-called charities were previously unknown to Americans but now were on the list of the most reviled. They were extraordinarily well funded by the Oil Kingdom. And they needed a lawyer. A lawyer who could help them win in a country that detested them. A country feeling the rage of the raw emotion of the wanton killing of family, friends, and neighbors. There were more than one million lawyers in the United States in 2001. They called only one—Jonathan Kent.

The representation fit Cabot, Lodge & Biddle's criteria for taking the case. It would be high profile and garner national press coverage. Better yet, these clients had petrodollars to burn to pay virtually unlimited fees and the case would generate millions in annual fees for years to come. Added to his three huge California class action cases, Jonathan would likely be the top money producer in the firm. There was another lucrative money angle. The firm now had several offices outside the United States, a growing energy practice, and was looking to open an office in Dubai or Riyadh, Saudi Arabia. Taking the case would open the door to opportunity for Oil Kingdom business.

To Trane and several others, especially the younger lawyers not completely jaded by dollars, it was a no-brainer. As in, don't take the case. They were aghast that the firm would even consider representing the money machines behind the killing of nearly three thousand innocent Americans. Trane, in full locomotive mode, was livid and practically barreled into Jonathan's office. He didn't mince his words. No Buddha of the Beltway or the Noble Eightfold

Path today. Trane was sizzling in the patriot's frying pan, standing menacingly in front of Jonathan.

"Are you fucking kidding me?! You're going to represent the bastards who bankrolled the savage attacks on us?"

"Whoa, slow down. The charities are the *alleged* money behind the attacks." Jonathan knew immediately that this conversation was not going to go anywhere but downhill. But even he was not prepared for Trane's full-on verbal assault, perhaps proving the point that only the ones who love you can muster such anger toward you.

"Alleged my ass and charities my ass. Follow the fucking money. You know damn good and well the money trail leads back to those sons of bitches. Where else did those jerk-offs who flew the planes get the money?"

"We don't know that. We represent a lot of companies alleged to have done bad things," Jonathan responded defensively, invoking the convenient safety shield of this is what lawyers do—ours is not to reason why....

"Cut the bullshit, Jonathan, you're talking to me, not the PR department or a bunch of naïve law school recruits."

"Seriously, Jack, our client list, like the clients of all Big Law firms, reads like a rogues' gallery of bad apples. You know this. We defend clients accused of doing all sorts of bad things. Look at our client cases.We represent companies accused of fixing prices, monopolizing markets, gouging consumers, screwing competitors, polluting neighborhoods, dumping poisonous chemicals into drinking water, selling dangerous drugs and products, swindling investors, destroying pension plans, cheating creditors, predatory lending practices, insider trading, corporate fraud, healthcare fraud, tax fraud, bank fraud, money laundering, screwing policyholders, stealing trade secrets, infringing patents, cheating customers, harming workers, pumping and dumping stock, racially discriminating. The list goes on and on. We'd be out of business if people were angels. But just because they are accused doesn't mean they are guilty. You of all people should know that."

"Save your sorry-ass stump speech for someone stupid enough

to swallow it. And by the way, while you were prattling on you forgot to mention the goddamn global warmers in the fossil fuel business who pay us tens of millions of dollars to help them skirt environmental regulations so they can burn up the fucking planet. Look, I take your point, but this is different."

"Is it really?" Jonathan knew that taking such a controversial case would cause concern with at least some in his Big Law firm but had convinced himself that lawyers are not their clients and therefore they are morally clean when representing companies accused of heinous acts. He even convinced himself that lawyers were almost morally *obligated* to undertake such representations, assuming, that is, that they were extraordinarily well paid for their professed ethical commitments. But he had the good sense not to go down *that* hypocritical road at this time while Trane was practically hyperventilating.

"You're damn straight it's different. This is not like some good client we have represented for years that has gone sideways on something. This is a group of bullshit shell companies for the Saudis that exist for one and only one purpose: to bankroll a cowardly war on us. We should be bombing those motherfuckers back to the stone age, not defending them, for Christ's sake."

"Jack, you're making a bunch of unwarranted assumptions. Talk about swallowing, you are swallowing hook, line, and sinker what you're hearing from the shock jocks on talk radio and reading in the plaintiffs' complaint."

"Tell that to the victims' families. Tell that to the rest of the world. Stop hiding behind some "every dog gets its day in court" slogan. Look, it only takes a couple of hours of digging to know that the fucking Saudis funnel all the money through those shell companies. And if you think anything goes on in that country without the royal family knowing about it … well, then you've got your head up your ass."

"Jack, have you been getting your information from Al Jazeera?"

"Are you serious? You think this is some parlor game?! Nary a sparrow falls in the Oil Kingdom without the royal family tracing its arc. The Saudis funneled all the money to the bullshit charities who provided it to the terrorists."

"Look, Jack, there are serious jurisdictional issues as to whether our clients can even be sued in the United States. They have no offices here and don't do business here. I should get them out on a motion, and it will all be over. The US is not the court of last resort. And then we can impress the Saudis where we are trying to open an office."

"Listen to yourself. Don't do business here? Are you shitting me! No, they just fund the killing here. Who gives a flying fuck about technicalities? Those guys provided the money, they should pay. Let some other soulless Big Law firm take their blood-drenched money."

"Look, Oliver Stone, you're too emotional about this. The controversy will pass, the younger lawyers will calm down, we'll make a lot of money, open another office, and grow our energy and global practices. All good."

"No, not all good. It's a damn disgrace. But I can see the horse is out of the barn. Look, I'm nearing retirement, and I'm not an owner of this place. But I think this is a big mistake. We're better than this, or at least we should be. We can make a choice. This is a civil lawsuit about money, plain and simple. It's not a criminal case where the defendant could go to jail. And there are plenty of other Big Law lawyers who would eagerly take those bastards' petrodollars. They don't need us, and we sure as hell don't need them."

"Jack, in the end, this will be good for our business. You'll see."

"Oh, that's rich. So now we're Michael Corleone? It's not personal, it's strictly business? You just might want to remember that with that line Michael started his transformation from war hero to mafia don. Think about it. Make no mistake about it, the cases we choose to take reflect our values. Look, Jonathan, I'm no tilter at windmills and I know we have bills to pay and we're in a dollars arms race with other Big Law firms. But do we really have to clutch corporate cash like maggots clinging to rotten fruit and vegetables? You know we don't. We have a choice. I'm with Winston Churchill: 'What's the use of living, if it not be to strive for noble causes.' In my book, there is nothing noble about defending those sons of bitches. I'll see you later." With that Trane stormed out in high dudgeon.

Cabot, Lodge & Biddle took the case. The firm raked in huge

fees and opened an office in Riyadh. For all the initial publicity, for years the case languished in a quagmire of technical legal motions mostly concerning, as Jonathan had predicted, whether the so-called charity clients could even be sued in the United States. Jonathan's brilliant technical legal maneuvering kept the case stalled at the starting gate year after year.

More than thirteen years after the case was originally filed, the plaintiffs dropped the Saudi charities as defendants and focused the lawsuit on the Kingdom of Saudi Arabia. At that time, none of Jonathan's clients had turned over a single document and not a single charity witness had provided a word of testimony. And by that time, more than ten thousand New Yorkers had been diagnosed with cancer related to toxic fumes from the destruction of the Twin Towers and the ensuing cleanup efforts. After reading those bleak statistics in his *New York Times*, Trane decided he needed some fresh air. Out on the street, he approached a liquor store. He looked in but kept on walking.

COURTS AND CORPORATIONS

Jonathan successfully resolved his three corporate cases in San Francisco but not before collecting more than $50 million in legal fees. In the cell phone and car replacement parts cases, Jonathan, relying on favorable legal precedent hostile to class-action lawsuits, succeeded in excluding the testimony of plaintiffs' economics experts by challenging the reliability of their opinions that the cases could properly be treated as class actions.

Without those expert opinions, both cases collapsed. Left unresolved was whether millions of cell phone subscribers and insured drivers were getting gouged by their carriers. For his brilliant lawyering, Jonathan was rewarded with more defense work from both corporate clients.

In the cigarettes case, the plaintiffs persuaded the judge that the case should proceed as a class action. Game on. Two of the other defendants settled shortly thereafter. One defendant paid $385 million and the other paid $675 million. The class plaintiffs told Jonathan that they would not settle for less than $850 million from his client. Jonathan offered $95 million and the plaintiffs countered with $2.3 billion. Settlement negotiations predictably collapsed.

Jonathan and his client were in full trial preparation mode. But he had one more shot at a pretrial victory before exposing his client to the risk of a jury trial and the $12 billion in damages the plaintiffs' Stanford University economist had calculated for the class. He would file a motion for summary judgment. In plain English, Jonathan would argue that the judge should avoid a jury trial altogether and declare his client the winner based on the facts the litigants were not disputing. Jonathan knew that was going to be a difficult argument to win. His legal filing needed to be crystal clear, accurate, and most of all, compellingly persuasive. As Judge Roy used to say to him about legal writing, "I want sentences so clean I can swim in them."

He enlisted the help of the best young antitrust legal thinkers and writers in the law firm. At the top of the list sat David Joseph, a young gay associate whose brilliance and talent Jonathan spotted early on. Jonathan recognized that David had superstar talent and went out of his way to mentor him and invited him to join his team. David enthusiastically joined and never looked back. He would become Jonathan's most valuable, indispensable team member and would eventually make partner and his own mark. Jonathan often thought that one thing Big Law was actually getting right compared to how it was when he started practicing was the acceptance and assimilation of the LGBTQ community. David would help Jonathan craft the winning argument.

The biggest challenge they had was an optical one. The plaintiffs alleged that the tobacco companies conspired for ten years to overcharge the tobacco wholesalers. In fact, the prices were the same or nearly identical most of the time, and the tobacco companies were garnering huge profits. At first blush, it sure looked suspiciously like a conspiracy. Jonathan and David argued that it was a conspiracy mirage. They argued that perfectly legal conditions in the tobacco industry resulted in price uniformity, not some midnight conspiracy. Following in the pioneering legal briefing tradition of the brilliant Louis Brandeis in the early twentieth century, Jonathan and David relied less on technical legal arguments and more on empirical evidence by providing example after example of American industries where prices are the same or nearly identical when there are only a handful of competitors selling commodity products. Their theme: this is capitalism in modern America. Their subtheme: and it's legal, baby.

They argued that the cigarette industry was what economists refer to awkwardly as an oligopoly—a concentrated industry with only a few sellers—just like most major industries in the capitalist United States. Like it or not, pricing in oligopolies tends not to be competitive, but not because of actual agreements, and the antitrust laws only outlaw pricing *agreements*. The point they emphasized was that there was nothing unusual or nefarious about their client's pricing practices. The same type of argument Jonathan had made in the cell phone case. In their favor were a string of pro-business Supreme Court decisions that tilted heavily on the side of corporate America in antitrust cases, all in the name, ironically enough, of "consumer welfare." They argued the case should end now.

The judge agreed. Reluctantly. He was dismayed by the lack of price competition and hand-over-fist money the tobacco companies were making but noted that conservative Supreme Court antitrust precedent dictated his decision. The hamstrung judge bitingly concluded his opinion by citing former president Herbert Hoover, a fervent capitalist, who once quipped that "the only trouble with capitalism is capitalists; they're too damn greedy."

It was a stunning victory. Two defendants had already paid more than $1 billion to settle. The trial would have been in San Francisco, and the plaintiffs' expert economist was brilliant and engaging and could more than hold his own with lawyers on cross-examination. Jonathan joked that the expert also had the two most valuable attributes a trial lawyer wants in an expert witness: he was tall and spoke the Queen's English. Jonathan appreciated all too well that books often are judged by their covers and a jury would likely be persuaded by the plaintiffs' expert's style of presentation even more than his substance. For all his trial prowess, Jonathan knew deep down he had dodged a bullet.

Before departing San Francisco to return to DC, Jonathan took a long run along Embarcadero to clear his head and think about something that was gnawing at him. The superstar had now been practicing at Cabot, Lodge & Biddle for fifteen years. He was enjoying unprecedented success and was being richly rewarded. Yes, he kept telling himself that he did not make either life's or Big Law's rules, that he would be master not slave, but the value neutrality of it all was starting to sound somewhat hollow and hackneyed. Yes, he could take pride in his technical legal prowess, but the grueling hours and the nature of his cases were giving him pause. Seven miles into his run, he had a flashback to his time with Trane in

Memphis years ago, when Trane quoted Dr. King—"Life's most persistent and urgent question is what are you doing for others?"—and Trane admonishing him to ask that question of himself from time to time. He wasn't sure about next steps, but for the first time in his dazzling career, he was starting to have serious reservations about what he was doing in his life. Years earlier in Paris he underwent some existential angst about the meaningfulness of how he was spending his life, but that was fleeting and not uncommon for a thoughtful young person. This was deeper and more persistent. He was feeling shallow. This feeling was not going away.

RAW DEAL

The last years of the first decade of the twenty-first century were no American dream for average Americans. They were a nightmare. The years 2007–2009 marked the longest and deepest economic downturn since the Great Depression. Unemployment hit 10 percent and poverty 15 percent. Households lost a staggering $16 trillion in net worth. Financial inequality continued to widen, with the rich getting richer while more than 93 percent of Americans felt the gut punch of declining net worth. For most, there was no Square Deal, New Deal, Fair Deal, or Great Society. Only a raw deal.

The culprits weren't hard to find. They would become clients of Jonathan and Cabot, Lodge & Biddle. They would also cause Jonathan to question more intensely whether the nature of his cases and the price of Big Law success were all worth it.

Banks, financial institutions, and mortgage lenders drunk with greed and recklessness drove the country off a financial cliff. Subprime mortgages ignited the financial fire. These were home loans lending institutions issued to people with lousy credit histories. They were high-risk loans, but banks bought them up by the thousands in bulk, bundled them in packages called mortgage-backed securities, and hoped to turn a quick profit by selling them. But junk is junk no matter how you package it or whatever highfalutin name con artists and their Big Law lawyers give it. Jonathan remembered an expression he had heard early in his career while traveling through the South on the milk cases: you can't perfume the pig. Junk is junk and stink is stink. CLB made lots of money defending junk and stink.

The financial recklessness and irresponsibility were astounding. As the banks continued to lower the mortgage interest rates to millions of customers who otherwise would not have qualified for the loans, demand increased for more new housing. With increasing demand came increasing housing prices. This vicious cycle started to be felt by 2005 as interest rates inevitably began to increase. This suppressed housing prices. Then: *wham!* All too soon, and predictably enough as night follows day, many subprime borrowers, known as poor people to most folks who don't speak in the masquerading tongues of financial argot, could no longer afford their mortgage payments. Banks euphemistically called this being "underwater." Those living the nightmare called it what it really was, being "in deep shit." Deep shit because millions of folks owed more on their mortgages than their homes were worth. The writing was on the wall. Foreclosures followed, banks stopped lending to poor people, evictions spiked, and housing prices fell through the floor. Not even a gasoline enema would be this painful.

By early 2008, Wall Street investment firms besotted by big bets on subprime mortgages began to collapse and file for bankruptcy. Showing no scruples and embracing socialism for the rich, they, hat in hand, shamelessly asked for taxpayer bailouts. If you were small and poor, you got crushed. For the mighty, you were "too big to fail." Multibillion-dollar automobile companies got bankruptcy protection and bailout programs. The feds lent a Wall Street giant $85 billion so it could remain afloat. Corporate welfare for the big boys.

A financial crisis in the country means opportunity for Big Law. Loot from the looters. Jonathan's clients included investment firms accused of major fraud in connection with the mortgages and the hopelessly complex financial engineering they used in their cupidinous attempt to spin straw into gold. Big Law, which created a lot of these products, salved their consciences by referring to them blandly as "financial instruments." Proctologists would have been proud. Jonathan's clients paid CLB more than $25 million to keep them one step ahead of the law and the people they screwed. The fraud was rampant. Jonathan's clients had all sorts of devious arrows in their fraud quiver. They deceived borrowers about the mortgage terms and eligibility requirements. They deceived them by concealing vital information, including huge monetary balloon payments at the end of the loans. His too-clever-by-half clients made loans to borrowers with no income, no job, and no assets, cynically calling them "NINJA" loans. Then there were the "Jumbo" loans, or large loans for luxury homes made to greedy borrowers who could not afford them, where the banks predicted that defaults were likely. The rogues' gallery would not be complete without clients who made hundreds of millions of dollars on loans that did not meet the banks' own lending requirements. They were all pigs with their snouts in the moolah trough. Dumb and greedy with satchels of money to pay silk-stocking lawyers to help them avoid a day of reckoning. Precisely the types of clients Big Law lusted after.

The financial fallout from the fraud-filled years leading up to and causing the Great Recession was enormous for the financial giants and manna from heaven for Big Law. Dozens of mortgage lenders, commercial and investment banks, and savings and loan institutions hired Big Law lawyers to settle predatory lending and securities fraud lawsuits in droves. More than 250 fraudsters paid more than $80 billion in penalties.

Cabot, Lodge & Biddle made tens of millions of dollars representing big banks and their executives in criminal prosecutions, Securities Exchange enforcement actions, state attorneys general actions, and private class-action lawsuits. While average Americans lost their homes and jobs, as small businesses collapsed, as the poverty level worsened, as most of America was gripped with fear and uncertainty, CLB had record profitability through the years of the Great Recession. As his firm entered the second decade of the twenty-first century, Jonathan had ascended to the top of the compensation ladder. Yet he wasn't feeling very good about the road he was traveling. He was itching for some change.

MONEY, MONEY, MONEY
IN THE WHITE BOYS' CLUB

By 2011, there was no going back. Big Law was seduced lock, stock, and barrel by the siren song of money. When their leaders boasted that their firms' core goals were to represent the biggest companies in their biggest litigation and corporate matters, they should have run out the ground ball and continued with "because that is how you make the most money and that is precisely why we exist." By then Big Law was ubiquitous in American life. There were multiple Big Law offices in every major city; in the biggest cities there were typically at least thirty. And by then virtually every Big Law firm in the country had made the pilgrimage to the Mecca of Big Law—New York City, where lawyers charge the highest hourly rates and *play* and *rest* are verboten four-letter words. Corporate deals and mergers to make giant corporations even bigger and industries even more concentrated? Handled by Big Law. Private equity vultures looking to hollow out companies and pocket their assets? Call Big Law. Biggest lawsuits challenging corporate conquest and consolidation, cheating consumers, and causing personal and environmental injury? Defended by Big Law. They infiltrated the judiciary, major federal agencies, and big business. An astute observer of legal trends, Trane likened Big Law to the locusts in the Bible, where Moses warned the pharaoh of Egypt that God would send so many locusts that they would "cover each and every tree of the land and eat all that is there to be eaten." To Trane, Big Law lawyers had become legal locusts.

Trane was now well past the age of sixty-five, but the firm kept him on to teach trial and litigation skills to young lawyers. Privately, Trane thought it was a colossal waste of money because the overwhelming majority of these young lawyers would never try any cases. Reflective, Trane had now been sober for close to twenty years and had mellowed some, but he was ever ready to cut the cant and call bullshit at the hypocrisy and direction of Big Law. He was also still a bit scruffy and disheveled, not quite rakish, but close. He never did quite master the sartorial skill of matching each shirt button with its proper hole, having particular trouble with the button by his navel and the right button on his collar. And one summer week, Jonathan noticed that Trane wore the same seersucker suit each day, attire not especially suited for masking sweat and tinkle stains.

For the life of him, Jonathan could not understand why Trane and other lawyers wore seersucker suits. He hated them. He never saw a man who looked good in one. To Jonathan, it appeared that the only men who wore them were either pudgy, shapeless, flabby endomorphs or skinny emaciated waifs, all of whom looked like they were allergic to exercise and were auditioning to be the local popsicle man. So why, Jonathan especially wondered in disbelief, did women fulfill *My Fair Lady's* Professor Henry Higgins's hope that they would be more like men and also start wearing them? To Jonathan, these ridiculous wrinkle suits lacked both style and charm. They, along with brown suits, should be tossed onto a raging tacky pyre, or at least be banned from courtrooms.

Donning a brown seersucker suit, right shirt collar unbuttoned, and his farcical Tony Lama boots, Trane wandered into Jonathan's office intent on ribbing him about the state of affairs in Big Law.

"Have you seen some of the stats of Big Law?" Trane asked indignantly. "Says here that the hundred largest law firms had annual revenues of more than $1 billion. Can you believe that? The article predicts that by 2020 there will be a number of firms making more than a billion, and partner profitability at the top firms will shoot through the roof."

"Yeah, the numbers do keep growing year after year. Firms keep getting bigger, and the revenues and partner profits feel like they're on a perpetually upward-moving escalator. At least they are at the best of the big firms. As I've told you before, Jack, Big Law is one big money chase."

"Big Law firms in soulless search of El Dorado in the crass hopes of paving their halls with gold. When Shakespeare asked in *As You Like It*, 'Can one desire too much of a good thing?' I guess the answer is no."

"Market forces, Jack."

"The old invisible hand shibboleth. The hand is not so invisible anymore."

"These are all market driven, even if we do have, as you are suggesting, corporate welfare."

"Yeah, yeah. A market full of money pricks. How about these associate salaries? I know it sounds like a partner's lament, but they're outrageous."

"Probably no more outrageous than what partners make. But do you think any intelligent, talented young lawyer would work the grueling hours and trudge through endless days of dull work, seven days a week, unless we paid them big salaries?" Jonathan asked matter of factly. "The only time they're not tethered to a computer or smart phone waiting for the next partner demand is when they are sleeping. Even then, I suspect most of them put their phones under the pillow with a partner alert function."

"Hmm, do I detect a little discontent and empathy for these young lawyers? Even so," Trane noted, "you're paying rookies close to two hundred thousand dollars and they can't even find the courthouse, much less know what to do once they get there. But I suppose you're right. Nobody with half a brain would grind it out doing all of this dull work if you didn't pay through the nose for them. God, the work is lousy for so many of them. What a waste of brain talent."

"Golden handcuffs, Jack. As if money is the answer to everything that ails associates in Big Law. Pay them enough to pay off crushing student debt and a lot more than they can make anywhere else, except at another Big Law firm that also grinds 'em down and spits 'em out. They're automaton billing machines, and the overwhelming majority will never make partner, and of those who do, only a few will ever come anywhere near the top. There is no way I would join Big Law if I were coming out of law school today. Of course if you quote me, I'll deny it," Jonathan cracked with a sly grin.

"What a racket. For the great majority, it's like that Tom Petty song "Runnin' Down a Dream"—they're runnin' down a dream that will never come to them, instead it's always cold, no sunshine. But look at what partners are now making. Says here that only twenty percent of all partners in the hundred largest firms have any ownership interests, but for those who do, they make an average of two million a year. At the elite of the elite, more than three million a year."

"Yeah, how does one live on three million a year?" Jonathan sarcastically asked.

"Very funny. I know those are just average numbers. Highfliers like you make three, four times that much."

"No comment."

"And you're a cheap bastard. You invest all your money. Probably in Warren Buffett territory by now. It never has been about the money per se for you, has it? Just a way of keeping competitive score and insuring your independence. But most of these rich white boys do love to spend their money on boy toys and gewgaws."

"You got that right."

"Their conspicuous consumption is straight out of Thornstein Veblen and *The Theory of the Leisure Class* with their insecure need to flaunt their wealth to boost self-esteem and feel superior. Mansions in tony neighborhoods, wardrobe closets bigger than average homes, second homes, luxury cars, wine cellars, exotic vacations, prep schools that cost more than most colleges, swank country clubs, kids' birthday parties that cost more than an average wedding, kids' weddings that cost more than average homes, coked-up high school kids driving beamers, the whole nine yards. For them, the superfluous has become the indispensable. Then the wealth workers—their financial advisers, personal accountants, therapists, professional trainers, nannies, housekeepers, gardeners, dog walkers, shoppers, concierge service providers. Like a vestigial caste system. Reminds me of what another Princeton guy, F. Scott Fitzgerald, once said: 'Let me tell you about the very rich. They are very different from you and me. Even when they enter deep into our world or sink below us, they still think they are better than we are. They are different.'"

"Okay, Big Law partners can make a lot of money, but we're a far cry from the private equity crowd, hedge fund managers, and Fortune 100 CEOs.

"And Big Law is not just a white boys' club anymore," Jonathan said half-heartedly, as he tried to muster a conviction he knew he didn't have. He also let slide the fact that he agreed with Trane's spot-on remarks about Big Law partners' insecurities and their outlandish spending proclivities. Yes, he made a lot of money, but he lived in a two-bedroom condominium, abjured most displays of conspicuous consumption, and invested most of the money he made. Jonathan, from early on, wanted to make money for independence, not superficial status, and the sooner he could achieve it, the better.

"Save the bullshit diversity apologia for the marketing folks. You and I and everybody else with a brain knows it's still a white boys' club. Just follow the money, and I mean the real money. Take female partners, less than twenty-five percent in Big Law. It drops below ten percent for racially and ethnically diverse partners. Down below five percent for racially diverse women. And you as well as I know that very few of them are anywhere near the top of the compensation ladders. Then there are the issues of isolation and alienation felt by so many minorities. No wonder the abysmal mental health statistics in Big Law are even worse for minorities than the rest of us. Don't tell me Big Law is not still a privileged white boys club."

"What do you want me to say? Change is slow, it takes time. We're trying, we're making some headway," Jonathan said, somewhat apologetically.

"Hell, Jonathan, I'm just blowing off some steam. I know some strides have been made. But CLB and Big Law have been shoveling the same bullshit story about diversity and women for years and nothing real ever changes. And don't kid yourself, this dizzying dollars arms race in Big Law will trump all these diversity and inclusion efforts. It will continue to be the same lip service and lipstick on the pig fifteen years from now. The Dead sang about it in "Uncle John's Band"—the same story, the crow told me, it's the only song it knows, nothing but a bunch of rosy morning talk about minority and female advancement and then it blows away before the sun sets."

"After all these years, I still shake my head that you even know who the Grateful Dead is. But then I felt the earth stop rotating around its axis when the hippie's hippie Jerry Garcia came out with a line of neckties. That was more disappointing than the complete sellout by Big Law, which was not hard to predict. Guess the deadheads weren't shelling out enough for Jerry's heroin fixes. Anyway, thanks for the uplifting talk. Let's save your jeremiad about a lost generation of trial lawyers for another day."

"Deal. I'll just keep truckin' like the do-dah man on this long, strange trip of life." As Trane walked away, he quoted one of his favorite sayings: "May you live in interesting times, my man."

TIME FOR A CHANGE

By the second decade of the twenty-first century, Jonathan epito-mized the zeitgeist of a rainmaker in Big Law. Partner compen-sation was a way of keeping score, an objective measure of relative value, or so Jonathan and many others allowed themselves to be-lieve. Jonathan was at the top of the compensation ladder with blue skies ahead. He handled huge cases and his phone was constantly ringing with new and old clients wanting him to defend them in their toughest cases. Riding high and truckin' along, he was growing restless with the direction of his career and the nature of his cases. He wanted some cases he could really believe in. Cases his clients *should* win because they were wronged and deserved vindication. Cases where he could answer, not duck, Dr. King's urgent and per-sistent question about what he was doing for others.

Encouraged by Trane to think more critically about his case selection and to live in interesting times, he had an idea. *Yes,* he thought, *I'll still work on the defense side, but I'll pick and choose my cases. There are, after all,* he thought, *plenty of cases where it feels good to be on the defense side. But I'll also start a plaintiff's practice at CLB where we'll take worthy cases on contingency for clients that can't afford our princely hourly rates. Cases in need of avenging angels. And I'll look for opportune pro bono cases where I might be able to make a small difference in the lives of ordinary people.*

Associates, already clamoring to work on his trials, would line up outside the door to get in on this action. But his plan, he an-ticipated, with its associated financial risks and commitment to provide substantial free legal services from fully engaged lawyers, would meet with stiff resistance from risk-averse management. Big Law litigation was a twenty-four seven hourly cash machine defending corporate interests, and Jonathan, a prime mover, was suggesting a paradigm shift, at least in his own practice, and a potential threat to maximum partner profitability. That type of disruption was bound to be unsettling to CLB's staid management, whose primary mission was to increase partner profitability year after year, preferably by double-digit percentage points.

The meeting included Baxter Hodges, the long-running managing partner; Oliver Truckle, the obsequious litigation department head who had never tried a case; Felix Quaestor, CLB's stiff, starched, and stilted bean-counting financial partner who represents public and private companies in deal work and governance matters; and a couple of senior litigation partners who mostly defend corporations in securities and toxic tort cases. Nobody from the small pro bono committee was there.

They congregated in the Biddle Room adjoining Hodges's spacious corner office, a portrait of Arthur Biddle holding a law book in two hands dominating the back wall. Water boiling in an antique Russian samovar for English tea and French macarons and madeleines served on Wedgwood bone china plates were on a side table. Jonathan brought bottled water.

"I assume you have all read my business proposal," Jonathan started, "and so I'll pause to answer any questions." Jonathan was taking the action right to them with an unstated assumption that of course his plan would be approved and then he would parry any assaults on it. In meetings, he typically let others speak first so he could get his finger on the pulse and determine what points he really needed to make, if any. Once again, King Lear—"Have more than thou showest, talk less than thou knowest."

"Well, Jonathan, I guess I don't understand why someone as busy and richly compensated as you would be looking for a change, especially a change where we take the risk of not getting paid for substantial commitments of time and resources," Hodges said. "You know, in litigation, other than patent infringement suits for big corporations, we are a defense firm for corporate clients working by the hour at substantial hourly rates. That model has served us very well. We are one of the most profitable firms in the country. As I'm sure you know, you have a number of partners who are still upset that you sued the FHM accounting firm."

"That was some years ago, and they weren't so upset that they turned down their share of our legal fees." It still irked Jonathan that some of the most vehement opponents of him suing the accounting firm were low-producing partners who contributed very little to CLB's bottom line. "But as I wrote in my business plan, there are plenty of corporate clients—like Hazard Materials—that find themselves on the plaintiff's side of cases. They can pay full freight. Others need help, and we can put skin in the game by taking the cases on contingency and, with rigid due diligence, identify cases with robust return on investment potential. In this dynamic age of innovation and disruption, there are scores of cash-strapped entrepreneurs who are getting trampled who have very attractive intellectual property and antitrust claims where we can be of help and make a lot of money by sharing risk/reward with them. And, my plan includes a more focused effort to identify worthy cases to take pro bono."

"Jonathan," Quaestor weighed in, "as the financial partner, I don't see the need. You already have the highest hourly billing rate in the firm, your cases generate our biggest profits, and you have more work opportunities than you can handle. It seems to me you should let well enough alone."

"Two responses. First, I think we can do even better financially by taking on risk. Hourly rates are like bonds; contingency cases like equity. Diversify the financial portfolio and swing for the fences in appropriate cases. But second, it's not just about the money. I want, hell, I need to do something other than be a tool for corporate clients every time they screw up and get their asses sued. I need more cases I can emotionally believe in, and quite frankly, I get hired in lots of cases where the other side is wearing the white hat. That's getting pretty damn tiring. I at least need some balance."

It was only a matter of time before Oliver Truckle, who continually showed a profound lack of appreciation for the prudence of silence over the prodigality of speech, said something inane, while chomping on a macaron no less. "But, Jonathan, why should we risk our reputation with corporate America by becoming plaintiff's lawyers?"

Jonathan resisted the urge to call him a witless muttonhead and to stop sucking up to Hodges. "Oliver, there would be no such risk. I'm not proposing that we become ambulance chasers. I'm proposing something far more judicious. We will vet our cases carefully and select only those that are consistent with our reputation for excellence and offer us an opportunity for a substantial payoff, unless we take the case pro bono, in which case virtue will be its own reward. More virtue would be good for the soul. And take it from me as one who has tried a lot of cases, corporate America is far more interested in hiring lawyers who can win, not whether you have ever been on the plaintiff's side. The very best civil trial lawyers can and do work both sides of the V."

"I'm also leery about your pro bono intentions," Quaestor said. "There is no need for CLB to deploy substantial lawyer time on big cases where we won't get paid. We can check the pro bono box by encouraging lawyers to contribute to legal aid groups and individual lawyers can take small cases from time to time. After all, we *are* a profit-maximizing enterprise, not an eleemosynary institution."

Talk about a lapsus linguae, did patronizing Felix really just say that? Jonathan thought. "Felix, you just stated the absolute bare minimum we should be doing on the pro bono front as a prominent law firm. To whom much is given, much will be required, or something like that. Look, I'm not suggesting we take on every pro bono case that comes our way. But I am emphatically saying that we should do more and that we should look for worthwhile cases that can make a difference in the lives of ordinary people. And let's not forget, we have an entire generation of younger lawyers who want more out of the practice of law than eighty-hour work weeks of tedious labor on behalf of corporate America. Something more enriching."

"Let's do this," suggested Hodges, in an effort to end a debate that could quickly go south. "Jonathan, you can start this plaintiff's practice, but let's take it slow and see how it develops. One case at a time. But make sure you get management approval before you accept any such representations, especially any major pro bono commitments. Deal?"

"Deal, thanks, gentlemen." *Okay,* Jonathan thought, *that was quick and easy. Perhaps too easy.* His instincts told him this was a mere formality to placate him and kick the can down the road. Hodges was a savvy and wily politician who always played his cards close to the vest. And, like the Roman general Fabius Cunctator employing delaying tactics to fend off the advances of Hannibal during the Second Punic War, Hodges was skilled in the art of avoiding a major confrontation. He gave Jonathan a small green light but retained full veto power over any proposed plaintiff's or pro bono case. Nonetheless, Jonathan decided to hope for the best and prepare for the worst. *One pragmatic step at a time*, he reminded himself.

DAVID V. GOLIATH

A few days after the meeting, Jonathan was retained in two antitrust cases he could believe in. One on the plaintiff's side, on
contingency, the other on the defense side where the plaintiffs were
uninjured corporations looking for a huge legal windfall.

Both cases were going to take him back to court in San Francisco, thanks to antitrust shenanigans coming out of Beijing, China,
and Seoul, South Korea. In the China case, he was hired to represent a small and promising semiconductor company based in Silicon Valley against a monopolist in Beijing backed ultimately by the
Communist Party. In the South Korean case, he was hired to represent a family-run industrial conglomerate, known as a chaebol,
which had been raided by antitrust regulators on three continents
for a long-running price-fixing conspiracy that jacked up prices for
computer, cell phone, and television screens. Jonathan was back on
his coastal bus.

Modern life would be inconceivable without semiconductors,
as Jonathan quickly learned as he dove in to tackle a new subject
matter. As one technologist observed, "Semiconductors are an innovative and technological miracle, where transistors ten thousand
times thinner than a human hair enable billions of them to fit on
a microchip the size of a quarter." When Neil Armstrong stepped
onto the surface of the moon in 1969 and proudly said, "That's one
small step for man, one giant leap for mankind," it was semiconductors that helped put him and Apollo 11 on the moon and return
them safely to earth.

Semiconductors were invented in the United States. They are

ubiquitous and indispensable to the economy and Americans' way
of life. Anything that is computerized or uses radio waves depends
on semiconductors, which are mostly created with silicon. They are
used in personal computers and peripheral products, in consumer
electronics, and wired and wireless communications systems. They
generate enormous revenues and eye-popping profits for the major
players. Revenues and profits that one monopoly-minded company
intended to protect by any means necessary. Legal or not.

Beijing Semiconductor Manufacturing Company was a leading
semiconductor company, globally and in the United States. Headquartered in Beijing, it was founded in 1990. In the complex hi-
erarchy of corporate ownership in Communist China, BSMC was
owned by Beijing Semiconductor Manufacturing Group, a state-
owned enterprise administered by the Communist Party–run SA-
SAC, or State-Owned Assets and Administration Commission.
From documents Jonathan was able to secure in the lawsuit, BSMC
was not content to be a major player in semiconductors. It wanted to be the biggest. Not just the biggest, but the biggest by far,
especially in the United States. Its avowed purpose: conquest and
control. By any means necessary, legal or not.

The semiconductor business is a tough nut to crack. It requires
investments in the millions, and the major players have patents
that give them protection from various sorts of competition. To
protect turf, the big boys constantly sue each other for patent infringement. Those lawsuits are expensive and deter a lot of companies from even thinking about getting into the semiconductor
business. With cunning calculation, BSMC had a two-step plan to
gain and maintain dominance. To conquer and control. The execution of BSMC's perfidious plan is what Jonathan challenged in
court under the antitrust monopolization laws.

Step One. BSMC set out to shrink the number of players in the
game. BSMC, with the ultimate financial backing of the Chinese
government, made an audacious bid to acquire a major American
semiconductor company. Wall Street was stunned at the extraordinary premium price BSMC put on the table. An over-the-top offer
the target company's board of directors could not responsibly refuse. The merger would make BSMC the biggest player in the game,

but it would first have to be approved by the US Department of Justice. Observers were surprised when the DOJ gave BSMC the antitrust green light. Pundits on both the left and right speculated that misguided geopolitical considerations greased the skids for BSMC. Either way, BSMC was now positioned to dominate in a vital sector of the US economy.

Step Two. With a dominant market position, BSMC continued to consolidate its power and vise grip on the market by locking up customers with exclusive long-term contracts and bundling product offerings by refusing to sell customers products they could only get from BSMC unless they also bought products from BSMC that they preferred to buy from BSMC's competitors. BSMC also aggressively used the legal system to thwart competition by filing a slew of expensive patent lawsuits against actual and even potential competitors. Finally, BSMC targeted young and promising start-up companies for acquisition. That strategy killed two competitive birds with one predatory stone. It eliminated the targets as competitors and enabled BSMC to add to its patent portfolio and intellectual property arsenal for attacks on other competitors.

One coveted BSMC acquisition target was a small company in Silicon Valley that was making innovative strides in the exciting, emerging technology areas of artificial intelligence and quantum computing. The company, AIQC, for artificial intelligence and quantum computing, was started by two brilliant Stanford University dropouts and had grown to eighty employees with $200 million in revenues. These were some seriously smart former college students. And they were on to something big. AIQC had financial backing from venture capitalists who were predicting that the company would soon do an initial public offering and grow into a multi-billion-dollar company. Apparently BSMC thought the same thing and made an unsolicited hostile takeover offer to buy AIQC. When AIQC rejected the offer, BSMC pulled out its anticompetitive play-book, lawyered up with two Big Law firms and a boutique firm with a former federal judge and sued AIQC for patent infringement. Suit was filed in San Francisco federal court.

The big brains at AIQC were not easily intimidated. AIQC knew that BSMC's patent claim was meritless. Nothing more than a misuse of the judicial system to tie up the young company in litigation. Force it to bleed legal fees, slow the advancement of science and innovation, and thereby snuff out its business dream. A predatory attempt to bring AIQC to its knees and force it to surrender and sell. Already frustrated by BSMC's anticompetitive conduct of locking up customers with long-term, exclusive contracts, AIQC and its investors concluded that BSMC was violating the antitrust laws. So the young company's brain trust resolved to fight. With a one-two-punch strategy, AIQC resolved to fight BSMC's meritless patent lawsuit and countersue BSMC for antitrust violations.

There was a big problem. Money. AIQC had a couple hundred million in revenues, but that money was needed to operate the business. Its cash reserves were marginal; the young company did not have the resources to both defend a patent lawsuit and prosecute an antitrust suit. AIQC needed a top-flight lawyer and firm to take the case on contingency. A capable, not crazy, lawyer willing to take the risk of investing millions and losing.

Given BSMC's mighty financial wherewithal and rules-be-damned conceit, AIQC needed a fearless warrior handy with staff and sling in this fight for its very life. What lawyers call a bet-the-company lawsuit. Jonathan Kent got the call. He believed in the case and thought AIQC's damages claim justified the risk. After an internal knockdown, drag-out fight at CLB, the fifteen-person management committee voted eight to seven to allow Jonathan to take the case on contingency. But this would not be the last Jonathan heard from the determined dissenters.

THE THRILL OF THE CHASE

Shortly before Jonathan got the call from AIQC, he received a call of quite a different nature. This time he was being asked to take over an antitrust price-fixing case that had been ongoing for several years. It was set to go to trial within a year, also in San Francisco. The client—Kwon Electronics—was a huge South Korean conglomerate that made an endless supply of products, including flatscreen panels for computers, mobile phones, and televisions. It was accused of conspiring with competitors in South Korea, Taiwan, and Japan to overcharge customers in several countries on five continents. Already it and several other companies had pled guilty to criminal charges of price fixing. Collectively, they paid more than $2 billion in criminal fines to antitrust regulators in the United States, Japan, South Korea, and the European Union. The antitrust cops in Brazil were hot on the trail. Now they were all defendants in the United States in a civil class-action lawsuit brought by companies that directly bought the screens from the defendants and then integrated them into finished electronic products for sale to consumers.

At first glance Kwon Electronics was unsympathetic and the case was a sure loser. But Jonathan saw something else. When he clerked for Judge Roy, he learned in the home builder supply price-fixing case that first purchasers in supply chains are the only ones that get to sue under the federal antitrust laws, yet they rarely suffer harm because they typically pass on any overcharges to their own customers, just like this case, where the big computer companies and cell phone and television makers undoubtedly passed on any flatscreen overcharges to their customers—the real victims of the price-fixing conspiracy. The big corporate buyers were just looking for a multibillion-dollar legal windfall. The challenge presented by a case legal pundits thought was a sure loser for Kwon, as well as the opportunity to stick it to a bunch of corporate grifters with an overreaching damages claim, riled Jonathan's competitive juices and convinced him to take the case. He let slide Oliver Truckle's high-handed comment, "Now this is our type of case—a flush antitrust defendant up shit's creek without a paddle but more than willing and able to pay us tens of millions of dollars at our standard rates to defend it before the case ultimately settles."

Kwon had been defended by typical Big Law litigation partners—sterling academic résumés, strong on paper and motion practice, short on jury trial skills. Those unimaginative lawyers, who were making millions running the hourly meter, had no inspiring ideas about how to win in light of the criminal guilty pleas. As one of their $1,800-an-hour partners asked in defeated resignation, "How the hell are we supposed to win when our client has already admitted it did it?" Not a bad question. But the client needed creative answers, not despairing questions, and a brilliant strategist and jury trial lawyer who might have some ingenious ideas to at least improve its settlement leverage. They needed an Arthur Schopenhauer talent who could hit a target no one else could hit, maybe even a genius who could hit a target no one else could even see. As it stood, it had neither. That was about to change.

The flatscreen case was known as the LCD Litigation. The technical name was Thin Film Transistor—Liquid Crystal Display. LCDs are panels, or screens, that are integrated into products such as computer monitors, laptops, mobile phones, and televisions that are then sold to consumers as finished products.

Not surprisingly, LCDs were and continue to be enormously popular with consumers. Flatscreens shrink the size, and certainly the depth, of some of consumers' favorite products. During the time of the conspiracy, annual global sales surpassed more than $50 billion. Until the mid-1990s, LCDs were manufactured and sold almost exclusively by Japanese companies. Then South Korean companies, including Kwon Electronics, entered the market, followed soon thereafter by Taiwanese manufacturers. The global market was flooded with excess LCDs. Supply overwhelmed demand, and prices predictably plummeted. All good news for consumers. Not so good news for the suppliers' profits. And big powerful corporations typically do not sit idly by while their profits perish. So they schemed.

The LCD suppliers decided that covert cooperation rather than crushing competition was a better way of pumping profits. Assuming, of course, that they did not get caught, always a tenuous assumption for such a daring, long-term undertaking. From early 1996 until the partners in crime did get caught in late 2006, the LCD manufacturers had created a global spiderweb of conspiratorial activities. With offices strategically placed all over the globe, including several in the United States, the price fixers conspired covertly by email and instant messaging, telephone calls, trade associations, rendezvous on golf courses and even bookstore coffee shops. When communicating their price-fixing intentions in writing, always a bad mistake for crooks to make, the dumb guys routinely included incriminating instructions to "destroy after reading," instructions many even dumber, dim-witted conspirators disregarded, helping to create a damning paper trail for the antitrust enforcers. It reminded Jonathan of the Detroit dolt who robbed an 8 Mile bar and then tossed his own wallet and license into the pile of the victims' wallets. Jonathan thought maybe these Southeast Asian conspirators were also doing Acapulco Gold water bong hits with Colt 45 chasers.

The conspirators' most brazen and favorite conspiracy meetings occurred in hotel rooms in Seoul and Tokyo. Not so clever, they dubbed them "Raise Price Meetings." Downright dumb, they took minutes of the meetings.

Dumber even yet, the conspirators sent their chief executive officers and presidents to the meetings to ensure that prices would be raised. No plausible deniability now. Each meeting was duly detailed in pages of minutes and distributed among the price fixers. For prosecutors and plaintiffs' lawyers, these incriminating minutes were a gold mine, a treasure trove of evidence that proved the point of an old Chinese saying that the palest ink is better than the best memory. This smoking hot, direct evidence was even better than the tape-recorded conversation between the CEOs of American and Braniff Airlines in the 1980s.

By late 2006, the jig was up. In a plea deal for lenient treatment, one of the cartel crooks ratted out the others, and the cartel was quickly busted by antitrust enforcers in the United States, South Korea, Japan, and the European Union. Every conspirator but one pled guilty to criminal price fixing. The one that didn't foolishly went to trial and was predictably clobbered. Clobbered as in a felony conviction, a $500 million fine, and several senior executives hauled off to federal prison. Jonathan thought, *No wonder criminal defense lawyers get paid in advance before trial.*

The follow-on civil class-action lawsuit of corporate buyers was considered a slam dunk for the plaintiffs. There were some technical defenses that might cause a nick here and a dent there in the plaintiffs' case, but it would not be credible for Kwon and the other defendants to deny participation in the conspiracy. Most of the defendants reasonably figured that it was defeat class certification or bust. And that would take a Hail Mary pass, maybe even literal divine intervention. But the sinners' prayers went unanswered, and several months after Jonathan entered the case, the trial judge, Sara Elston, ruled that the case would be treated as a class action. The settlement dominoes began immediately to fall. Three months before trial, the class plaintiffs had settled with every defendant but one. Jonathan's client.

Now settlement was off the table. The class plaintiffs had already collected $900 million in settlements. Their PhD economist estimated total damages of $2.4 billion. The plaintiffs were playing with house money. They were willing to roll the dice with a jury trial unless Jonathan's client was willing to pay $1.5 billion. With $900 million in their pockets, they wanted another $1.5 billion from Kwon so they could recover $2.4 billion, or 100 cents on the estimated damages dollar. Jonathan and his client knew that the expert's damages estimate was outrageously inflated. But there was no denying the obvious: trial would be risky, very risky. This was no time for conventional trial strategy or the faint of heart.

RUMBLE IN THE JUNGLE

As the LCD settlement negotiations collapsed, Jonathan received some good news in the semiconductor case. BSMC had picked the fight by suing AIQC for patent infringement in retaliation for AIQC's refusal to sell itself to BSMC. AIQC countersued. Now the trial judge granted Jonathan's motion to toss BSMC's patent suit as meritless. The judge even agreed with Jonathan's argument that the patent claim was "frivolous." Just like that, AIQC's case went from defense to pure offense on its antitrust monopolization claim. For good measure, the judge scheduled the trial six months after Jonathan's LCD trial was scheduled to conclude. Jonathan could hear Trane saying, "May you live in interesting times." The next year certainly was going to be a whirlwind for him.

By the time of the semiconductor and LCD cases, Jonathan had assembled a core trial team. Given how sparse trials are in Big Law, these were coveted spots for young lawyers who harbored any hopes of ever seeing the inside of a courtroom. The team was tight and exceptional, and the members played well-defined roles. By Big Law standards, where reams of lawyers clocked bloated hours on big cases, Jonathan's team was small. More Navy SEALs than infantry soldiers.

First there was David Joseph, by then a young partner who was in charge of the overall day-to-day management of both cases. If Jonathan was the chief executive officer, David was the chief operating officer of the cases. He would also handle some of the trial witnesses, including the oppositions' damages experts. A musician in his youth, David was a brilliant young lawyer who worked tirelessly, was meticulous and attentive to detail, and had a facility with the mathematics used by expert economists in antitrust cases. David finished law school at night at the University of Baltimore while he worked full time at the World Bank. David was Jonathan's indispensable trial team member.

Working closely with Jonathan and David was JP Hale, a newly minted partner and University of Virginia law graduate. Like David, JP graduated in the very top of his law school class, was unflappable, and was wonderful with witnesses, jokingly referred to as the witness whisperer. JP was a federal judicial clerk for highly regarded trial and appellate judges before he joined the firm. He would devote most of his time developing and marshaling the evidence in the pretrial discovery process and working closely with Jonathan to refine case themes and stories. Maya Gibson—senior associate, African American, and University of California at Berkeley honors law graduate—was another budding superstar and can't-miss future trial lawyer, as long as she got the opportunities. Maya was the point person on all legal filings, and there would be countless filings. She also worked with Jonathan developing the testimony of the main client witnesses.

The final two core team members were Ruth B. Greenfield and Kaori Settite, both Asian Americans. Ruth graduated number two in her Georgetown Law School class, was a judicial clerk for a prominent federal judge, and was now a third-year lawyer at the firm. Her mother adored Supreme Court Justice Ruth Bader Ginsburg and named her Ruth after the pioneering jurist. Ruth's mother never could have imagined that her diminutive black-robe hero would become the "notorious RBG" with her own bobblehead doll. The next-generation RBG, Ruth, was point on all legal research issues and an on-call utility player. Kaori was Jonathan's indispensable go-to paralegal whose organizational skills were second to none. The cases could never run as smoothly as they did without Kaori's contributions.

The team worked at a furious pace to prepare both cases for trial. The LCD trial was first up and just around the corner. As he did for every case and trial, from the start Jonathan figured out the story he wanted to tell the jury, set the strategy, marshaled the evidence, and adjusted along the way as circumstances dictated. One of Jonathan's favorite aphorisms he'd learned from Trane was that there are no surprises at trial, only insufficient preparation and imagination. Over the years, Jonathan developed an acute appreciation for the role of imagination in jury trial work, from envisioning how the trial story should be conceived and executed to the role of intuition and creativity to make for a morally compelling narrative for the jury. But he also never forgot Thomas Edison's practical observation that vision without execution is just a hallucination.

Jonathan convened a team meeting to refine the LCD trial strategy. This was going to require deft finesse and plenty of boldness. JP made sure there were easels in the conference room because Jonathan felt naked without them. He habitually drew pictures, charts, and graphs and prepared bullet-point talking points. Typically, at the conclusion of Jonathan's strategy meetings, somebody would click pictures on their smartphone camera and work them up for distribution to the team. Jonathan kicked off the meeting with a depressing question.

"Okay, folks, how are we possibly going to win this antitrust case where our own client and its CEO have pled guilty to criminal charges of price-fixing, where our CEO spent a year in jail, the CEOs of the other conspirators have also pled guilty and have agreed to be cooperating witnesses for the plaintiffs, and one more thing, none of our South Korean witnesses speak English?"

"So tell me again why we are not settling?" the ever-practical Maya asked in resignation.

"That ship has sailed. The plaintiffs have $900 million in the bank. The contingency-fee lawyers will get at least 20 percent, or $180 million. They feel like they have nothing to lose by going to trial," said Jonathan matter-of-factly.

"I don't blame them," chimed in JP. "By their calculations, they are going to win on liability. To them, the only question is how much they are going to win and whether to add a Bentley or Lamborghini to their luxury car collection."

"They already have those. Think Cessna or Gulfstream," Jonathan corrected, drawing sighs from the group. "Besides, these class-action plaintiffs' lawyers settle virtually every one of their cases. Every once in a while, they need to try one to prove they aren't afraid to go to trial. It increases the threat potential in future settlement negotiations. So I ask once again, how are we going to win?"

"Let's set the table, as Jonathan likes to say," suggested David, the protégé, "and first talk about what the plaintiff must prove to win."

"Just a second," Jonathan requested as he stood up to walk over to one of the easels to write it down. Just as he would do for the jury.

David resumed. "First, they have to prove there was an LCD conspiracy from 1996 to 2006. Second, they have to prove that our client was part of that conspiracy."

"Based on the evidence," JP sarcastically remarked, "I don't think you need to go to Harvard to prove the first two points," a reference to the lead plaintiffs' lawyer, which the team understood.

"We'll get to our defenses," David said, moving on, "so let's first finish with the plaintiffs' proof requirements. It's not enough for them to prove a conspiracy and our client's participation in it; they also have to prove some injury to competition for buying and selling LCDs."

"That won't be hard either—oh, sorry," JP blurted before apologizing for veering off course again.

"Maya, what's next in the proof chain?" asked David.

"Well, I think we all agree that the real fight in this case goes to the next two points. So, Jonathan, point number four on your easel is this, and it has two parts. The class plaintiffs must prove that they bought LCDs in the United States. And they have to prove that the agreement to charge higher prices was effective. Meaning, our client and the coconspirators actually stuck to their agreement and charged higher prices all those years."

"Yeah," Ruth weighed in, "that was a big ruling we won when Judge Elston ruled that if the sales took place outside of the United States, then they were out of the case. Great argument, David!"

"That's right," Maya agreed, "so the plaintiff must prove they bought LCDs at inflated prices in the United States. If they prove all that, then the case just becomes a counting contest of how much extra they paid."

JP couldn't resist jumping ahead again. "We know they bought some LCDs in the US, everybody agrees with that, but here's the rub: Did they actually pay inflated prices for those LCDs?"

"That is the rub," David said, nodding in agreement, "and our expert and cross-examination of their expert will give the jury a lot to think about."

"Which brings me to point number five," Maya wrapped up. "If the plaintiffs can prove the first four points, they still have to prove with accuracy the amount of damages they are entitled to recover. That's the counting contest."

Jonathan had written all five points on his easel. "Okay, you masters of the courtroom, how are we going to win?"

"I feel like that's a trick question," JP said, somewhat guardedly. "Isn't the real question not how are we going to win, but how badly are we going to lose? Aren't we really talking about damage control and not embarrassing ourselves by losing the biggest jury verdict of the year?"

"Remember, genius is hitting a target nobody else can see. This team is too young to remember the Rumble in the Jungle, but that's how we are going to win." Jonathan was smiling and animated. He turned to Ruth and asked, "You have no idea what I'm talking about, do you?"

"Not a clue."

"The Rumble in the Jungle was a heavyweight championship boxing match between the reigning undefeated champion, George Foreman, and the former champion, 'I am the greatest' Muhammad Ali. The fight took place in Zaire in October 1974, dubbed by some as the greatest sporting event of the twentieth century. It was historic. Foreman was considered invincible. Some feared that the dynamite his punches packed might kill Ali. But Ali, a prohibitive underdog, won with an eighth-round knockout."

"I still don't understand," complained a still-confused Ruth.

"Ali employed a rope-a-dope strategy to beat the younger, stronger Foreman."

"Boxing and ropes and dopes?" Maya smirked.

"Yes, ropes and dopes. Ali would lean against the ropes, cover-up, and let Foreman punch away without landing fatal body

blows or kill shots to the head. Ali would take strategic shots at
Foreman. This went on round after round until Foreman tired and
faltered in round eight. Ali then seized the opening and pounced
with a combination of punches that knocked out Foreman. Just
like we're going to take a flurry of early plaintiffs' punches before
knocking them out at the end of the trial."

"Sounds great, but as you always say, the devil is in the details,
so how are we going to do this? How are we going to avoid having a
hallucination and getting our brains beat in?" quizzed JP.

"You watch, these plaintiffs are going to overwhelm the jury
with all the evidence of an LCD conspiracy. With great fanfare
they will parade in all the guilty pleas, notebooks of the Raise Price
Meetings, reams of emails and telephone logs. Witness after cooperating witness speaking through translators about the conspiracy.
They'll talk about a sinister coverup. They will punch themselves
out for a few weeks proving their strongest point. They'll be like
the basketball player who always goes to her right hand and doesn't
work on her weaker left hand."

"I'm a tennis player. I like the forehand/backhand analogy better," offered Ruth.

"We'll work on the best analogies, but Jonathan, are we even
going to defend against the conspiracy charge?" asked David.

"That's when we lean against the ropes. Soft resistance. On
fringe points where we will have some credibility and can take some
strategic shots, like when the conspiracy started. When did it end?
Was it really one uninterrupted conspiracy? All the points that go
to the effectiveness of the conspiracy and the proper amount of
damages, which we all know are our real defenses. Like Ali did to
Foreman, we'll find our strategic spots and throw some jabs. But we
can't blow our credibility. If we do, we're toast. The jury needs to
know that anytime one of us or our client speaks, we're shooting
straight."

"Is this where we get to your fact versus opinion testimony trial
speech?" asked JP.

"You've learned well, young Jedi. As did I from Judge Roy. The
first two questions, was there a conspiracy and did our client participate in it, are both fact questions. Yes or no answers. The facts,

documents, and eyewitnesses either tell the conspiracy story or they don't. And we all know how that story is going to play out."

"So what about opinion testimony?" asked Maya.

"That's the first punch in our one-two knockout punch. Plaintiffs are relying on expert opinion testimony for points three, four, and five. Point three, competition in the US was harmed. Point four, plaintiffs paid inflated prices because the conspiracy was effective. Point five, the total damages are $2.4 billion. Never forget the soft underbelly. We're going to pound and pound that soft belly of theirs. Like Rocky pounding away at Apollo Creed's rib cage, knocking the air right out of him. All of those hot-air opinions are based on assumptions, selective use of data and models, and we're going to suck all of the hot air right out of them until they are nothing but a pool of drool. Oh, and there's one other thing. I have a trick up my sleeve, the second of the two knockout punches, but more on that later. David, take over about what you and I discussed our goal should be."

David went to another easel to write as he went along. Jonathan flashed a proud smile.

"Okay, we know their expert economist opines that global damages amount to $2.4 billion. On cross-examination, my goal will be getting admissions that whittle down the number. But let's first talk about what our expert will say.

"Of course it would be great if our expert said the damages are zero. But that wouldn't be credible if the jury finds there was a years-long conspiracy, which they almost undoubtedly will. And if the choice for the jury is zero or what the plaintiffs' expert tells them, there would be too great a risk that the jury would just go with the plaintiffs' estimate. So we decided on a different strategic option. Our expert will attack their guy's mathematical model, correct his mistakes, and say that even if you used his model, the damages couldn't be more than $40 to $62 million. When I cross their expert, I should be able to whittle down his $2.4-billion figure and get him to admit that his damages estimate is not one number but a range of numbers."

"Great job, David," interjected Jonathan, "so the strategy is to get the jury thinking about damages as a number between what our expert says it is and the low end of the range of their expert. That's what we have learned from three different mock jury exercises with our consultants."

"That certainly was an eye-opener," Maya said, shaking her head. "The mock jurors were all over the place and really didn't pay any attention to the legal instructions."

"That's right," Jonathan agreed, "and the real jurors will likely do the same. What else?"

"For all the bad conspiracy evidence," Maya remembered with hope, "the mock jurors didn't believe these plaintiffs were hurt by the conspiracy and most of them were reluctant to award them big damages."

"Why not?"

"Because these plaintiffs, mostly big corporations themselves, buy LCD screens and assemble them with other parts to make and sell computers and mobile phones and televisions. They just pass on their costs to people like the jurors and us, the people who buy the finished products. So they don't think these huge corporate plaintiffs were hurt at all. Just like our real jurors might not believe these screen buyers were hurt to the tune of billions of dollars."

"But wait," Ruth protested, "Judge Elston will follow the law and instruct the jury not to consider whether these plaintiffs passed on any overcharges to consumers and will instruct them just to focus on the prices Kwon and the coconspirators charged these plaintiffs."

"She will indeed," Jonathan agreed, before dismissing the point, "and it will likely go in one ear and out the other. At least for some of the jurors. Once the seed of cost pass on is planted, it will be impossible for the jurors not to wrestle with that issue when they consider the proper amount of damages to award these particular plaintiffs. It is unlikely that our jury will have much sympathy for these corporate plaintiffs, some of which are multibillion-dollar corporations. And how sweet it will be to stick it to some of these non-tax paying corporate opportunists looking for a legal windfall with an artificially pumped-up-damages claim. One of the reasons I took the case."

"Is that your trick up your sleeve?" asked Maya.

"No, the jury will figure out that issue on their own. The evidence will be clear that nobody buys LCDs as stand-alone products. They buy them and then resell them as part of computers, phones, and TVs. The jury is not going to think that multibillion-dollar sellers of computers and cell phones, some of the biggest names in the tech world, were hurt by the conspiracy. They are going to think that those corporate giants just turned around and stuck it to the consumers.

"I have an even better trick up my sleeve. But we have to limit the damages to under the low end of their expert's range. If we do, the class plaintiffs won't recover a single penny from our client. Like Ali, we will be the greatest!" Jonathan joked.

Smiling, Ruth rolled her eyes. She and the others were learning in real time that trials and trial preparation with a talent like Jonathan sure beats the hell out of what most litigators do.

CROSS-EXAMINATION

The run-up to the LCD trial was intense. Staring at a potential loss of $2.4 billion invites visits from the Goddess of the Moon to rattle trial lawyers with night terrors and many sleepless nights. And she who must be feared whispered in Congress's ear when they decided that the judge, in antitrust cases, *must* triple any amount of money the jury awards to the plaintiffs. That could put the exposure at $7.2 billion in the LCD case. Trial lawyers who lose multibillion-dollar verdicts are haunted by visions of aisle clean-up at the Piggly Wiggly.

One week before trial, Jonathan and team checked into San Francisco's Le Méridien hotel across from Embarcadero Plaza. They set up litigation war rooms in three conference rooms on the second floor. Super paralegal Kaori handled all the logistics. When the trial team arrived, everything was up and working and ready to go.

Friday late afternoon before trial, Jonathan decided to shut down work and take the team to dinner. Their choice. Big mistake. Every one of them was online searching their screens for the best restaurants in San Francisco. Jonathan heard some of the best arguments, of any type, he had ever heard over the competing choices. Hungry, ultimately the team went with Maya's pick, Alice Waters' Chez Panisse restaurant across the Bay Bridge in Berkeley, where Maya had gone to law school. To complement the wonderful food, especially the black truffles and winter vegetables with Indian spices, Jonathan ordered some bottles of Kosta Browne pinot noir from the Russian River Valley. The team needed this downtime for the grueling trial that lay ahead.

Trial started Monday morning at nine o'clock with jury selection. A jury was seated by the end of the day, including two jurors Jonathan thought would be good with numbers; a young rebellious-looking woman with tats covering her neck, brunette hair shaved on one side and streaked in purple, green, and pink on the other, and a lower lip pierced with three rings; and an assistant professor of sociology at San Francisco State University whose PhD dissertation was titled "Tallness and the Woman Athlete: A Critical Study of Outsiderness and Normalized Gender Height Bias." Jonathan told the team he felt good about their jury.

Just as Jonathan had predicted, in his opening statement, plaintiffs' counsel went almost all-in describing "one of the biggest antitrust conspiracies of all time." For effect he wheeled in a cart of notebooks claiming they contained the "mountain" of evidence proving the conspiracy. He had a chart with the faces of the CEOs of the eight LCD companies, mug shots after they had been booked and fingerprinted. In flowing and hoary rhetoric, he talked about how the purpose of the antitrust laws was to protect free and open competition, even telling the jury that antitrust law was the "Magna Carta" of American capitalism. Jonathan thought that last line likely didn't resonate with the sociology professor and Ms. Rainbow Hair. What the lawyer barely mentioned, however, was damages, perhaps fearing, like many inexperienced trial lawyers, that the jurors would be offended about talk of huge dollars too soon. So instead he told the jurors that they would hear from a PhD economist who had "conservatively" calculated "very large damages."

Jonathan agreed with many trial lawyers that the opening statement is usually the most important part of the trial. The first time the jurors get to hear an explanation of the lawyer's case. But general rules always give way to the circumstances presented. Jonathan knew, rope-a-dope, that his knockout punches needed to come late, during damages evidence and the drama of witness examination. So he gave a short opening. Mostly telling the jury that there are always two sides to every story and asking them to keep an open mind, as he knew they would. Then he zeroed in on fact versus opinion testimony, emphasizing that plaintiffs' evidence of competitive harm and damages would be the product of opinion testimony.

Opinions that were unreliable and grossly overstated. It was a bold promise and could backfire if the jury liked the plaintiffs' expert and disliked his expert. But Jonathan was paid to make tough judgment calls. He felt good about this one.

The plaintiffs put on three weeks of conspiracy evidence, made longer because many of the Asian witnesses' testimony had to be translated. Maya did most of the cross-examination of these witnesses and scored good points. All in all, Jonathan was sensing that the jury was more bored than incensed. And defense lawyers get tetchy when juries get angry.

Then came the plaintiffs' last witness, their damages expert. Some people try but simply cannot conceal their contemptuous arrogance or wipe a perpetual smirk off their face. Dr. Russell Lame was one of them. A PhD economist, Dr. Lame was not a professor. He instead worked full time in a litigation consulting firm. In other words, he was a full-time gun for hire. A courtroom mercenary. Jonathan felt a jolt as he zoned out for a few seconds and imagined Trane singing Pink Floyd's "Money" while Lame was having a gas making quite a stash with litigation cash. Dr. Lame quickly explained his opinions and said he had created something called a statistical regression model to show harm to competition and to calculate damages. His condescending words and body language suggested that all of this should be self-evident to this or any other jury of ordinary Americans. He testified that he had calculated global damages in the amount of $2.4 billion. With a look of smarmy self-satisfaction on his smug face, he volunteered that his damages estimate was a "conservative" estimate, drawing raised eyebrows from Judge Elston and a few chuckles from the gallery.

David was assigned the cross-examination. He was a young partner with very good trial instincts. When cross-examining an expert, Jonathan had taught David not to wade into the expert's wheelhouse. You likely won't pin him down or shut him up. Cross is about control, and you never want to lose control of the witness. Stand on firm ground, like facts and admissions the expert must make or risk looking like a shameless shill for his side, which of course is precisely what he is. After many skull sessions with Jonathan, David refined his strategy with two overarching goals for his cross of Dr. Lame: whittle down the $2.4-billion damages figure and get the schmuck to admit that he estimated a broad range of numbers, not just a single figure. David had worked with Jonathan for several years now and dreamed of an opportunity like this. He was ready.

"Good afternoon, Dr. Lame. We have never met before. My name is David Joseph."

"How do you do?"

"Fine, thank you. I would like to start by seeing if there are some things you and I can agree on. Sound fair to you?"

"Sure, that sounds fair enough, I guess."

Some people just can't help being smug, Jonathan thought.

"Dr. Lame, I have reviewed your résumé, and it appears that you have testified in three jury trials in the past ten years. Is that correct?"

"Yes, it is."

"And you have testified in depositions forty-five times in the last ten years, correct?"

"I don't have my résumé in front of me, but that sounds about right."

David corrected him. "Actually, Dr. Lame, you do have your résumé; it is Tab 1 in the notebook I handed up to you before we started." David was keeping Lame on a tight leash.

"Oh, okay. Yes, I see it now. Yeah, forty-five times."

"Now each time you testified in your three jury trials, you testified for the plaintiff, correct?"

Stammering, Lame said, "Oh, oh, I'm not sure, but I don't disagree."

Yanking the leash, David said, "Well, if you need to review your résumé to refresh your recollection, please do so."

"That's okay."

"And each of the forty-five times you testified in a deposition, you testified on behalf of the plaintiffs, isn't that also true?"

"Let me see. Oh, yeah, that's true."

"In fact, sir, in the last ten years, you have never testified on the behalf of a corporate defendant, have you?"

"I guess not."

"Dr. Lame, the jury doesn't want you to guess. You have never testified on behalf of the defendant, isn't that true?" David knew Michael Corleone's line about keeping your friends close and your enemies even closer. He wasn't going to give Lame an inch of running room.

"Yes, that's true."

Jonathan, feeling proud, thought David was off to a great start. He was firm but polite and in ten minutes exposed Lame to be a plaintiff's jukebox witness. Pay him the money and he'll sing the song of plaintiff's choice. Grab the cash and make a stash. David resumed.

"Dr. Lame, let me switch gears and turn to another topic. In this case you are charging the plaintiffs $1,300 an hour for your time, correct?"

"That's my standard rate, yes." Out of the corner of his eye, David thought he saw Ms. Rainbow Hair snort.

"And you agree, do you not, that you have a staff of twelve other people working with you on this case?"

"I'm not sure of the total number, but I do have a staff working under my supervision."

"We have your billing records right here. Would you like to take a look and confirm the number?"

"No, no, I'll take your word for it."

"Not my word, Dr. Lame, your word and the number of staff members listed on the billing records you send monthly to the plaintiffs' lawyers, correct?"

"Okay, yes."

"Now your billing records are at Tab 2 of the notebook right in front of you, so please feel free to check, but you would also agree with me that your firm has already billed the plaintiffs $3.4 million in this case?" David was making sure that the jury was getting the message that every admission he was getting was not some lawyer trick but coming straight from Lame and his own records.

"Let me double check; that sounds high. Okay, yes, that's right." Audible gasps in the courtroom.

"And you are a fifty percent owner of your consulting firm, correct?"

"Yes."

"And last year you personally made $4.5 million doing litigation consulting work, correct?"

"That's correct. I'm paid appropriately for my work."

"Appropriately, did you say?" David asked, with just a light hint of incredulity at Lame's self-satisfaction of making at least more than twenty-five times what any of the jurors made in a year to offer bought-and-paid-for opinions.

"Yes, appropriately."

"By the way, your litigation consulting work is your full-time job, correct?"

"I don't know what you mean."

"Really? I mean you work full time at the firm where you are a fifty percent owner, correct?"

"Oh, yes. That's correct."

Jonathan thought, *a jukebox millionaire witness. This dipstick doesn't come close to my expert, Professor Jennifer Applebaum of UCLA, who teaches economics to undergraduate and graduate students.* If the jury has to choose between Lame and Applebaum, Jonathan was feeling good about his chances, especially with the sociology professor who very likely was going to listen to a full-time female professor over a full-time male mercenary.

David moved on to his final line of questions.

"Dr. Lame, a few questions about your damages calculation. This is an estimate, correct?"

"Yes, but an estimate based on regression analysis, a well-accepted method for calculating damages."

"An estimate, correct?"

"Yes."

"Based on a model you constructed, correct?"

"That's correct?"

"A model you constructed for this litigation?"

"Yes, to calculate damages in this case."

"Your model and the math you used is so complicated that you didn't even try to explain it to the jury on direct examination, did you?"

"I'm not sure how to answer."

"Right. You didn't explain all of your equations that you used to come up with your estimate, did you?" David was subtly making the point that Lame's model was a black box that plaintiffs were implicitly asking the jury to take on faith. If they liked Lame, that might work. But if they didn't, it would be easy to reject his opinion.

"Well, I could if you want me to."

"Not my job, sir. You had your chance when your lawyer was asking questions."

"Objection, Your Honor, argumentative," the plaintiffs' lawyer objected.

David had made his point. "I'll move on. Dr. Lame, this case is the first time you have ever done work in the LCD business, correct?"

"Yeah, but I don't see your point. My model could apply to lots of industries."

"So the answer to my question is yes, this is your first time working in the LCD business, correct?"

"Yes, as I just said." Lame just couldn't suppress his smugness or his smirk, not even when he was being paid $1,300 an hour to try to win over the jury.

Jonathan glanced at the jury and sensed a real dislike of Lame.

"You agree with me, don't you, Dr. Lame, that $2.4 billion is an overstated estimate of damages in this case?"

"I don't agree at all."

"Well, you agree that your estimate is for total global damages, correct?" David walked over to an easel and wrote "$2.4 billion."

"Yes, that's correct."

"And did you know that Judge Elston has ruled that these class plaintiffs can seek damages only for purchases they made in the United States?"

"Well, I can easily pull out the non-US purchases."

"We'll get to that. But first, you estimated that overcharges could be as low as 2 percent and as high as 10 percent, right?"

"Yeah, I did."

"But you decided to go with the 10 percent figure, correct?"

"Yes, I think that's a justifiable figure?"

"And based on your own model, 2 percent is also justifiable, correct?" So much for the "conservative" estimate.

"Yes, I suppose so."

"The total global purchases are $24 billion, correct?"

"Yes."

"And ten percent of $24 billion is $2.4 billion, correct?"

"Correct."

"But you estimated that only 40 percent of those sales occurred in the United States, correct?"

"That's correct."

"And 40 percent of $24 billion equals $9.6 billion, correct?"

"I'll trust your math."

"Do you need a calculator, Dr. Lame?" David had Lame on the run.

"No, no. Forty percent of $24 billion equals $9.6 billion."

"You agree that 10 percent of 9.6 billion is 960 million, so, based on your estimate of a 10-percent overcharge, that would amount to $960 million in damages, correct?" David wrote the number on the easel after crossing out $2.4 billion.

"Yes, that's correct."

"So the first adjustment we need to make to your damages estimate of $2.4 billion is to lower it to $960 million based on a 10-percent overcharge, correct?"

"Yes, that's correct if we're only talking about US sales."

"But if the overcharge was only 2 percent, as you yourself estimated, then the damages would be $192 million, correct? Two percent of $9.6 billion equals $192 million, correct?" David wrote that number on the easel.

"Yes, that would be the model's result."

"Your own model's result, correct?"

"Yes."

"Now this range, $192 million on the low end and $960 million on the higher end is quite a swing, wouldn't you agree?" This was a heads-I-win-tails-you-lose trap question for Lame. If he said yes, he made David's point. If he said no, he would look like a foolish liar.

Buying time, Lame responded, "I'm not sure what you mean. Those are the results of my model."

"Yes, your model. Your model shows a swing of $786 million, doesn't it?"

"Yes, the difference between $960 million and $192 million is $768 million."

Jonathan had told the jury in his opening statement that they would show that Lame's opinion testimony was unreliable. The jurors were now seeing it with their own eyes. So David asked, "Dr. Lame, that's a huge difference in your model results, isn't that fair to say?"

"I don't agree or disagree. It is what it is."

"And what it is, *is* a *staggering* difference of close to a *billion* dollars based on your own model, correct?"

"*Staggering* is your word, not mine."

"*Staggering* is your model, not mine. I have no further use of this witness, Your Honor." The sociology professor bowed her head to conceal a smile.

GENIUS SEES THE TARGET

Jonathan thought David's cross-examination of Lame was masterful. It gave him precisely what he needed for closing argument. He predicted the jury would like his expert's rebuttal testimony, and she in fact did well and handled her cross-examination skillfully. If he could get the jury to debate damages in the range of $40 million and $192 million, there would be cause for celebration. Other than Professor Applebaum, Jonathan only called two other witnesses. One from the client, handled by Maya, and an expert on Asian ways of doing business, handled by JP.

The case was ready for closing argument. Jonathan listened carefully to the plaintiffs' argument, didn't hear anything he had not anticipated, and decided to stick with his prepared remarks.

In a navy blue pinstripe suit, white shirt with thin blue pinstripes, emerald-green tie, and black polished shoes, Jonathan rose, walked to the middle of the room, and addressed judge and jury.

"May it please the court. Good afternoon, ladies and gentlemen. I stood before you five weeks ago and told you in my opening statement that the real issue that you will need to decide is not whether there was a conspiracy—there was. No, the real issue is whether the conspiracy was effective. Whether it caused the harm concocted by Dr. Lame's mathematical models. And whether the plaintiffs in this case, sellers of electronics equipment, were hurt to the tune of hundreds of millions of dollars. The evidence proves that these plaintiffs have tried to oversell their claim to you. Let's take it step by step.

"The conspiracy claim first. According to the plaintiffs, there was a single, uninterrupted conspiracy for ten years. They didn't come close to proving that overreaching claim. Now let me say once again that my client should not have gone to those Raise Price Meetings in Tokyo and Seoul. And there were agreements at those meetings. But the evidence showed two very important things. First, those meetings lasted four years, not ten, and my client didn't attend all of them.

"The second thing the evidence showed was that the agreements often fell apart soon after the meetings ended. Remember how our expert, Professor Applebaum from UCLA, showed you actual pricing data? Remember when she came down off the stand, stood right over there, and went through my client's actual sales of LCDs and compared them to the agreed-upon prices? How much lower my client's actual prices were? What that proved is that my client is what economists call a cartel cheater. In plain English, that just means that my client was a price cutter. My client didn't charge the agreed-upon prices—it charged much lower prices. And it's the actual prices that need to be accounted for. The conspiracy, plain and simple, was ineffective.

"That brings me to point number two. I promised you in my opening statement that their evidence of harm and damages would all be opinion testimony. I kept my promise. The horse they rode was Dr. Lame, a $1,300-an-hour full-time litigation consultant who has never testified on behalf of a defendant. Plaintiffs have paid him more than $3 million. Dr. Lame just badly missed the mark. As the trier of fact, you get to judge the credibility of the witnesses. Not just what they say, but also how they say it. When my partner Mr. Joseph was cross-examining Dr. Lame, did you notice Dr. Lame's body language? Did you notice the distortions of his face, the contortions of his body? Did he seem to you to have any confidence in his mathematical model that he ginned up for this trial? You get to judge.

"They are the plaintiffs. They have the burden of proof. If their damages claim is riddled with mistakes and is unreliable, you can reject it. You can reject it completely. You remember Mr. Joseph's cross-examination questions of Dr. Lame. Dr. Lame admitted that his $2.4 billion damages calculation was overstated. Overstated by at least $1.4 billion, by his own reckoning. Dr. Lame also admitted he had calculated a range for damages, not just one number. That range swung wildly from the low end of $192 million to $960 million on the high end. How reliable is that? And then with a straight face he told you that his high-end pick was a 'conservative' estimate. Please, do not be conned."

Jonathan made a mental note that the sociology professor rolled her eyes in disgust and Ms. Rainbow grunted. He had very little doubt that, in the eyes of those two jurors, Lame had no chance against Applebaum. That contest is where Jonathan was headed next. All the jurors were taking notes.

"Ask yourselves this question: How reliable is Dr. Lame's black-box model when it varies by $768 million? Judge Elston will give you instructions before you deliberate, and she will tell you that you can use your common sense in your deliberations. Ladies and gentlemen, Dr. Lame's opinions do not pass the common sense test.

"They do not pass the math test either. That's why we called Professor Jennifer Applebaum as a witness. Professor Applebaum received her PhD in economics from Stanford, served one time as the chief economist of the Antitrust Division of the Department of Justice, and has taught economics courses to undergraduate and graduate students at UCLA for fifteen years. Her classes include statistics and mathematical models. Unlike Dr. Lame, Professor Applebaum is a full-time teacher and must write and publish papers evaluated rigorously by her peers. Dr. Lame has not published a single paper in a professional journal.

"Like she would do in the classroom, Professor Applebaum studied Dr. Lame's statistical model and concluded that it is unreliable and therefore his damages estimates are worthless. Actually, *worthless* is my word. You'll recall Professor Applebaum's more charitable words, 'Dr. Lame's calculations do not accurately measure what they are trying to measure.'

"So I asked Professor Applebaum if she could correct Dr. Lame's mistakes and, using his own model, calculate damages if one just assumed the plaintiffs' conspiracy allegations were true. She did. You remember her testimony. In Professor Applebaum's professional, scholarly judgment, Dr. Lame's model would still be unreliable.

But even so, correcting for all his mistakes, the proper amount of damages would be in the range of $40 to $62 million."

Jonathan paused and retrieved the easel David had used in his cross-examination of Dr. Lame. He placed it right in front of the jurors. Jonathan then put a red line through the $192 million number and wrote $40 million, and a red line through the $960 million number and wrote $62 million. His instincts told him there was no more to say about Dr. Lame.

Jonathan finished by thanking the jury. He told them he was confident that they would render a just verdict.

After the jury went out to begin their deliberations, Jonathan convened a team meeting back at the hotel. Now was the time for the trick up his sleeve. Trane, who had flown out from DC to watch Jonathan's closing argument, joined them.

"Okay, folks, $300 million is our magic number," Jonathan started.

Trane interrupted. "Before you begin, let me just say that this team did one hell of a job. I read the trial transcript as it was delivered each night, and you were all great. You were up against nearly impossible odds. You are going to lose, but you can hold your heads up high. You have a real shot of getting a verdict in the low range of their expert's calculations. If you get a $300 million verdict, that would be an outstanding result given the terrible facts on your side."

"Thanks, Jack, but we're not done yet," Jonathan said anxiously. "Any verdict of $300 million or under and we don't pay a penny."

"How the hell does that work?" asked an incredulous Trane.

"Glad you asked. Ruth, do you have the legal memo you've been working on?"

"Right here. Jonathan is right. The law is clear on this point."

"Explain how that works again," requested JP.

"Go ahead, Ruth, the simple version," Jonathan admonished.

"Okay, the idea is pretty straightforward. The law only allows a plaintiff a single recovery for her damages. But the antitrust laws triple the amount of any recovery. Our jury doesn't know this and doesn't know that the plaintiffs have already recovered $900 million in settlements."

"I get it," said Trane, the quick-witted old fox. "That's why

$300 million is the magic number. $300 million times 3 equals $900 million, money those plaintiffs already have."

"Exactly," said Ruth. "Even if we lose, our client wouldn't have to start paying unless the damages award is more than $300 million before tripling. It's called set-off."

"I'll be damned. Are you positive that's the law?" Trane asked.

"Positive," Ruth replied with confidence. "There aren't many cases on the subject, but I read each one many times."

"Ruth is right. I read them also," Jonathan said reassuringly. "That is why David's cross of Lame was so crucial. He got that jackleg to admit his low-range number is $192 million. Three times that equals $576 million. And that is why Professor Applebaum's testimony was so important. She destroyed Lame's calculations, was extremely credible, and drops the damages to $40 to $62 million. We have a damn good shot at getting the jury debating a range between $40 million and $192 million."

"Yeah," Maya agreed, "after Professor Applebaum came off the stand and just talked to the jury, the sociology professor and Ms. Lip Ring were furiously taking notes."

"So here's the plan," Jonathan directed. "After the jury returns with its verdict, we will fill in the actual amount times three in Ruth's memo and ask the judge to set it off the $900 million in settlement dollars. If the verdict is under $300 million, we declare total victory."

The team was still in their meeting when Jonathan got a call on his iPhone. It was Judge Elston's' deputy clerk. The jury had a verdict. The team piled into taxies and raced back to court. The jury had deliberated for only a few hours.

Not a good sign for the defense in a long, complex trial. Did the jury even consider the defendant's evidence? The verdict form was long, but there were only three decisions that mattered. Yes, the jury found that Jonathan's client participated in the LCD conspiracy. Yes, the plaintiffs proved that they had suffered damages. No surprises yet. Waiting for the next announcement was excruciating. On the line that requested the amount of damages, the jury foreperson, the sociology professor, wrote $40 million. Jonathan finally exhaled. The very lowest damages amount on the table. The jury lanced Lame and completely accepted Professor Applebaum's testimony.

Giant corporations looking for a legal windfall with an over-reaching damages claim were going home empty-handed. Jonathan smiled as he remembered one of his favorite southern sayings from his milk price-fixing days: pigs get fat and hogs get slaughtered.

Outside the courthouse on the front plaza, the lead lawyer for the plaintiffs told the press that they were gratified with the jury's verdict. He went on to gloat that the $40 million verdict would be tripled to $120 million, and told the press it was "a great victory for the class I'm privileged to represent." Jonathan declined to comment.

One month later, Judge Elston granted Jonathan's motion to offset the verdict against the settlement dollars. His client, found liable for participating in a ten-year price-fixing conspiracy, walked away without paying a penny to the big-corporate plaintiffs. Asked by the press to comment, Jonathan was terse in an email response: "We are gratified with Judge Elston's decision."

FAMILY IS WHERE THE HEART IS

The news was not unexpected. When you reach the age of nine-ty-eight, death is not far away. Improvements in health science and technology as well as advances in nutrition and sanitation have extended average human life expectancy but only by staving off premature death. Only a minuscule percentage of the population makes it to one hundred. Death itself is still the inexorable fate of human beings. The elixir of immortality is quest, not conquest. Doctors do not officially declare that a person dies of old age or natural causes, but by and large that is how many people would prefer to end their sojourn on planet earth. A long life lived well with a quiet and peaceful end. That is how the candle went out for Jonathan's maternal grandmother. Her name was Harriet, but everyone called her Hattie.

Jonathan got the news a week after the LCD verdict. The funeral and gathering were going to be held in southwestern Ohio, just north of Cincinnati, where Hattie lived her entire life. Hattie was predeceased two years by her husband of seventy-eight years, Ed, and one daughter. Her surviving daughter, Pam, Jonathan's mother, would be there with her husband and Jonathan's father, Bob. Jonathan's two sisters, Susan and Jenny, would also be there. Susan divorced five years ago. Jenny and her husband, Dan, as well as their two children, both in college, would also be there.

Hattie wanted a funeral with a Catholic mass. Until her last peaceful breath, she still harbored hopes that Jonathan would become the first American pope, conveniently overlooking the numerous prerequisite check boxes left blank on Jonathan's papal scorecard, starting with practicing Catholicism. But Hattie did not want a mournful affair. Secure in her faith and the life she had led, Hattie devoutly believed that she was going to reunite with her husband Ed and deceased daughter once she passed through the pearly gates of heaven. Hattie had also lived her life with gusto and encouraged a post-mass gathering to celebrate her life and enjoy each other's company. The family honored both wishes.

Jonathan did not see his parents or sisters very often. They all lived in Ohio, he in DC. With his work schedule, he tried to visit once or twice a year, but typically made it only once. It had been more than a year since he had last seen them. This visit, a memorable vacation they had all taken together three years earlier would dominate the evening's conversation. Jonathan excepted, the family was short on means and money but long on love. Jonathan's sister Jenny loved Leo Tolstoy's novel *Anna Karenina* and liked to say that if Tolstoy was indeed right that all happy families are alike, then shared loved must be the single common denominator that makes it so. A lot of love was shared that evening.

Hattie had always dreamed of traveling to Rome and visiting the Vatican and the pope. Pam, Jonathan's mother, gently tried to temper her mother's lofty expectations by telling her that the supreme pontiff did not sit for personal visits and likely would not make an exception for Hattie.

Jonathan's parents also longed to go to Rome, but the expense was beyond their means and the fear and uncertainty of international travel were too daunting for them. Jonathan had an idea and an offer they couldn't refuse. The trip was on him, and he would lead the way. So Jonathan met his parents, Jenny and Dan, and Susan at the Cincinnati airport and they flew to Rome to see the marvels of what ancient writers called the Eternal City built on seven hills. Once accurately described as Caput Mundi, or the Capital of the World, Rome long ago ceased to be the center of the universe, but its endearing charm endures in its history, monuments, relics, and people. The family's memories were fond ones.

"Mom, I still can't believe you got on that airplane. The first time in your life that you flew somewhere," Susan teased.

"Yeah, and the last time also. I don't like flying." Pam confessed something everybody already knew. "But that was fun flying in first class, and I admit it was a wonderful trip. But no more airplanes for me."

"I was so excited to see Rome," Jenny offered. "I'm not quite sure what I was expecting, but Rome was great."

"Forget all of the Roman relics," Susan exclaimed, "how about lucking out with a hot driver who was our guide! Giuseppe. Remember how he stretched out the pronunciation of his name? Jew-SEP-Pay. Distinctly pronouncing both p's and accentuating the accent on the second syllable? Too funny."

"That did crack me up," an amused Bob remembered. "He said he worked in California for two years and said he was amazed at all the different types of food we have in our country. Who but a crazy Italian could get so excited about burritos, avocado toast, and Cobb salads? When he said he had never eaten Indian food before, I thought he and Jonathan would never shut up about all that stuff I can't even pronounce!"

"That was hysterical," Dan joined in, "and Giuseppe would say in America you have all this variety and can eat foods from all over the world. But not in Rome. He complained that all you get to eat in Rome is Italian food. Cry me a river. Remember how he described it? It was nothing but 'big pasta or little pasta, thin pasta or thick pasta, straight pasta or curly pasta.' That was pretty damn funny."

"And, Jonathan, great job picking the hotel, just a few minutes from the Spanish Steps," Susan complimented in appreciation. "My room was spectacular."

"Yes, the Portrait Roma, that was a terrific hotel," Jonathan concurred. "Wonderful rooftop views of the city. Remember that one night we each got a glass of wine and just stared out at the beautiful city and tried to have a recap conversation of the day until that obnoxious asshole—sorry, Mom—from Lichtenstein, who thought he was Tacitus, Livy, Suetonius, and Edward Gibbon all rolled into one as *the* expert on all things Rome and Roman politics, tried to horn in and lecture us? Leave it to Susan to say, 'Excuse me, buddy, but this is a private party.'"

"Jonathan," Susan volunteered, with a self-satisfied smile of another family member not afraid to take on all comers, "you really liked the Piazza di Spagna, the public square at the bottom of the Spanish Steps. All of those people, and you dragged us into the museum there that is dedicated to John Keats, who used to live there, and that other English poet."

"Yes, the Keats-Shelley House. Just kidding, but England has more than the two poets and the other poet you're talking about is Percy Bysshe Shelley. He wrote beautiful lyrical poems, like two of my favorites, 'Music, When Soft Voices Die' and 'Love's Philosophy.' Keats and Shelley were both Romantic poets who became great friends and both died young and in Italy. One of Shelley's best poems, 'Adonais,' is an elegy on the death of Keats. I especially like Keats's beautiful poem 'Bright Star, Would I Were Stedfast as Thou Art,' about one lover's desire to remain in the company of her lover forever. Very moving. Keats understood the impermanence of life. His tombstone, at Rome's Protestant Cemetery, does not bare his name, just the engraving, 'Here lies one Whose Name was writ in water.'"

"Yeah, I remember you said visiting that museum brought back a lot of memories for you," Jenny noted suspiciously as she raised an eyebrow. "At one point I didn't think you were ever going to leave. Speaking of memories, Mom, what do you think Hattie would have thought about St. Peter's Basilica and the Sistine Chapel?"

"Oh wow, she would've loved it all. And Jonathan, she just loved it that you took us all there."

"Can you imagine the cost of building Saint Peter's today?" Dan asked in wonderment. "Not even Bezos, Buffett, and Gates combined could pick up that tab."

"Yeah, it took truckloads of indulgences to pay that bill," Jonathan sarcastically provoked.

"After seeing it, I can believe that it took more than one hundred years to build," Bob noted, ignoring his son's zinger about how the Vatican paid for its fancy digs.

"Not bad when your architects include Raphael and Michelangelo," added Jonathan, deciding not to push the envelope any further.

"How about the emotional intensity of Michelangelo's *Pieta*, the marble depiction of the body of Jesus on the lap of Mary after the crucifixion?" commented Susan. "That is beautiful. And the only work he ever signed. He supposedly said, 'I saw an angel in the marble and carved until I set him free.'"

"What an artist Michelangelo was," Bob pointed out admiringly. "All of his paintings and sculptures we saw, and then to think he also painted the ceiling of the Sistine Chapel. What a genius. What did Giuseppe say he was called? Il Divino, the Divine One."

"You can get churched out in Italy, but I did like that small church by the Piazza Navona," Susan remarked.

"Oh yeah, the San Luigi Dei Francesi, with the three masterpieces by Caravaggio, one of my favorite artists. He was a master of the canonical technique called chiaroscuro, using strong contrasts between light and dark for emotional and dramatic effect. Da Vinci, one of Dad's favorites, was also a master," Jonathan informed the family. "*The Calling of Saint Matthew, Saint Matthew and the Angel,* and *Martyrdom of Saint Matthew.*"

"My mom probably would've liked that church more than St. Peter's," Pam reflected. "As splendid as St. Peter's is, she would've liked the smaller churches that aren't giant tourist attractions."

"Hey, guys, excuse me, but I have to make a quick work call," Jonathan apologized. "It will only take a few minutes." He ducked out of the room to take the call.

"It's good to see Jonathan," acknowledged Susan. "It's been over a year. Just wish the circumstances were better, Mom."

"You know my mom adored him. She was so proud of all his accomplishments. Probably bragged about him more than I do."

"Oh yeah, the Christ child," Susan good-naturedly snarked. "Jenny and I know all too well about it. Not Jonathan's fault Hattie thought he hung the moon."

"Hattie couldn't understand why Jonathan wasn't married by now. She would say there have to be a lot of women out there who would love to be with a rich, handsome lawyer," Pam lamented. "Not to mention the *grandchildren* he could have given us."

"He says he dates, just hasn't found the right person yet," Jenny commented, with a tone that suggested a healthy bit of doubt.

"Yeah, he had a girlfriend in college, Michele, I think was her name, but we never met her. I think they were pretty close, but Jonathan once told me they broke up after graduation because he was going to law school and she to graduate school. I think he was really close with her. Wonder what happened to her. He mentioned some girl in law school, and now that he's living in DC, we don't get to meet any of the women he dates," bemoaned Susan. "How are sisters supposed to steer him along in the right marital direction?" She laughed. "He told me he sees a Georgetown doctor off and on, but nothing too serious."

"Give the guy a break," Bob pleaded. "He's a partner in a hot-shot law firm and works all the time on those huge cases. Seems like he works seven days a week. Hell, he's on a work call right now. He's famous. He'll find the right woman at some point. Better not to rush things."

"Oh, you mean like I did, Dad?" Susan asked defensively.

"Now hold on, I didn't mean that at all. Your ex was a jerk and you're better off without him. Your mom and I never did like that guy."

'I'm back," Jonathan announced. "Sorry, I had to make that call."

"Jonathan, remind me of the name of that park in Rome where your mother kept giving all of the sidewalk musicians money. I thought she was trying to send us to the poor house."

"The Villa Borghese gardens, just off the Spanish Steps. They call it Rome's 'green lung' because of all of the trees, orange trees, and flowers."

"I loved that place," enthused Susan, "and I couldn't get over how big it is right in the middle of Rome."

"Jonathan, at the Roman Forum, remember the Bocca della Verita, if that's how you say it?" Dan teased. "That was the ancient stone carving of a bearded man's face, where legend has it that it will bite off the hand of anyone not telling the truth. Lawyers are duly warned to keep their traps shut around it!"

"Very funny, Dan. Don't give up your day job for stand-up comedy, you'll go broke."

"Dad, you thought Mom gave away all of your money to the musicians at the Villa Borghese gardens, but how about all the money she threw into the Trevi Fountain?" Jenny asked in a loving, mock tone. "Sure, I thought the marble statue of Neptune surrounded by tritons was pretty cool, but not enough to throw away all our meal money!"

"Ha, ha, young lady," Pam responded, "you laugh now, but as the legend has it, I'll be the one returning to Rome since I threw coins into the water."

"I'm with you, Mom," agreed Jonathan. "I also threw some coins into the water to ensure a return to the Eternal City. Dreamed about going there in college. I don't think I could ever tire of Rome. Wonderful people."

"And the food was wonderful too. I liked the place where we had pizza. A whole week in Italy and we only ate pizza one time," Pam pointed out, half complainingly.

"Hey, Mom, you weren't in Kansas anymore. Lots of wonderful food in Italy besides pizza," Jonathan joked.

"I'll ignore that remark. What was that place called?"

"It was in Trastevere, across the River Tiber, where Julius Caesar once lived. Cleopatra too. We ate at Pizzeria ai Marmi. Thin-crusted pizzas fresh out of a wood-fired oven and we drank some great Fontodi Chianti Classicos. As the Italians say, a night of la dolce vita, the easy-going sweet life."

"That was a great day and night," Susan remembered fondly. "Lot to be said for the easy-going sweet life. Too much of a rat race and keeping our heads above water back home, at least that's how it feels way too often."

"Well, I agree it was a great night. I loved all the art and history in Rome, but what I really liked was the dinner with family and pizza. It felt like home, with all of us together. And that was our last night in Rome. The dinner reminded me of my own mother. Hattie loved nothing more than evening meals and conversations, and even better yet, meals on holidays with her family. I sure wish I could have another meal with my mom." As Pam's eyes teared up, Jonathan reached over and gave his mother a tender hug, and she lovingly tapped him on his shoulder. A boy will grow up to be a man, but even a highly successful man of influence will always be his mother's son. "It was a terrific trip. Thank you, Jonathan. It's wonderful to have you all here right now. It's how things should be. Life sure does go by way too fast. Hattie is smiling down on all of us right now."

"Mom, the Italians have a saying that you would like," Jonathan offered. "It's 'La familiglia e la patria del cuore,' or, family is where the heart is."

"That is a good saying, and the dinner was wonderful," Bob agreed. "Best vacation ever. With Hattie's passing we all realize once again that life is too short and family is the best. I love this family. One more time, a toast to Hattie and family."

"Hear, hear."

Jonathan gave his family members hugs and said his goodbyes. In the morning he would be back on the plane to DC and work. His mom gave him an extra-long hug and said she loved him very much and asked that he visit more often. As he lay in bed before sleep, he thought about the different roles we play in life. Before he stepped onto the plane in the morning in DC to head to Cincinnati and his grandmother's funeral, he was Jonathan Kent, superstar trial lawyer. A man of renown, status, and accomplishment. Now, for the past twelve hours, he was just Jonathan, son, brother, brother-in-law, and uncle. Just one of the family. Was the family proud of him? Yes, they were, more than he probably appreciated. But it was Jonathan the family member, not Jonathan the performance artist on a big stage, they loved. The love and laughter and tears and simple joys of life he shares in their company. They understood he was different, that he mostly operated in a world foreign to them, but it didn't matter. To them, he would always be Jonathan, their son and brother. Since before Jonathan was eighteen, he was determined to escape the life of his parents, but he could never escape their unconditional love. Nor, he realized, did he ever want to.

AMORALISM AND ADDICTION

For one day at Hattie's funeral, Jonathan played the role of son and brother. It was cathartic. Back in DC, his role as quintessential twenty-first rainmaker, a role that he had relished early in his career but was now having serious reservations about, swiftly reared its head. Cabot, Lodge & Biddle peddled the same trope as the rest of Big Law: we are corporate America's first stop in the defense of bet-the-company litigation. Handling those types of cases propelled Jonathan to the top. To remain there, he was expected to routinely reel them in. Now a major pharmaceutical client of the firm was in serious trouble.

This was not Jonathan's client. The client attorney, Brianna Jackson, was a female African American partner—one of only three—who specialized in mergers and acquisitions, not litigation. She did deals, not lawsuits. Her client, Analeptic Chemicals, now needed the very best and was demanding that Jonathan handle the litigation. Jonathan had no interest, but he liked and wanted to help his partner, and bringing in a major matter like this would certainly boost Brianna's compensation and standing in the firm. Baxter Hodges and Oliver Truckle were breathing down his neck to take the representation that promised to make the firm $10 to $20 million.

CLB was no different than its Big Law competitors. It had an amoral, elastic conscience when it came to defending clients willing to shell out that kind of money. Jonathan knew this all too well. He had mastered that game in his climb to the top. Now he was feeling trapped. This wasn't like the LCD case, where major corporations were squaring off and just fighting over money. Sure, Kwon Electronics was a bad actor, but the corporate plaintiffs were no saints, either. Nothing at stake but money. This was far different. An entire supply chain was profiting while people—lots of down-and-out people—were dying and getting strung out. This time it was opioids and the bucks that poured in for defending those who made, sold, and distributed drugs that hooked their users and wrecked their lives. Big Law was going to feast on the litigation fees generated by the opioid crisis in America, and CLB wanted a seat at the banquet table. With Analeptic Chemicals, they got their seat. Jonathan reluctantly took the case.

The statistics are staggering. Since 1999, more than three quarters of a million people have died from a drug overdose. The main culprit is an opioid. The addiction rates are rising. And the crisis is ubiquitous. Opioids are drugs cultivated from a poppy plant that ultimately can be manufactured to make morphine, opium, and heroin. They are typically used for pain relief and treatment. The drugs intercept pain signals to the brain and thereby reduce pain thresholds. An overdose can suppress breathing and slow heart rates to a stop.

Opioids are highly addictive. Not hard to understand why: they make pain go away. But only for a little while. They induce a feeling of happiness as they flood users' brains with dopamine. But when the high subsides, hopelessness, agitation, and sadness take over. Years ago, these drugs were called "narcotics" but were sinisterly rebranded as opioids, a sterile, less-threatening sound, like ominous-sounding *global warming* got rebranded by unprincipled political consultants to more benign-sounding *climate change*, or bombing the hell the out of civilians became *collateral damage* and tribal genocide became *ethnic cleansing*. Major pharmaceutical companies had reassured the medical community that patients would not become addicted to prescription opioid pain relievers. Those reassurances caused providers to prescribe opioids at alarmingly increasing rates. Soon, brand-name drugs would flood the market across the country. Names like OxyContin, Percodan, Percocet, Actiq, Nuecynta, and Hysingla. OxyContin, what some call hillbilly heroin, in particular was touted as a "wonder drug" for patients suffering from chronic pain. Unscrupulous marketing campaigns and false research created huge supply and demand, so much so that by 2012, researchers estimated that there was one bottle of OxyContin for every adult American. Jonathan soon realized that the United States was inverting the infamous criticism from the communist revolutionary Karl Marx that religion is the opiate of the masses; in twenty-first-century America, opioids became the religion of the masses.

Fatal addiction rates and deaths are the result. People became addicted to prescription pain relievers, heroin, and synthetic opioids such as fentanyl. In time the daily death rate from drug overdoses would rise to a morbid 192 people. On the streets crack cocaine was referred to as the "devil's dick" and Oxy as the "devil's balls." Strung-out users, desperate for their fixes, stole from family members and neighbors. They busted into pharmacies and robbed elderly ladies walking home from church. Parents lost life savings spent on treatment and patrolled pawn shops in search for heirlooms stolen and sold by their own children. The Centers for Disease Control and Prevention in Atlanta concluded that prescription opioid abuse constituted an economic burden in the country of more than $78 billion a year.

It wasn't long before criminal investigations and civil lawsuits followed. The targets were big and rich. Really big and really rich. Major pharmaceutical companies and their distributors. National pharmacy chains. The entire supply chain, for that matter. Then there are the major banks that launder billions of cartel cash from south of the border looking to cleanse that cash by investing illicit drug proceeds in expensive commercial real estate and other so-called legitimate enterprises. Dangerous drugs like fentanyl-laced heroin flowing north into the United States, and billions in junkie cash flowing south only to boomerang back north to banks and Wall Street loan syndicates. From each according to their addictive need, to each according to their deadly greed.

Big Law scrambled to defend these "blue-chip" clients. There were no conscientious speed bumps on the roads to those clients facing serious legal jeopardy because they would pay small fortunes to armies of lawyers to defend them. Analeptic Chemicals exceeded all lofty expectations by paying CLB $15 million a year. Brianna Jackson got a substantial compensation raise. Oliver Truckle proudly touted the representation on CLB's website.

Some opioid defendants pled guilty to felony counts of wrongdoing. Not Jonathan's client. Others had to file for bankruptcy protection. Not Jonathan's client. Companies pled guilty to false claims charges that they were working to prevent opioids from getting into the hands of people who didn't need them, when in fact they sold opioids to doctors (pill mills) they knew were providing them to nonpatients. As more evidence of wrongdoing came to light up and down the opioid supply chain, more players copped deals to staunch the legal bleeding. Settlements in the several hundreds of millions of dollars and more. One blockbuster settlement with a major pharmaceutical company and its distributors rang the register to the tune of an astonishing $26 billion. Several banks paid nine- and ten-figure money laundering fines.

Ultimately, Jonathan was able to negotiate a comprehensive settlement for Analeptic Chemicals for $1.4 billion. As in billion, with a B. Only in America: Wall Street reacted favorably to the news. Analeptic's stock rose 22 percent. Jonathan thought, *Talk about the rough beast of decadence and slouching toward Gomorrah*. As a reward, Analeptic hired CLB to defend it in an antitrust case where the pharmaceutical giant was monopolizing the market for a critical drug for seriously ill patients by keeping lower-priced generics out of the market with a series of bogus patent lawsuits and cosmetic product changes that forced the lower-priced generics to spend years seeking FDA approval before they could sell their cheaper drugs to the needy patients. Another partner took the lead after Jonathan declined to take the case, using as his excuse the need to prepare for the upcoming AIQC trial when, in fact, he vowed to himself he would never represent Analeptic again.

To celebrate the opioid settlement, Analeptic rented a private room at the Capital Grille Steakhouse in DC for drinks—plenty of twelve-year-old Macallan Double Cask scotch and a case of 1995 Château Lafite Rothschild at $1,750 a bottle—and dinner for Jonathan and more than a dozen firm lawyers who worked on the case. Jonathan, a wine connoisseur, declined the vintage vino and left his plainly grilled salmon and asparagus half eaten. That same day, 130 people died from opioid abuse. Jonathan was thinking this might be the last straw.

GOLIATH'S WATERLOO

Jonathan had assembled a different team of lawyers for the opioid litigation. He provided supervision but let a couple of senior partners who did not generate their own work manage the day-to-day defenses to get everything up and running. He was perfectly content to do as little as possible to help Analeptic Chemicals. In the meantime, he needed to prepare for the semiconductor antitrust trial in San Francisco. He loved this case and loved his clients. He would go to trial with his crackerjack LCD team. David Joseph and JP Hale, Maya Gibson and Ruth B. Greenfield. And, of course, Kaori Settite. Once again the team left DC a week before trial and decamped to the Le Meridien hotel across from Embarcadero Plaza.

For weeks, CLB's financial partner, Felix Quaestor, had been importuning Jonathan to settle the case. He didn't seem to fully appreciate that settlement is the client's call, not the lawyer's. Quaestor hated risk, hated contingency cases, hated representing plaintiffs, and hated this case. He had voted to decline taking it and had lobbied hard to persuade other management committee members to vote no. He missed by only one vote. The parties did one mediation, but it fast fell apart when BSMC refused to put an offer on the table. That was just fine by Jonathan, as he was chomping at the bit to get BSMC in court. Quaestor and Truckle tried to pressure Jonathan to make an offer on the courthouse steps. He ignored them.

Antitrust monopolization cases can be long and complicated and dominated by expert economists and technical jargon. Boring. Trane had warned Jonathan early in his career that most antitrust lawyers seemed more interested in impressing the economic experts than with preparing and presenting a persuasive case for the jury. Economic evidence would be important at his trial, but Jonathan was not going to let it drive the story. Ultimately, Jonathan understood that every trial is about people, their motives, their characters, their incentives, their foibles and frailties, and their strengths and weaknesses. Jurors relate to human beings, not to mathematical models and equations and abstruse econometric jargon. No jury in history ever returned a verdict for one side by declaring that it had the best regression models. No jury ever said to the losing side that they would have decided the case in their favor if only they had seen more statistical equations from their economist. Jonathan had always remembered what former president Lyndon Johnson, who in private spoke in earthy and salty language, once said to one of his top economic advisers: "Did it ever occur to you that making a speech on economics is just like pissing down your leg? It seems hot to you, but not to anybody else." Jonathan had no intention of pissing down his leg in front of the jury.

One week before trial, in their hotel litigation war room, Jonathan called a team meeting to put the final touches on their trial story and strategy. JP had already set up the easels. Jonathan kicked it off.

"Good morning, folks. This is a monopolization case. We have a complex subject matter—semiconductors, artificial intelligence, and quantum computing. We have some complex economics involving statistics and regression analysis. And, we have a defense team that will trot out every defense under the sun while they tergiversate and prevaricate. But we will keep our story simple and straightforward. It will be easy to understand. And it will pack a moral punch."

The teacher wrote on an easel—BOUGHT AND BULLIED.

Jonathan continued. "BSMC bought and bullied its way to a monopoly position. And its bad behavior hurt competition and it hurt AIQC. Now it's the jury's chance to say enough of this bad behavior and award damages to AIQC. So, Maya, get us started by setting the table for what we will need to prove to win a jury verdict and hold on to it in the appellate court."

"Sure. The first thing we need to prove is that BSMC is big. We say that the market, the arena of competition, is the semiconductor market. Heck, the word semiconductor is even in BSMC's name! BSMC has a dominant position in that market. That's what makes it a monopolist."

"What's BSMC's defense to that point?" asked JP.

"Their economist doesn't really dispute that point. Instead he tries to finesse it by saying that the real focus should be on a small segment of the semiconductor market. On artificial intelligence and quantum computing, where our client is strong. In that segment, BSMC is not big and dominant according to him."

"That's nuts," scoffed David. "That's like saying that a car company that sells 65 percent of all cars is really just a small fry because it doesn't sell a lot of one type of car, like luxury cars. It's still a dominant player in the car market."

"Precisely," Maya agreed, "and BSMC's own documents refer over and over to a single semiconductor market. They even have a strategy document that Jonathan especially likes. It's in Mandarin, but roughly translated reads, "We like being the big dog in semiconductors because only the lead dog gets a change of scenery.""

"That's funny," laughed David, "and we also have our nuclear weapon again. Professor Applebaum from UCLA. She's terrific in front of a jury, as we all know, and she's great on the relevant market issue. She'll give us great testimony that BSMC is a monopolist in the semiconductor market."

"Great," David said, "so if we prove that BSMC is a monopolist, what's the next thing we have to prove, Maya?"

"Once we prove the monopoly element, we have to prove that BSMC did bad stuff to hurt its competitors. More technically, we have to prove that BSMC engaged in exclusionary conduct that hurt, not helped, competition. We have to prove that BSMC got and has maintained its monopoly position by bad conduct, not by building a better mouse trap."

"That's our simple story," JP asked, "that BSMC bought and bullied its way to the top?"

"Exactly," Maya answered. "They used their unlimited financial might to pay a ridiculous premium price to buy a leading American semiconductor company to get their dominant position. That was step one. Step two was to tie up a huge customer base with long-term and exclusive contracts. They sue competitors with bogus patent lawsuits, and they force customers to buy products from them that the customers prefer to buy from AIQC and others if they want products they can only get from BSMC. Under the antitrust laws, we are on solid ground if we can prove this pattern of conduct, and we can prove it."

Maya continued. "This proof of bad conduct gets us into the red zone. Sure, BSMC has an expensive and fancy economist who will sprinkle holy water on all of this conduct, but Professor Applebaum takes him apart. She will also show the jury how BSMC has been charging extra-high prices and raking in sky-high profits. Profits you never see in competitive markets."

"Agree," nodded David, "so how do we get into the end zone?"

"We have to prove that BSMC damaged AIQC's business and we have to prove the amount of damages."

"Reenter Professor Applebaum," Jonathan chimed in. "She has identified business AIQC has directly lost because of BSMC's bad conduct, and she has made reasonable projections of future lost business because of BSMC's exclusionary conduct. In her professional judgment, AIQC's damages are $635 million."

Jonathan wrote the number below BOUGHT AND BULLIED on the easel. So it read:

BOUGHT AND BULLIED
$635 Million

"In the LCD case," Jonathan continued, "we did rope-a-dope. In this case we are going to do jujitsu. BSMC's lawyers are not going to be selective and focus on their best defenses. Instead these Big Law defense lawyers are going to challenge us on every point, no matter how small. They will say they are not big. They will say even if they are big, they're not bad. They'll say even if they are bad, they didn't hurt competition. Then they will say even if they are big and bad and hurt competition, they didn't hurt AIQC, and AIQC has failed to prove reasonable damages. They will even play the blame game and argue that any damage AIQC claims is a self-inflicted wound. And if they lose, they will appeal and hope to get a panel of judges who worship at the altar of Federalist Society ideology and enthusiastically deep-six every antitrust case they can get their hands on.

"So, we will take all of their thrusting and energy and turn it right back on them and complete our story in our closing argument. We will tell the jury that once we vaporize all of BSMC's smoke screens, let's talk about the only real issue in the case. That issue is the proper amount of damages. The same strategy we used in LCD, but from the other side."

In just after three and a half weeks of trial, the case was ready for closing arguments. Jonathan knew all too well that there are ups and downs in every big trial, but overall he felt good about the evidence. He put on a streamlined case. His Stanford drop-out clients were brilliant and poised and held up well on cross-examination. The jury was not going to have to stretch to believe that AIQC was on the cusp of being another spectacular Silicon Valley success story unless a ruthless giant tried to squish it.

The defense did pretty much what Jonathan had expected. They exhibited a certain purblindness, challenging everything and conceding nothing. Even when confronted with their own documents that undercut them. BSMC's defense lawyers were one speed—aggressive to the point of being hostile and seemed to have permanent scowls and sneers plastered on their faces. Maybe that overt aggression would curry favor with a monopolist client hellbent on worldwide domination, but Jonathan seriously doubted that it was playing well with this San Francisco jury.

In his navy blue suit with thin light blue pinstripes, white shirt with thin blue pinstripes, emerald-green tie, and polished Allen Edmonds black shoes, Jonathan stood before the jury and immediately reminded them of the theme of this case. That "BSMC bought and bullied its way to its monopoly position." That BSMC's conduct hurt American semiconductor competition and hurt AIQC. He then walked the jury through each element of AIQC's claim, reminding and showing the jury the most compelling evidence in support of each element. He demolished each defense BSMC had offered up until its legal levee broke and it had no place left to hide. It was exposed and it was naked. To this point he had resisted the urge to mock, but now he went in for the ridicule kill.

"Ladies and gentlemen, all of BSMC's excuses and defenses, all of its twistifications, remind me of an old defense I read about long ago. Before law school. I read it in a book in college, a book by Charles Dickens, the guy who wrote about Scrooge in *A Christmas Carol*, and it was the best of times, it was the worst of times in *A Tale of Two Cities*. Dickens wrote a lot of books in his time. In his book, *The Pickwick Papers*, he wrote about a defense that reminds me of what BSMC's lawyers are trying to sell to you.

"It goes like this. Back in England in the nineteenth century, this guy kept a goat in his yard. One day the goat got loose, wandered over to the neighbor's yard, and ate the neighbor's cabbage. The neighbor demanded one pound in damages for the cabbage the goat ate.

"So what was the goat owner's defense? It was a beauty, just like BSMC's defense. The goat owner first argued that there were no cabbages. He then argued, if there were cabbages, they weren't eaten. If there were cabbages and they were eaten, they were not eaten by a goat. But if they were eaten by a goat, they weren't eaten by his goat. And if they were eaten by his goat, his goat was insane!"

As the crowd in the gallery was laughing, the judge pounded her gavel and instructed that "there will be silence in the courtroom." Jonathan thought he detected a grin at the corner of the judge's mouth, but that might have been wishful thinking on his part. He resumed.

"Ladies and gentlemen, don't we know who ate the cabbage in this case? That brings me to my final point. The damages that BSMC's conduct has caused AIQC."

Jonathan briefly reminded the jurors of how Professor Applebaum calculated those damages. He then placed his easel in front of the jury and wrote $635 million with a green magic marker and asked the jury to award that figure as just compensation.

The jury began their deliberations at nine o'clock on Thursday morning of the fourth week of trial. They finished that same day at three o'clock. AIQC won.

The jury did not award the full $635 million. They awarded AIQC $605 million. Once again, Jonathan had delivered a stunning victory. And the $605 million would be tripled by the judge to $1.815 billion. Jonathan thought, *1815*. He smiled, recalling something he learned when he visited the Hôtel des Invalides in Paris, that 1815 was the year a monopolist of another sort was resoundingly defeated. Napoleon Bonaparte, who had conquered much of Europe, suffered his final defeat at the Battle of Waterloo and then abdicated four days later, ushering in nearly one hundred years of relative peace in Europe. BSMC had vanquished a number of competitors on its relentless quest to conquer and control, but in this San Francisco courtroom, with Jonathan Kent and his small team on the other side, BSMC had just met its own Waterloo.

As Jonathan walked out of the courthouse, he was approached by two young professional-looking women who extended their hands to congratulate him. They introduced themselves as Anne Little and Helen Elion. They said they would like to speak with him about a potential lawsuit when he had some time. Said it had to do with intellectual property and theft and how it hurt their business. Said there was some urgency to the matter. They each give Jonathan a business card and said they hoped to hear soon from him. Anne's card read Dr. Anne Little, Co-president of Memory Solutions, Inc., and Helen's card read Dr. Helen Elion, Co-president of Memory Solutions, Inc. Jonathan was intrigued.

GENIUS AND NOBLE CAUSE

After Jonathan and team returned to DC from the AIQC trial, he did a background investigation of Drs. Little and Elion and their company Memory Solutions, Inc. What he found intrigued him even more. MSI was located in Mountain View, California, home of many high-tech companies. The company and its ten science-trained employees worked out of cramped, rented space and were otherwise quietly and unobtrusively ensconced in an environment of entrepreneurial and intellectual fecundity. Jonathan quickly realized that MSI had the Silicon Valley vibe of the obscure company that would explode onto the scene as a supernova and become a brand name. Much like AIQC. Unless, like AIQC, a predatory beast came hunting for it.

MSI seemed to be a perfect marriage of founder genius and societal need. Jonathan learned that the need to develop a cure for Alzheimer's is overwhelming. More than six million Americans are afflicted with the degenerative disease, mostly age sixty-five or older. He thought about his own aging parents. They still had their mental faculties, but the onset of a dementia disease like Alzheimer's would be physically, emotionally, and financially devastating to them. More seniors die of Alzheimer's than die of breast and prostate cancer combined. Two thirds of the afflicted are women. Alzheimer's strips a loved one of dignity and quality of life and typically imposes extreme hardships on spouses and children, who often become primary caregivers. Jonathan's research showed that healthcare experts estimate that more than eleven million Americans provide unpaid care for Alzheimer's victims. It's a death sentence with an ignoble ending. Anne Little and Helen Elion were dedicating their lives, their very existence, to finding a way to make it all go away. Lives in pursuit of a noble cause. He had a case he could pour his soul into.

Jonathan learned in Rome that the Latin verb *gignere* means "to give birth or bring forth," and is the root of the word genius. To the ancient Romans, all humans have a guiding spirit from birth, called a genius. Drs. Little and Elion were born with a guiding spirit, and their high-octane IQs blew the top off of the intelligence thermometer. Their guiding spirits and intellectual wattage were propelling them to bring forth a cure for Alzheimer's, a disease that had prematurely robbed Dr. Little of her beloved grandmother and Dr. Elion of her favorite aunt, her mother's only sister. Both died in their sixties. Dr. Little, a Stanford PhD, and Dr. Elion, a Johns Hopkins PhD, met as postdoc researchers at Duke University's Department of Neurology, a leader in innovative Alzheimer's research. There, they met two bioengineering professors who, with a business partner, founded a start-up company in cardiology ultrasound in the humanitarian hopes of inventing and bringing to market better diagnostic tools for heart diseases. Inspired by that laudable example, they packed their bags and founded their own startup company in Mountain View, an area with lots of brainiacs and potential angel investor money to help them lift off.

Impressive on paper, the good doctors overwhelmed Jonathan in person. Brain power? Sure. Intense focus? Unquestioned. But it was the humanistic passion for their work they exuded that had won him over. Perhaps they were somewhat naïve to the take-no-prisoners way of the business world, but Jonathan had chalked that up to their relative youth and business inexperience and their own sterling integrity. Besides, he thought, they were young scientists devoting twelve hours a day, seven days a week, to finding a cure for a pernicious disease, a cure that would benefit humankind. The fact that they didn't turn on a lie detector every time they talked with an unscrupulous potential business partner said more about unsavory predators than it did about the good doctors. Jonathan had no doubt that he could fend off any attack in court that tried to suggest that Drs. Little and Elion were rubes who did not deserve just compensation for the theft of their pathbreaking work.

Jonathan of course ended up taking and winning their case. Once again, he had gone to trial with his terrific team. David Joseph and JP Hale. Maya Gibson, now a partner, and Ruth B. Greenfield and Kaori Settite. And once again Jonathan had received immense pressure from the litigation department to disband his team so other young, trial-starved lawyers could get inside a courtroom. He deflected and temporized and kept his team intact. They were loyal to him, and he to them. They were enormously grateful. And lucky.

But the $3-billion jury verdict almost never happened. Once again, risk-averse Felix Quaestor and Jonathan's quisling litigation department head, Oliver Truckle, led the charge to derail the representation. MSI, like AIQC, did not have the resources to pay lawyers millions of dollars running the money meter by the hour. There would have to be a contingency-fee arrangement. Both Quaestor and Truckle, whom Trane said "didn't know shit from shinola when it came to evaluating a plaintiff's case," called MSI's claim "a dog." Predicted it would be a huge money pit for CLB and predicted that MSI would lose, and even if it won, the verdict would be small and insufficient for CLB to recover its substantial investment. So much for their legal acumen. If Jonathan had lost his shirt in a losing effort in the AIQC trial, there is no way management would have given him the green light to represent MSI on contingency. But he won and CLB raked in quite a stash, so he narrowly got the nod to fight the good fight for MSI.

Quaestor and Truckle were persistent. One day before trial, Jager Pharmaceutical made its "last and best offer" (Jonathan remembered in the south they would have said "that possum's on the stump")—$15 million if MSI dismissed the lawsuit *and* transferred its eighteen valuable patents to Jager. Jonathan and his clients were insulted. Quaestor and Truckle were ecstatic. They exerted immense pressure on Jonathan to convince his clients to take the deal. Jonathan told them both to go to hell.

WAITING FOR GODOT

After the tremendous MSI victory, the trial team needed to decompress. Except Jonathan, who had to prepare for an appellate argument he had been hired to handle in New York federal court concerning the applicability of the US antitrust laws to business conduct that takes place outside of the United States

David organized and hosted. When the philosopher Plato throws a dinner party, as recounted in the *Symposium*, the guests talk about the meaning of love and the desire for wisdom and beauty. When young Big Law lawyers throw a dinner party, they talk about themselves and work, work, work. But they do have one thing in common with the analytical Athenians—in vino veritas.

David started. "I'll offer the first toast. To Jonathan. Trial lawyer extraordinaire, mentor and protector of his own."

"I'll second that," JP chimed in. "Do you realize that we have now done three major jury trials with Jonathan in just the past five years?"

"It's incredible," agreed David. "There are litigation partners in the firm who haven't done three jury trials in their entire careers."

"Three? Try one!" exclaimed Maya. "Until the LCD case, I didn't think I'd ever get to do a trial at our firm. Most of the partners are strangers to courtrooms. Now that I have been in trials and have seen Jonathan in action, I can't imagine many of the partners ever relating to juries. Until I actually prepared for and did a trial, I couldn't believe just how different—and *fun*—that work is from the everyday grind of regular litigation! And all the focus is on the emotional messages we want to convey to the jury. It's great. And what I never realized before doing a trial is just how worthless almost all the discovery folks obsess over really is once you start preparing for trial."

"No kidding," agreed JP. "LCD was my first trial, and I was a rookie partner. Being in a jury trial is a whole new world. I was beginning to think I would never get to do a trial. Like waiting for Godot, waiting for a trial that likely will never happen. Life for young Big Law litigators. I had my résumé out and was eyeing a potential assistant federal prosecutor's job. One of the first things Jonathan told me about trial work he said he learned from his judge, Judge Luke Roy. Trials are great because you get to be the playwright as well as producer, director, and lead actor. That is *so* true. And that's what makes trial work so much fun. Nothing beats the drama and then waiting for the jury's verdict. And once you've taken a case all the way through trial, you look at discovery and how to prepare a case from a whole new perspective. Man, it's crazy how much time is wasted in discovery on stuff that just doesn't matter."

"Totally agree. I'm now a senior associate and the only one in my class who has done a jury trial," joined Ruth. "Most of the associates don't even hope anymore. And they're not learning anything about how to get a case ready to go to trial."

"Why should they hope?" Maya scoffed. "Hardly any of the partners bring in jury trial work. And if they ever did, they would have to get Jonathan or maybe a couple of other partners involved because they wouldn't know the first thing about how to try a case."

"Yeah, I don't know how they do it," lamented an exasperated David. "I couldn't do this year after year after year without going to court. That would drive me insane. Jonathan told me that he would never join Big Law if he were coming out of law school today. Pretty sad."

"Sad? Insane? It's killing the young lawyers," added Ruth. "Work is pretty much twenty-four seven for most of them, us, and it's drudgery. The Chinese complain about what they call a '996' work life—9:00 a.m. to 9:00 p.m., six days a week. Heck, that's better than twenty-four seven monotony. The same thing over and over and over. Just bouncing from one case to the next doing discovery and writing briefs, mostly about discovery. And never going to trial."

"I have four words for you. Dis-cov-er-y," Maya groaned slowly and deliberately. "Push the rock up the hill, watch it fall back down. Push it back up, watch it fall down. Watch the case settle and start all over. That's all most of them do. And it's around the clock. No wonder most leave."

"No shit. In one of my other cases," JP complained, "I think I have written and received from the other side at least five hundred emails about discovery disputes. Usually after nine o'clock. It's crazy. I wake up every day and wonder, *What bullshit discovery fight will the day bring?* And sure enough, some stupid issue pops up that I need to chase down. I think I'm destroying my brain."

"Same here," moaned Maya. "These battles are endless and almost always over documents that don't mean a damn thing in the case."

"Yeah, and it just seems to get worse and worse," bemoaned David. "Meanwhile, Drs. Little and Elion are using their brain energy trying to find an Alzheimer's cure. I often question what the hell I'm doing with my life. If I had to do it all over again, I think I would study biology. I think it would be cool to work in the life sciences and biotechnology. Lots of revolutionary stuff going on. Did you see that two women won the 2020 Nobel Prize in chemistry for developing a method for genome editing? Something called CRISPR-Cas9 or something like that. Allows them to rewrite DNA in human cells. An American, Jennifer Doudna, and a French woman, Emmanuelle Charpentier. First time two women won the Nobel together. And Maya, Doudna is a Berkeley professor. "

"Golden Bears! That is so cool. So much for the stupid chestnut that women can't do science. Can you imagine if gene editing would enable doctors to wipe out a bunch of diseases like sickle-cell anemia or Down's syndrome? Or autism? Who knows, even Alzheimer's maybe. Better yet, edit out the gene that causes discoveritis!" Maya exclaimed. "If the monotony of being a discovery lawyer wasn't bad enough, computers and smartphones are going to enslave and kill us all."

"You think?" Ruth asked sarcastically. "Talk about revolutionary stuff, computers and smartphones are turning us into electronic slaves. At least the rest of you are partners and have some control over your lives. You folks don't expect it from younger lawyers, but we have plenty of asshole partners who expect you to be on call twenty-four seven, including weekend nights. No wonder three quarters of the associates have acute cases of sleep bruxism, grinding and gnashing their teeth all night, worrying about how to please unreasonable and insecure partners."

"I know, I see it," sympathized David. "And it's usually stupid shit that could be dealt with during normal business hours. Just a bunch of insecure jerks and control freaks flexing their little bit of power. Like some mutant form of the Napoleon complex. Another candidate for gene editing!"

"Absolutely," JP chimed in, forgetting Jonathan's pet peeve he got from Trane. "Pretty picayune stuff usually. Sometimes I really wonder if many of the partners have any lives at all away from the office."

"I can answer that—*no!* So let me ask you elders this question," imposed Ruth, the only associate. "Why have you stayed around as long as you have?"

David poured more wine for everybody, anticipating that tongues were about to loosen some more. Lost on the entire group was the cardinal rule of fine wine consumption—it should be sipped and consumed slowly to celebrate life, not guzzled to fuel its commiseration. Jonathan once joked that is why despondent Russians prefer to quaff vodka rather than sip an impeccable red.

"I've been here the longest, so I guess I'll start," David graciously volunteered. "If I'm being honest, I'm not sure I'd still be here if not for the trials these last several years. When I started, I loved the prestige of the job and of course the money. And in the early years, I got great training in research and writing, well, some better than others. It's weird, but the older I get, the more I realize that a lot of the partners are actually pretty lousy writers. Really stilted and lots of hackneyed legalisms that never pull you in as the reader. I think half of them are incapable of writing a brief without the word *disingenuous*. Anyway, a lot of cases have some interesting facts, but they're almost always anticlimactic because they either end by motion or settlement. But until I started to do trials with Jonathan, which *I love*, it was just really long hours of the same old type of paper pushing and meeting bullshit deadlines imposed by senior lawyers."

"Do you think you would even still be here if you hadn't gotten the trial opportunities?" Ruth asked, in a way suggesting she already knew the answer was no.

"You know, Ruth, honestly I'm not sure," David responded reflectively. "It wouldn't be any different at another Big Law firm, and it's hard to walk away from the money I'm now making. But I know I would've explored my options more seriously if I hadn't gotten on Jonathan's trial team. Before that, I had no passion for what I was doing. Nobody else in the firm comes close to consistently offering the trial opportunities like Jonathan. He's such a wonderful mentor. And to make matters worse, the firm unrealistically expects young partners to get their own clients and produce their own business. If you don't, you're just running in place until they ask you to leave. And that increases your neurosis and turns your hair prematurely gray."

"Yeah, that's bullshit," JP added emphatically, whose own young full head of dark hair was starting to show strands of gray. "How in the hell is a young litigation partner in Big Law supposed to get hired as the lead lawyer on a major case, much less a trial? That just doesn't happen anywhere. Seriously, like some client is going to hire me over Jonathan to handle its monopolization case. Get real. Management has their heads in the clouds, or someplace else … Ruth, you talk about *associates* having sleep bruxism, young partners have already ground down their teeth and are in a twenty-four seven state of clenched teeth worrying about how the hell they are going to bring in business."

"I agree, the business-generation expectations are total bullshit. Just an excuse to weed out most of us after they squeeze every last

billable hour out of our overworked bodies. At least as young lawyers we are getting trial experience with Jonathan," Maya added,
somewhat hopefully. "I suspect we're all hoping that these experiences will give us a springboard to get our own clients someday."

"That's exactly right, at least for me," David declared. "That's
my hope. Candidly, I don't know why most of our fellow young
partners are sticking it out. We all know they're miserable and just
waiting for the ax to fall. Maya's right, it's basically a slow weed-
ing-out process. Two drones enter, one drone leaves, two drones
enter, one drone leaves ..."

"More like ten enter, nine leave. So Ruth, why do you continue
to stay?" JP inquired.

"It's funny, but I suppose I'm the unicorn among associates. I'm
actually getting trials, great trials, and I'm loving it. I don't love the
long hours and weekends, but at least the cases are fun and I feel
like I'm developing the skills to fly the nest at some point. When I
listen to fellow associates, they're absolutely miserable. Long hours,
dull work, and no real light at the end of the tunnel. And I don't
think any of them are fooling themselves about their realistic pros-
pects at the firm. They know it's just a matter of time before they
bolt or are pushed out."

"Exactly. That's just why so many leave early, even the really good ones," David assessed in resignation. "Hate to say it, but
they're probably the smartest ones, or at least the ones with bal-
anced values. Even if you make partner, the pressure just gets worse
because you'll be gone in several years if you don't have your own
clients. I suppose if you are a rainmaker like Jonathan who has
trials and makes a fortune, Big Law is pretty good, but for most
everybody else, it sucks. I think the psychiatrists make a fortune off
of Big Law partners at every year-end around annual reviews and
compensation time!"

"No kidding. After I made partner, I couldn't believe how much
bitching and complaining partners do about their comp. So much
self-worth tied up in their comp. But in fairness it's hard to imagine
people doing this except for the money," JP evaluated. "If you're a
Jonathan, you make generational wealth. But even if you can make

it to the middle of the pack by the time you're fifty, you're likely talking about two to three million a year. If you don't stupidly spend it all like a lot of partners, you can actually save enough to retire early and do something else with your life."

"That's not happening. I can't believe how many partners blow through their money. Many of them don't have investments other than their 401(k), and some of them don't even max that out. It's crazy. But it's still really long odds for associates and even young partners to make it even to the middle of the pack," David responded. "And then there is the personal toll. The long, never-ending hours and the pressure and anxiety. I think half the partners are on Xanax."

"Tell me about it," Maya lamented. "Your personal life is close to nil, especially with the digital leashes of computers and smartphones. Even when you're with spouse or kids, if you have any, you're consumed with work and constantly checking your phone, especially for the younger folks. And don't get me started on the complex calculus for women about whether to have kids, how many, and when to do the strategic timing. You need Stephen Hawking and Big Blue to figure that out!"

"When you think about it, it really is a warped system," JP said.

"What are you getting at?" Ruth asked, suspecting she already knew the answer.

"Just think about it," JP challenged. "The top-paid partners make a fortune and even the partners in the middle of the pack make a few million a year. But a lot of them are insecure and fear it will all go away. I get that. And the system only works if there are armies of associates and young partners like us billing hours twenty-four seven to create the huge cash pile. It's one big, giant back-breaking, soul-crushing pyramid."

"Yeah, back in the day, the few Egyptian pharaohs got all the glory but the legions of folks who actually built the pyramids were condemned to lives of broken bones and early deaths. The rainmakers in Big Law are the modern-day pharaohs, and we're the grunts who build their fortunes!" David groaned. "And it's the nature of the beast, only a few get to be the pharaohs."

"Pharaohs indeed. At our firm and other Big Law firms, the

highest paid partners make more than thirty times what associates make," noted Maya. "We should change the name from rainmakers to Pharaoh Partners!"

"Yeah, and like the pyramid builders, the work most associates do sucks," chimed in JP. "Endless hours on the discovery treadmill. But that brings in all the money for the partners to take to the bank. Like I said, what a fucked-up system. The young lawyers work like dogs and have virtually no hope of ever making partner, or at least anywhere within a million miles from the top. And the only thing that keeps folks here is a few hundred thousand dollars a year and a modest year-end bonus. Look, I realize most of the outside world would take one look at our salaries and say, 'Cry me a river and stop your whining, you spoiled, overpaid assholes,' but that doesn't mean it all doesn't still suck. It certainly looks a lot different on the inside than it does from the outside, except to the spouses and significant others who know the painful truth about living with absentee lovers."

"Yeah, probably, and not to sound like a pathetic ingrate," Maya protested, "but a bonus only if you bust your ass and bill a gazillion hours. Just a few crumbs off of the partner banquet table. But I know we aren't really complaining about our money, it's the overall grueling quality of life in Big Law that sucks."

"Do you think Big Law life will change anytime soon?" Ruth despondently asked the group as she poured everyone some more medicating wine.

"Not at all," David emphatically declared. "Zero chance of that happening. The New York work and money ethos will still set the pace. And it's brutal. More money begets more money. It's a fairy tale that a certain amount of wealth causes complacency and the opportunity to pursue other things in life. Big Law partners just want more and more money. That's not going to change. Look at all those rich partners around the country working past sixty-five and into their seventies. You hear them say, 'I love what I do,' or 'To me it doesn't feel like work.' That's bullshit. Talk about self-delusion. In reality, they love the money and have lived this twenty-four seven life for so long they wouldn't know what to do with themselves if they retired from Big Law. They've lost all ability to even imagine an alternative world, much less imagine a change in lifestyle. So they pull the security blanket even tighter around themselves and go into denial and cling to the money and the job. Actually, it's sad."

"Jonathan might beg to differ about the complacency part," JP challenged. "He says half the partners are content and lazy and spend too much time on the golf course. They still want more money, they just don't want to work any harder for it. You know he loves obscure words. Says that many partners are fudgelling, pretending to work when they have nothing to do, and need to be feagued in the same way old horse trainers used to enliven sluggish horses — by sticking live eels or peeled raw ginger up their asses. Cracks me up."

"That's funny. I heard him say that to Oliver Truckle," David agreed, "but we all know that there is no turning back, no backsliding on the money. More money means more work, which means more money. It's a hedonic treadmill where more money just means more expectations and desires. It's a rainmaker's ballgame. Pharaoh Partners, as Maya says. I like that. That's why you see these partners at the very top New York firms leave to go elsewhere for a few more bucks. Seven million a year? Not enough, I want eight. Eight million a year? Not enough, I want nine. On and on. And to what end? They're so warped."

"Big Law partners should read Saul Bellows's book *Henderson the Rain King*. Like the book's protagonist Eugene Henderson, their inner voices are saying, 'I want, I want, I want,'" JP slowly intoned. "It's like what the philosopher Schopenhauer calls the wheel of Ixion, just an endless cycle of wants, satisfaction, then more wants. Like Ixion, they are eternally bound to a revolving wheel chasing more and more money and never satisfying their desires."

"Wow, ply JP with vino and he goes deep. Looks like we have come full circle," Maya concluded, by way of wrap up. "As our firm and Big Law compete to get the biggest cases, trial opportunities for younger lawyers will continue to dry up faster than water in the desert. For younger lawyers, pushing paper and dis-cov-er-y will be their life. Pardon my French, but it's like that Warren Zevon song "My Shit's Fucked Up"—something like I had a dream, oh well, it's all fucked up and shot to hell. Not exactly Bellow or Schopenhauer but it hits the target."

"It's getting late, folks, and on that note, we should probably call it a night, so hit your Uber apps," David said as he stood up for one last toast. "Here's to hoping we have many more trials for clients as remarkable as Dr. Anne Little and Dr. Helen Elion. And here's to hoping that Jonathan continues to try cases until he is one hundred years old."

"Amen!"

HELPLESS CHILDREN

No doubt life in Big Law is grueling and often dull and dispiriting, but real hell on earth is the fate of hundreds of million children around the world. Experts estimate that more than 150 million children are in child labor and more than 25 million are in forced labor. Governments and NGOs (nongovernment organizations) call it what it is: child slave labor. This barbarism in the private economy produces staggering annual profits of $150 billion for global corporations.

These corporations profess to believe in open and free markets. In theory, market forces would push up labor wages to competitive levels, at some expense to owners' profits. Child slave labor not only corrupts morals and basic human decency, but this savage system also corrupts the market by artificially depressing labor costs so corporations can profit thereby. The more Jonathan learned about how child slave labor was endemic in the global economy, the more appalled he became and wanted to do something about it.

Child slave labor is ubiquitous, especially in impoverished rural areas in third-world countries. Products pumping their profits off the beaten backs of kids under the age of twelve include clothes, coffee, cigarettes, cell phones, sugar, chocolate, shoes, toys, gold, and even cobalt ore for lithium batteries that power up all sorts of electronic devices. And many of the profiteering companies are headquartered in the United States.

A few of those corporations were Jonathan's intended targets for a pro bono lawsuit in the United States. Two lessons Jonathan learned doing his plea-bargaining study in law school stuck: deprivation and degeneration and dehumanization will persist when, as Judge McCracken had said, "society don't give a fuck," and to look for progress one pragmatic step at a time. Of course he couldn't solve the problem of global child slave labor, but with a lawsuit, he might at least be able to hold some corporate enablers accountable and seek compensation for some of the victims.

Jonathan cared. Wanted to help defenseless children. But first he would need to convince the wary management of Cabot, Lodge & Biddle and familiar firm foes to see past "business conflicts" and let him take the case. A conservative US Supreme Court would be another potential obstacle on the path to progress and justice.

Child slave labor is particularly acute in West Africa, including in Ghana and Côte d'Ivoire (in English, the Ivory Coast), where there are more than 1.5 million children working on cocoa plantations. Cocoa is a valuable commodity, especially for chocolate candy and desserts. Finding the cheapest sources, an avowed goal of profit-maximizing cocoa purchasers, led them directly to West African plantations where slave children brandishing machetes whack away at cocoa stalks for no pay or less than a dollar a day, fourteen hours a day, six days a week, and live in subhuman conditions. All so sweet-craving consumers can bite into chocolate treats and slurp syrup emanating from enslaved hands.

That is what a class of former child slaves was trying to prove in a federal court in Washington, DC. The litigation had been ongoing for years with several trips to intermediate appellate courts. To date, it was an endless procedural contest over the threshold issue whether the federal courthouse doors were open or closed to hearing the legal claim. Thus far, the atrocities were being shielded from accountability by legal technicalities. Now, it was looking like the latest appellate decision was finally going to open the door and let the child slave victims try to prove their claims in the trial court. But the slavery supply-chain defendants appealed to the US Supreme Court to have the case dismissed on a bunch of legal technicalities. If the Supreme Court refused to consider the appeal, or allowed the appeal and affirmed the intermediate appellate court's decision allowing the case to be decided on the merits of the claim, the child slave victims were going to need the help of a superstar trial lawyer to take on the multibillion-dollar corporate defendants who were sparing no expense enlisting the aggressive services of a cartel of Big Law powerhouses to defend them with a scorched-earth strategy.

The very best trial lawyers have a few quixotic genes in their bodies. Jonathan was no exception, and he was clamoring to find a pro bono case to satisfy his soul. He got the call. Cheryl Benton, a law school classmate and high honors graduate like Jonathan, had dedicated her career to public interest law. She was a director of Lawyers for Justice and Human Rights (LJHR). Cheryl and LJHR were helping to orchestrate the prosecution of the child slave labor case. In law school, especially Gladstone Bulldozen's civil procedure classes, Cheryl witnessed Jonathan's legal brilliance and fearlessness. She had also casually followed his career from afar and knew he was just the knight errant she needed, assuming she could persuade this high-profile Big Law litigator to take what would be a hugely expensive case pro bono. She didn't have to try hard. Jonathan accepted immediately on two conditions: he would need to clear legal conflicts and his CLB management would have to approve the representation. He knew instinctively that Felix Quaestor was about to have an apoplectic fit.

The defendants included a who's who of manufacturers, purchasers, processors, food and beverage companies, and retail sellers of cocoa beans. Jonathan was pleasantly surprised that none of those defendants were current clients of CLB. No legal conflicts. Now for the really hard part. Jonathan was self-aware. He understood that saying no to the top producer in the firm was not something management would do cavalierly. But still. It's one thing, he thought, to get management buy-in to take an expensive plaintiff's case on contingency, where at least there is the prospect of a big payday, but it would be quite another thing to take a pro bono case that could risk pissing off corporate clients who don't want to have to defend lawsuits in the United States for their offshore conduct. He anticipated opposition from the traditionalists and paleoconservatives, as well as from the pusillanimous, toadies, tightwads, and timorous. But he was resolved.

They met in the Cabot Room, an oil painting of Lowell Cabot

donning a double-breasted suit from Anderson & Sheppard, on Savile Road, hanging prominently behind the head of the table. If still alive, no chance this patrician pretender would even consider taking the case—DOA. The Cabot Room is where the fifteen-person management committee deliberated on a monthly basis. Much to Jonathan's disquietude, the oleaginous Oliver Truckle had connived to get voted onto the committee, by the slimmest of margins. Jonathan believed but could not prove that Baxter Hodges put his thumb on the scale for the bootlicker. Felix Quaestor, a long-time management fixture, was there. So too, the even longer-serving Hodges, the seemingly permanent managing partner who ruled with an iron fist inside a velvet glove. Hodges kicked off the meeting.

"Okay, Jonathan, why don't we give you the floor. The committee understands that you feel passionately about taking this case and will listen respectfully to your views. As the firm's top producer, you've earned the right to be heard. But I should tell you at the outset that a number of your partners think it would be a colossal mistake for CLB to represent a class of plaintiffs from West Africa against major corporations we would like to call our clients."

Jonathan resisted the urge to bellow out "Ugh." Hodges's coy reference to a "number of partners" was just like him. It was Hodges who believed it would be a colossal mistake, and he was signaling his no vote for all to hear. "Thanks, Baxter, and thanks to the committee for hearing me out." Better be on good behavior, he thought. He appreciated that there were some legitimate opposing viewpoints, but it galled him to think that he was going to have to beg CLB to allow him to do something about a humanitarian tragedy. He took some comfort knowing that numerous lawyers, especially the younger ones, were tripping all over themselves to join the cause.

"Let me first say we have no legal conflicts. None of the defendants is a current client."

"Yeah, and if we sue them they'll never be clients of the firm." Felix Quaestor couldn't help being a smart-ass.

The second dagger drawn. Jonathan continued. "I've done factual due diligence, and the allegations in the lawsuit seem to be well supported. Child slave labor is all too real, it's horrific, and the corporate defendants are lining their pockets with blood-drenched dollars. Perhaps that might be of some relevance if CLB ever wants to represent any of these defendants in the slavery supply chain." Jonathan's way of parrying the assault with "FU, Felix."

"Here's what has yet to be challenged by those wonderful defendants. The child slave victims, the plaintiffs, are kids. Some from their own country, others trafficked in from neighboring West African countries. Many receive no pay, others less than a buck a day. They are treated like commodities. They are forced to work fourteen-hour days, six days a week. They are fed scraps of food. They are whipped and beaten by brutal overseers. They are locked in rooms at night and not permitted to leave the plantations. As you would expect, many try to escape. If caught, they are beaten and tortured. There are many eyewitnesses to the degradation and dehumanization of desperate children getting their feet cut open and forced to drink urine for the crime of seeking freedom. Folks, this is all happening to innocent kids, for Christ's sake!"

"Look, Jonathan, nobody is saying that's good, but these corporate defendants are not the ones enslaving kids," offered the witless and tone-deaf Oliver Truckle.

"Not directly, Oliver, but they are the enablers," Jonathan riposted, as always with compelling data at his fingertips. "Combined, these scofflaws control production, and they know full well what is happening on the plantations. The sons of bitches even successfully lobbied Congress not to pass legislation to curb child slave labor. With their economic clout, they could stop these atrocities tomorrow. But they don't give a damn about these poor, innocent kids. All they care about is a cheap source of labor to suppress cocoa prices and increase their profits. It's sickening. All for products that contribute to obesity and diabetes, no less. They have orchestrated a slave-based supply chain. Not to be overlooked, these kids aren't white, they're black. American companies profiting from black slave labor. Hmm, sound familiar to anybody?

"And there's more. They protect the cocoa supply chain with exclusive buyer/supplier relationships with the farmers. They provide technical and financial assistance and even give the farmers money for their personal use. Sound like bribery to anyone? They do all of this from US headquarters and regularly send their henchmen to Côte d'Ivoire to inspect and oversee quality control and production practices and then report back to HQ, where financing decisions are made. So don't tell me these defendants aren't responsible for enslaving kids."

"Okay, I think we get the picture," said a nervous Hodges, fearing that if he allowed Jonathan to continue reciting despicable facts, he would lose control of his committee and Jonathan would get an approval vote, an outcome Hodges was lobbying behind the scenes to prevent. "I'm not a litigator, but Oliver, our litigation department head, and others have told me that the legal claim is a long shot at best and that the Supreme Court, with a corporate-friendly majority, thank goodness for our clients, will likely reject the attempt to use American courts to seek redress. What say you?"

Of course that lickspittle Truckle was stabbing him in the back, Jonathan thought. With his fluorescent bow ties and periwinkle argyle socks, the little popinjay is afraid of his own shadow and lives in mortal fear of anything that "might offend corporate America." God help the twit if he ever stepped foot in Judge Roy's courtroom. "The legal claim is one for aiding and abetting child slave labor in violation of the ATCA—the Alien Tort Claims Act. Without going into too much detail, the ATCA allows claims in US federal courts for violations of the law of nations. Recognized claims include genocide, war crimes, torture, and supporting terrorism. I doubt that even the current Supreme Court would rule that child slave labor doesn't qualify as a violation of the law of nations."

Another committee member, Dean Douglas, a banking partner, asked, "Does this Alien Tort law really allow foreigners to sue in American courts for conduct outside the United States, and don't you agree, Jonathan, that our corporate clients would prefer that we fight that issue, just like other Big Law firms, with sterling reputations I might add, are doing so on behalf of the defendants?"

Given CLB's client base, fair enough questions, Jonathan supposed. "Dean, as to your first question, the answer is yes, such lawsuits are allowed, but in limited circumstances. As a critic of what you like to refer to as terminological inexactitude in legal documents, the Supreme Court has ruled that the ATCA applies to foreign conduct only if it 'touches and concerns' the US. Lot of potential wiggle room there. If the Supreme Court does decide to hear the slave labor defendants' appeal, that issue could very well be the only issue they tackle.

"As to your second question about whether our clients would balk at us for taking the case, who's to say, but I suggest that we not be too cynical. And not suppose all corporate clients think alike or have the same interests. For example, on behalf of a number of American corporations, I was in the Second Circuit Court of Appeals not long ago arguing that the US antitrust laws apply to foreign price fixing under certain limited circumstances. Hasn't hurt our business. Besides, not all our corporate clients are troglodytes, and some might even think this lawsuit is a noble cause. I sure as hell hope so. Some might even be repulsed by our Big Law competitors siding with slavery enablers."

"I doubt that," the cretin Truckle protested self-righteously. "I think corporate America appreciates that lawyers are different than their clients, and everybody is entitled to a defense."

The dumbass just unwittingly served up a softball for Jonathan. "Yeah, I said the same thing years ago when we represented the Saudi charities after 9/11, and Jack Coltrane shredded the argument to pieces."

"How so?" Truckle really was not smart.

"I'll answer that question, but first, if clients really are nuanced and savvy enough to separate lawyers from the clients and cases they take on, then there should be no business conflict issue in taking the child slavery case." Out of the corner of his eye, Jonathan saw Hodges glaring at his stooge, Truckle. "But the underlying premise of value neutrality in civil litigation is a myth. A fiction to assuage the conscience. We get to choose our cases, and when we choose, we make value choices. We know that those choices overwhelmingly come down to money: if we stand to make a lot of money and the client can pay, the easy default option is we take the case. We don't fret over the underlying nature of the case. We don't sit in judgment of our clients, but let's not fool ourselves about our values. First and foremost they are about money.

"And let's not hide behind the shibboleth of every client deserves a defense. True enough in criminal defense work where people can go to jail, and by the way, the only criminal defendants we represent are of the white-collar variety, almost always well-paying corporations that risk fines but, of course, not jail time.

"Not every defendant in a civil lawsuit deserves a defense, certainly not one provided by us. That's a choice we make. And I, for one, would choose not to defend corporate enablers of child slave labor. But I would choose, and I do choose, to represent the victims of that heinous system. If this isn't a violation of the law of nations, I don't know what is. I want to hold the slavery enablers accountable for their moral reprehensibility and represent the tragic victims in the hope of getting them some compensation. In the hope that through our legal system, in our federal courts, we, Cabot, Lodge & Biddle, can help make progress toward the dream of freeing poor and innocent children from this savage system of slavery."

The room was silent. No partner in his or her right mind would speak in opposition, at least not openly in that moment. Baxter Hodges was feeling trapped, but this modern-day Fabius Cunctator didn't just fall off the turnip truck. He knew better than to call for an open vote. So he delayed. "Thank you, Jonathan. As always, you have spoken eloquently and certainly have given the committee plenty to mull over. Let us adjourn for now so the committee can continue to give your request consideration."

Jonathan thought, *They're going to fuck me. I need another hook.*

ANTITRUST SUPER BOWL

It didn't take long for Jonathan to find his hook. For several years Cabot, Lodge & Biddle was one of dozens of law firms that represented Centillion Intelligence, a leading high-tech, search-engine provider headquartered in Austin, Texas, with offices throughout the world. Founded by two MIT- trained physicists in Boston in 1995, as the company grew it relocated to Austin, allured by Texas's no state income taxes as well as the warmer weather and funky vibe where folks walk around in "Keep Austin Weird" T-shirts and listen to the likes of Willie Nelson, John Prine, and Stevie Ray Vaughan at the iconic Austin City Limits. But Centillion was primarily motivated to relocate to the city that was rivaling Silicon Valley as the tech center of the universe because of the abundance of talent and the synergies created by the proximity of so many tech companies.

Jonathan had never represented Centillion. The legal work CLB did for Centillion was primarily patent litigation and international tax and transfer pricing matters. Centillion was not the company's original name. As internet use exploded, so too did internet websites. The young startup devised efficient ways to search those websites with software called "crawling," index what they found, and then serve up those findings in helpful ways to users. For example, if a user was sitting in a MIT dorm room and wanted to find a crab shack, Centillion's search engine, and its innovative DQ (data quality) algorithm, would find shacks in and around Cambridge and Boston and place them at the top of the screen. But, if the same person was in Pakistan and wanted to eat crabs in Karachi, Centillion's browser would first direct her to nearby places in that city.

The young physicists were better at fermions, bosons, and quantum field theory than marketing, advertising, and consumer choice and unimaginatively named their promising company ICIS, as in internet crawling, indexing, and servicing.

Clunky, but all well and good until 2014 when Northern Iraq and Syria were overrun by a radical group calling itself the Islamic State, or more commonly known in the West as ISIS. ISIS, which sounds identical to ICIS, was confusing to consumers, some of whom already believed that there was a secret cabal of technologists attempting to control minds and take over the world. ICIS needed a name change and made the change in 2015 to Centillion Intelligence. It took a gargantuan database to store the exploding number of websites and respond to the billions of daily queries the company was receiving. By 2015, Centillion was the dominant internet search engine and its new management (the founders retired in 2007 with net worths approaching $30 billion each) was smitten by the stentorian sound of Centillion. They also thought it was cleverly symbolic to name their company after a staggeringly large number, given the size and scale of their computational power—centillion is the number 1 followed by 303 zeroes.

By 2020, Centillion had a market cap of a trillion dollars and revenues in the hundreds of billions. The corporate giant followed a familiar path to dominance. In the twenty-first century, it acquired more than one hundred core and complementary businesses to fortify, protect, and grow its expanding business. Many press pundits and those in the blogosphere called it an empire. Now, so too was the Antitrust Division of the Department of Justice. They sued Centillion for unlawful monopolization. The company needed a lead trial lawyer to defend what was being described as the looming "antitrust trial of the twenty-first century." Centillion intended to do what many corporations do when faced with a bet-the-company lawsuit: interview four or five firms and then select their lead trial lawyer. CLB was invited to audition, but only if Jonathan A. Kent was available and willing to commit to being the lead trial lawyer in a case that would be close to all-consuming.

From his early college days to law school, to his clerkship, and throughout his career, Jonathan dreamed of being the lead trial law-

yer in a case of this magnitude. It was the equivalent of every young
baseball player's dream of hitting a grand slam, in the bottom of the
ninth, with two outs, down by three runs, a full count, in game seven
of the World Series. This is what Roy Hobbs would do. Now Jonathan was getting a chance to compete for the at bat. He wanted it, he
could taste it, but he also wanted his child slave labor case. And he
knew all too well that Baxter Hodges and even Oliver Truckle would
move heaven and earth to convince him to represent Centillion. The
prestige of such a high-profile case, as well as the tens of millions
of Centillion dollars that Felix Quaestor could count each year for
several years to come, would burnish CLB's reputation and pump its
partner profits. Jonathan had his hook.

No Cabot Room meeting. This time, hat in hand, they came to
him. Unlike many partner offices that serve as shrines to their egomaniacal occupants, Jonathan's office was spartan rather than show.
Plain and spotless desk from a flea market. A few secondhand guest
chairs. Unadorned walls save for two impressionist reproductions:
Renoir's *Ball at the Moulin de la Galette* and Monet's *The Artist's Garden at Giverny*. Not much else but a computer, telephone, the Oxford
English Dictionary, Scientific American's *Science Desk Reference*, David
Bevington's *The Complete Works of Shakespeare*, and two easels and
markers, legal pads, and pens. Hodges and Truckle and the two Centillion client attorneys knocked on his door.

"Good morning, Jonathan," Hodges started. "I see you still don't
spend any of your bountiful compensation on office furnishings. This
Centillion case is a tremendous opportunity for you and the firm, but
Oliver tells me you're not sure you can commit. That hardly sounds
like you, Jonathan. Is that true?"

"I agree, it is a once-in-a-lifetime opportunity for the firm and
me, but as you know, I already have a full plate and am not sure I can
make the commitment." Jonathan was trying to be coy, but Hodges
knew him too well and sensed there must be something up his sleeve.

"Being busy has never stopped you before from taking on one
big challenge after another. I know you want to take plaintiff's cases.
Is that it, you have reservations about defending an alleged monopolist?"

"Come on, Jonathan," Truckle practically shouted, once again jumping to conclusions before his opponent played his hand. "This is our core business and this is exactly the type of case CLB wants and needs. Why are you turning your back?" Jonathan thought back to the Rush Street jazz club his last night with Judge Roy—Truckle's mind is on vacation and his mouth is working overtime.

"Oliver, who said I'm turning my back?" Jonathan calmly asked. "I simply said I have reservations."

"I suppose some reservations are fine, Jonathan, but this case is the Super Bowl of antitrust litigation. And if Tom Brady was put on this earth to play in the Super Bowl, you were put here to play in this game, on the Centillion team," Hodges said.

Jonathan thought, *Well-played, Baxter. I'm not arguing that point.*

"I appreciate the compliment, Baxter, but let me tell you the reservation I have." He could hear Trane channeling his inner Deadhead and saying the cards ain't worth nothin' if you don't lay them down. Now was the time for Jonathan to get truckin' and play his hand. "Yes, I want to be in the DOJ/Centillion game, but I also want to be on the team that is trying to help child slavery victims. As professionally motivated as I am to take the antitrust case, I'm just as emotionally motivated to try to help the helpless victims of a savage system. I want to know that my law firm stands with me."

Checkmate, or is it? Hodges didn't survive this long as CLB's leader without quick wits and his own ability to think several moves ahead. "You know, Jonathan, independent of this meeting, I've been thinking a lot about how we can proceed with your pro bono case," Hodges dissembled, as Jonathan was calling to mind William Blake's *Augeries of Innocence*: *a truth told with bad intent beats all the lies we can invent.* "I think I have a workable solution."

"Let's hear it."

"Right now the parties in that case are waiting to see if the Supreme Court will take the appeal, nothing is happening in the district court, so there is no need for us to decide right now. Our appellate litigators are predicting that the court will take the appeal. If the court does take it and reverses, that would undoubtedly be the end of the case." That was the bet Hodges was making, fervently praying for. "Either way, let's see what the Supreme Court does before we make a commitment and enter an appearance."

Jonathan knew Hodges was making a reasonable proposal. No sense stirring up partners and potential client controversy if the Supreme Court was going to gut the case in any event. "I can live with that, Baxter, but I want to be very clear about one thing. If the Supreme Court refuses the appeal, or takes it and affirms, and the case proceeds to litigation and a trial on the merits, I want to be lead trial lawyer and will have to consider all my options if the firm fucks me over. Am I clear?"

"You have a way with words. I understand you very well, Jonathan." A master of strategic delay on difficult decisions, the wily Hodges was living to fight another day. "So you're in on the Centillion audition?"

"I am. Let's get it and win the case."

GAME ON

Over the course of his career, Jonathan's life, like his cases, had a been a series of sensations, a series of ephemeralities. Memories fading, many to extinguishment. His bus ride had taken him a long way since his law school procedure classes with the inestimable Gladstone Bulldozen and his clerkship with the remarkable Judge Luke Roy. He had been involved in matters and events that reflected Americana for overlapping generations but dominated by the one referred to as the Baby Boomers. Competition and conquest, country music, corporate accounting, cigarettes, cell phones, and car insurance. School lunch milk and airline travel. Banks and Ponzi schemes. September 11 and the Great Recession. Semiconductors and computers. Opioids and Alzheimer's. On his bus ride, he had sought the independence that motivated him from early in life. Fear and escape.

Failure at early love only intensified his desire for professional success and independence. Money was always a means to that goal and, secondarily, a way to keep score in the brutally competitive world of Big Law. He had seen the mountain and scaled it. But his laurels would not allow him to rest. Just the opposite. Like his literary and cinematic baseball hero Roy Hobbs in *The Natural*, he wanted the evanescent goal of being "the best there ever was." Roy Hobbs, of course, was a fictional character. So, too, was Jonathan's goal. What started as his professional aspiration melded into his life's aspiration. The two were one.

The Centillion antitrust case was being described as the biggest antitrust case in twenty-five years. Taking and winning the case would get him closer to his imaginary Hobbsian goal, putting him at or very near the top of the list of America's most celebrated trial lawyers. Earlier in his career, Jonathan had dreamed of a moment like this, and now that the audition was over, he was one phone call away. Should the call come, nothing but nothing would stop him.

Jonathan got the call. It lasted twenty minutes. He had one condition. The next day it was announced that Jonathan was Centillion's lead trial lawyer. Jonathan agreed with Abraham Lincoln that one bad general is better than two good ones. Ships sink in storms and battalions die in battle when a cacophony of voices drown out the single commander's voice charting the course. Jonathan insisted on command of the overall strategic direction of the lawsuits, not a trial by committee that happens when big corporations hire several Big Law firms, and their egomaniacal lawyers, to defend them.

There would be some internal firm controversy, but it took Jonathan a nanosecond to figure out his team. So he reassembled them all. David and JP. Maya and Ruth and Kaori. Several others would be added to the team given the size and scope of the lawsuits, but they would be the core trial team. This was going to be a clash of the titans, and Jonathan needed his very best. He had waited a long time for this case. He did not intend to lose.

GETTING READY

Monsters are scary. For as long as human beings have been communicating with one another and telling stories, monsters have haunted the imagination. Monsters are egocentric, they are heartless, and they devour and destroy. Monsters personify imperfection. Nobody roots for the monsters.

Jonathan knew that the developing zeitgeist of the 2020s was Big Tech equals Leviathans. Certainly to influential federal and state politicians and the antitrust regulators. The government, invoking an image of Cyclops guarding the cave, called Centillion an internet gatekeeper. His new client wasn't just being portrayed as big, Jonathan recognized, it was being portrayed as bad, as a heartless beast devouring and destroying anything in its path.

Jonathan understood all too well that he could not win the case if the monster description went unchallenged. One of the things he did successfully in the AIQC monopolization trial was to portray Beijing Semiconductor as a monster, a heartless monopolist that had bought and bullied and devoured all that did not bend to its selfish will. To win, he must portray Centillion as an innovator, not a beast. Innovators challenge the status quo with the creation of a new order of things, and that gives rise to plenty of enemies, typically with partisan passions. His defense must be impassioned and strategic, not uninspired and sluggish. Jonathan appreciated that he must bring home the theme that Americans appreciate success, not annihilate it.

So, this splendid warrior wondered, what is the new order of things that this innovative client has brought forth? Can he persuade judge and jury that it is a hill to die on? Jonathan convened a team meeting. Everybody by now knew the drill. JP made sure there were easels in the conference room.

"The *United States v. Centillion*," Jonathan intoned. "It's going to be a long slog. Discovery for a year, probably two. Trial doubtful for another three years. Maya, what's the antitrust claim?"

"The government claims that Centillion is monopolizing a market for general search services."

"Thanks. And, JP, what do we know already?"

"We know that the DOJ is going to use the *Microsoft* case from twenty years ago as a blueprint for how to prosecute this case."

"Exactly. Ruth is preparing a strategy memo that lays out exactly how the DOJ proved its case against Microsoft, and we will use that as a starting point to prepare an outline of the allegations against Centillion. That will give us a good start for developing our trial proofs, which we will use as a roadmap to win the case."

"And I'm dissecting all the reports from Congress, and the information they relied on, to supplement Ruth's memo," JP volunteered.

"And Maya and I are coordinating with the other defense firms on offensive and defensive discovery strategy," David added. "Thank goodness they get the fun of all of the initial document reviews to cull the documents so we can focus on what really is important and relevant."

"Great," Jonathan remarked. "But let's change gears a bit. David, you and Maya are taking the lead on defending the Centillion witnesses in depositions, and JP and Ruth will be on point for figuring out the depositions we want to take, mostly of our client's competitors and business partners, right?"

"Yes," David acknowledged, "everything is in the works."

"We'll talk about experts at our next meeting. What do we know about the DOJ lawyers who will try the case?" Jonathan asked.

"Jonathan, only you would make every case some lesson from James Bond in *Casino Royale*," Ruth laughed as she shook her head in amusement.

"Sean Connery and Pierce Brosnan were great as Bond, but Daniel Craig is my favorite Bond. What a line from *Casino Royale* when he ordered a vodka martini and the bartender asked the question made famous by the prior Bond movies: 'A vodka martini. Shaken or stirred?' The answer: 'Do I look like I give a damn?' That was the best. An announcement that there was a new Bond at MI6. Please continue," encouraged Jonathan, doing his best Daniel Craig as James Bond smirk. In the *AIQC* case, Jonathan had traveled to Beijing for a settlement conference. While there, he hiked the Great Wall and visited many wonderful sites, including the spectacular Yonghe Temple (the Palace of Peace and Harmony), a Tibetan Buddhist temple and monastery, where locals wanted his picture, convinced he was James Bond as played by Daniel Craig. The highlight of his trip.

"According to *Bond*, in a poker game you never play your hand, you play the opponent across the table," Ruth dutifully droned.

"Obviously an overstatement, but just as we want to know everything we can about the judge, we want to get the skinny on our opponents across the table," Jonathan explained, as if they were MI6 agents.

"I'm pulling the bios on the lawyers and will circulate them," Ruth volunteered. "It's a combination of career government lawyers and a few lawyers recruited from private practice to beef up the trial team. The main lawyer who will likely take the Google depositions is from private practice."

"Good, I look forward to getting the bios and learning something about our adversaries," Jonathan casually concluded as he drew the meeting to a close, not expecting to find anything too surprising.

ADVERSARIES

It is not unusual for the DOJ to fortify its trial team when investigating and then bringing major civil lawsuits. Especially when the government brings a monopolization case against a high-tech giant. In the *Microsoft* case, the government even retained a prominent lawyer from private practice to be its lead trial lawyer.

As it launched its investigation of Centillion, the government intended to hire an additional two, possibly three, lawyers with civil antitrust and high-tech experience to work exclusively on the case. For a younger lawyer looking to make a mark, gain invaluable experience, and find a way to separate herself from tens of thousands of other Big Law senior associates and young partners, the Centillion case represented a once-in-a-lifetime opportunity to get ahead. A win would bring career cachet that would open doors that otherwise likely would remain firmly closed. For a young partner who always took ownership of her career, who was brilliant, talented, and ambitious, who aspired to join the unicorn club of top female trial lawyers, the Centillion case was the ticket.

Better yet, the DOJ wasn't looking to add just another body to the case. A fear many a talented younger lawyer has about working on huge antitrust cases is getting relegated to being a cog in the wheel, far from any meaningful skills-development action. An infantry soldier as the case settles into years of trench warfare. Or Big Law life. No, the DOJ was interviewing for two significant positions, one to work with the lead lawyer preparing the government's expert economists and one to lead or colead the effort to marshal the factual evidence to prove that Centillion was an unlawful monopolist. Not surprisingly, the DOJ was inundated with Big Law ré-sumés. It winnowed the field to a handful of folks whom it brought in for interviews. Joni Shannon was one of them.

Joni worked in a Big Law firm based in California with offices in San Francisco and Los Angeles as well as fifteen other American cities and London, Tokyo, Hong Kong, and Singapore. She was excelling as a young partner but was frustrated with life in Big Law and her firm's weak bench of top-drawer trial lawyers. Desperately concerned that her career at her firm was going to be nothing more than playing second fiddle to a second fiddle.

Joni brimmed with intelligence, had enormous self-discipline, and was exceedingly well organized. She prepped and prepped for her DOJ interview, her first job interview since interviewing for a law firm job after her judicial clerkship. Already steeped in antitrust law, she reread the *Microsoft* case, scoured Centillion's public disclosures, and read everything she could get her hands on about trying antitrust cases. She even read the trial transcript of the *AIQC v. BSMC* monopolization case, never even considering that more than a year later Centillion would hire Jonathan Kent as its lead trial lawyer. She thought it was manna from heaven—Jonathan's trial strategy, ironically, would be her guide, the potential winning roadmap for the Centillion case. She was ready for her interview.

There were five DOJ lawyers in the room, but the interview was conducted by a senior lawyer, Mark Landry.

"Good morning, Ms. Shannon, thanks for taking the time to come to DC for this interview. It's a huge and important matter, and we're only interviewing the best." A flattering way to start by Mark.

"Thank you very much, Mr. Landry, I'm excited to be here for this terrific opportunity. But please, call me Joni."

"Fair enough. And please call me Mark. We have your résumé and your glowing recommendations, but why don't you start by telling us a little bit about yourself, like where you're from and how you became a lawyer?"

"Sure. I grew up in the Berkeley, California, area. My dad is an architect and my mom, who died last year, owned and operated a jazz café off the Berkeley campus."

"I'm sorry about your mom," Mark said, offering condolences.

"Thanks, she was an extraordinary woman. I miss her every day."

"I can only imagine. Did she inspire you to become a lawyer?"

"Not directly. She was a loving but demanding mother. One of my earliest memories of what she said to me as a very little girl was, 'You are going to college.' That was never in doubt. She demanded top grades in school and was forever telling me I could be anything I wanted to be. She never tried to direct me toward any particular path but instead encouraged me to explore and find my passion. Mom instilled a lot of confidence in me. Sort of the sky-is-the-limit mentality. And lots and lots of music. I started piano lessons when I was six. Still play."

"Well, you of course followed your mother's command and went to college. I see you did your undergraduate work at UC Berkeley. What did you study?"

"I majored in film with a minor in journalism. I actually considered Buddhist Studies but quickly realized that the path to nirvana was not likely to get me a job." Joni had learned that only those with cool self-confidence can flash a sense of humor in a serious job interview.

"Funny. Why film?"

"It was interesting, and when I started to think about law school, I thought it would be helpful. And I think it certainly has been."

"How so?"

"It's all about storytelling, like trial work. I learned about the craft of writing different types of stories for an audience. I studied how to tell emotional stories that capture an audience's attention. How to write interesting dialogue and conversation, how people actually talk in modern life. I worked on documentaries, not just the recounting of facts, but how to broaden the lens so to speak to get a view of larger issues. How to develop narratives and put things into context. How to explore issues from different points of view. I took three courses in screenwriting and one on the American detective in fiction. In my journalism courses, I concentrated on communications, not just with texts but also with pictures, video, and sound. To get behind a camera to see how a story might be viewed not just by the speakers, but mostly by the intended audience. I learned an invaluable saying that it's not so much important what the speaker says but what the listener hears. All of those courses I think go hand in hand with how to prepare a compelling story to tell in a courtroom."

"That's interesting. You know, Joni," Mark posited, "a lot of antitrust lawyers, like me for instance, were economics or business majors in college. Why not you?"

Joni sensed she was being tested. "I actually took a couple of economics courses and a couple of statistics courses, and they have been useful. As you know, a lot of antitrust lawyers don't try cases and don't want to try cases. That's not me. I want to try cases. And trials are not about theories and graphs and equations, they're about people and human motivations. I think my film and journalism courses are far more useful in developing skills in persuasion and telling stories that emotionally have an impact on judges and juries. I learned in a philosophy course that reason is a slave to the passions and that most people make decisions based more on emotion and biases than reason, one of the points Daniel Kahneman makes in his insightful book *Thinking, Fast and Slow*. And he's a psychologist who won a Nobel Prize in economics. There's a reason economics is called the dismal science."

"Touché. I like that, and I liked Kahneman's book," Mark conceded. "So, number three in your law school class at UCLA, that's impressive. How did you pick UCLA?"

"I was lucky enough to get into Stanford and Berkeley," a sly yet humble way of saying I could've gone to the school of my choosing, "but I thought I might want to do trial work related to film and entertainment, so I chose UCLA."

"And you clerked on the Ninth Circuit Court of Appeals?"

"Yes, I did. For Judge Mary McKinnon. She was great, taught me a lot about legal writing and how to write persuasive briefs, and as much as I enjoyed my clerkship, it made me realize even more that I wanted to focus on civil litigation in trial courts."

"So after your clerkship you landed at your current firm and have been there ever since?" Mark asked.

"That's right. I started private practice in litigation with a focus on antitrust, made partner a couple of years ago, and now here I am. In some sense it feels like everything I have done in school and private practice has been a long training exercise for this opportunity."

"Well, I think I can safely speak for the others, Joni, that you are certainly well qualified for the job. So let me give you the floor. Why do you want this opportunity?"

Joni knew this question was coming and was ready. "I guess you're not surprised that I figured you would ask a question like that. I don't want to sound like I've rehearsed a canned response. This is from my heart and my head. First, as my mother taught me, thank you for considering me for this opportunity. I believe in this case. I think Centillion is a monopolist and I think that it has maintained its monopoly by exclusionary conduct. Like Beijing Semiconductor in the *AIQC* monopolization case, Centillion bought and bullied its way to dominance. They are thwarting innovation, a key to a dynamic economy, especially in the internet/ information age. This is an important case, and I want to be on the team that does and should win. I think consumers and the country would be better off with more competition in such a critical high-tech field. Everybody, rich and poor alike, increasingly depends on their computers and smartphones and those devices' search capacities to carry on in life.

"Choice is important. It's important for the economy and important for our democracy. Concentrated power in a critical area of our lives is not good for consumers or citizens. One firm should not be allowed to consolidate power and dominate that important space. One of my favorite lawyers of all time is Louis Brandeis, who, as you know, served on the Supreme Court. Brandeis once said something that I think is really important. He said concentrated wealth is a threat to our democracy, that we must make a choice. We may have our democracy or we may have wealth concentrated in a few hands. But we can't have both. This case is a choice in favor of democracy, and I want to help win it.

"During my clerkship, Judge McKinnon taught me many valuable lessons, the first being to take ownership over my own career. Assume nobody is going to hand me anything. My mom also taught me that lesson. Judge McKinnon said that it is especially true for women in the law. She said female trial lawyer role models will be few and far between in Big Law, and that is why it is particularly important for me to own my career. In my own firm, for example, there is only one female partner who has been the lead lawyer in a jury trial, and she's on the East Coast doing mostly white-collar cases.

"Well, from day one I wanted to be a trial lawyer. Not exactly sure where that came from, maybe my film and screenwriting classes, but I wanted the drama of the courtroom. That has been my passion. And the intellectual part of my brain wanted to work on the most complex cases. That's why I like antitrust. Competition is critical for the economy, and antitrust provides the rules of competitive engagement. Americans love winners but only if they play by the rules. We don't like bullies, and monopolists are economic bullies. Just like Centillion.

"My firm, like most of Big Law, offers a lot of excellent training in many areas, but learning how to try cases by actually trying them, quite honestly, is not one of them. So, to get better, I need a new and different challenge. I have worked on many tough cases. I know how to work them up to get them ready for trial, just what you're looking for, but I also want to be on the team that works up a very tough case and then takes it to trial. I can do this. I'm ready. And I'll work long and hard as a loyal teammate until we bring home a victory. I really want this opportunity. So the last thing I want to say is thank you for allowing me the opportunity to compete for it. I won't let you down."

Laughing, Mark said, "Wow, Joni, I think you're ready to do the closing argument!"

Peter Young, the other senior lawyer who had been a keen but unobtrusive observer and who had yet to speak, stood up. He looked around. Walked over to the window and looked out for a few seconds. Turned around, looked straight at Joni, and asked in a commanding voice that would permit no equivocation, "Joni, there are two positions we need to fill, one working with our expert economists and one working up our offensive case against Centillion. If given the choice, which do you prefer?"

This was it. Joni stood straight up and knew she was about to close the deal. Making sure to make eye contact with all five DOJ lawyers before looking Peter straight in the eyes, Joni gave a resolute one-word response, "Centillion." The other four followed Peter's lead and welcomed her to the team.

GOOD NIGHT SWEET PRINCE

Jonathan had spent his entire career doing meticulous preparation for difficult cases. He was a master. Always poised and unflappable. Always choosing just the right words to convey his message. Now he felt lost and totally unprepared. What do you say to a friend and mentor who has been diagnosed with stage four pancreatic cancer and given but a few more weeks to live? Jack Kenneth Coltrane lived a hard life, and now he was suffering a painful death. Jonathan did not subscribe to the view that through suffering comes salvation. Suffering is just suffering, and his good friend was suffering in a lot of pain. Nothing good or promising about that. He knew this was the last time he would ever talk with Jack. And so, at that very moment, Jonathan knew that there was no place on earth he would rather be, where he needed to be. Trane was taking opioids when Jonathan walked into his hospice room.

"Good morning, Jack," Jonathan began, somewhat tentatively. Trane looked terrible.

"Good morning, Jonathan. Thanks for stopping by. Come on in."

Jonathan took a seat close to Trane's bed. "How are you feeling this morning?"

"The opioids help, but otherwise I feel like shit." Death looming, Trane apparently was not now going to start pulling his punches.

Or his sense of humor. A nurse walked in and solicitously asked, "Mr. Coltrane, do you want me to put a sheet over you?"

Without missing a beat, Trane, in a mock tone of seriousness responded, "Nurse, that is *precisely* what I'm trying to avoid in the little time I have left here on the good planet earth."

Jonathan just smiled. *Trane to the end*, he chuckled to himself.

"So I hear you're representing Centillion," Trane acknowledged, changing the subject. "Good for you. From what little I know about the case, looks like it's going to be a Microsoft do-over."

"You haven't been around the office in more than a year now. How did you hear that?" Jonathan had known for years that Trane had the uncanny ability to know just about everything that happened in the firm.

"Well, I'm not dead yet, for Christ's sake. Besides, I still have my sources... and my computer."

"Yeah, I guess information is easy to come by these days," Jonathan extemporized as he slowly tried to figure out what to say to his dying friend.

Trane helped him out. A voracious reader, he asked, "You got time to read any good books these days?"

"Finished Don Winslow's harrowing Mexican drug cartel trilogy—talk about the heart of darkness—and thanks to you, I read the Gabriel Allon, Jack Reacher, and Harry Hole books when they come out, usually on the plane. Formulaic stuff but good reads."

"Missed out on Winslow, but the others are fun reads and great characters. I always thought you had some Gabriel Allon in you. With your brooding and love of visuals, maybe, like Allon, you can dispose of evildoers and restore artistic masterpieces if this lawyer thing doesn't work out for you. I always liked Allon's mentor, Ari Shamron. But how about anything a little more serious?"

"Actually, I recently stumbled onto a book by an existential psychiatrist by the name of Irvin Yalom at Stanford called *Becoming Myself*. Interesting memoir. An older man now, Yalom says he was inspired to write it by a line by Dickens in *A Tale of Two Cities*: 'For, as I draw closer and closer to the end, I travel in the circle nearer and nearer to the beginning.' Yalom is a very good writer with a gift for insightful dialogue."

"Time does have a way of taking us back to beginnings. Maybe that's what Faulkner meant in *Requiem for a Nun* when he wrote that 'the past is never dead. It's not even past.' Anyway, sounds like this

Yalom guy has interesting things to say about death and dying and the human condition."

"He does." Quickly changing that subject, Jonathan asked, "How about you, Jack, any book recommendations?"

"You know I turned eighty a few years ago. One of those milestone years, I suppose. I found myself drifting in two directions. Reflections on luck in life and Dante. If you haven't read Michael Sandel's book *The Tyranny of Merit: What's Become of the Common Good?* check it out. Lot of insights about how to think about winners and losers in American life and the bitter divide in our politics."

"Isn't he a philosopher at Harvard?"

"Yeah, as a Princeton and Yale guy, I won't hold that against him. Like John Rawls before him, another Harvard guy, he zeros in on fairness and justice and the myth of individual achievement not discounted by luck and factors beyond an individual's control."

"How so?" Jonathan knew that Trane was in his element.

"Take elite colleges like my alma maters. The overwhelming majority of kids who get into the Ivy League schools come from the richest families. The admissions deck is completely stacked in favor of the rich. And of course those who make the most money in this country by and large are college graduates, especially from the top schools."

"In other words, there is more than individual talent and effort at play?"

"Exactly. Being born rich is not some individual achievement. That's nothing to brag about. It's nothing but damn good luck and good fortune, so to speak. That's the hubris of it all. Like I alone can fix it and I got my money and success all by my own hard work and merit. That's bullshit. Sandel is not saying that effort and talent don't count—of course they do—but a lot of luck and favorable circumstances play their parts also."

"That's interesting. I busted my ass in college and law school to get top grades. And I've busted my ass for thirty years to get where I am. But if I'm honest, I've had a lot of luck along the way."

"For starters, being white and male. You had nothing to do with either, but those have been real advantages for you in Big Law. Just look at the numbers—the success odds heavily favor those who are white males over any other combination of race and gender. It's not even close. And you can't take credit for either your race or your gender."

"Can't deny that. I remember years ago you and I debating whether Big Law is still a white boy's club. Sad to say, but you were right, it pretty much still is. Certainly at the top of the compensation ladder."

"Sad indeed. But think about the role of luck more broadly. Take the rich as Croesus guys like Warren Buffett, Bill Gates, Jeff Bezos, Elon Musk. All white boys with Ivy League connections, by the way. Imagine if those geeks had been born just 150 years ago. They'd be plowboys not plutocrats. Nothing but pure luck that they were born at a time and in a system where the particular skills they have enabled them to be billionaires a hundred times over. No one is saying they're not smart as hell and brilliant at what they do, but the timing of their birth and the system they were born into made it all possible for them to be spectacularly rich with the particular skills they have. They can't take personal credit for that. And don't get me started on the folks who inherited their way on to the *Forbes* list of billionaires. That's not achievement, it's nothing but staggering good luck. And that's just fucked up. You can be a dyed-in-the-wool capitalist and still support reasonable limits on how much silver is in the spoon the little trust babies of the world get to inherit."

"At least the system allows for someone like me who started closer to the bottom to make it to the top through hard work and ability." Jonathan thought, *Here Trane lies knocking on death's door, and we quickly go deep in a conversation as if we were back at the office, charged with solving the world's problems.* No pity or pathos, no mawkishness and maudlin words for Trane. He didn't need to wallow in his fate. He was eighty-four and facing death stoically. He lived for intelligent conversation about life and literature, fairness and justice, race and opportunity, and he was getting it with Jonathan, like an unspoken dying wish.

"Come on, Jonathan, you're a one-off. Yeah, there are folks like you who start from not much and make it big, but that's the exception, not the rule. You're a left-handed shortstop and there aren't too many of those. Income inequality is getting worse and worse, and that's not good for our democracy. It's like what the cosmologists say about the expanding universe: things are moving farther apart at an accelerating rate. If you start rich, you stay rich. If you start poor, you stay poor. And the gap continues to widen between rich and poor. As far as I'm concerned, that's an existential threat to our democracy. And it's utter bullshit when one political party dominated by a bunch of soulless dingleberries invokes the bogeyman of socialism every time somebody proposes to do something to benefit the common good or the least fortunate. For crying out loud, have Americans forgotten how to engage in critical thinking? Those bastards simply want to infantilize voters so they can perpetuate the growing economic and political inequality and keep minorities from voting and getting fairer opportunities. With their slavish devotion to a narcissistic, would-be autocrat and their irrational hostility to science and democratic norms, they've become nothing but a gaggle of little limp dicks and cuckoo chicks. Like the wonderful Marvin Gaye used to sing, make me want to holler and throw up both my hands."

"I agree that it's a sad state of affairs when stupid sloganeering and cult worship substitute for intelligent discourse on important policy questions. But are you and Sandel saying that economic and social upward mobility are myths?"

"Of course not entirely, but it's increasingly becoming so. That's why Sandel zeroes in on what he calls 'meritocratic hubris.' What I call smug assholes. The notion that rich and poor alike deserve their fates. Like it's some fucking moral reward or punishment whether you are rich or poor. Like good luck and good fortune, or lousy luck and bad fortune, are irrelevant. They're not. They are critical."

"Damn, Jack, it's good to be here talking with you. You're a noble warrior for a more humane world." Sensing Trane was tiring, Jonathan decided to move the conversation along. "I'll read Sandel's book. Sounds like lots of folks should read it. So tell me why you've been reading Dante."

"Rereading, actually. I first read the *Divine Comedy* in college. Thought it was an extraordinary feat of imagination, but otherwise moved on."

"So why rereading?"

"After I crashed and burned on you before the Birmingham milk case, I knew I had hit rock bottom. First Nixon's election in 1968 and then my near-death bender, those two times I felt lower than whale shit."

"Jack, you didn't do anything to me. You and I both know you have a disease."

"Yes, I do. But after that third trip to rehab, my wife, Mary, divorced me. By the way she died last year. Respiratory failure."

"Sorry to hear that."

"She was a good woman. Deserved a lot better than I was able to give her. Mary divorced me. My two kids graduated college and stayed on the West Coast. My career as a practicing attorney was over. Hell, I even lost my dog, Winston. God, I loved that dog. I needed to find another way, or I was going to die. As John Lennon sang in "Watching the Wheels," I had to get out of the big time, get off of the merry-go-round, I just had to let it go."

"And rereading the *Divine Comedy* helped?"

"It did. I also tried to learn about Zen states and being more accepting of things I can't control and focus on the bigger picture of life. Not to stress over every small detail in life."

"That's a hard ask for a lawyer. We spend 90 percent of our time obsessing over small details. What a life, huh?"

"True enough. But I needed to let it go. I took breathing lessons and meditation classes. And I decided I needed to reflect more on my interior. Not what so-called society expected of a Princeton and Yale grad, expected of a Big Law partner. Who am I to me, not who am I to others? And that led me back to Dante when I got out of my third stint in rehab."

"How so?"

"As you know, the *Divine Comedy* recounts Dante's trip through Hell, Purgatory, and Heaven. In the beginning of the *Inferno*, Hell, there is a wonderful passage that described me. Dante says, 'Midway upon the journey of our life I woke to find myself in a dark wood, for I had wandered off from the straight path.' That struck a chord. I had a choice to make. A choice of life or death.

"A popular theme in books and movies about the wayward or prodigal son who loses his way only to find redemption," Jonathan noted.

"The world would be a much better place if there was more redemption and, as Dr. King was fond of saying, a constant attitude of forgiveness. Anyway, it was in the telling by Dante that helped me find some peace and equanimity in my life. With Virgil as his guide, Dante journeys through the nine circles of Hell. Souls relegated to Hell for lack of self-control, greed and gluttony, slaves to material wealth, and souls consumed by anger. Those were all causing me Hell on earth."

"Jack, I think the biggest transformation I saw in you when you returned to the firm was the disappearance of raging anger. You clearly seemed to have learned some self-control and a degree of contentment with who you are. Privately, I thought you were the Buddha of the Beltway."

"Glad you kept that to yourself. It wasn't easy to improve my self-control and temper my anger. But it had become a matter of life and death for me. There were times I wanted to scream at life's injustices. When I wanted one more trial, just one drink, to be back in the action, but I let it go. And it saved my life."

"More Dante?"

"More Dante. It was always interesting to me that the final circles of Hell, where the worst lost souls are consigned, relate to fraud, deception, betrayal, and treachery. I felt I was committing those things to myself."

"To thine own self be true."

"Polonius from *Hamlet*, yes. Well, I hadn't been. I was betraying myself for the expectations I thought others had of me. I had been a fraud and deception to myself. I didn't even really know myself; I was more concerned with how others saw me. And I never liked what they saw."

"Jack, when I finished my clerkship with Judge Roy, he gave me a laminated card with a quote from the sixteenth-century humanist and essayist Michel Montaigne about how nothing is as important as acquiring the knowledge to live life well and naturally, and he says, 'the most barbarous of our maladies is to despise our being.' I have his complete essays on my nightstand and read some most nights when I'm in town."

"Your Judge Roy is a fabulous judge, one of the best, and Montaigne was a brilliant essayist. That's a wonderful quote the judge gave to you. I wished I had read Montaigne early in my life. Might have helped me not despise my younger self and focus on how to live life well. As I approach death, I'm okay with who I became later in life. By the way, Montaigne has a wonderful line about not worrying about how to die because nature will tell you perfectly how to do it, fully and adequately. Don't I know that now."

"Well, Jack, you should feel good about who you are and the man you became later in life. So back to Dante."

"Dante left Hell and the visionary Beatrice replaced Virgil as his guide through Purgatory and then partially through Paradise, when St. Bernard took Dante on his final journey."

"Should be required reading, along with Montaigne."

"You still know how to get my goad. Anyway, as Dante ascends the Celestial Ladder, he is quizzed on the virtues of Faith, Hope, and Love. He finally enters the Empyrean, where he finds souls blessed in love and peace. Dante is overwhelmed by the power of love. A love that gives purpose and meaning. A love that enables inner peace."

"So Dante found supreme love in his Christian God."

"He did."

"How about you, Jack?"

"Well, I've always been an Episcopalian, often casually so. But what I find so beautiful about the *Divine Comedy*, besides the extraordinary, adventurous imagination, is the ultimate simplicity of a journey from egocentricity to a consuming passion for something other than self."

"Years ago I had something of a similar experience standing among the gravesites at the American Cemetery in Normandy.

How all of those very young men committed the ultimate act of unselfishness and sacrificed their lives so that others then and even now could live in peace and freedom."

"Amen. I regret that I never did make it to Normandy; that would have been enriching. Anyway, Dante inspired me to be less egocentric, to keep faith and hope and work on love and charity. To temper judgment, give the benefit of the doubt, and to strive for empathy. To stay true to myself and not be consumed by how I am perceived by others."

"Jack, you learned very well. Your intelligence and gifts were always on display for all to see. Then you returned from your own hell a changed man. A kind man and a beloved man and partner. Jack, you gave love and love was returned to you. I suppose it was some kind of good fate that you would spend the rest of your career as a marvelous teacher for younger lawyers who learned so much from you. You continue to be an inspiration in ways that you'll never know. You're a special man, Jack, and you made the world a better place, certainly a more interesting place, in your eighty-four years. Those of us who had the good fortune to know you will always remember you as a one-of-a-kind, wonderful man."

"Jonathan, that is very kind of you to say. Beautiful words for a dying man to hear. Look, I don't have much time left, and I would like to get some sleep. This visit has meant the world to me, Jonathan. I love you, son." With those parting words, Trane drifted off to sleep.

Jonathan remembered Horatio holding a dying Hamlet in his arms: "Now cracks a noble heart. Good night sweet prince, and flights of angels sing thee to thy rest."

Outside of the hospice building, Jonathan wept uncontrollably. "I love you, son" were the last words Jonathan ever heard from Jack. Jack Kenneth Coltrane died one week later. In his will he left Jonathan his copy of the *Divine Comedy* with an inscription: "To Jonathan, my dear friend and trial lawyer extraordinaire, may you find love and peace, Jack."

PREPARATION

Over time, Trane's death would profoundly affect Jonathan. Eighty-four was not too young to die, Jonathan reasoned, but emotionally all he now had left of Trane were cherished memories, many of which he realized would inevitably fade with time. But the memories that would never fade were of a dying friend and mentor calling him son and exhorting him to find love and peace. Trane was a brilliant man with a passion for the precise use of words. To find connotes a search for something you don't have. Something missing. And Trane was exhorting Jonathan to find the love and peace he was missing. Trane, ever the mentor and teacher, had implied that Jonathan, too, needed to focus on—even find—his interior and be less concerned about chimeras and external validation. To let go of his one-dimensional existence and live a fuller life. Jonathan knew Trane had peered deeper into him than he himself was willing to go. Like now, with the press of the Centillion case and a return to his monomania for work. Some things, Jonathan knew all too well, are easier to avoid by distraction.

Ruth had sent Jonathan and the team an email with links to the web bios of the DOJ lawyers who were prosecuting the Centillion case. There were fifteen links. Jonathan clicked open the first two, Peter Young and Mark Landry, the lead lawyers. He perused their bios, looking specifically for cases they had tried. He was not surprised that there was not much to find. He had other emails to attend to, so he closed out of Ruth's email, figuring he would check out the other bios another time.

Then Jonathan turned to another matter. Of extreme strategic importance for preparing a winning case for Centillion. The trial proofs memo. Jonathan used one in every case. Starting with the law that will govern the case at trial, the memo maps out what the DOJ must prove, Centillion's best defenses, legal and factual, and the documents and testimony Jonathan would need to present Centillion's best defense. The memo, always a work in progress, disciplines the team to stay focused on the essentials and never take their eyes off the ball that will win the case. It is also a powerful stimulant for courtroom visuals, which Jonathan thought about daily.

JP and Ruth had finished their initial research and prepared a solid first draft of the memo. With documents stored electronically and ten three-ring binders of hard-copy documents, Jonathan put a do-not-disturb sign on his door and did his iron-butt study session. He had a prodigious capacity for concentrated work. Like Sherlock Holmes "throwing his brain out of action" to focus on a single issue. For three twenty-hour days (naps on the floor) and one all-nighter, he studied, thought, studied, and thought some more about one issue: how to win. He had four easels in his office and used them all. He then revised JP's and Ruth's draft memo until he liked what he saw. And Jonathan was excited about what he was seeing. There would be many more revisions as the case progressed, but barring some significant unforeseen developments, he thought he and the team had a winning trial formula. They could and were going to win the antitrust trial of the twenty-first century. As always, success or failure would ultimately depend on execution.

That execution would include the defense of Centillion witness depositions. Before any of the depositions in the case began, both sides agreed to meet again to see if they could reach agreement on how to conduct the remaining discovery. They had done this early on to discuss protocols for the enormous document discovery and that had worked out reasonably well. Now they were doing the same for the depositions.

This meeting, although long, also went reasonably well. The lawyers on both sides conducted themselves professionally and stayed focused on the task at hand, often a rarity in big cases. It became immediately clear at the meeting that the DOJ's day-today point person for the Centillion depositions was Joni Shannon. Peter Young, one of the senior DOJ lawyers, was also going to be involved. To break the ice and work out the details of the schedule, both sides decided that Joni, for the DOJ, and Maya, for Centillion, would meet the next day for a working lunch to prepare a draft schedule.

Jonathan was an enthusiastic proponent of getting to know your adversary. Professionally, it helped to promote civility, usually an evanescent aspiration in take-no-prisoners litigation. Strategically, it is difficult to play the person across the poker table if you don't know anything about her except what you read on the internet bios. Bios that invariably are shameless puff pieces. Reading those suppressions of truth, what lawyers call suppressio veri, you would think no litigator in America ever lost a case, wasted a client's money, or performed anything less than Houdini acts in impossible-to-win cases. Jonathan mocked the malarkey, quipping that if he were a corporation looking to hire a lawyer, he would hire the first lawyer who posted something like the following: "I recently tried a tough case and got my ass kicked all over the courtroom. Let's be real, I lose sometimes and don't pretend I'm a cartoon superhero like every other trial lawyer you will ever read about. At least I'm honest about it."

So Maya had a working lunch with Joni. They were roughly the same age and both had gone to Berkeley, Joni for undergrad and Maya for law school. On opposite sides, each standing in the other's way of a once-in-a-lifetime opportunity for a young, aspiring trial lawyer. Having more in common than not, a mutual respect developed almost instantly between these two magnetic personalities.

The business side of the meeting went faster than either had anticipated. Although both were on guard and realized that the other, like herself, was gathering intelligence, they engaged in a friendly conversation about self, job, and career while they enjoyed their lunch.

"So, Joni, how do you like working at the DOJ?"

"So far so good. You probably know by now that I interviewed specifically for this job," Joni offered, proceeding openly but cautiously.

"I do. I think it's great. Obviously, it's a terrific opportunity. I just hope you lose!" Maya fenced, in a friendly, competitive way.

"Ha, same to you. As you know, we have years to go before this case ever gets to trial. I suppose a lot can happen along the way."

"Yeah, these cases are really interesting, but I do wish they were a lot shorter. They consume your life. I just wish it didn't have to be for years," Maya lamented.

"I agree. I didn't work on anything this big in my prior firm, but discovery in civil lawsuits is ridiculous. We're off to a good start here, I hope we can continue that way."

"Me too," Maya agreed. "I can tell you, one of the many great things about working with Jonathan is, he says, if you have a discovery dispute, don't wage an email war with the other side, just pick up the phone and talk it out. If you can't resolve it, then go to the judge. So, I suggest we do that here."

"Totally agree. I get so sick and tired of snarky emails at 10:00 at night or on a weekend afternoon. About a snarly adversary, I can't count the number of times I thought to myself, 'Get a life.'"

"I hear you. So I suggest we start with good intentions. I'm on point for us, you for the government, if a discovery or schedule dispute comes up, and we both know that they will, you and I will get on the phone and try to work it out."

"Deal. What did Margaret Thatcher say? If you want a speech, ask a man; if you want something done, ask a woman?"

Laughing, Maya added, "Yes, and Thatcher also said the cock may crow, but it's the hen that lays the eggs."

"That is too funny. I need to remember that one." Drinking some water, Joni then asked, "So how did you like Berkeley? You know I went there undergrad? The library's Free Speech Movement Café was my home away from home."

"I saw that. I liked Berkeley a lot, or I guess as much as any normal person can actually like three years of law school. And I know what you mean about the café. Great food and hangout."

"Did you consider taking a job in San Francisco or in the Valley?" Joni asked.

"Thought about it a lot. Even clerked half a summer in San Francisco, but my family is on the East Coast, and I wanted to be closer to them, especially my grandma, who passed away a couple of years ago."

"Maya, I'm so sorry to hear that. I lost my own mother a couple of years ago. Think about her every day," Joni said, her eyes starting to well up.

"Joni, my grandma died of heart failure. How about your mother?"

"A rare disease. Something wicked called acute myeloid leukemia. Same disease that killed the brilliant Nora Ephron, one of my mom's favorite writers and directors. There are no known causes, and the survival rate after diagnosis is abysmal. It was an awful way to go for my mom, an extraordinary woman."

"I bet she was," Maya softly consoled. "Do you have any brothers or sisters?"

"No. Just me. My dad is still alive and working. He's an architect in the Bay Area."

"What did your mom do before she became ill?"

"She was so cool. She had me early in life. She had me right after college, so she put off going to graduate school and worked as an office manager of a tech company in San Francisco. She changed academic directions after she started working, and in the evenings she started her MBA at Berkeley and then finished her last year full time."

"Wow. Did she stay at the tech company after she got her MBA?"

"For a few years. But this is another reason she was so cool. When I was thirteen, she lived her dream. One of mom's favorite sayings was by the wonderful female novelist George Eliot, who said, 'It's never too late to be what you might have been.' So, off the Berkeley campus she opened a jazz café. Jazz at night, mostly local Bay Area artists, but often some big name would drop in, and she included a small vegetarian menu and featured California and Oregon wines. The club is still going strong."

"Wait, I know the place. I think I went there once to hear a San Francisco sax player who was really good. Wow, that was your mom's club?"

"Life's Illusions."

"Yes, that's it! I was there, can you believe it? Great name."

"You know where she got it?"

"No, but I'm sure there's some story behind it."

"There is. Mom got the name from Joni Mitchell. That's why I'm Joni. Named after the fabulous singer/songwriter Joni Mitchell. Mom loved her."

"Joni is a great name. My mom and grandma named me Maya, after Maya Angelou. Strong and brilliant woman. My grandma loved her poem 'Still I Rise.' 'You may trod me in the very dirt, but still, like dust, I rise.'"

"Another remarkable woman. Glad you got your name from her. Maya, I don't think anybody will ever trod you in the dirt!"

"Thanks. So why Life's Illusions?

"So Mom loved Joni's song 'Both Sides Now.' Beautiful in its mournfulness and lost love. The illusions of love and life. Mom just loved that song and thought Life's Illusions would be a great name with a personal touch for a jazz club. Joni Mitchell actually visited the club once. That was really special. She signed a photo of her and mom. It's a great photo. Still proudly hanging on the wall in the club."

"Joni, I'm really sorry for your loss. Your mom sounds like the coolest person."

"She was."

"Let's do a selfie. When the case is over, we'll do another one to see whose hair went gray first!" Maya clicked the photo and emailed a copy to Joni. Foes yes, friends becoming.

HAUNTINGLY FAMILIAR

Jonathan had arranged with the client for the team to spend a week at Centillion's bustling regional center in the South of Market (SoMa) area of San Francisco, a growing Geekistan like Austin, for witness interviews and initial preparation for depositions. The plan was to fly out on a Sunday afternoon, do five full days of work, have a client dinner Friday night, and then fly back to DC on Saturday morning. Maya had debriefed Jonathan and the team about her working lunch with Joni Shannon and had mentioned that Joni's deceased mother had started a Berkeley jazz café called Life's Illusions. All along, Jonathan had intended to tack on a couple of extra days to the end of the trip and made a mental note to possibly check out the club.

Centillion gave the trial team an intense, two-day crash course on its business operations that were pertinent to the case. Then, on Wednesday, Thursday, and Friday, the team split up and conducted interviews of twenty-two Centillion employees. All in all, Jonathan was satisfied with a productive week and was feeling even better about the chances of success at trial.

Friday night was a time to relax with some of Centillion's in-house lawyers who were working on the case. The Geeks picked Greek. They dined at Kokkari Estiatorio, a fabulous Greek restaurant serving meals and wine that would satiate Zeus and Dionysus. At the dinner, Ruth distributed the DOJ bios, with photos, of the lead lawyers as well as Joni Shannon, who was in charge of the DOJ's day-to-day offense against Centillion. Maya also showed the group the selfie she had taken with Joni.

Jonathan was struck by three things when he saw Joni's bio. He didn't know that she had clerked for Judge Mary McKinnon on the Ninth Circuit Court of Appeals. Judge McKinnon had authored a number of high-profile decisions. To Jonathan, the most important by far was her March 2020 decision affirming the dismissal of a copyright infringement lawsuit brought by the estate of the front man for the band Spirit, claiming that the rock band Led Zeppelin ripped off the opening notes to their emotionally draining, celestial megahit "Stairway to Heaven" from Spirit's song "Taurus."

Jonathan didn't care if the claim was true or not, just like he didn't care whether it was Leibniz or Newton who first invented calculus—they were both geniuses and their inventive genius helps us better understand the nature of space, time, motion, and optimization. Calculus "is the language God talks," in the words of the genius Richard Feynman. That is beautiful. Okay, a rock song is not quite calculus, but to Jonathan, Jimmy Page and Robert Plant created an artistic, aesthetic thing of beauty with their entire eight-minute masterpiece. Some works of art, he thought, should just be enjoyed and left undisturbed. A great work of art, like a great book, takes on an existence independent of the creator/author once it is out in the world. The mortal artist/creator might disappear, but the immortal masterpiece endures. Shakespeare died more than four hundred years ago, but *Hamlet* is alive and well. Jonathan always thought that it was supremely ironic that the Impressionist painters attempted to capture momentary glimpses of people, places, and events, and by so doing, preserved them forever. Joni Shannon was fortunate to have clerked for Judge McKinnon, he thought.

The second thing that struck Jonathan was Joni's web bio photo. It was in black and white but looked hauntingly familiar. He asked Maya to show him the selfie and compared the two photos. There was indeed something hauntingly familiar, but he moved on, finished his dinner, and returned to the hotel to get a good night's rest. That didn't happen. He barely slept at all. Just before nodding off, he experienced something of a hypnagogic hallucination providing premonitions of what appeared to be his immediate future.

In the morning, the rest of the team headed back to DC. Jonathan stayed back and went for his usual run along Embarcadero, through Fisherman's Wharf, up the hill, past Fort Mason, over to Crissy Field, and then reversed course, past the Ferry Building to the base of the Bay Bridge, and back to the hotel. He was still restless. He drank some water, munched on a Granny Smith apple, and decided to wander aimlessly wherever his walking shoes took him. For several hours up Nob Hill and Russian Hill, to Pacific Heights, over to Oracle Park, then on to the Mission District, Haight-Ashbury, the Golden Gate Park, over to North Beach, Telegraph Hill, through Chinatown, and back to the hotel again. His mind awhirl in agitated thoughts. After a night and then day of internal debate, he called Taufiq, his Moroccan driver, and asked him to take him to a jazz club in Berkeley that night called Life's Illusions.

LIFE'S ILLUSIONS

Taufiq was in a chatty mood, swelling with pride as he talked about his young son's soccer games and his daughter's swimming and music lessons. "Mr. Jonathan, aren't kids great?" he exclaimed. And he talked about the majesty and mystery of his beloved Morocco and renewed an offer he had made several times before. "Mr. Jonathan, please let me know if you ever want to go to Morocco. I would love to show you my country." His friend Taufiq would no doubt make a wonderful traveling companion, but the past, not the future, was preoccupying Jonathan just then as they crossed the Bay Bridge and headed north to Berkeley.

The music didn't start until 9:00 p.m., but Jonathan figured he would get there by 8:30 to get a seat, have some light fare and wine, and ease into a relaxed state to hear the night's featured act, a piano jazz trio from Mendocino. One wall at the entrance was covered with photos of artists and celebrities who apparently had visited the club. Jonathan was immediately seated, but he did spot photos of Bay Area celebrities Carlos Santana, Johnny Mathis, and Clint Eastwood, who produced and directed the film *Bird*, about the life of Charlie Parker, a jazz sax player who was a leader of bebop. Jonathan ordered a warm cauliflower salad and some fresh spring rolls. The wine menu was surprisingly extensive and included a selection of wines made by extraordinary female winemakers. There were red zinfandels by Helen Turley, cabernets by Cathy Corison and Geneviève Janssens, and pinot noirs by Merry Edwards. Inviting choices all, but seemingly randomly, Jonathan decided to try a Domaine

Drouhin Dundee Hills pinot noir by Veronique Boss-Drouhin. The choice did not disappoint.

The music started just after nine. The musicians—on piano, double bass, and drums—looked to be in their late twenties and clearly had played together for several years. The first set ended around nine fifty. It was very good. As Jonathan was sipping his newly discovered velvet treasure, he felt someone approaching from behind his right shoulder. It was Joni Shannon.

"Excuse me, Mr. Kent, but I thought I recognized you so I thought I would come over and introduce myself. I'm Joni Shannon. I'm one of the government lawyers in the Centillion case."

Surprised, Jonathan quickly recovered and rose to greet her. "Well, isn't this a small world. Nice to meet you, Ms. Shannon, but please, call me Jonathan."

"Will do. How do you know about this club? Have you ever been here before?" Joni asked with excitement in her voice.

"First time. Maya Gibson told me she had a productive and delightful lunch with you and you had mentioned it. I've been a longtime jazz lover. I'm here for the weekend, so I thought I would check it out." Jonathan was growing increasingly anxious but so far was not showing it.

"That's great. My mom started it. She died a couple of years ago, but my dad and I still own it. Mom used to run it, but we hired a manager to handle the day-to-day operations. This was her dream. Her passion. She poured her heart and soul into this club. I visit when I can, and that's why I flew in from DC to be here this weekend. Trying to carry on her legacy, I suppose."

"I'm sorry to hear about your mom; she must've been quite a person."

"Oh, she sure was. I see you're drinking her favorite Oregon pinot, Domaine Drouhin. Maybe you know this, but Veronique Drouhin was born in Burgundy and makes outstanding wines. France even awarded her the Legion d'honneur, their highest award of merit. Mom met her once. Is this also one of your favorites?"

"Actually, I never had it before. I saw it on the wonderful wine list and for some reason decided I'd give it a try. Pretty random actually. It's divine, like a velvet treasure."

"Ha, must be good karma or something. Funny, but that's just how Mom described Veronique's wines, velvet treasures. Anyway, I won't keep you, just wanted to stop by to introduce myself. I guess we'll be seeing a lot more of each other during the case. Oh, by the way, congratulations on your AIQC victory. I read the entire trial transcript. Lot of good ideas for the Centillion trial. I learned a lot from you. Enjoy the music and thanks for checking us out. Tell your friends!"

"I will indeed. And thanks for stopping by and saying hello. It's a real pleasure to meet you, too, Joni. I suppose we'll be seeing each other down the road in the litigation. Oh, try to forget what you read in the *AIQC* case. Take care." Jonathan softly shook Joni's hand and involuntarily held it for perhaps a second or two longer than a conventional shake before letting it go.

Jonathan didn't know much about strokes, but he thought most of the warning signs were there as he sat down. He felt numb, dizzy, out of breath, and was having trouble seeing. He felt everything was a blur. His ears were ringing, and his hands were trembling. After a few minutes, he regained his sight and composure. But he still felt as if he were having an out-of-body experience, like his entire world had just been turned upside down, like nothing would ever be the same again, like he had just discovered his own parallel universe and was suddenly a stranger to himself in both the real and alternative worlds.

Forcing himself to concentrate, the third thing that had struck Jonathan about Joni's web bio was her date of birth. A December birth. End-of-school conception. That could fit. Maya's color selfie with Joni was one thing, but seeing her—seeing those eyes in person—was quite another thing. Those beautiful, luminescent, emerald-green eyes. Could it really be true? Jonathan had to leave. Immediately.

Heading toward the exit, he walked past the wall with the photos. Pictures really are worth a thousand, revealing words. Yes, it could be true. There, he saw two photos. Yes, it is true. The photos confirmed it. The owner, Joni's beautiful mother, in a photo with Joni Mitchell, simply signed "Love, Joni." The next photo was the mother and Joni Shannon, both with emerald-green eyes. There was no mistake who the mother was. Now there was no mistake who Joni is. Jonathan's daughter. He could barely breathe. Here, at Life's Illusions, Jonathan profoundly realized that he really doesn't know life, at all.

EMERALD GREEN, DARKER THAN JADE

Back at the hotel, Jonathan stared at his computer. He knew if he opened it up, clicked on his Centillion search engine, and typed in three words, he would read the painful truth. If he didn't, he could continue to exist in a quasi-state of suspended animation, where time ground to a halt and all brain activity stopped. A shield protecting him from a brokenhearted past and now a very uncertain future. He knew that typing three words would confirm death, resurrect memories, and change his life forever. Of that he had no doubt. It was already happening.

He opened his computer, ignored the new emails, typed in the three key words that would conclusively reveal what had already ceased to be a mystery to him: "Michele Shannon obituary." The page popped right up and contained a number of links. It took him only a few seconds more to find the one he was looking for. Taking a deep breath, he clicked on it. On the left was a color photo; on the right, a string of words that would have to wait. Stunned and transfixed, he could not take his eyes off the photo. Michele as a vibrant, radiant young woman. As he remembered her. Before acute myeloid leukemia ravaged her body and beautiful face. In the photo, her face was so mesmerizing, her smile so striking. It appeared to be a three-dimensional picture. And the eyes. Her unforgettable eyes. Emerald green, darker than jade, a verdant green hue with high transparency, like a brilliant gemstone. A color of freshness and renewal. Eyes that long ago looked into his in a way that only passionate lovers who inhabited each other can. Eyes that a fateful choice he made thirty-seven years ago were lost to him forever. Eyes that indelibly imprinted themselves in his consciousness with the same luminous animation as those that danced and sparkled off the beautiful photo on his computer screen.

Jonathan eventually forced himself to read the words. He read only with his right eye, because his left eye was spellbound by the photo of lost love. He learned that Michele was survived by her husband, Michael Shannon, an architect, and a daughter, Joni, an attorney. An animal lover, Michele was also survived by her two faithful dogs from a local rescue, Ellie and Siena. After college Michele received her MBA from UC Berkeley. For twenty-two years she pursued her life's passion as the owner and manager of a popular Berkeley jazz café called Life's Illusions. Many young jazz artists who found success got their start at Life's Illusions.

Fluent in French, Michele loved to travel. France and Italy were her favorite destinations, Paris and Rome her favorite cities, but her boundless energy and restless curiosity took her to twenty other foreign countries. She hiked the Great Wall in China and the rugged hills of the Isle of Skye in Scotland. She witnessed the Great Migration of wildlife in Tanzania and boated through the amazing Amazon tropical rainforest. In Morocco she went camel-trekking in the Sahara Desert and scaled the Atlas Mountains. She was a lifelong cycling enthusiast and avid swimmer. At the funeral, her daughter Joni sat at a piano and played her two favorite songs: "Clair de Lune" and "Both Sides Now." In lieu of flowers, the family requested donations to the Leukemia & Lymphoma Society. A service and celebration of life, specifically requested by Michele, was held at a Berkeley funeral home where friends were encouraged to say a few words about Michele and her remarkable life. Michele was cremated. Per her wishes, her ashes were scattered where the Russian River flows into the Pacific Ocean between Jenner and Goat Rock Beach. Jonathan was too numb to cry. Nor could he sleep. He recalled a line from Dante's *Divine Comedy* that was ringing painfully true for him: "There is no greater sorrow than thinking back upon a happy time in misery."

SHELLY AND JAK

In sorrow and misery, happier times came rushing back to him. Jonathan never knew Michele as Michele Shannon. He knew her by her birth name, Michele Parker. In his two years of prelapsarian innocence with her, he called her Shelly, inspired by the romantic poet Percy Bysshe Shelley. He was young and enchanted by the mellifluous and euphonious soft sound of the name. So he called her Shelly. A romantic spirit and soul. She whimsically called him Jak, the three letters of the alphabet that rhymed with the long vowel A.

Jonathan remembered reading somewhere that memories associated with smell are the most powerful, vivid, and emotional. All these years later, he could still smell the sweet lavender scent of Shelly's body. A fragrance.

Fragrance, a beautiful soft word, like her name. Shelly. He remembered the sweet intoxicating drift into the gateway at his nostrils and into his entire being. Lavender. Shelley loved lavender. How she rhapsodized about her love for France. She spoke the language and yearned to stroll through the streets of Paris, hand in hand with Jak. She dreamed of seeing the museums, especially the Musée d'Orsay and the impressionist paintings she so adored. Ah, to see the Côte d'Azur, she dreamed. She longed to lounge in the luscious lavender fields of Luberon north of Aix-en-Provence and east of Avignon. Then saunter along the Promenade des Anglais in Nice and smell the cool breezes of the Mediterranean Sea followed by a night or two in Eze Village, the scenic hilltop medieval village with spectacular overlook views of the Mediterranean. And his young amore dreamed of strolling the streets of Rome, holding hands, and treasuring the relics and ruins of the timeless place founded by Romulus and Remus. For two dream-like years, Shelly believed her dream was their destiny. Both a beautiful dream and destiny. For two wondrous years, Jonathan, Shelly's Jak, shared it passionately with her.

Shelly and Jak, Jak and Shelly. For two years they were inseparable. They inhabited each other. It was as if everything that happened in the world was a code only the two of them could understand. Where a simple eye-contact response communicated ineffable meanings only Shelly and Jak could understand. Where words weren't necessary to simultaneously say I understand and I love you. As they caressed, Shelly once told Jak that a soulmate is a person, when meeting that special other person, meets the half that is her own. The young soulmates loved the old poets. Quoting the Romantic poet Shelley, dear friend of poet John Keats, Shelly was fond of telling Jak that "soul meets soul on lover's lips." Jak was Shelly's soulmate. She believed something wonderful happens when soulmates meet. They are struck by love and a sense of belonging to one another. By desire. Passionate desire. A refusal to be apart from one another, ever, even for a moment. She cherished Keats's poem "Bright Star, Would I Were Stedfast as Thou Art," and its lyrical expression of a desire to remain in the company of her lover forever, to have Jak's head rest on her breast and feel it gently rise and fall as she breathed, awake forever in a sweet unrest, and to let her die if this could not persist forever.

His episodic memory darted with alacrity to the time they visited the Art Institute of Chicago. Shelly, a literature and art history double major, adored the impressionists and the Institute was featuring a Renoir exhibition, including paintings on loan from Paris's Musée d'Orsay. Those paintings included four dance- themed paintings: *Dance at the Moulin de la Galette, Dance in the Country, Dance in the City,* and *Dance at Bougival.* Shelly and Jak had been taking ballroom dance classes, and Renoir's dance paintings were another secret code between them. As if Renoir had painted them especially for the young lovers. Why Jonathan was hypnotized when he saw them again in Paris so many years ago.

Shelly taught Jak how to be carefree, silly even. How to giggle. How to tickle and be tickled. How to have lovely fun. Together, they learned how to be emotionally and physically uninhibited. Jonathan remembered how they taught one another the gift of anticipation. They talked and moved slowly with inexpressible love and joy. How, as Jak, somehow everything, no matter how seemingly disconnected, had a connection to and a path back to Shelly. Neither could have ever imagined a disunion of this mystical two into one or, by that time, a life apart.

Jonathan remembered the evening he surprised Shelly by softly singing "Edelweiss." That special night Jak was able to hold the moonbeam that was Shelly in his embracing arms. Remembering, he felt ashamed that he was not there with her, holding her ravaged body in his arms, softly caressing her bald head, as her rare form of cancer stole her last breath and extinguished the effervescence from the true love of his life. It was thirty-seven years ago, but now, just like that, Shelly was gone, like the evanescence of a beautiful dream that seemed so vital yet vanished so quickly.

Looking back over the long arc of his life, never did he feel so dynamically alive as those two extraordinary years with Shelly. The one, the only time, in his life he experienced romantic love. The exhilarating experience of love's poignant possibilities.

For all of her music loves, Shelly's favorite artist was the incomparable Joni Mitchell. A soulful musician, songwriter, intelligent and romantic storyteller, and accomplished painter. She was introspective. She displayed a vulnerable honesty about love and the human experience. Angelic voice. Beautiful and hip. Cool personified. Jonathan thought, in great dismay, how cruelly coincidental that Joni Mitchell wrote beautifully sad songs about failed relationships, "A Case of You," "Help Me," "The Last Time I Saw Richard," and "Woman of Heart and Mind." Shelly promised Jak that on their first visit to Paris they would play Joni's song "In France They Kiss on Main Street" and she would shower him with kisses on the

Champs-Élysées. And, of course, there was Joni's song "Both Sides Now," where it was her Jak who would painfully bring home for Shelly the lines about the illusions of love and life. Shelly loved Joni Mitchell. She even named her daughter and life's passion after her kindred spirit. Jonathan remembered Shelly's favorite poem, the poet Shelley's "Music, When Soft Voices Die."

Music, when soft voices die, Vibrates in the memory; Odours, when sweet violets sickens, Live within the sense they quicken.

Rose leaves, when rose is dead, Are heaped for the beloved's bed;

And so thy thoughts when thou art gone, Love itself will slumber on.

Jonathan remembered that once, lying in bed in the afterglow of a night of especially passionate lovemaking, naked bodies enfolded and Shelly softly stroking his hair as his head rested peacefully on her warm breasts, she assured him that her memories of him, like the poet Shelley's invocation, would be permanent. Her music loves will live on in her memory, she whispered, and her abiding love for him will slumber on after he's gone.

For the first time since learning of Shelly's death, Jonathan cried. The past is never even the past.

OMNE TRIUM PERFECTUM

Jonathan composed himself. His mind drifted back to the first time he uttered three magical words to Shelly. The mystical magic of threes. In Latin, she had told him, omne trium perfectum means that everything that comes in threes is perfect. As in two soulmates consumed with one another in mind, body, and spirit. Jak's three perfect words to Shelly: "I love you." She said them right back, with three more perfect words, "I always will." OTP was their secret code for I love you. For I always will.

Time fades most memories, but not all. Memories are of things gone, that's why some haunt and others we try to suppress. But some plumb our deepest emotions, making them indelible and ineradicable. Thirty-seven years later and Jonathan was trembling remembering the fateful choice he made.

Shelly had lied to him about her abortion intent, but now it seemed so obvious to him. He thought, *If I had been better attuned to Shelly's feelings, I would have realized that Shelly's choice was inevitable.* She was never going to abort the child she wanted to be theirs and, no matter what, was *always* going to be hers. He was scared and feeling trapped. Not Shelly. She implored him to "use your imagination. Why can't you believe in us and what, together, we're capable of? The two of us, soon to be the three of us? Why can't you see that together we can make our lives work? Make it all work beautifully. Our three lives. Jak, OTP. Omne trium perfectum. Just the three of us. It will be perfect. A life of love is the best plan of all, Jak. Don't you see that? That's the plan we should hug and embrace."

Only now could Jonathan put it all together. Shelly had given him one last chance to show a true love for her. To compromise, even potentially sacrifice so they could have a shared life of Shelly, Jak, and months from then, Joni. Jak's body was hers, but in the moment that mattered most, not Jonathan's soul. It was inaccessible to her. How could he not have had faith in her and a life with her and their baby? So, like Lady Macbeth, Shelly had decided that a "false face must hide what the false heart doth know."

Jonathan now realized that Shelly's face was a false face because of course she had Joni, not an abortion. False heart, Jak would never learn because a part of Shelly never really stopped loving him. That tragic night was the last time anyone ever called him Jak. He would never know that no one else ever again called her Shelly. Jonathan had made his choice, had moved on with his life, but now he recalled the last line of Tennyson's poem "Tears, Idle Tears": "O Death in Life, the days that are no more."

THE RIVER'S END

Jonathan emailed his assistant, Mary, and said he was going to stay in San Francisco for several more days to tend to some other business matters. Not quite accurate. Instead, he rented a Mini Cooper Convertible and headed north to Guerneville and to Highway 116 to follow the Russian River to Jenner and the Pacific Ocean. Jonathan was not a mystical man, but he was overwhelmed with a feeling that it was more than just coincidence that a place he had fallen in love with years before was the precise place where Shelly had her ashes scattered. His rational faculties told the calculating probabilist that it was just coincidence that he happened to see Shelly that magical night in the college library, but love at first sight suggested romantic fate and not statistical probabilities was the reason. Now, it seemed to Jonathan, romantic fate was once again uniting them in some ethereal, astral way where love and leaps of faith guide the soul. It was fate that had brought Jonathan and Shelly together for the second time, here where a mighty river meets a majestic ocean and merge into one, just as it had once been for the two of them. Where the waters' unity creates something special, just as the erstwhile lovers' unity created something special: Joni.

The celebrated barrister now had some important decisions to make, and this revered place is where he intended to make them. So he booked a room at the River's End Inn in Jenner with its breathtaking views of the Russian River and Pacific Ocean. Where Shelly's spirit now permeated the serene space.

Shelly had lied to him about her abortion intent. For a fleeting moment, Jonathan was angry, but his anger quickly subsided, and sadness overcame him. He had forced Shelly's hand. He was adamant that she have an abortion and then they would carry on as if nothing had ever changed. Shelly, wiser and more mature, knew there could be no going back. Jonathan forced her to choose him without their baby. Shelly wanted him with their baby. She was willing to settle for their baby without him. But she was not willing to live without *her* baby. Still, with feelings of love, Shelly freed Jak to allow him to be Jonathan. Jonathan's career, his fear of ordinariness and subservience, working some job answering to the boss man, frightened him as a young man and controlled his immature judgment. He was incapable then of seeing past the moment. Shelly realized that, and so she put on a false face to hide a false heart. Jonathan realized that Shelly, ever wise, made a loving choice. A loving choice for him, her, and Joni. There are no do-overs in life, which is why, he realized, he felt such sadness and remorse. Choices have consequences, and he was slowly appreciating that he had made the worst choice of his life thirty-seven years ago.

Jonathan ruefully realized that Shelly had made the correct choice. A wise choice. Without self-pity, he now understood that Shelly could not continue in a relationship with him. Not on his uncompromising terms. Not when his uncompromising terms meant that there would be no Joni. Not when he refused to embrace Shelly and their baby and take a leap of faith that, together, they could live a wonderful life of love. Joni would allow them to live the dream, not extinguish it. How prescient, how wise Shelly had been back then to unpack time and have the imagination to envision how Joni would have fulfilled, not imprisoned them. That a life with the three of them would have been anything but ordinary. Life with Shelly and Joni would have been extraordinary. OTP, omne trium perfectum, Shelly had sagely said. The three of them would have been perfect. She had said to him "that a life of love is the best plan of all," but he was too consumed with self to hear her. Three more perfect words: life of love. He was slowly realizing that would have been the best life of all.

Shelly's prescience was more than a vision. Jonathan saw the evidence. Real, live, walking-around evidence in the person of Joni. Conceived in passionate love. Carrying his DNA. A rippling effect he, in fact, has on the world, even if now, with Shelly's death, he is the only one who knows it. Shelly's beauty and eyes and intelligence and special traits and his lawyerly ambition. His flesh and blood but a man Joni only knows as a quinquagenarian litigation opponent. A stranger. His own biological daughter had looked him right in the eyes and held his hand and saw and felt nothing but a stranger and someone she needed to defeat in court. A trial lawyer adversary, not a father. A supreme cruel twist of fate. The emotional consequential fate of his myopic rational choice.

Shelly must not have told Joni. So what did she tell her? Jonathan thought obviously Joni doesn't know that he is her biological father. There is no way she could have introduced herself so cheerfully to him at Life's Illusions without revealing such knowledge. Or being on opposite sides of the Centillion case without confronting him with the truth. Or telling him without irony or sarcasm "I learned a lot from you." No, he thought, Joni doesn't know.

But why not? Shelly, Michele, had married and was married when she died. It certainly seemed plausible that she had decided to make a clean break from her past, move two thousand miles west to San Francisco, and start a new life with Joni on the West Coast. Whatever her reasons, it became clear to Jonathan that Joni did not know that he is her biological father. Shelly must have had her reasons for not telling Joni.

So, he thought, what do I do now? Do I tell her? He was overwhelmed with a feeling of bittersweetness when he learned that the young woman he had met at Life's Illusions was his daughter. Bitter because he was realizing what a tragic, selfish decision he had made thirty-seven years ago. Joy because Shelly was a gift to the world and now Joni, her daughter, with his DNA, was extending that gift. Jonathan betrayed Shelly's trust and love once before. He was not going to do it again. He decided that he would take his cue from Shelly. She, after all, raised Joni to be the wonderful young woman she is now. Yes, Shelly must have had her reasons for not telling Joni, reasons no doubt grounded in a consuming love. He would not interfere, not because, again, he did not want Joni. He did. No, he would not interfere because he had never stopped loving Shelly. The only romantic love of his life.

Shelly was the only love of Jonathan's life, and that is why *Madame Bovary* haunted him so much the summer between college and law school after Shelly told him she never wanted to see him again. The line came back to haunt him again: "Emma tried hard to discover what, precisely, was denoted by the words joy, passion, intoxication, which always looked so good in books." With Shelly, Jonathan, then Jak, for two enchanted years discovered the intoxication of passion and joy with a soulmate, with an angel in life. Jak discovered this wonderment not in a book but in his real heart-pumping, blood-coursing-through-veins life that he shared with the ebullient Shelly whose emerald-green eyes and lavender scent provided permanent reminders of a life of love that could have been his if only fear and blind ambition and a failure to imagine the possible—the possibility of so many things he and Shelly could have done together—had not clouded his vision and turned love and life into an illusion.

He took a walk down to the water. To where he imagined Shelly's ashes were scattered. At a distance from the elephant and harbor seals. As he strolled aimlessly, Jonathan thought about the concept of the eternal self. He had lived long enough to understand the philosophers' point: there is no eternal self. Yes, there is connective tissue with one's past self, but Jonathan understood that he is not the man today he was thirty-seven years ago. And he could make choices. Out of fear of being ordinary and his desire to be elusively great, he had singularly pursued career and ambition, money and fame too. False idols in hindsight. Love had not been his life's plan. Not shared love with a wife and daughter. A tragic mistake.

Peering out to the ocean, he imagined Shelly's seraphic face, that beautiful face with her dazzling emerald eyes. He remembered an extraordinary lover. She taught him joy and laughter, intimate physical exploration and experimentation, sharing and caring and the beauty and loveliness of emotional vulnerability to a soulmate.

In death, she was teaching him something more about love and guiding him toward wisdom. But wisdom, Jonathan understood, was not something that is taught by another. He must find it himself.

As he continued to walk, he thought about Judge Roy and Vietnam and Hamburger Hill. He thought about all of those very young men buried at the American Cemetery who died on the beaches of Normandy. The sacrifices they all made for something bigger than self. For other human beings. He thought about Nicole Laurent's philosophical words at the American Cemetery: "If faced with a difficult choice, just hope you do the honorable thing." He thought about his very last conversation with Jack Coltrane. And Jack's fatherly hope that Jonathan—"son"—would find love and peace.

His mind wandered back to Shelly. Why was there love at first sight? Why was it so intense, so open, so exploratory, so free? A love where emotional vulnerability was so liberating. Shelly, ever wise, had told him the answer was simple, "because you are you and I am I." Shelly would lovingly mock him for assuming that everything has a rational explanation, a rational reduction. She told him that love between two people is an emotional attachment whose manifestations are their own explanations. That's the beauty of true love.

True love is what Shelly showed and gave to Jak. She once told him never to forget something her beloved Bard of Avon had said about love: "All creatures in the world through love exist, and lacking love, lack all that may persist." Jonathan, remembering Jak, scooped some water out of the ocean and whispered, "Shelly, my love, it's time for me to show Joni some love."

Jonathan had a plan, and this time it wisely included love. Maybe it would also help him find some peace.

PARENTAL LOVE

Back in DC, reality came around to hit Jonathan with some more depressing news that seared his soul. There would be no justice, no vindication in federal court, for the child slave victims. No pro bono case where Jonathan might find some salvation by fighting for the most noble of causes. Not a case of money changing hands, or not, typical of his civil litigation practice. But a case on behalf of the most helpless, the most vulnerable, cruelly subjected to lives that are nasty, brutish, and short. The US Supreme Court took the case and then put an end to it. On a technicality, describing the slave enablers' domestic conduct as nothing more than "general activity common to most corporations" and therefore beyond the reach of the Alien Tort Claims Act.

The appalling facts of the savage system of slavery were never challenged or refuted. No corporations would be held accountable. Global corporations would continue to profit from the enslaved labor of defenseless black children. Hodges and Truckle and the CLB management could now breathe big sighs of relief that their superstar trial lawyer would not be championing a pro bono cause of freedom for enslaved children, potentially to the chagrin of corporate clients, but would rather be focused entirely on the lucrative Centillion case. Jonathan was crushed.

After a few days of more reflection and introspection, Jonathan reread the Centillion trial proof strategy memo. He was convinced even more that he had a winning strategy. Plus, his side had the "X factor." Jonathan in the courtroom. The senior lawyers on the other side were likely competent, but in the courtroom, they weren't

Jonathan. He was an extraordinary performer in court. Jonathan had dedicated his career, his entire life, to winning an antitrust case like this in the courtroom. Now he knew he had a path to a Super Bowl victory, a crowning achievement. A victory that would inch him even closer to his dream of being recognized as the best there ever was. A capstone that would not vanish like a puff of wind. This superstar trial lawyer realized it was all right there before him. It was within both his reach and his grasp. It was that close.

The father realized something else. Inevitability. His win would be his daughter's loss. There was no other way. Trials are zero-sum games; one side wins, the other side loses. It's that simple. Joni had left private practice for this once-in-a-lifetime opportunity, an opportunity to catapult her fledgling career as a trial lawyer. The man who was a stranger to her, her own biological father, could be the one to dash her dream and break her spirit. Jonathan had vowed that nothing would stand in his way to victory. Only one thing could stop Jonathan.

Thirty-seven years ago, Jonathan did not let Shelly's pregnancy and Joni's impending birth interfere with his career. He would not repeat that mistake. Now, Joni's birth, her existential being, the love a father could not help but feel for his daughter, would be the reason that Jonathan would withdraw from the case and prematurely end his career. For once in his life, he would submerge his ego and ambition and make a sacrifice for someone else. For the daughter he knew he should have raised. For the love he still felt for Shelly. For the love he now felt for his biological daughter. Time and space and circumstance do not set boundaries on parental love. Knowing that Joni was in the world unleashed a protective love that only a parent can feel for a child. Joni and the government might still lose the case, but not because Jonathan would be in the courtroom standing in Joni's way. Joni was his biological daughter and now that he knew it, he profoundly realized he loved her and would show his love the best way he could.

The Centillion trial was a few years away, but this was still a momentous decision. Jonathan of course understood that he could not provide the real reason why he was withdrawing from the case and resigning from the firm. Nor could he responsibly just walk out the door with no explanation at all. So he provided an honest but incomplete explanation. He told client and CLB that he had to deal with a personal issue that would require his full-time attention for the foreseeable future. No, he answered to the immediate questions, he was not sick or dying. And no, he did not want to take a leave of absence in lieu of resignation and retirement. This was something he had to do.

Then he knew he had to address the hardest part of all. By now, Jonathan was mentor and friend to each member of his terrific trial team. They were his closest colleagues in the firm. Top-tier talent and wonderful people.

The news of his decision spread at the speed of light and sent shockwaves throughout the firm. If there was any fixed star in the CLB constellation, it was that Jonathan Kent would be in a courtroom somewhere trying a high-profile case. That he would walk away from a trial-of-the-century case was a mind bender that stumped everyone. Most especially his tight-knit trial team.

They were all in the conference room when he walked in, looking anxious and morose. Each had stayed in the firm for one and only one reason—to work with Jonathan and try cases. Now it was inexplicably disappearing from them. It was surreal. There was David Joseph and JP Hale, Maya Gibson and Ruth B. Greenfield, and Kaori Settite. He knew he had to keep it short. He reassured them that he was not dying, no diagnosis of a life-ending disease. He told them simply that there was something personal he had to address and he needed to leave to do it. Imaginations were running wild. Misty eyes all around, for these extraordinarily smart folks could not be easily fooled—a towering figure like Jonathan Kent doesn't just wake up one morning with an epiphany that he needs to do something else in his life. This *was* his life. He was obviously hiding something.

Jonathan told them some good news. There would be a new lead trial lawyer from another firm, but Centillion wanted them to continue to assist on the case. They had become invaluable and were genuine contributors. He then addressed each one individually with kind words of encouragement. He assured them that their futures were promising. He thanked them for the wonderful work they had done together and wished them the best. Jonathan's parting words were that he hoped he would see them down the road sometime. Those were the last words he spoke at the firm. He walked out of the conference room and straight to the elevator, got off at the lobby floor, and exited the building, never to return.

EPILOGUE

Bicycling through Provence, Jonathan marveled at the vibrancy yet delicacy of Luberon's luscious lavender fields. Endless enchanting beauty and heavenly scents. He even asked a local to snap a photo of him on his iPhone, donning a T-shirt emblazoned with Life's Illusions, in a tranquil field with the sublime Senanque Abbey in the background. Jonathan hopped back on his bicycle and pedaled to the picturesque countryside of Manosque, the Riviera hill towns, and then onto the beautiful descent to the Mediterranean at Cannes and up the coast to Nice.

After a few nights in Nice and Eze, with their stunning views of the Mediterranean, Jonathan flew from Nice to Marrakesh. There in baggage claim Taufiq was holding a sign that read "Mr. Jonathan." Taufiq would serve as his friend and guide as they adventured through the magical, mystical lands of Morocco. Carpe diem. Seize the day and let tomorrow take care of itself. As Joni Mitchell sang in Shelly's beloved song "Both Sides Now," in living every day something's lost, but so too is something gained. And so for Jonathan the temporary journey that is a human life moved on to see what tomorrow brings. Still alone, but at peace with himself.

It was December. Her birthday. Joni received a note from the Leukemia & Lymphoma Society. An anonymous donor made a contribution, in the name of Michele Shannon, in the amount of three million dollars with a simple message: Omne trium perfectum. With tears in her eyes, Joni stared out the window and wondered.

CPSIA information can be obtained
at www.ICGtesting.com
Printed in the USA
LVHW091257030322
712547LV00015B/126